Secrets of Starlight and Shadows

NEVERLAND NOVELS COLLECTION

BAILEY BLACK

For the girls who flirt with danger, fall for the broody ones, and never follow the map.
May your secrets be juicy, your shadows well-behaved, and your starlight always a little unhinged.

Looking for some love in your life? Bailey's contemporary romances range from sweet to spicy, with everything in between.
Find your love story...

Romantasy Adventures

The Lost Darling
    Second Star to the Right
    Island of the Lost
    Secrets of Starlight and Shadow—The Neverland Collection
    Lucky in Love
    All I Want For Christmas
    Resting Grinchface
    Rooted in Blood and Thorns

Sweet and Spicy Contemporaries

Falling for You
    In Too Deep
    Temptation
    Beautifully Broken
    The Love-Hate Duet
    Unexpected
    Breakups and Bouquets
    Love Me Like You Mean It Anthology
    Say You'll Be Mine

THE
LOST
DARLING

THE LOST DARLING

CHAPTER 1

Wednesday

Three drinks down and I'm convinced this bartender has magic hands. She's found a way to mix rum and a half dozen other concocktables together until it tastes like a liquid dessert. Her sweet, pineapple slice of heaven is exactly what I need to forget the utter shit-storm my life has become in the last six months.

I pull the mini umbrella out of its ice bath, place the Maraschino cherry between my teeth, then pop the stem. I close my eyes and suck on the little round fruit until all the flavor has faded away, then bite down. The cherry alone is a treat, but paired with whatever else is in my cocktail, *chef's kiss*.

A few more rounds, mixed with the spritzers I drank earlier, and I might be able to forget that I walked in on my sister six months ago, legs spread, my boyfriend's hands cupped around her perky double-d's, while she bounced on his cock. Unlikely, but with every ounce of alcohol I swallow, I get that much closer to temporary peace.

"You okay there, Wens?"

The simple answer? No, but life hasn't been simple for a long time. I open my eyes and smile at Kierra, my sister's maid of honor, the liquor lifting my lips even though I'm beyond pissed.

My sister broke her pinky promise. That was supposed to be my job. I should be the number two in command.

I was supposed to help plan this weekend's festivities, picking which booze cruises we went on during the day and which bars we bounced to after dark. I would have made sure she had a spotlight dance at the strip club we went to last night and kept Boobs-McGee from drinking too much so she wouldn't cause a scene, because that's the maid of honor's job.

Instead, I'm just the sister of the bride. Not even a bridesmaid in the wedding or a ridiculous adult flower girl. I'm a guest with a pity invite to the bachelorette party.

I'm the reject.

The girl the bride was forced to bring along that pretty much everyone ignores.

Tyle—said sister...twin sister... who is getting married in two weeks to my ex-boyfriend—and I have been planning our weddings since we were innocent, star-eyed ten-year-olds who found Leonardo DiCaprio back in his *Titanic* days on cable TV. That man was fine as sand during the late nineties and has only gotten better with age. He made me realize I had a thing for the preppy, blonde-haired, blue-eyed heartthrobs.

And my sister had a thing for what was mine.

"I. Am. Peachy." I take another sip through my paper straw in my cup (hate those) and frown when I pull more air than yummy goodness. My glass must be broken. It might even have a hole in the bottom.

So did the one before that.

And the one before that one, too.

I hold the empty drink up, signaling to the wizard behind the bar that I'm ready for another round of her signature drink, *a kiss me on the lips.*

I have no shame in ordering it, but I wonder how many guests our bartender has honored with its name. I bet her drink makes for some great tips and even better stories.

If I were working behind the bar, I'd kiss every hottie that ordered one. Male. Female. Unicorn. It doesn't matter anymore. A broken heart opened me up to all sorts of things I never thought I'd do. If it's not illegal and will make me forget the searing pain in the center of my chest, I'll try it.

Right now, our bartender has her eyes set on a tall drink of broody goodness, probably deciding if he's worth a little lip-locking. I vote yes, but there's no telling what this chick is into. For all I know, she may have a vag badge. I'm not hating that prospect. She's a gorgeous girl I'd happily lend my lips to. Yet, I fight a smile. Tyle would have a fit if I kissed a girl this weekend. She's still living in the past when it comes to relationships because, as much as she deserves to have her perfect weekend ruined (in her eyes, kissing the wizard would cause waves), I'm trying to be good.

That's what family does. They respect each other. Even if my sister doesn't know what it means to leave well enough alone, I know my place.

Kierra takes the scalloped glass from me and sets it on the bar top, a concerned frown on her face. She stares at me for an uncomfortably long amount of time. I don't know what she expects to come out of my mouth.

Venom about the wedding?

Curses to her name for stealing my job?

If that's the case, she's going to be sorely disappointed because the one thing I'm not going to do is give Tyle a story by making waves. That's the ocean's job. Mine is to cruise through this weekend in a drunken haze and make it to Monday morning.

I hiccup and cover my mouth with my hand, laughing between each breath of air.

"You should go back to the boat and get some rest." Kierra took on the role of *Mom* for the group this weekend. I should be grateful. Without her intervention last night, I would have ended up with more than another tattoo on my forearm. Nipple rings were *this* close to happening. I'm grateful for her presence, but I'm still mad at her.

She helped my sister not pick oleanders for the table decorations.

She didn't suggest the sweetheart, A-line gown that hugged Tyle's curves in all the right ways.

And she didn't talk my sister out of sleeping with my boyfriend.

Or marrying him.

Although if I'm being fair, by the time Kenny proposed to Tyle, I couldn't claim him as mine anymore. Whatever. It's all semantics. Either way, my sister is marrying my ex six months after our breakup, and it's fucked.

"I'm fine." I hiccup. "I just need another one of these." Hiccup. I reach for my glass, but Kierra slides it out of reach. I frown at her, ready to give her a piece of my mind, when the wizard appears again.

"Here you go, honey." Our bartender says as she sets another delicious piece of heaven in front of me.

I snatch my drink before Kierra can steal it away. I don't know how the bar babe saw me, but I don't care. I'm grateful. Memories I'd rather not relive are burning through this haze of alcohol, and I need to extinguish them. "What do I owe you?"

"Nothing." The chick steps back and tilts her head, signaling down the bar. "That guy bought it for you."

"Oh!" I say as Kierra murmurs my name—Wednesday—in a warning tone.

The bartender steps away, turning her attention back to paying customers. A temporary moment of disappointment that she wasn't the one who noticed me is replaced by a new flicker of excitement. This whole weekend, all eyes have been on Tyle. This is the first drink someone outside the wedding party has bought me. I'm not gonna waste it or an opportunity to talk to a hot guy.

Tall, dark, and broody stares at the flat screen above the bar. There's a football game playing, probably a re-run, but he seems interested in it. Tattooed fingers curl around a tumbler of amber liquor, bringing the glass to his lips as he studies the screen.

I take a sip of my yellow-orange goodness and smile against the straw. It's heaven in my mouth. Just like the other three. Or was it four? I don't know, and it doesn't matter. My goal is to stay numb this weekend, and this man is helping me reach the finish line. The fact that he's eye candy is an added bonus.

Kierra grabs my arm as I slide out of the stool. The sheer white cover-up I have over my bright red bikini slides down my shoulder, exposing my sun-kissed freckles. Tyle takes after our mom. Her natural brown hair, before she bleached it, was four shades lighter than mine, her lips fuller, her waist smaller. I look like our dad. Darker. Thicker and just... more.

"What are you doing?"

I shrug and back-step away from Kierra. She doesn't try to stop me, probably because she knows the effort is futile. Considering all the things I've almost done this weekend, me talking to a guy is the least of her worries, but it doesn't keep Kierra from scowling as I creep away.

"It's only polite for me to thank the sexy stranger." I flash Kierra a grin we both know too well. It was Tyle's go-to back in the day when she was up to no good. I don't know what my plans are for this guy. Probably nothing more than a little shameless flirting, but knowing that Kiera will tell Tyle and that Tyle will be jealous makes me happy.

A few tiny waves won't hurt anyone.

"Wens..." Kierra warns again.

"Relax, *Mom*. I'm just gonna say thank you. Maybe chat him up and get some more free booze. What's the worst that can happen?"

CHAPTER 2

Wednesday

I'm nervous.

Which is stupid because the guy who bought my drink isn't even that hot.

Okay. That's a lie.

He's kind of gorgeous.

Tattoos of twisting designs and symbols I've never seen before cover his arms, chest, and down to the band of his black bathing shorts, while his defined back has a giant map of a tropical-looking island. There's not a spec of color in the art. Just shades of gray and black against copper skin and deep-set muscles.

He's got a nineties-style fringe, where the hair is short in the back but falls over his brows in a sexy just-been-fucked kind of way. His eyes, a blue that parallels the deepest parts of the ocean, hold mine as I approach. He knew I'd come. A quick upturn of his lips against his glass confirms my suspicion. He doesn't look at me. His gaze is fixed on the flatscreen above a shelf of liquor, but I can feel static building between us the closer I get.

I lean against the bar and try not to puke as I smile. My nerves are running rampant, like a teenage girl with a crush in my system. It's been years since my heart stuttered this fast. If this guy was blonde, it would be game over. I wouldn't even try to fight my needy lady bits. I'd give in right now, in the single-stall bathroom down by the pool, and screw him until my legs don't work right. But his hair is dark, and I haven't had *that much* to drink yet. So, logic still has some say in my life.

"Hi." My head spins from the rush of adrenaline. I sip my drink, using the cool liquid to ground my body. From afar, this man is beautiful, but up close, he's an anomaly cut from marble, too pretty to be real.

And he's looking at me.

Not Tyle.

Me.

My sister isn't far, just six seats down the bar, chatting with a random man she met on the boat. It would have been nothing for tall, dark, and broody to look past my plain brown hair and boring hazel eyes. Tyle's bleached blonde strands and big blues have a way of luring men into conversation. Although, Mr. Broody wouldn't have been the first to buy her a drink today, which could be why the cocktail was sent to me.

I try to push back the fear sneaking into my thoughts away. Guys have always noticed Tyle first and used me to be by her side.

My ex—Kenny—was the only man I knew who chose me over her. She could have had him in high school when she threw herself at him. Literally. Naked on the trampoline at a party after graduation. But he left her there, sloppy and crying (because she lives for the drama), to find me.

Tyle has always been everything I'm not, even when we were younger, but when Kenny and I were together, I was more than enough. Someone noticed me. Wanted me. I was on cloud nine until my world came crashing down. In what felt like an instant, I wasn't good enough for him anymore.

I wonder if that's the predicament Tyle is in now. If Kenny has grown tired of her, but is in too deep to let go. If so, I don't feel bad. Karma is a bitch, and her retribution is more than deserved.

It would explain why Kenny and Tyle gave each other a hall

pass this weekend. They decided that what happens at the bachelor and bachelorette party stays here.

No questions.

No regrets.

One last hoorah.

I take another sip of my drink as the mental image of Tyle ruining my brand-new couches creeps into my mind again. Only this time, Kenny's scarlet hair is as dark as night and his face is replaced by my new friend's.

I feel sick again, but this isn't a nervous kind of sick. It's a heart-hurting, gut-retching reminder that the man I loved chose my sister, kind of sick mixed with the dark thoughts that I will never be good enough.

Don't get me wrong, I'm still pissed at both of them for the betrayal, but I know I did nothing wrong.

Outside of never granting backdoor access, I gave Kenny anything he wanted. I was everything a girlfriend should be, sometimes even more, but the insecurity of not being good enough has embedded itself in my DNA and it's morphed into a passing thought every time someone looks at me. Most days, I can silence the clamor with a drink. Others, I can barely look at myself in the mirror.

Today, I'm choosing to drown the voices.

Today, I refuse to let Tyle win. This may be her weekend, but it's my life. If I want to get blackout drunk and hook up with a stranger I will because I am enough! Cheers to me!

My hand moves faster than my mouth is ready for and some of my drink spills over the rim of the glass and onto my chest. It's cold and my flimsy coverup does nothing to keep the sticky liquid from dripping between the girls.

"Shit," I mumble.

Tall, dark, and broody chuckles. The rumble of his voice vibrates deep in his chest and somehow has a direct connection with my lady bits. The poor girl has finally woken up after a temporary celibacy streak and set her eyes on this unfortunate soul.

"Allow me." He grabs a handful of bar squares and presses the small white napkins to my chest.

Sober, pre-broken-hearted Wednesday would have taken a step back to excuse herself, clean herself up, take a mini bath in the sink, then dry her tits under the hand dryers. She would be embarrassed and probably sneak away when no one was looking, then go home and fantasize about what could have happened had the stars aligned.

That version of me disappeared one heartbreak and two drinks ago.

This newer, freer me likes the heat burning through the napkin from McBroody's touch and she ain't stopping him. He runs his fingers across my collarbone, between the peaks of my breasts, and down near my belly button until his rough calluses grip my hips.

I forget how to breathe. Every fiber in my body is set alight with need and I let out a laugh I banished when I hit puberty.

"I missed a spot." He leans closer, oblivious to the embarrassing noise I made. His tongue swipes against the sensitive skin of my neck, nowhere near where my drink spilled.

I'm not complaining.

Desire spreads from my center, lighting me up from head to toe. It's exhilarating. I haven't felt this good since... no. I'm not thinking about the dickhead who broke my heart right now. Not when this man is making me feel So. Good.

"I think I got it," Mcbroody whispers in my ear. He pulls his lips away, just far enough for me to turn and look at him.

There's a brief moment between us, one where static bounces and electricity cracks. It's barely a second. Just long enough for me to back away if I don't want this.

But I do.

Oh, god. I do.

I see it in his eyes the moment he gives in. The man without a name growls, the feral sound deep in his throat, then devours me. His lips find mine, hungrily taking everything I have to offer and then some. Our tongues dance together, roaming, exploring, fighting for dominance. One hand cups the back of my neck while the other fists the sheer material of my cover-up. He pulls me onto his lap and presses our bodies together until there's not even enough room for a bead of sweat to drip between us.

I close my eyes, lost in his lips. The world tilts on its axis, spinning fast enough for me to feel the rush but slow enough that I'm not sick. This feeling, this exhilarating, life-changing, lust-falling sensation has nothing to do with the alcohol I've been drinking. It's him and the way my body reacts to the hardness pressing against my center through his shorts.

He fists my hair, wrapping the sea-sprayed locks that are more knots than loose waves around thick fingers, and pulls my mouth from his. My roots scream, not used to the tingle of pain vibrating through my scalp, but I like it. It pours gasoline on the wave of heat in my belly, making me powerless to the man who thinks I'm something more than what life has let me be.

"Do you want to get out of here?"

Yes! A hundred times, yes... but I shouldn't. The old version of me liked to play it safe, driving just under the speed limit and checking twice for motorcycles. I never trusted dating sites because of the *MTV* show *Catfish* and, up until a few months ago, I'd never had a one-night stand. I've always been a go-slow and feel-the-guy-out kind of girl.

Then, six weeks after Kenny broke my heart, I let loose. I got my first tattoo, drank my heartache away, and found new friends to numb the pain. I realized that, at twenty-one, I was barely living. I existed to make a paycheck and to keep my ex happy.

But I didn't like who I was becoming, so I took a break from the sleeping around part. I swore I wouldn't give myself to someone who didn't care about me, and I've been searching for someone who fits that bill for the last two months.

But this is vacation, and I like how this man's eyes trailing over my body makes me feel. Maybe it's the alcohol, but I doubt I will regret hooking up with him when I sober up.

Still, there are some necessities a girl needs to know before riding a new love stick. Like Mcbroody's name, his relationship status, what he does for a living, etcetera. Might as well start with the easy stuff. "Maybe. You got a name?"

"Peter," he breathes, those perfect lips drifting to the side of my neck again.

Peter.

I smile, letting myself linger in the moment instead of thinking. I feel Peter's hand slide to my hip and up my back, fingers toying with the strings of my top. I feel his hardness protest against the thin fabric keeping us apart. I feel like I don't care if I'll regret my next move in the morning.

"Wens!" Kierra yells.

I clench my teeth and groan.

Peter sinks his teeth into my shoulder, pulling a squeal of delight from my lips, and then leans back to swallow what's left of his drink. I try to relish the moment and ignore Kierra, but she calls my name again, making it impossible for me to ignore her. It figures she'd be a cock-block.

Just not for my sister because, you know, that would have been helpful.

I force a smile and look her way. Kierra's waving like a maniac to get my attention. "The boat leaves in five!" She gives two thumbs up and waits for me to acknowledge her before walking away.

"Cute nickname." Peter's hand slides down my arm and I shiver as he leans back against the bar. "Is it short for Wendy?"

I don't like the space between us. It makes me anxious. I inch closer until my arm touches his annd the thread of tension in my chest thins. He smirks and uses his other hand to sip from his glass.

"No."

Although that would have been perfect. Peter and Wendy, like the fairy tale. Destined to have our lives intertwined in adventurous harmony. If starlight wishes came true and book boyfriends were real, I'd be in a magical land with a morally gray prince who gives orgasms just as often as he gives glaring side glances. But my life isn't a story book and I'm not anything special.

"That's a name I could get behind, but no. I drew the short end of the stick."

Peter watches me, waiting for more of an explanation. I don't know why but I feel like I need to tell him the history of my name. It's an urge, a desperate ache I fear I won't quench if I don't explain.

I don't have much time left and missing the boat isn't an option. I'm not sure which island we're on or how far we are from the hotel. So, I give Peter the gist of our family's stupidity in one big breath.

"There's a long-standing family tradition of picking a name that starts with a W. Well at least the firstborn girls have a W. It's open season for everyone else. I'm sure there's a Wendy somewhere in the family, but my mom was a hippie without a creative bone in her body and named me Wednesday."

Peter grins a deliciously dark grin that makes me wish I had more time with him. But again... not lucky. He takes my hand and kisses my knuckles. "It was a pleasure to meet you, Wednesday."

"Wens!" Kierra calls again. She taps her wrist and then throws her hands in the air.

I guess my time is up.

"I've got to go." I press a quick kiss to his lips, one I wish was longer and ended with our clothes on some crappy motel floor.

Fate would throw a beautiful weekend savior in my face only to take him away before any actual saving could be done.

Probably for the best, though. Tyle would lose her mind if I stole her thunder by hooking up with someone before she could. Last night had a strict no-dick rule. It was our first night in town and Tyle wanted to make sure we had at least one whole evening together.

Tonight, however, is fair game and Peter would have been perfect. A distraction from my thoughts. Bragging rights that I hooked up first and a more than decent memory of this trip to look back on. If only time was on my side.

Oh well.

At least I got a kiss out of him. "It was nice to meet you, Peter. Maybe I'll see you around."

"Count on it, Darling."

Wednesday

A tingling sensation skirting down my spine has me peeking over the edge of my eReader, shade from my hat the only thing saving my eyes from the blinding Florida sun.

Somehow, the rays seem brighter reflecting off the white concrete and cerulean blue water than it does back home. I don't think I've ever been as tempted to wade into a pool as I am today. Sweat drips down my body in places that have never leaked before in their lives, and it's only mid-morning. I fully understand why everybody runs around half-naked down here. It is literally too hot for clothes.

My eyes take a moment to adjust to the brightness, too used to staring at the darkened screen of my eReader. I wish they hadn't. I should have kept my gaze on the words and not searched for what triggered my spidey sense. I was a lot happier two seconds ago.

"Aou-aou-aou! Sexy mama! Get it, girl!" The bridesmaids I'm forced to spend the weekend with whistle and catcall.

My sister struts down the pool deck, swinging the end of her dress like she's a tigress. She's doing the walk of shame, only today it's a walk of pride.

I shake my head and go back to my book. I don't want to hear about Tyle's sexcapades. Watching her rub how much she loves Kenny in my face every time they're together is hard enough, but hearing how little she respects him makes me angry.

Why take him from me if she was going to cheat?

Why ruin my life just to play with his?

"So, how was it?" Samantha, one of my sister's bridesmaids, asks.

"Oh, my gosh, guys." Tyle sits on the edge of Michelle's lounge chair. At least, I think that's her name. I honestly don't remember. Tyle has six bridesmaids and the only person I actually know is Kierra. Everyone else is a friend from work.

People my sister considers to be more important in her life than me.

Tyle pushes her long bleached bangs out of her eyes and gives us her I've-got-a-story face. "Have you ever given a blowie so bad that while you were doing it, you knew it sucked, but the guy didn't say anything, so you just kept going?"

I roll my eyes and stare at the paperwhite screen, but the words in front of me are a jumbled mess. I try to focus on them, but the longer Tyle talks about her one-night stand the more pissed off I get.

I think the arrangement she made with Kenny is fucked. You shouldn't need to venture out for something new if you love someone. When her future husband was mine, I never thought about another man. Hell, I didn't even read romance books because he was all I needed.

Clearly, Kenny didn't feel the same way.

"I knew the moment I started sucking on his crooked thing that everything was wrong." She giggles. "But whatever. I was drunk and it was fun. He got his happy ending—one way or another—and I got some serious man candy to add to my lady spank bank."

A bridesmaid wearing a bright blue bikini and boobs the size of my head hands Tyle a seltzer beer. Apparently, only alcoholics drink liquor before dark, and regular beer is for college kids. I don't know who made these rules, but all the girls swear by them. Even Kierra.

I sip on my orange-mango mimosa, inwardly giving every one of them the middle finger, and do my best to tune out their conversation.

Tyle isn't the reason I haven't been able to focus. It's not the book either. Believe me. I can get down with some Fae high lords. It's the guy from last night who's got my mind swimming.

Peter.

I haven't felt a fire like the one that shot straight to my lady bits since Kenny kissed me on the Farris wheel my senior year. I thought the lusty haze I felt for tall, dark, and broody was because of the drinks I had, but I'm still thinking about Peter. Still getting a tingle between my legs that I don't dare satisfy while sharing a room with seven other girls.

I know it's not likely that I'll see him again. There are seven main keys in Florida, but almost seventeen hundred little islands. I have no idea where the booze cruise took us yesterday. The pamphlet I saw at the hotel said we started in Key Largo, but we went to six other bars, all of which claimed to be secret hot spots, plus we drank on the way to each location. For all I know, we were taken to some private island that is only accessible by boat. The chances of Peter's and my path crossing again are slim, but damn I hope they do.

"What!" My sister squeals, pulling me out of my thoughts. "Wednesday! You found a man last night?"

Tyle shimmies and shakes, trying to make what I think should be a sexy gesture with her body. If that's the coordination her boy-toy got last night, it's no wonder the man didn't say anything about the BJ. If she were to try harder, the poor guy probably would have thought he stuck his dick in a meat grinder.

"I want all the dirty details, you little whore." Tyle scoots to my lounge chair and wiggles herself beside me.

Five years ago I would have shifted onto my side and cuddled up next to her. The guys at school loved to see us close... fucking pervs. But we're not sixteen anymore. We're twenty-one and I have a hard time even looking at my sister these days, let alone giving her snuggles.

I pull my legs in close and then turn sideways to sit on the chair's edge. I doubt Tyle notices the inch of air between us. She hasn't noticed the wedge she created the summer we turned fifteen growing wider with each passing year. Why would she notice an extra inch?

"Not sure what to say. I can't remember very much. That last bartender was amazing."

"Oh, em, gee. She made me something called a Purple Hooter Shooter." Tyle looks at the girls and raises her eyebrows. "Y'all... best thing I put in my mouth all night."

I force a smile at her joke while bile climbs my throat. How is she okay with this? How is she okay with Kenny doing the same thing? Pressing his lips against some other girl's neck. Touching her like he cares. Taking all of their intimate moments and sharing the tricks that are solely hers with someone else.

I shudder, unable to take it anymore. I'm used to my mind straying to Kenny's sex life, especially at the beginning of their relationship. Wondering how many of the moves I taught him he's used on my sister. It still makes me sick, but this is somehow worse because a small twisted part of me hoped Kenny would use this pass to give us one more chance. Our last bedroom romp was horrible. He was frustrated because he couldn't get it up, and I was a mess thinking I was the problem.

Turns out the problem was that I wasn't Tyle.

I may be crazy, looking into the sideways glances Kenny sends my way or the extra second eye locks, but... I don't know. I thought he wanted to give us closure.

I would have ditched Tyle's bachelorette party in a heartbeat to show up at Kenny's door because he used to be a great lay. Mostly I wanted to climb onto his cock and ride him until he is at the brink of coming and then walk away. That man deserves a severe case of blue balls after how he screwed me over.

But the bragging rights that Kenny still wants me would have been the ultimate slap in the face to Tyle.

I smile inwardly, thinking about the conversation we would have had after the fact, but of course, things didn't pan out that way. Instead, Kenny is sharing what used to be our intimate tricks with someone new. Once again, throwing it in my face that I'm not good enough.

I skip the straw in my glass and take the rest of my drink like a shot. I can feel judgy eyes on me as I gulp half of a champagne flute in one swallow, but truthfully I couldn't care less about what these bitches think.

Fun fact about Tyle and me... we're different. Besides the ugly truth that I'm not a heartless whore, who's paid to look like a blonde Kardashian, I have no gag reflex.

We both know that she'll choke the moment her mouth gets full. That's why she mumbles *drunk* under her breath as I swallow. She knows that no matter how hard she tries, I will always suck dick better than her.

Am I proud of that?

Eh... It's not something I flaunt, but today it feels good.

I moan and wipe my mouth, channeling my inner porn star just for the sake of adding more awkwardness. I'm ninety percent sure Tyle's oral exam last night was meant to be practice for the wedding night. Kenny loved to try and choke me with his monster —and believe me it's a monster—but I never gagged. *Better get practicing, bitch.*

"I'm heading up to the room." I don't give anyone a chance to respond. The chair tips when I stand. Tyle squeals like the helpless little bird she is as she falls to the floor. Her friends scramble to help her back onto her feet, fussing over superficial scrapes and dirt.

As for me... I steal Tyle's seltzer beer and take it with me. I may not be a fan of this shit, but she took what was mine.

It's only fair I return the favor.

Wednesday

I think my sister's sole purpose in life is to torment me.

She knows I hate the ocean.

Not the beach. I like the feel of sand and tiny shells between my toes. I like sitting on the shore as waves cool my sun-kissed skin. I love relaxing with a book and a bucket of something tasty while birds fly across the sky. I even enjoy laying on a foam board and riding baby waves onto the skinny water while gliding across the sand.

And I can get behind watching man candy play volleyball, or football, or even frisbee so long as it requires him to have his shirt off.

What I don't like is being in water that's more than waist-deep. Which is why I hate the glass-bottom-boat tour she's scheduled for today. Its sole purpose is to prove just how much more than waist-deep the ocean is. We haven't passed over any coral or a noticeable seafloor in hours. I haven't seen a fish, a dolphin... nothing. There's just a never-ending swipe of blue on a much too big canvas both above and below the water.

Even if the bottom wasn't plexiglass and I couldn't see beyond the hull, I would still hate this boat. The double-decker, one hundred and twenty-foot vessel is fully air-conditioned and staffed with a captain, three servers, as well as a fishing crew. It is the Titanic of glass-bottom tours, minus the sinking.

But even if this boat were the infamously sinkable cruise ship, where I was guaranteed a hot hookup, a lifeboat, and a multi-million dollar diamond at the end of our voyage, I would still despise it, just like I despised yesterday's sportfish.

Because I can't swim.

My worst fear is falling into the water and drowning. It's so bad I can barely go by a pool. I'm terrified someone will throw me in thinking the prank is harmless and I'll inhale too much water and die.

My logic may be dramatic, but I have my reasons. I never used to be like this. When we were little, I loved being in the water. I still love it. If we go someplace with a pool, I usually find a chair at the shallowest end and stay next to the steps, dipping my toes in.

On the rare occasion I venture deeper, I stay on my feet. I don't like floats or rafts because they can drift to the deep end, and I won't go in if the water is the slightest bit cold. Shivering half-naked isn't my idea of fun. Most of my friends know about my fear of water and they're respectful.

But I'll never forget the summer Tyle dared her boyfriend to throw me into the community pool. He tossed me in the shallows, but at the time, I didn't know.

All I saw was light filtering through from above.

All I felt was the suffocating pressure pushing my body deeper and deeper until my skin scraped against the cement floor.

I was underwater for less than ten seconds, but every tick of the second hand felt like hours. Kenny immediately jumped in and pulled me to the surface. I clung to him, desperately trying not to cry while our friends laughed.

I wasn't in any real danger, they said. The prank was harmless, but I felt like I had been violated. I didn't talk to my sister for the rest of the summer, and I think that's the moment I started pushing our circle away. I couldn't trust any of them.

My hand shakes just thinking about how easy it would be for

something similar to happen again. At least there's a bar on board to alleviate some of my anxiety and two stories to lounge on. Although, for some reason, being on the top deck makes me queasy. Maybe it's seeing all the water around me, a stretch of deep blue that haunts my thoughts like a never-ending nightmare.

"Thanks." I stuff a five-dollar bill into the tip jar and immediately bring the rim of my glass to my lips. I close my eyes as I take the first sip of what will probably be many glasses. My concoction, liquid marijuana, is cold and bitter with the right amount of sweetness.

"You make the most delicious sounds."

I choke on my green drink. The little hairs on my arms stand on edge. My body is angry at my sudden stupidity of confusing a cocktail for air, yet excited because I recognize the voice.

Peter wipes a calloused thumb across my chin, erasing tiny green droplets that missed my mouth. I wonder what he does for a living to have such textured hands, or if the roughness is from lifting weights. He's got the body to show for that kind of hard work. All sharp edges and smooth lines.

Peter's lips lift in a smile that demands to be kissed. *God, he's pretty.*

I still haven't figured out how someone as beautiful as him is single. Or maybe he's not. Maybe he's married and a shitty husband, or in an open relationship. I know nothing about him and I don't want to ask.

Does that make me a bad person? Probably.

But as long as I don't do anything crazy my conscience will survive. I lean in for a hug as the boat rolls over a large wave. It throws me off balance. I stumble backward, spilling half my drink onto the bartender's table.

Peter wraps his arms around my waist and pulls me close, steadying me on my feet. "Easy, Darling. It would be a shame to lose you so soon."

My arm goes around his neck on instinct. Being this close again is dangerous. Yesterday's desire paired with today's anxiety is a lethal combination. I hope no one needs the bathroom for a while because if things go my way, we'll be occupying it for a long time.

We lock eyes and his gaze devours me in a way I wish his lips would. Heat climbs my cheeks and I'm smiling again, feeling like a kid with her first crush all over again. "Thanks."

Peter smells just like I remember. Rich, with a hint of earth, sage, and bad decisions. The scent penetrates my senses, making each one itch to be satisfied.

His fingers play with the strings of my forest green bikini top. I stole this one from Tyle's suitcase because it reminded me of Peter. Not this Peter but the one from the story about Neverland and in a roundabout way it made me feel close to this Peter.

It made sense at the time, but now as I think about the choice again, it sounds crazy. I look into *this* Peter's eyes and fall deeper into their abyss. Like the ocean, their deep-set blue makes me quiver, but for a more enjoyable reason.

Peter's grin shifts into a goofy one, wide, two dimples on display. For a moment, I can see it. Him being some grown-up version of the boy who refused to age, hardened by life but still playful at heart. I imagine him flying and crowing and causing chaos only to find his way into my bed once the sun goes down because, let's be real, fantasizing about a kid is weird, but thinking of a grown man who left his fictional girlfriend for me... way better.

I push the ludicracy away and make a mental note to find some kind of *Peter Pan* retelling when I have cell service again. "What are you doing here?"

Peter doesn't let me go, even as my hand slides down his bare chest, feeling the baby hairs that cover those dark tattoos. I trace a line with my finger, following it from his collarbone to his sternum. His muscles are hard, warm, and the line keeps going. It intertwines with more than a dozen lines, creating new paths on his body. I'm lost in the gorgeousness that is him...until his deep whisper brings me back to reality.

"I wanted to see the beauties beneath the sea." His voice sends a shudder of delight through me. I can't explain it. The warm, needy sensation that trails through my veins like liquid gold.

But I like it.

"Although, I'm not complaining about what I found above it." His finger traces a small circle on my lower back. "What about you, Wednesday? What are you doing on this boat?"

"Oh, you know, fulfilling my mission to help my sister check every box on her bachelorette bucket list." I roll my eyes because this particular ocean tour ends with optional snorkeling and she has every intention of losing her top in the water. The only reason I agreed to come is because it is an adult cruise. The last thing we need is a pissed-off parent because her pepperoni nipples scarred some kid for life.

I hear Tyle's voice carry across the room. I can recognize her anywhere, and it's not even a twin thing. Tyle just has that voice—high-pitched, notoriously upbeat, and all-around fake.

"Worst idea ever," my sister declares, talking to her bridesmaids. She struts across the teak, her heels *click, click, clicking* as she sways her hips. Every step is exaggerated, meant to draw the eyes of anyone who will look. Tyle doesn't care if it's male, female, or gender-neutral so long as people pay attention to her.

She frowns when she sees me, her eyebrows drawing into a straight line. She signals her pose to hang back, and they do, staring and whispering amongst themselves with sinister grins as Tyle walks toward us.

I look Peter in his royal blue eyes, knowing the game that's about to begin, and see all possibilities of what could have been fading away. The moment his gaze settles on her, I feel it in my soul.

It's game over for me.

CHAPTER 5

Wednesday

My stomach twists into a dozen knots. Nerves, disappointment, alcohol, and the rocking of the boat merge together and morph into nausea. I fight the bile climbing my throat. Throwing up everywhere would give me an escape from what I'm about to witness, but I don't want to leave.

There's an invisible string between Peter and me, pulling tighter and drawing us closer with every minute we're together. If I believed in love at first sight, I'd tell the world that's what this is because my body craves Peter's touch as much as my ears beg to listen to his voice. A small part of me has hope that this unexplainable bond between us is enough to evade Tyle's thirst trap.

Still, I can't stand the thought of Peter touching me if he falls under my sister's spell. It hits too close to home. The pain from my last relationship is too fresh, the bandaid covering my scars ripped off by what's about to go down.

I move my hand from the waistband of Peter's bathing suit, my fingers having just found the curls at the end of his happy trail, and step backward.

Peter's grip loosens, but he still holds my waist. His hands burn my hips, heat from my anxiety and neediness mix together. I arch my back, putting as much distance between us as I can. He lets me go with a frown.

Tyle flashes her signature smile, showcasing perfectly white veneers as she comes closer. I'm sure she assumes she's already won, my pulling away the white flag. I'm not going to fight over a man, no matter how much I like him, and she knows it.

Tyle glides the tips of her manicured nails down the curves of Peter's arm. The same feeling I get when she kisses Kenny blooms in my chest—a tightness that spreads from my sternum to my back. It squeezes the air from my lungs and shoots needles down my spine.

I hate this.

Watching her take what could have been mine.

Again.

Kierra asked me once, back when we were in high school, why I allowed Tyle to walk all over me. She assumed I let my sister flirt with the boys I liked and willingly turned my back when she made them hers under the bleachers.

The truth is that every time my sister manipulated a man into choosing her over me another crack set in. Another voice of doubt and discouragement whispered in my mind until there was no point in trying anymore.

It didn't matter if Tyle had a boyfriend or not. She couldn't stand the thought of a guy looking at me and so she made him only have eyes for her. She lived for the attention and then discarded him once she had it.

Today is no different.

I could easily lean into Peter and hope this energy bouncing between us is enough to dissuade her charms, but I don't want a man who would choose my sister over me. I want someone who ignores Tyle's pretty face and sees her for the snake she is.

If Peter falls into her thirst trap, I'm better off without him. Even if a small part of me already hurts at the thought of letting him go.

"O.M.G. Your tattoo is fabulous," my sister purrs.

I watch Peter, mentally preparing for the grin that has sent butterflies a flight within me to flash for Tyle. The only man I knew who could resist her seductive blue eyes and ruby-red lips gave in to temptation. It took years, but she got her way.

I don't have high hopes for today.

Tyle is sex in heels, whereas I'm a bookworm with some extra love on my hips and hair that's lucky to see a blow dryer on the weekend. She's the kind of woman men fantasize about. While I'm the girl they leave their kids with and not think twice about it before walking out the door.

Peter's blue eyes darken and shift in color. Black spills into them like ink in water until there isn't any azure left. He clenches his jaw, showing one tick of frustration, and then it's gone, wiped away as if it never existed.

The bartender at the counter behind us hands Peter a glass of amber liquor. I don't remember him ordering, but he must have, probably when I was lost in the patterns of his tattoo. He brings his lips to the tumbler and takes a sip without so much as sparing a passing glance at my sister.

Tyle forces her grin wider. Men don't usually respond to her this way. She's used to them chasing her like love-drunk fools but Peter is impassive and barely acknowledges her existence. If I know my sister, like I think I do, it's eating her alive.

Tyle presses her chest against Peter's arm and her pretty white-tipped nails run down the length of his spine and stretch wide, touching the muscles of his bare back.

I turn away from them and ask the bartender for a cup of water. I don't feel so good again and I don't think drowning my thoughts in alcohol is a good idea. Not when Tyle can see I'm bothered.

I refuse to give her the satisfaction.

"Is that a picture of Neverland?" Tyle asks, her voice a whisper of seduction. "*Peter and Wendy* is my favorite Disney retelling."

Liar. It's mine and she knows it. I force the huff of breath to ease out my nostrils, slow and controlled. It's just one more thing to add to the list of items Tyle took from me.

"Don't touch me," Peter growls, jerking his arm away.

The sheer hatred in his tone makes me jump. I should be scared or at least put-off. Logically, I know a man who reacts to a woman with such harshness is dangerous. I shouldn't feel the tingle of lust between my legs, but dear god, it's hot watching him reject my sister.

Tyle holds her hands up, mock-surrenders, and steps to where he can see her pouty face. "Sorry, pumpkin. I didn't realize you had a kink."

"Peter, this is my sister Tyle." The introduction is like ash in my mouth. I know it's what she's been waiting for. After all, in her eyes, married or not, I will forever be her wing-woman. The only reason I'm even bothering is because I'm curious as to what Peter will do next.

"Oh, my God. Your name is Peter?" Tyle squeals and touches his arm again. Peter's gaze narrows on her hand. He frowns, but Tyle is oblivious to his discomfort. "I have some role-play fantasies I'm dying to try if you're into that kind of thing."

Peter grips his glass until his knuckles flash white, somehow managing to keep his features indifferent. He lifts his tumbler of whiskey, ice clinking along the sides, but pauses before drinking.

"Sweetheart, you couldn't handle me in bed." He takes a sip of the whiskey, his gaze trailing from Tyle to me, and then grins. "But I have a feeling this one here knows how to have a good time."

"Wednesday?" My sister scoffs. Her eyes roll so hard I'm surprised they're still in her head. "Please, she's so vanilla. Her boyfriend dumped her six months ago because he got bored screwing her. Poor thing hasn't had a man in her life since." She touches my arm, pho-sympathy on her face. "Bless your heart, darlin'."

The nagging burn of tears pricks my eyes. Tyle knows how to hit me where it hurts. She knows her betrayal is a barely closed wound on my heart, one she likes to poke and reopen any chance she can.

I force the knot of hurt in my throat down and try to smile. If I do anything else, even something as deserved as defending myself, the dam will break free and I'll be a blubbering mess. That's what she wants though. Isn't it? To destroy what little chance I might have with Peter by any means necessary.

I almost wonder if Tyle is even attracted to Peter doesn't fit our usual go-to man, or if she just wants his attention because he's talking to me.

I know I said I don't want a guy who would leave me for her, and I stand by that, but I don't understand why she can't just respect what's mine. Why does she always have to take, and take, and take? It's not enough for her to marry the only man I've ever loved, she has to screw my rebound too.

Peter doesn't miss a beat. He looks me in the eye again and that dark matter I can't explain swirls in the blue of his irises. I've never seen anything like it. It's fascinating, so much so that I almost miss his response. "Vanilla is my favorite flavor."

My jaw drops at the same time Tyle's nearly hits the floor.

"Come on, Darling." Peter reaches for my hand and threads our fingers together. His touch is colder than I remember, but the tingle of nervous energy in my palm offsets the chill. "You and I have some unfinished business to attend to."

"Oh, my God!" Tyle squeals, her voice reaching an octave only dogs should hear. "You're him! You're the guy from the bar last night." She turns her attention to me, a disappointed frown tilting her lips. "Jesus, Wednesday. How could you forget a hunk like that?" Her eyes drag back to Peter with an *I'm so sorry* look. "Yeah, she forgot all about you. Couldn't tell us a single thing, not even your name."

"I promise you, Cabinet, your sister did not forget about me." Peter's thumb rubs circles against my skin. His touch is steady, soothing. "If I were a betting man, I'd say Wednesday was trying to save me from the likes of you, but what she doesn't realize is that I've dealt with monsters that have slimier tentacles than yours." He pauses, smirking to himself. "Although, I will say you give those beasts a run for their money."

"My name is Tyle," she mutters through clenched teeth.

"And I don't care." Peter releases my fingers to wrap his arm around my waist. I lean into him, my heart racing, my mind replaying the last five minutes. I've never seen a man blatantly reject Tyle before.

And he did it for me.

CHAPTER 6

Wednesday

Peter and I walk to the stern of the boat. There's only one couple back here with us. A man in a button-down shirt with hula-girls on it and a woman with a big purple hat that shadows most of her face. The woman leans into the man, touching his arm when they talk, pressing her body close.

"Do you think they came together or are they having some boat-loving fun?" I wonder out loud. I watch the couple, curious about what outsiders see when they look at Peter and me. We look about as matched as Oreos and whiskey. Separate each one is amazing, but together...not so much.

Peter stares off at the horizon. His brows are pulled close together, his thoughts far from where we stand.

"Peter?"

"Hmmm?"

"You're not having buyer's remorse. Are you?" Something falls into the pit of my stomach—a knot, or maybe my heart. It's hard to say, but it leaves me feeling hollow.

Maybe I jumped to conclusions, thinking he was better than the rest.

Maybe he likes to argue and that show of power was foreplay.

Maybe I read our situation all wrong.

That last thought makes me sad. I hope not. Peter makes me feel good and worthy of attention. Forever being in my sister's shadow has messed with my confidence. It got better when Kenny was around, but the floor fell out from under me with that one. I hate the doubt I'm feeling, but better to find out now that I'm being used than three years from now and have my heart incinerated again.

"If you want to go back to Tyle, you can. She won't care." I force myself to laugh because I feel like I'm crumbling. "Hell, it'll probably turn her on if you reject me now."

"Darling." Peter threads his fingers through the hair at the base of my neck and pulls me close until our chests are pressing against each other. He looks me in the eyes with unwavering confidence and inky darkness spills into the deep blue of his irises. "There are a million women in existence throughout the universe, but there is no other soul in all the galaxies like yours. I would choose you over her every day, with every breath."

No one has ever said something so beautiful to me. My knees buckle and I reach for the deck railing with one hand to steady myself. I feel like I'm standing naked for all the world to see, all of my insecurities exposed because for the first time in months, I feel something more than hazy lust and anger.

I feel vulnerable.

It's crazy that a man I met only yesterday has such control over my emotions. It doesn't make sense, but the terror that Peter will walk away and never see me again is as real as the sweat dripping down my back. It's unwelcome and inconvenient and messy, but it's there.

"So...what's wrong?" I whisper.

"I'm trying to decide what to do with you." He pauses. His fingers pull at my roots again, inching our faces closer together. I stare into his eyes. That beautiful blue swallows the black ink that dances within his irises. They're normal again, a blue ring surrounding onyx pupils. *How do they do that?*

Peter's fingers unfurl from my roots. He turns and sits against the edge of the boat. "Play a game with me, Darling."

"All right." I mimic his pose. My heart beats faster, doubling in speed with each thump. I take a deep breath and convince myself I'm okay. We're slow-cruising. Taking our time so everyone aboard can enjoy the scenery. The seas are calm-ish and clear. The chances of me falling overboard are one in a million and, even if I did, I'm fairly confident Peter would save me.

I. Will. Be. Fine.

"Truth or dare." There's a glimmer of mischievousness in the way he asks. The kind expected from a teenage boy just before they do something stupid. Peter is a far cry from a teenager. If I had to guess, I'd say he's in his mid-twenties and no part that I can see is *boy*.

"Truth." Dares are dangerous. He could tell me to disappear with him and I would, in a heartbeat, because my soul feels like it's splitting in two. An ache resonates in my bones that's only quenched when his hands are on my body. Maybe I should have said dare.

"Okay. Ask away."

I laugh, confused by his response. "That's not how the game works. You're supposed to ask me a question."

Peter drags his teeth across his bottom lip. The movement is slow. Deliberate. Meant to make me look at his mouth, and I do. I remember the way his lips felt, how his tongue moved expertly. I imagine it's just as skilled on other parts of the body. I press my thighs together, embarrassed by the wetness pooling in my panties.

"Scared of the answers, Darling?" He eases closer, dropping his voice to a gruff, sexy low. "I know something is looming in your mind. I can see it on your lips."

"Am I that obvious?" I tuck wayward strands that have wiggled loose from my braid behind my ears. They tickle my nose and cheeks, blowing in the breeze. The feeling isn't uncomfortable, but the fact that Peter can so clearly see through my guard is.

"You possess the beautiful ability to display how you feel without using words. All I need to do is look at you to see your little mind running in circles. Ask me what you want to know, Darling." He touches my chin and the rough pad of his thumb brushes over my bottom lip. "I'll only ever tell you the truth."

My cheeks heat again, proving his point that I can't hide how I'm feeling. Peter chuckles at my embarrassment. I let out a slow breath, then meet his gaze again. I need to look him in the eye for this. "Do you have a wife? Or girlfriend? Or someone who would be upset at what we're doing?"

He tilts his head, thinking. "I am neither formally nor informally committed to anyone, but I'm sure there are plenty who would be unhappy that you have my undivided attention."

Neither a lie nor a truth. The sneaky bastard kept his word.

"Your turn." Peter takes my hand in his and flips it over. He traces the lines on my palm with the edge of his nail. Pressing hard enough that the sensation tickles but doesn't hurt. "Favorite color?"

"Really?" That is such a loaded question. My favorite color changes with my mood. I can never pick just one. Even as a child, I would ramble off four or five at a time, never the same ones in a row. "I don't know. Green, I guess. What about you?"

"Blue, like that of the sky." He glances upwards, a playful grin on his face, but there's a shadow of sadness that looks out of place. "My turn. What is your greatest fear?"

"Wow. Going deep. Um... drowning. I can't swim."

"And you're on a boat?"

"Never claimed to be the sharpest crayon in the box."

"Well, Darling, I was going to ask if you were daring, but I think I have my answer." He smirks again. I don't think I've ever seen a man as happy as him. It's like the weight of life doesn't fall on his shoulders. My job, all the bills I have to pay, and the decisions I've made in the past make it hard to enjoy life. But Peter... he's pure joy wrapped in tattoos and muscles. "You're the bravest girl on the boat."

"I wouldn't go that far. More like stupidly eager to please."

Peter's hand covers mine. He turns my wrist over and kisses my knuckles. His lips are pillow-soft and they send a surge of excitement all the way down to my toes. "I want the biggest truth of them all, Darling. Whatever the answer, you cannot lie. Promise me."

"I promise," I say, anticipation sucking the breath from my lungs.

"Would you come away with me, Wednesday? Leave your sister's pettiness behind and have the adventure of a lifetime." He squeezes my hand in his, holding onto me with so much hope that it radiates off him in waves of yellow and gold. "There is so much I can show you. So much we can do together. You'll never have to worry about anything again. What do you say?"

I laugh, unsure of how to respond. This is crazy. No sane woman runs away with a man she just met, even if he is panty-dropping hot. This is how women go missing and end up trafficked. I can't leave. I won't leave.

But this is just a game.

I can pretend for a few minutes that Peter is everything he seems to be and more. For all I know, he's a wealthy businessman ready to whisk me away on a private jet to some tropical island. That would be nice. I toy with my thoughts, imagining what it would be like to disappear and live extravagantly without worrying about money, or my sister, or any part of day-to-day life.

Tonight, I'll go back to my hotel and we'll all go out one more time before heading home tomorrow. Maybe I'll see Peter again before I leave. Maybe I won't. Either way, what harm can come from playing a game and giving the answer I wish could be true?

"Yes."

"I was hoping you'd say that." He presses his lips to mine but they pull away far too quickly. "You're perfect, Darling. Absolutely perfect."

Without warning, Peter pushes my shoulder and I fall backward, over the ledge of the boat. The cold Florida water hits my skin and sucks the air from my lungs before I can scream. My arms flail, and my legs kick, but they don't work together. A shadow passes over the sun's rays as they permeate through the water.

Someone will come for me.

I'll be okay.

A burning ache spreads in my lungs with each second that ticks by and I realize I'm alone. My body is desperate for air, and the longer I'm without it the harder it is to make it cooperate. My limbs get heavier. Harder to move, but I push through the pain.

Today is not my day to die.

I will fight until my heart quits because as hard as my life is, as much suffering as it's caused me, I'm not ready to give it up. There's too much I haven't done. I want to get married and have kids and travel the world. I want to find the little moments and live within them. This can't be the end.

I don't know how much time passes, but a breath of ice coats my skin.

And then it all goes dark.

CHAPTER 7

Peter

I kick the edge of the doorstep before crossing inside, knocking the dirt off my boots. It's been decades since I stepped into the realm of the living. I forgot how long the journey from the mirror pool to the tree house is and how taxing it is to go from The Triangle to Neverland.

I'm tired.

Too tired to clean up a muddy mess.

Wednesday has yet to wake, the journey was more strenuous on her than me. She turns in my arms and hugs close to my chest. Her mouth falls open and drool drips down her cheek, pooling against my skin. I force my mouth to hold steady and fight a grin. The war against my emotions begins now. Before she realizes what I've done or who she is.

Casper Greenbrier, my right-hand man, sits in the faded wing-back chair by the window, a tattered novel in his hands. Waiting for me. "Taking a page out of your brother's book, Peter?"

I shake my head, ignoring the dig. I'm nothing like James. Not anymore. "This one is different. It's her."

"How do you know?"

I look at my shadow. The part of my soul I sacrificed to save the only person I've ever loved. The devils I bargained with gave him free will and the ability to leave my side, taking my gift of flight with him. A cruel corollary to the promise made, but that's what the Fae do. They twist the truth until it becomes so convoluted that it can only be a lie.

Back then, if I knew the true price of saving Wendy Darling's life, I would have found another way.

My shadowself leaves the comforts of the counter he perches on. He walks to me along the wall, taking his time, knowing Cass is judging his every step.

The funny thing about my shadow, he may be his own being, but our thoughts are connected. I can feel his excitement and fears despite being inches away or halfway across the world, and he can read my mind. Whether or not he listens is another story.

Today, he seems amicable. My shadow slides along the floor to place his feet on top of mine and climbs into my skin. He slithers, getting comfortable. Even though he's made himself home inside me again the past two days, it's jarring having him there. Two minds. One body. Forever at war with each other.

The power I lost bleeds out of Shadow and into my veins, igniting like sparklers in my blood. On Earth, the sensation was an annoying tingle, painfully waiting to be awoken. Here, I'm connected to the Island again. We're one, like we were so long ago.

It feels good.

I let out a controlled breath and school my features into passiveness. The only tell that his power, my power, flows through me again is the onyx in my eyes. Shadow's presence fills them, masking my blues with his darkness. I didn't realize he could do that until I saw my reflection yesterday. He and I haven't been together since that fateful day.

"Holy shit," Cass mumbles. He sets the leather-bound book on my end table and stands. "It is her."

I nod, the gravity of Wednesday's presence falling harder against me. Cass's kin created the curse I live with. He and his siblings, Belle and Emmit, are the only Fae on the island, but none of them were there that night. They don't know everything I sacrificed or what her soul's return means for all of us.

Cass has an idea. He's the only person who understands what I've done. What I've condemned us all to. I see the moment he realizes what having Wednesday in Neverland could mean for The Lost. "How did you get the Darling here?"

"By doing something she'll never forgive me for."

Cass rubs the back of his neck and sighs. There are two paths into Neverland: through the sky or a portal. Neither of which can be navigated with a fully beating heart. I carry the guilt of every soul that crosses into this realm. Most were brought by James or happenstance, but it's because of what I did that they are eternal prisoners of the island.

"Sounds about right." Cass stares at Wednesday's chest, watching the rise and fall of her lungs with each breath. His brows draw together as the dots connect before him. "She's still alive? How?"

"A little bit of luck mixed with a lot of magic." I lift my chin toward Wendy Darling's old room. I haven't been there in ages. The sheets are probably dust-covered, along with the rest of her furniture. All of Wendy's personal items are with James. I have nothing left of her but haunting memories and an empty space. "Think she'd like that one? Or should I give her my room?"

"No. That one should be good. With any luck, it'll trigger a forgotten memory and make the transition easier." Cass walks to the kitchen, if it could be called that. The tree houses don't have modern amenities. Appliances like a fridge or stove are useless without gas or electricity, but I have cabinets with cups and plates and a drawer of silverware. Cass doesn't reach for those. Instead, he grabs a bucket from under the counter, a clean set of sheets, and a wash rag. "Sit with her. You've had a long night. I'll get the room ready."

I sit in the chair by the window, setting most of Wednesday's weight on my lap. The poor girl is still out cold, her breaths a slow, steady intake as she sleeps. I watch her while Cass cleans, reliving our last moments together in my mind.

The terror of witnessing Wednesday die and the regret of using her weakness against her hangs on me. I don't miss this part of my shadow.

The feelings.

Shadow took those with him a long time ago and I was comfortably numb, free of ailments like pain or sorrow. Until his excitement hit me like a sledgehammer to the face the other day. He called to me, begging me to join him in the human world.

And so I did.

I think the fear he holds is the most jarring. I feel it like it's my own. Strong. All consuming.

If my shadow found Wednesday, that means James could have, too, and that makes Shadow's bones shake.

After all these years, James never stopped searching for Wendy's reincarnation. Girls, boys, dogs… if he thought there was a chance our Darling had returned, he took them. Killed them in hopes they'd survive the journey and disposed of the bodies when they didn't. It physically hurts me to think about what could happen if he discovers Wednesday.

"It's ready."

I meet Cass's gaze. He gives me a sad smile. We both know Wednesday can't stay. It's too dangerous, but we have to find a way to keep her safe. At least if she's with us we know she isn't with him.

"She'll never trust me." The admission is a knife to the chest. People like me don't get second chances. Not after what I've done. But Wednesday's beating heart is the missing piece. The antidote to our curse. Our second chance if I can figure out how to break the curse without permanently taking her life.

I stand, careful not to drop Wednesday in the process. She's pitifully light, but I'm drained. It's been so long since I've wielded magic. I forgot how taxing it is.

"She might. It just depends on how she wakes."

Meaning which emotion is prevalent. Neverland holds the soul in their last moment of life. I'm hoping that Wednesday's beating heart didn't trap her in an eternal state of fear. It's taken Scarlett—one of our Lost souls—decades to manage her terror.

Wednesday doesn't have that kind of time.

"I need you to be her hero, Cass." A knot lodges in my chest, but I know this is for the best. Wednesday needs to trust someone on the Island. She needs an ally. I can't be that person for her. "No matter the cost, keep her safe from everyone. In her eyes, I'm the bad guy. Let me be her villain. If she hates me, it will make my next move bearable."

I lay Wednesday on the bed and touch her cheek one last time. I doubt she'll let me get this close again. Probably for the best. I've already let myself fall too far down an old path.

"Peter."

"Tell the others to play along, Cass." I pull the thin sheet he found over her shoulders. Water bleeds onto the fabric from her bathing suit. Green under white. The colors of life and death. "I'll set the plan in motion when she wakes. After that, she's all yours."

Cass frowns. He believes there's another way, but he's wrong. My soulmate gave her heart to my brother, and I gave away my soul. There was always a chance the Gods would allow her to live again, but the Fae made sure we could never be together.

If Wednesday's heart is claimed before James can find her, the curse will be broken.

I think.

I hope.

CHAPTER 8

Wednesday

I suck in a sharp breath, jolting myself awake. All I see around me is darkness, a black hole void of light or shadows. I remember the darkness as it pulled me beneath the water. The way its cold hands wrapped around my neck, pushing me deeper into its trenches. No matter how hard I clawed, I couldn't reach the surface. My lungs burned and my chest felt like it was being torn apart.

I touch my chest, desperate to feel my heartbeat. Its consistent *thump, thump, thumps* make me sigh a breath of relief.

I survived.

Somehow, someone must have pulled me out of the water, gave me CPR, and brought me...here. Wherever here is.

The flame of a lighter flickers in the room. I sit up as someone's thumb rakes against the wheel. Light. No light. Light. No light. Until, finally, the flame holds steady, pressed to the wick of a candle or something similar.

Shadows reach out from the darkness that covers us like a blanket. Another candle is lit, this one at the base of the wall at the far end of the room. Yellow light stretches up, touches the bare wood, and kisses the hue of the beam strewn beside it.

One by one, the perimeter illuminates. I follow the path with my gaze, taking in each shadowed item in the room. There's a dresser on one end. A small desk and chair are on the wall across from it. I'm in a bed, this much I can tell and the mattress beneath me is soft, the blankets light.

I curl my legs in, folding them to sit crossed. Each new light is a piece of the puzzle. It's terrifying, not knowing what's coming next, but exciting, too. Like unwrapping a present at Christmas.

The next candle lights beside the bed and I scream as dark eyes stare into mine. I swing on instinct and a hand curls around my fist. Tingles spread from the touch of his skin down my core and that's when I realize whose eyes I'm looking into. I recognize them as I would my own in a mirror.

Peter sits in a chair, arms crossed over the wooden frame where his back should rest. There's something different about him, a coldness I didn't notice on the boat or the bar.

"I was wondering when you'd wake," he says, and even his voice has an edge to it. "I hoped you'd still have that fire in you. Death is unpredictable. Sometimes people come back... different."

Flashes of memories come back to me in broken pieces. My skin heats as it remembers the way Peter's hands felt on me. My neck tingles in the place his lips caressed. I reach up and touch that spot, a small smile lifting my lips, but then I remember his palm on my chest and the cold rush of water that came after.

"You pushed me." I don't realize I said the words out loud until Peter nods once, his eyes chained to me.

"Dying is the greatest adventure of them all." He says it in such a childlike way, filled with wonder and unhindered belief, I can't help but laugh once.

"I don't want to die, Peter." My voice cracks when I say his name, revealing how vulnerable I am. I hate that my insecurity is out there for him to see. I'm not this person. I don't cry in public, I don't get mad and blow my top. I'm the calm twin. The one everyone turns to when shit hits the fan. I keep the world together when everything falls apart, but I'm breaking. "I didn't want any of this."

"Liar!" Peter stands and throws the chair in one swift movement. It shatters into a dozen pieces across the room. I flinch out of reflex and he snarls.

"Take me home, Peter." I cross my arms. "Or so help the stars in the sky, I will make you regret bringing me here." I narrow my eyes and glare, hoping my paper-thin armor doesn't fall apart. I don't know how I'll make him regret bringing me here—wherever here is—but I will find a way.

Peter frowns but nods, visibly at war with himself. His expression softens and he sighs. "I'm sorry, Darling."

I drop my arms and try not to cling to the hope that I've won the argument. The cynic in me says that was too easy, but the terrified, pissed-off woman in me is squeezing that shred of hope to the point of suffocation.

Peter drops his head back. He looks at the ceiling, staring with determination, searching for something far off in the distance, beyond the walls that cage us.

"All is not lost," he says after a long pause. Those dark blues, nearly black with whatever swirls inside them, find mine. "There's still time."

"Time for what?"

He smirks. A devilish grin devours the sweet, boyish innocence he radiated. "Tick. Tock. Tick. Tock. Never fear time on a broken clock. Don't worry, Darling. While you're here, we'll be sure you have fun."

"I don't want to have fun, Peter. I want to go home!" He can't do this. He can't keep me here. In this room. On this island.

Peter ignores me and chants the same confusing rhyme as he leaves me on the bed. The candles blow out as he crosses the room, one by one, each step casting a new web of darkness.

"Peter!"

He stops just before the last bit of light is snuffed out. There is no gust, no breeze that would extinguish the fire. Nothing to make sense of the darkness coming for me.

The hackles on my arms stand on edge. I've never been this

scared. It's an instinctual fear. A nagging feeling like the one I get when walking into a parking garage by myself. "Where am I?"

Pink and yellow light pours into the room from the windows. Not as bright as the sun rising, but that dim, in-between hue where both the sun and moon are in the sky. It happens too fast for time to have changed and yet I can't deny what I'm seeing with my own eyes.

Peter looks over his shoulder. Shadows fall over half his face, cloaking him like a bandit in permeable darkness. "You're in Neverland, Darling."

CHAPTER 9

Wednesday

Peter doesn't shut the door when he leaves.

It's open, tempting me to run. Taunting me with the hope of freedom.

I've never been kidnapped, but based on my limited experience on the matter, drawing from all the smutty stories I've read, I do not want to try to escape through that door. There's a good chance this opening is a trap or that someone is standing guard, waiting for me to do the obvious.

Yeah... not gonna happen.

Looking around the room, there's not much to see. The walls are bare and the furniture is minimal and the faint hue of a yellow light seeps from the hallway into my space. I don't think I'm on the first floor of the house. Kidnapper logic dictates the bedroom window should be blocked, maybe even barred. Truth be told, I'm surprised I'm not in a basement or chained to the bed or... something. *Maybe I've read too many books.*

I walk across the room, trying my hardest to keep the pitter-patter of my feet quiet. The house is still. Scarily so, without a single noise carrying into my room. I pad to the window and stare at the world outside, even more baffled.

This is a treehouse.

A literal, sitting on limbs, made from wood, surrounded by leaves, treehouse. *What the fuck?*

Rope bridges connect this house to more tiny log cabins, crossing over and through. I don't even know how many trees there are. Oaks, pines, and laurels intertwine to shield the houses in dense foliage. All of which are at least ten feet off the ground. I can't say for certain how many houses there are, but it's a good number. More than a handful. Which makes me wonder how many people Peter has under his thumb.

How many women has he kidnapped over the years?

Most importantly, what does he do with the girls?

My throat goes dry at the thoughts running through my mind. People don't live in groups like this by choice. There has to be some incentive, something Peter can offer them. Fresh meat for the men to dip their sticks in. I chew on my bottom lip, letting it all sink in. So long as this isn't a Dahmer-type compound, I'll be okay.

I've got this.

Sure, being kidnapped by a possibly crazy hottie isn't ideal, but all the great romances start off this way. Maybe Peter will be the broody, possessive type and not want to share. I'll take that over the alternative.

I rack my brain, trying to think of some stories I've read with the forced proximity trope. The first one that pops into my head is *ACOTAR*. Tampon—I mean Tamlin—and Feyre had a good run. He stole her away first, and then her fairy mate forced her into spending time with him, but it all worked out in the end.

Hades and Persephone are another good one. They eventually fell in love after a whirlwind adventure... so to speak.

Uhh... my mind draws a blank after those two, but I'm sure there are more success stories out there. I know I've read more. I will be fine! *Keep telling yourself this, Wens.*

On the bright side, I don't see any lights. All the windows of the other treehouses are dark, making me wonder what time it is.

The in-between hues of the day give me hope that everyone is either sleeping or working.

I chew on my lip, debating whether to make a run for it tonight or wait and see what I'm being forced into. There are downfalls to both scenarios, but I wager that I have a small advantage right now.

Peter thinks I'm weak, probably too tired and scared to make a move. I'll only have the element of surprise once. Now is the best chance I've got. If I get caught, I can adjust my strategy and try again another time. I just wish my only option wasn't the window.

I hate heights.

The lock on the glass is ancient and the frame pushes open instead of sliding upwards. Carefully, I lift the latch that holds it shut, terrified it'll make a noise. I let out a small, triumphant breath when it's unlocked and look over my shoulder.

No one is watching me.

No one heard the click of metal letting loose.

I try to rein in my excitement. The cynic in me insists something will go wrong with my plan. Be it now or once I'm on the ground running, I need to be prepared for the worst.

But that doesn't stop me from hoping for the best.

I press my hand against the cedar window frame. Slowly, carefully, I push it open. The hinges squeak. In a normal house, the sound would barely be heard over the whoosh of a running air conditioning and the little noises of life being lived. Here... it's too quiet.

"There's a front door, you know."

I freeze at the sound of a male voice. It's different from Peter's. Lighter. Not so baritone. The man behind me chuckles as heavy steps echo off the walls. I swallow the lump in my throat and stand up taller. He doesn't know I planned to run.

I was hot.

I opened a window.

End of story.

I turn to face the intruder and lose all train of thought. Eyes the color of maple leaves in the fall drag over my body, making me aware that I am still in Tyle's string bikini. My hair is probably a matted mess and my makeup is probably running and ruined. For a second, I hope he isn't scared off by my appearance, then mentally scold myself for caring. Captor number two may be a nineties DiCaprio replica, but he is not a love interest. End of story!

My new warden takes his time, drinking in my curves while I shamelessly admire the outline of his body. Even in the dim light, I can see his shirt stretched across his pecs. Tan, or maybe brown, cargo shorts hang low on his hips. I bite the corner of my lip and come up with a new plan.

Divide and conquer by any means possible.

If I can get this beautiful creature on my side, I can learn about Peter and the island, find some leverage and then get the hell out of here.

"You, Darling, are going to give Peter a run for his money."

I lean against the window sill and arch my back. The girls, still wet from my unwanted swimming adventure, probably shine like headlights through the sheer cover-up.

Mr. DiCaprio looks unashamed of his gaze falling to my chest and excitement shoots through me. I have two dream-worthy men under one roof, one of whom checks every box on my panty-dropping list and the other who's a bad decision waiting to happen. Both of which look like they'd be a wild ride. These are dangerous waters. "Is that so?"

Blondie wiggles a sandwich-filled Ziplock baggie in the air and then tosses it onto the bed. "I thought you might be hungry after your journey. Coming to Neverland can take a lot out of a girl."

My stomach growls in response. I don't know how long it's been since I last ate. I had lunch by the pool with the bridesmaids, but that was hours ago, if not longer. "What is it?"

"Peanut butter and jelly," he declares as if it's the best sandwich in the world.

Oh. Damn. I can't eat that, but do the islanders know about my allergy? Are they actively trying to finish what Peter started? Or is this sheer coincidence? "How do I know it's not poison?"

"There's no fun in killing you, Darling." He taps the tip of my nose as he says the nickname Peter coined.

I think the statement is supposed to be reassuring, but all I hear is the unspoken *yet*. The lingering promise of torment, even if it's only a never-ending longing to go home.

"Peter has bigger plans for you." He chuckles and walks to the edge of the bed and grabs the sandwich out of the bag. He takes a bite, not waiting to swallow before asking, "Am I dead yet?"

I fight a smile and cross my arms. I don't know what to make of this guy. Peter is all broody and blah, while his new warden is rainbows and sunshine. Talk about emotional whiplash. "Doesn't seem like it, but the jury's still out. It could be slow-acting poison."

Blondie smirks and extends the sandwich to me. "Then we die together. What do you say? Be the Capulet to my Montague?" He laughs again—a deep belly-rumbling chuckle. "I'm joking. It's just a sandwich. You've had a long day. You should eat something."

"Can't. I'm allergic to peanut butter." I shrug.

"Oh, shit. Really?!" Blondie stammers, all playfulness gone. "I'm sorry." He runs out of the room, baggy and sandwich in hand. A door kicks down the hall, probably hanging against a wall.

I stand there, waiting to see if he comes back. I mean, who does that, just leaves mid-conversation?

Blondie returns a couple of minutes later with two glasses of pink juice. He hands me one with a serious, apologetic look on his face. "I brushed my teeth, just in case you're like allergic allergic."

His minty breath makes me want to smile again. This guy is tumbling through my defenses with his charm and I've barely known him for five minutes. I need to batten down the hatches and prepare my lady bits for war. This is a game of skill, with a high possibility of a bedroom romp. There's no time for butter-flies or any of that bullshit. "I mean, I am, but only if I eat it".

"Good to know. I'm Casper, but everybody here calls me Cass." He folds one arm over his stomach and bows while extending his other arm outward.

The gesture reminds me of the ringmaster at a circus I went to once when I was a kid. That man had the same exaggerated move-ments, the kind meant for putting on a show. I'm sure that's all this is. A show of deceptive trust to lure me into a false sense of safety. Well, two can play his game.

"Wednesday." I bring the cup to my nose and sniff. The pink stuff smells sour, like lemonade, but also sweet. "Is this gonna kill me too?"

"A bit paranoid, aren't you?" Cass chuckles again. There's a hint of mischievous playfulness in his question, the kind you expect a twelve-year-old to have with every word that comes out their mouth, not a twenty-something-year-old.

"Humor me. Peter tried to kill me and then kidnapped me when I survived. And now I've got you, a new player on the board, bringing me food and drink not even five minutes after he tells me I'm stuck, and I quote, in *Neverland*. Can you blame me if I'm on edge about everything?"

"Fair point." Cass takes my cup and downs half of the juice, pink at the bottom and yellow on top, in one big swallow. He holds up one finger as he swallows, keeping us in a suspended state of silence even after he's done. "Nope, not dead. I think it is safe to say that this drink here." He points at my glass. "Is not going to kill you."

"You're lucky you're cute." I lift my cup and take a sip. The flavor is unlike anything I've ever had before...in a good way. It's sweet and tangy and burns my throat, but it's delicious. I didn't realize how thirsty I was. My stomach grumbles again, reminding me that it, too, is needy. "What is this?"

"Cloudberry lemonade."

"I've never heard of it."

"The cloudberries are only grown on the island and in two regions of the world. Although somehow one of your chain restaurants has managed to mass produce it and sell their lemonade during your summers." He pauses, staring off into space before mumbling, "I need to have Emmit look into that."

"Who's Emmit?"

"My brother. You know..." Cass walks over to the window and stares out. into the forest. I can't see the sky from here. There are too many trees, but I imagine it's clear and the evening stars are just beginning to poke through the hazy sky. The simplicity of knowing that I'm under the same shifting sky as Kenny is comforting. It shouldn't be. I shouldn't be thinking about my cheating ex, but that's the problem with love. When it's true, the heart never lets go. There will always be memories and triggers to remind you of what you've lost. Moments when you find comfort in the past, no matter how painful the present is.

"Are you thirsty?" Cass asks suddenly.

I wiggle my nearly empty glass in the air.

He rolls his eyes, laughing again. "Not what I was offering. Come on."

Cass hops onto the windowsill like a spider monkey. He crouches, extending one foot onto the roof, and holds his hand out for me.

I hesitate, my fear of heights trickling into my consciousness. Leaving this room sounds great, but not out of that death trap. "I thought you said there was a front door?"

"Where's your sense of adventure, Darling?"

"Back home, with all the clothes I'm not wearing." I gesture to the barely-there bikini.

"I'm not complaining." Cass winks.

I roll my eyes because that's such a guy thing to say. The normalcy of his comment is a good distraction. My mind has gone off the deep end, drawing up ways I can fall to my demise once we step outside.

Cass laughs, apparently amused by my reaction. "Fine. Fine. I know someone who's about your size. She'll have something you can borrow." He wiggles his fingers and glances down at his outstretched palm. "What do you say, Darling? Are you ready for your first adventure in Neverland?"

No, but this is what I wanted—help out of the treehouse and someone with an in to give me information. Match that with Cass's lust-filled eyes and I'd say my plan is already in motion. I just wish there was another, safer way out of this treehouse.

CHAPTER 10

Wednesday

We scale the roof and jump down onto a platform. I hold in my nerves and follow Cass. Step by step. I don't have a problem with heights, per se. It's the falling part that makes me nervous. I kind of wish this *was* Neverland. At least then I could hold on to the happy thought of being free and fly if I slip.

The roof is easy. It's solid. Steady. It's the next part of our journey that makes me want to turn back and wait for another opening to present itself.

Rope bridges connect one treehouse to another. The planks are secured with loops on each end and that's it. There are no handrails to hold onto. No supports to offset the rhythm of movement. The boards wobble and tilt with each step, throwing me off balance. Walking on them by myself might not be bad, but Cass's extra weight makes going from one house to the next nearly impossible.

I drop down to my hands and knees after the first half-dozen steps. Crawling seems safer. I can grip the boards with my fingers. I close my eyes and try to trick my brain into thinking I'm on solid ground as I inch forward.

Cass is rambling, probably telling me things about Neverland

I should be listening to, but all I can hear is the sound of my heart in my ears. *Thump. Thump.* Deafeningly loud.

"Woman." He sighs.

I look up. Cass has made it to the next platform while I'm still somewhere between Peter's treehouse and where I'm supposed to be. He shakes his head and jogs back to me. The bridge wobbles from side to side, tilting me to the left and right. Left and right.

I take a slow, steady breath. If I focus on my breathing I can regulate my heart rate. Once I get that back to normal, I can make it across the bridge to something solid.

"You're gonna get us caught if we go this slow." Cass crouches low and turns his back to me. "Get on."

"You've got to be joking." I try to laugh, but it sounds like a strangled cry.

Cass looks over his shoulder, hazel eyes meeting mine. "Afraid not, Darling, and I'd like to be thoroughly inebriated by the time Peter figures out you've left the room. So..." He taps his back.

A barrage of what could go wrong streams through my mind, but that's not what makes me pause. It's the thought of relying on someone I'm not sure I can trust, and the temptation of being that close to someone who is basically my kryptonite. I know that's the last place my mind should be, but trauma does weird things to the brain. I hesitate, refusing to crawl the remaining inches.

"Come on, Darling," Cass whispers. He looks around, his gaze bouncing to two of the treehouses in front of us like he's about to tell me a secret, before finding my gaze again. "We both know you want to ride me."

I laugh and the knot of stress in my chest releases. "You're insufferable."

Cass winks because, in his mind, that is an acceptable rebuttal. I give in and climb on his back. He's solid, all muscle between my legs while strong fingers grip my thighs. I wrap my arms around his neck and unintentionally breathe him in. He smells like the forest, like earth and pines, with a hint of vanilla. It's nice.

He carries me to the first platform and then across two more bridges before setting me down on the doorstep of a small treehouse. I'm dizzy from how fast my heart is racing, but grateful. I don't think I could have made it across all those the bridges by myself.

"Is this your place?" I ask, curious to see what's hidden in his closets, both metaphorically and physically.

I can't decide what I think about Cass yet. He's got the same playfulness that Peter had on the boat...before pushing me overboard. The kind that makes me want to smile and forget the reality of my situation. But then there's the serious side of him that clashes with his personality.

He doesn't seem too keen on Peter, which is a win in my book. Driving a wedge between them should be cake if they aren't buddy-buddy, especially once I spread my legs for him. I've already decided it's going to happen. Even if it doesn't help my cause because he's the second hottest man I've ever met. I have high hopes he can put my vibrator to shame in the orgasm department and will be sorely disappointed if I'm wrong.

"I'd rather cut my left nut off than live with the woman who owns this treehouse." He scoffs, turning the handle.

The door isn't locked, which makes me wonder about the rest of the treehouses. Once I figure out who I'm dealing with, I might be able to break into them and find some leverage. I'm not beneath blackmailing someone if it'll help me get home.

"Come on." Cass lights a lantern by the door and carries it across the open room.

I stay close and take in every detail. There's not much to see inside. A small couch. A table and chairs. There's nothing on the walls. No pictures of friends or family. At this rate, blackmail might be more complicated than I thought.

Cass stops in front of a door and opens it. He goes straight to the dresser, like he's been here before, and rummages through the drawers. I sit on the full-size bed. This room is similar to the one Peter had me in, with the same bare necessities. Dresser. Bed.

Nightstand with an oil lamp. The only difference is the layout. The rooms are flipped.

"Try these on." Cass tosses me a pair of jean shorts and a white shirt with a raven on it.

I step into the shorts and pull them over my hips. They're tight. I can't button them, but they are high enough on my waist that they won't fall down either.

Cass watches me. Hungry eyes drinking in every inch of exposed skin. "We'll need to find you something better, but those should work for tonight."

"Does Neverland have a mall?" I'm joking. I have yet to see anything resembling the twenty-first century in either treehouse. No refrigerator. No stove or TV. Hell, the rooms don't even have a light bulb. I doubt the shopping is up to par.

"The Pirate's Market has just about everything."

"Pirates?" I pull the shirt over my head. It has cutouts on the sides, but it's not too revealing. Better than walking around half-naked all night, I suppose. "Like in the stories?"

"What stories?"

"You know of Peter Pan, the boy who doesn't grow up. Captain Hook. Tinkerbell and the Lost Boys." I pull my hair into a ponytail with the tie on my wrist. Cass is looking at me like I have two heads. I don't like it. "What?"

He steps forward and takes both my hands in his. "Promise me you won't tell anyone what you just told me, Wednesday."

"Oh...kay. Why? The story is like a hundred years old. Everyone knows it."

Cass frowns and shakes his head. "Not everyone. I would bet my life few, if any, of The Lost know that story exists. If anyone found out..." He chews on the corner of his lip. "They just can't. Please, Wednesday. I'm begging you."

"All right. I promise, but you owe me."

"Anything, Darling." He squeezes my hands tight and then sets them free. "Name it and it's yours."

"For starters, you can stop calling me Darling. It's creepy. My friends call me Wens."

"Bless the stars, she considers me a friend!" Cass wraps his arms around my waist. He spins me around once, then sets me on my feet, an infectious grin lifting his lips at the corners. "Come on. We have about an hour or so until Peter rears his ugly face. I need a drink or ten before that happens. What do you say?"

"I'd say a drink sounds like heaven about now."

"Well, my lady, your chariot awaits." Cass turns his back to me and crouches low again.

I laugh and climb onto his back.

Neverland, here I come.

CHAPTER 11

Wednesday

It's official: Nature is not my friend.

Her leaves are pokey, her roots raised specifically for tripping, and she's filled with bloodsucking creepy crawlies that seem to only drink O-negative blood. Thank heavens for my sneakers. If I would have been in heels or flats before nearly dying this afternoon, I would be screwed.

"Maybe this is a bad idea." We stop at the edge of the tree line, just out of reach of the firelight. There are about a dozen people gathered near a bonfire in the sand. Most of them stand around the flames, listening to music my parents grew up on from an eighty-style boombox.

"Worried I'll run away?" I tease, but the idea looms in my mind. The only thing stopping me is that I have no idea where I am. The woods are a maze with no defining markers.

Cass's chuckle sends a flutter rolling over my skin. "Are you that eager to get away from me, Darling?"

Cass specifically? No. I like him, even though I know I shouldn't. It's easy to forget the gravity of my situation when we're together. His lighthearted playfulness erases all the worry and dread weighing on my heart, but the fact of the matter is that if there was a chance for me to get away, I'd take it. I'd leave all the warm-fuzzy feelings in a heartbeat if it meant I could go home.

"Worried?"

"Of course!" Cass takes my hand and twirls me around, then pulls me into him in one swift movement. "Half those fuckers will try to steal you from me the moment I walk away, and I'm not ready to let you go yet."

"Who said I was yours?" I ask, unsure of the signals I want to send. I've seen Tyle use men to get what she wants, and it's always ended with the guy getting hurt. The guilt that I'm doing the same with Cass doesn't sit well in my soul. That and Peter still lingers in my thoughts, even though I wish he wouldn't.

Disappointment passes across Cass's face. The reaction is brief and gone as quickly as it came, replaced by a flash of teeth. "No one, but I want you to be mine because you're gorgeous and your soul burns brighter than any star in the sky."

My cheeks heat and a smile tugs at my lips. I've never heard anyone say something so beautifully odd before.

Cass takes my hand, not pushing the conversation further, and leads us to the party. I don't feel nervous when the first set of eyes land on us or even the second. It's the third, fourth, and fifth that make my heart race. I wiggle my fingers and try to pull my hand back. Cass takes the hint, sensing my social anxiety and he sets me free but stays close, wordlessly claiming me as his.

"Who's this?" The voice comes from one of the men near a wooden cornhole board. I'm not sure which one. All of them are looking at me with a mix of curiosity and lust. Four shirtless bodies stare, each one just as beautifully muscled as the next, watching my every move.

"The new darling." A girl with a *we don't do well with strangers* expression says. She crosses her arms, glaring as she takes in my appearance. "Your ass is too big for those shorts."

"Stars and Scars, Heidi. You were new once. Ease up." A pretty Hispanic with long dark hair, in cutoff jeans and a gray tank top, nudges the first girl—Heidi— with her elbow. "I'm Aria, and this is Scarlett."

"Wednesday," I say, trying to seem friendly even though my guard is up. Are these more kidnappers? Or people Peter has stolen and brainwashed?

Cass jerks his chin to the guys and rambles off their names in one breath. I don't know who is who. No one waves or gives any signal for me to match a name to a face. They just stare, a few sipping on their mason jar glasses, like they couldn't care less I'm here. I almost wonder if the boys do it on purpose. So I can't identify them to the police when I finally make it home.

"I need to take care of some business. You gonna be okay on your own for a few minutes?" Cass asks.

I look up at him, realizing that his height seems to be the norm and my five-foot-five stature is small, even by the girl's standards. Their legs are long, their bodies lean. I'm short, with a few extra pounds here and there. Insecurity bleeds into my soul. Tyle was always thinner than me, strikingly beautiful like these girls.

And I'm just... me.

It makes me nervous to be left alone with these people, but I put on a mask of confidence. Fear can be manipulated and used to make someone do stupid, reckless things. I may be shaking in my Converse, but this isn't my first rodeo. I can fake it with the best of them. "I'm a big girl. Don't worry about me."

Cass flashes his teeth. "It's not you that I'm worried about." He leaves me to myself and heads to talk to the group of guys by the fire.

One of them, a dirty blonde, holds my gaze the longest. I can't help but notice the similarities between him and Cass. Same nose. Same kiss me lips and dimpled smile. I'm guessing he's the brother Cass mentioned.

"You're going to get Casper in trouble," Scarlett, the Asian chick beside Aria, whispers. Her gaze darts to Heidi, who nods in encouragement before she adds, "You shouldn't encourage him."

"Maybe I want to cause a little trouble." I smirk, feeling

triumphant to have figured something out. Peter has a jealous side. Good. I'll kill two birds with one stone named Cass.

I sit on the picnic bench beside Scarlett and watch Cass's features morph from the playful, boyish spirit I've spent most of the evening with to a serious one. I hate to admit it, but watching him turns me on. He checks every box on my fuck-them-without-second-thought list. Assuming he swings his dick with the same confidence he talks to his friends with, I won't have to fake it when I seduce him later.

"Oh, boy," a feminine voice, I think Aria says. I turn to her as she smiles against the rim of her jar, taking a sip of a powder-blue drink.

"What?"

"Nothing." She glances across the sandy knoll to the men and their meeting. "I just know that look."

"And?" I don't have a look. I'm tempted to tell her as much, but I get the feeling that she wants to stir the pot. There can't be much to entertain people here.

Aria tilts her head, her grin stretching wider. "It means that we all need to be shit-faced before Peter discovers you're catching feelings for Cass. You drink, new girl?"

"Sometimes." I try to mask my reservations, but I don't do a good job.

Heidi stares at me for a moment, distrust dancing across her features as she studies me. "How did you say you got to Neverland?"

"I didn't."

Cass returns in the nick of time with two wooden cups in his hands. I hide a breath of relief. I don't want anyone to know too much about me. Anything I give these people could be used to track me down again after I escape.

"Causing trouble?" he teases.

"Not yet," Aria answers with a wink. She seems to be the friendliest of the bunch. Heidi has done nothing but throw daggers with her eyes at me, and Scarlett has barely looked up from her hands. They're an odd bunch. In the outside world, I doubt they'd be friends, yet somehow, on this island, they work. "But I've got a feeling mischief is brewing just beyond the horizon."

"Most definitely." Cass's dark eyes trail my every movement. Every tiny shift of my weight and blink of my eyes. The intensity of his gaze makes me shiver.

Peter gave me the same nervous butterflies and he turned out to be a murderous creep. How do I know Cass isn't just as twisted? The pretty boys are the most dangerous and I have a feeling the ones on this island bring a different kind of peril.

"Thanks." I sniff the sparkly pink drink before tasting it. It smells sweet, like something I would order from a bar, which makes me hesitate. How did Cass know I'd want a fruity drink and not something with some bite?

"Scared, new girl?" Heidi taunts, pure venom dripping from her tone. Her lips lift into a sinister smile.

I roll my eyes and bring the cup to my lips, then take a swallow. The drink tastes like cotton candy, pure sweetness without a hint of bite. It's the kind of cocktail that sneaks up on you and gives you a good time until you find yourself puking over a bush an hour later. "What is this?"

"Faery Wine."

I smile, my lips lifting on their own, and welcome the way the wine melts away my resolve. I was wrong. The wine isn't sneaky. It packs a punch straight out the gate and hits my nerves after the first taste.

The buzz flitters through my whole body. It's a flying kind of feeling that enhances every touch. I feel the wind caress my skin. I feel grains of sand tickle my toes and the pink light of both day and night bathe me in its glory. Each new sensation is better than the last. I take another sip, a bigger one this time, desperate for more.

"Easy, Wens." Cass frowns, his copper brows pulling together. "This is a sipping drink. Enjoy the ride." He takes the glass from my hands and sets it on the table and links his fingers with mine. "Dance with me."

"Crazy For You" by Madonna croons through an old boom box. Cass twirls me once, then pulls me into his hard chest. I stumble, my feet two steps behind me. He compensates for my missteps and holds me tighter, ensuring I don't fall on my face. We sway, taking tiny steps in the sand.

"I've waited centuries for you, Wednesday," he whispers, the tip of his nose brushing against my neck, just under my ear.

"That's nice," I mumble, the words a distance ping in my mind.

I close my eyes and let Cass guide me, giving him total control of my body. The world is a swirly haze of music and emotions. This wine is potent. I've only had a few sips and I can feel every chord the speakers sing vibrate against my skin.

Cass's lips press against mine, tenderly asking permission to deepen the kiss. I want to open my mouth and let myself fall head-first into this drunken headiness, but my mind won't let me. It strays to Peter and what it felt like to be in this same position only hours ago.

I like Cass. I like how he makes me forget I've been kidnapped. I like how each breath I take around him is light and the longer we're together the less bitter I feel about being here.

But he's not the blue-eyed madman who set my world on fire. A man I hate so deeply yet can't seem to erase the imprint he left on my soul.

"Am I interrupting?" Peter's voice rumbles.

"Uh oh." Heidi snickers.

I open my eyes, pissed that not only is Peter fucking with my mind, but he's here, physically cock-blocking me. I glare at him over Cass's shoulder, inwardly pleased at the scowl on his face. "As a matter of fact, you are."

"I need a word," Peter demands. He crosses his arms over the loose-fitting tee that covers his chest.

If I look hard enough, I can see the dark lines of his tattoos. I remember tracing them, touching his smooth skin and the way lust shot to my center. My nipples harden beneath my shirt as the same needy heat pooling again. "I'm busy."

"It's not a request."

"Considering that I don't belong to you, I don't care." I step out of Cass's hold and take his hand.

I'm frustrated, and not just sexually. How dare Peter show up and demand that I talk to him? He was the one to leave my room without giving me any answers! Chanting a stupid tick-tock rhyme that made as much sense as telling me I'm in Neverland. I march toward the tree line and drag Cass with me.

"Where are you going?" Peter demands.

"To finish what you so rudely interrupted," I say reactively. I stomp over fallen limbs, purposefully trying to make as much noise as I can.

"Wednesday!" Peter shouts.

"Can't hear you!" I march and march, taking us deeper into the woods. My stupid lady bits are dripping with need. Arguing with Peter is almost as much of a turn-on as touching him is, which only makes me angrier. I don't want to be attracted to that psychopath!

"Where are we going?" Cass asks, not bothering to hide his amusement.

I stop in the middle of the woods. I was so lost in my thoughts that I almost forgot I dragged him into my mess. I look around, not recognizing a single thing around me, and sigh. "I don't know."

The fire from the party faintly glows through the brush behind us. I half expected Peter to stomp after me in a man-fit, demanding I do what he says, but he just let me go. I don't know why, but I'm disappointed.

"Want to come back to my place?" Cass asks. There's no innuendo in his question. I can't tell if he's being genuinely nice or hoping I'll make good on my word.

I glance over my shoulder, still hoping Peter will storm

through the trees and drag me away. I give him three heartbeats before deciding he must be calling my bluff.

If Peter thinks I'm not going to screw Cass, he's got another thing coming. I'm going to scream so loud that everyone on the island will blush from embarrassment. I want to douse that tiny spark of jealousy with gasoline and watch his world burn.

I trail my gaze over Cass's lean body, noting the way his shirt falls over the muscles of his chest. This may be a show for Peter, but that doesn't mean it won't be fun. "Lead the way."

CHAPTER 12

Wednesday

Cass's treehouse smells like a garden. Aromas of greenery and jasmine and sage, mixed with the sweet scent of flora, fill the air.

He turns the knob of an oil lantern as we step inside, lighting the small space. Unlike the other two rooms I've been in, there are no tables or chairs in the main room. Books upon books lie in stacks on the floor while trinkets fill his shelves.

"Are you thirsty?" He walks to the kitchen counter while I make my way to the shelves that line the walls. The oddities are chaotic. A button. A watch. A deflated red balloon. Toy car. An empty matchbook. Every item is broken in some fashion, and yet he keeps them.

"What is all of this?"

I turn around. Cass has two cups in his hands. I shake my head, uninterested in whatever he has to offer. The Faery wine is wearing off. There's a pounding behind my eye that's getting stronger the longer I stand in the light.

"Pieces of people." He sets both glasses on the counter and strides toward me. His fingers graze my hips. "Things that washed up on the shore over the years. Little moments from someone's life they once cherished, now forgotten."

"How are your hands so cold?" I shiver, wondering what they'd feel like around my neck. I've always liked ice in the bedroom; the way it awakens the nerves and enhances an orgasm.

"Forever frost," Cass whispers into my ear. He pulls me backward and presses my ass against him. His breath caresses my skin. His lips less than an inch away. "It coats the inside of the pitcher."

"I've never heard of it." I arch my back and press into the hardness on my thigh.

Cass reaches up and wraps his fingers around my neck. I groan, thrilled he has the same desires as I do. He turns me around, controlling my every move, and looks me in the eyes. "You'd never heard of cloudberries before tonight, yet you've drunk their lemonade."

"Is this why you brought me here? To tell me about ice that never melts and sober me up some." I touch Cass' chest. My fingers run between the muscles of his pecs and down his abs. I want him more than I should for reasons that make me blush. Selfish, dirty reasons that are as shallow as I want to come to the deviousness of I hope Peter finds out what I've done.

Cass's breath hitches. He inches closer. "Are you sure this is a good idea?"

No. I run my fingers through his hair and pull his mouth to mine. My first thought is of Peter and how his tongue is more skilled, but he's gone from my mind the minute Cass's hand slides up my shirt. He cups my breast and squeezes until my eyes pop open. He's rough, which is what I need because I need to be punished. What I'm doing is wrong on so many levels. But it feels. So. Good.

Cass tugs the strings of my bikini loose. It falls to my lap, discarded, and he pulls my shirt over my head. He sucks my left breast into his mouth and lifts me onto the counter. I drop my head back, unfazed by the thunk it makes as I hit the cabinets.

"Wednesday," Cass breathes against my skin. "We should stop."

"I don't want to." I lift his face to mine to make his lips stop talking, but he pulls away.

He looks me dead in the eyes and says, "You're drunk. I don't want you to regret this tomorrow."

Warmth pools in my heart. It figures I would find the only gentleman in the world on an island I'm trying to escape from. A pang of guilt stabs me. I should walk away and find somewhere safe to sleep, but I need Peter to hear my screams echoing through the trees and I want Cass to be the man who satisfies me. He's hot, and I think we would enjoy each other.

But I won't force him to do anything he's uncomfortable with.

"Stop being such a gentleman, Cass. Either you make me feel good tonight, or I'll find someone else who will."

Cass doesn't hesitate; he crashes his lips against mine, kissing me with a hunger I've never felt. Strong hands slide under my thighs and before I know what's happening, he's lifting me in the air and carrying me to the bedroom.

Cass's room is dark and I'm too into the moment to take in the scenery. He drops me on the bed and quickly strips while I work to take my shorts off. A moment later, he's on top of me, equally as bare, and kissing my lips. My neck. My shoulder.

His hands roam my body, toying with me, giving me as much pleasure as he can without letting me come. He keeps me just behind the line of ecstasy until my hips buck, and I'm panting, greedy, wanting more of whatever he'll give me.

Eventually, he positions himself, and somehow, through a lusty haze, I remind him, "Condom."

"I can't get you pregnant," he says, lips a breath beneath my ear.

"I've heard that before." I arch my eyebrows. He can't honestly think I'm stupid enough to fall for that line.

"Scared your birth control won't work?"

I push on Cass's chest. He shifts onto his side, and somehow, there's not a single fat roll on his body. Mine would have wrinkled and looked disgusting in that position. "How'd you know I'm taking birth control?"

He traces the thin line on the inside of my arm. The scar is only visible thanks to the tan I got in the Keys.

"I like covering my bases." He presses his lips to the sweet spot on my neck. "Kids aren't in the future for me, Wens. Even if you weren't protected, I'm sterile."

My eyes flutter closed. It's been a long time since someone made me feel this good. The need to feel him, and what's left of the wine, gnaws away at my restraint. I slide my hand between us and angle my hips until his perfect, heart-shaped tip slides inside me. Cass finishes pushing himself in, and I gasp as I stretch to accommodate his thickness.

Everything after that is a blur of passion. It's been months since I've let anyone down there and almost two weeks since I've touched myself, thanks to Red Week and the bachelorette party. I writhe underneath him, unable to control myself as an orgasm rocks my body.

"You are perfect," Cass mumbles, his release a close second to mine.

When we're done, Cass rolls off me and walks to a room I assume is a bathroom. I lay on the bed, breathless, covered in sweat, while his warm seed drips out of me. I cringe, disappointed with myself. I've never let a man come inside me before. That's always been my stipulation. They either have to wear a condom or pull out. I wanted to save this one thing for my future life partner, and I let my ego and hormones ruin the only precious thing I had to give.

"You okay?" Cass tosses me a wet washcloth.

I wipe myself clean and sit up. Hopefully, gravity will pull whatever is left inside out so I can pretend that part of tonight never happened.

"Getting clingy already?" I deflect.

"I'd be a fool not to." Cass leans down and cups my neck, then tilts my head upward to kiss my lips. "You are a treasure,

Wednesday. I'm not ashamed to admit that I want you all to myself."

My heart flutters, elated to have such beautiful words spoken to me. I'm sure they're fake. Men don't say such treasured things and mean them after only knowing someone for a few hours. Still, Cass makes me feel special.

If only my head would stop wishing the words had come from Peter's mouth.

CHAPTER 13

Wednesday

I wake in a bed that is not my own, in a room that is too bright.

The sun shines through curtainless windows, painting wooden walls in hues of pale pink and yellow. For one beautiful moment, I forget everything that's happened in the last twenty-four hours. But as I push myself upwards on a crisp, white bedsheet with no blankets, everything comes back with painful recognition.

My head hurts a little, the aftermath of drinking too much, but overall I feel fine. Well, as fine as I can be considering the situation.

"Mornin'." Cass leans against the doorframe, a white t-shirt falling just below the band of his khaki shorts. He looks good with a shirt on but even better without it. I fight a frown, remembering all the things we did last night.

I don't feel bad about sleeping with him. My body is my temple and he worshiped it better than anyone has before, man or woman. I only wish I hadn't been so stupid as to let him come inside me. The gift I had for my life partner is lost.

As pretty as Cass is, things between us will never be long-term. He is a means to piss off Peter and pass the time. Possibly even help me find a way home. And I am the new girl. Someone he can have a little fun with as long as we stay casual.

That's all.

"Hey." My voice is scratchy from all the yelling. At least I managed to do one thing right last night.

"Thirsty?" he asks. I nod, and Cass brings me the cup he's holding. A small wooden thing whittled from what looks to have been a thick tree limb. The bark has been carefully peeled off, and the inside hollowed. "Careful, it's warm."

The cup is neither hot nor cold in my hands, but I'm careful to bring its contents to my lips. Heat rises to my nose, along with the smell of honey and something floral. I doubt his tea will pack the caffeine punch I'm used to getting from coffee, but it tastes surprisingly good. "Thanks."

"Has anyone ever told you how beautiful you look in the morning?" Cass stares at me, a glimmer of hope and a whole bunch of unspoken emotions I don't want to deal with shining in his eyes.

"Has anyone ever told you that your flattery balances a thin line between sweet and obsessive?"

"Does it bother you?"

"Surprisingly, no." I'm shocked as the words leave my lips, but even more taken aback as I realize they ring true. It's kind of nice having someone be kind to me after they've gotten down my string bikini. Kenny's chivalry faded after the one-year marker, and one-night stands aren't known for hanging out once the deed is done.

Cass is the first hookup to stick around. He could have disappeared or sent Peter to fetch me to get me out of his hair. Instead, he's here. I guess it wouldn't hurt to be nice.

"Just saying, though, if you end up stalking me or become one of those obsessive weirdos, I know a guy who likes to...you know..." I run my thumb across my neck and give him a murderous glare.

Cass laughs, not the least bit intimidated by my threat. In all honesty, I doubt Peter would do anything to harm him. I have a feeling they're friends, or at least bygones. But it sounded semi-decent as I said it.

"Peter isn't usually so dubious." Cass leans forward. His thick fingers clutch the footboard and his forearm muscles flexing with each shift of his weight. "When he's not fighting his demons, he's an all right guy."

"Your definition of all right and mine are different."

Cass smirks and I find that sober me enjoys the shape of his mouth just as much as drunk me does. "Just wait, Wednesday. You'll see the side of him we all do. It just takes time."

"That's something I don't have a lot of, Cass. Time." Something punches me in the stomach. Regret... maybe? It feels a lot like regret, but I shake it off and chalk the sensation up to a hangover. I don't have the energy to deal with emotions like that. "I'm leaving the first chance I can. Whatever you want this thing between us to be... It's got a short shelf life."

Cass takes my hand. He flips it palm up and traces the lines with his finger. It's alluring. I find myself fascinated by the simplest things, like his chest rising and falling, and I'm anxious to hear him speak. I can't justify the need to stay by his side but it's there, running through my confusion and hesitations.

"One thing you should know about Neverland, Wens. Time is relative. Our days stretch on forever if you want them to, or they can end in an instant and night will rise. We're stuck in the same span of time, moving neither forward nor backward while the world carries on without us. Forever in the twilight hours. You say what we have has a short shelf life; I say it has a life, and that's good enough for me."

I shake my head, unable to fight the smile. Never have I heard a man speak with such heart or in so many riddles. It's flattering and confusing all at once. My mind feels drugged trying to make sense of it all. "You're unreal, Casper. Where did you come from?"

"A forgotten land called Wescroff, but my origin doesn't

matter. What does matter is that you need something decent to wear." Cass releases my hand and the haziness in my mind clears. "As much as I love seeing you in all your glory, Peter would have my head if I let you out like that."

"Damn, so it's not a nudist island?" I stand, my girls and all their glory out on display. I don't have a stitch of clothes on.

Cass adjusts himself over his shorts. "At times, maybe, but not when it comes to you." He tosses me a shirt and my cutoffs from last night. "The shower is over there if you want to freshen up. The water will flow once you step under it and there's a towel beneath the sink."

"Is it on a sensor?" I bend over to pick up my bathing suit.

"Something like that." Cass groans and his fingers grip the foot of the bed, those eyes narrowing on me. "Hurry up and get ready before I change my mind and keep you here with me all day."

The Pirate's Market isn't a market, but a series of shops along a long boardwalk that connects to docks stretching into the bay. Each storefront is built the same, made out of thatched huts with roofs crafted from dried palms.

Unlike Cass's treehouse, which is comfortably cool, the shops here are hot. Whatever system he and Peter uses to aerate their treehouses needs to be shared with the pirates because I'm sweating.

"How's about this?" Cass holds up a tie-dye shirt with vinyl lettering that reads, *Boyfriend wanted. Apply within.*

I laugh and throw the first shirt I touch at his chest. The clothes are in heaps. Piles on top of piles, completely unorganized, set together with no rhyme or reason. It's fun looking through everything, but it is starting to eat at my anxiety.

"Would you say the position is filled then?" He winks and drops the shirt onto the pile nearest him.

I roll my eyes and go back to searching. So far, I've found two pairs of shorts, a one-piece bathing suit, and a sundress that should fit. I'm still searching for some underwear or, at the least, another bikini to rotate the bottoms with. "Where does this stuff come from?"

Cass ties a coconut bra around his neck. It's too small for his muscular frame, falling nowhere near his chest, and puts a pink mouse-ear headband on with it. "The pirates call Neverland the Isle of the Lost."

"So, you're saying all of this is stuff people misplaced?"

"I'm saying things are often forgotten once they make their way to Neverland. The people who lost what you hold don't even realize it's gone."

"That's sad."

"It is what it is." He tosses his headband back onto the stack. It gets buried amongst the masses, discarded again instead of finding a new life with us. "There's another shop by the pub we can try."

"Okay. Who do we pay?" I look around, searching for a shopkeeper.

Cass shakes his head and takes my hand. "Human habits die hard. We don't pay for things that are already free."

He holds me close and guides us down the walk. I take in the scenery. Smoke billows out the chimney of a windowless shop. Music plays on a corner, flowing from a small guitar. Two men engage in a game of cards. Life is being lived on this side of Neverland. It gives me hope for some normalcy because I've only seen people party where we're from.

Cedar burns from somewhere around us. Not the chimney, that smells of spice and pork. This scent is different. It tickles in my brain, summoning a memory I can't quite place.

I look behind me for the origin, but the flavor fades. I look ahead of us and rise on my toes to see over the shoulders of the men in our path. I quickly find a large black hat with a red feather and a dark cloak over broad shoulders. Something in my chest comes alive, tingling with recognition. The man—I don't know why I'm assuming he's male, but it feels right in my soul—stops walking.

Cass is talking a mile a minute, probably giving me the back-story of these shops or rambling about the bird perched on the roof across the way. I don't know. His words are garbled, lost down a tunnel along with my thoughts.

All I can see is the cedar-smelling man. All I can think about is how his scent wraps around my chest, drawing me closer.

He turns, looking around as if he, too, can sense me. Dark stubble covers the side of a strong jaw, curving to match a long scar that marks his cheek.

Cass grabs my arm and pulls me between two buildings. He pins me against the wall, pushing me so hard against the wood the back of my head hits. His lips are on mine before the pain can register. His tongue hungrily pushes my mouth open, sweeping inside, taking all thoughts about the Cedar-smelling man with him.

He kisses and kisses until I'm a needy, hungry mess, and then Cass pulls back. His breaths are short—his lungs just as deprived of oxygen as mine.

"What was that for?" I ask.

"It's been too long since I've felt those lips." He kisses my neck and I shiver with delight as he sinks his teeth into me, lightly nibbling.

"You're ridiculous." I laugh, a flush of heat rising to my cheeks. I ache to be touched again. I take a deep breath and remind myself about who is using who. If Cass wants my body I'm happy to give it to him, but I need to keep my head clear. "What about my clothes?"

"Where we're going, you don't need any."

CHAPTER 14

Peter

"Y ou've been busy."

"You know what they say about idle hands." Darling drops a canvas bag on the ground at her feet, then falls into the chair beside the window. She picks up Cass's paperback, *Frankenstein*, flips to the description on the rear cover, then sets it down with a frown. "Why am I not surprised you're a horror fan?"

Her gaze bounces around the room, never staying on one thing for more than a few seconds before jumping to something else. My house is simple. Not as bare as some of The Lost, but less decadent than the others in our enclave.

I have a wall of shelving, filled with books that have shown up over the years. A small wooden table with two chairs to match. The end table and wingback by the window, and a handful of bowls on the counter that hold fruit.

I gave up on living possessions such as photos and decor ages ago, but I never could let go of the books. I don't read them. Reading was Wendy's passion, not mine, but each leather-bound novel reminds me of her.

Some of the books were found on the island. Those are the oldest, the ones Wendy hand-picked and read aloud to John and

Michael when they were little. Others I collected once I figured out how to cross between the realms. All of them bring me back to little moments suspended in time.

At first, it was a way to keep Wendy with me after she was gone. Neverland makes you forget and I never wanted to forget her. Now, they sit on my shelves, collecting dust until Cass finds it in his heart to pick one up or clean them off.

I haven't forgotten, but sometimes remembering is its own punishment.

Wednesday's eyes finally settle on me. Chocolate brown with flecks of emerald and gold throughout. Uniquely Wendy. So much of the old soul penetrates through to her new life.

"Cass said I had to be here. Care to tell me why?" She crosses her arms, those pretty brown eyes narrowing.

"You sleep in my bed. Not his." I let years of frustration bleed into my voice. Anger at my father for arranging the marriage between Wendy and James when he knew I loved her. Bleeding admiration at Wendy's dedication to her vows. The constant ache, as if being stabbed, with every whisper, every gentle touch James placed upon her skin, and every skip of my heart for when she stole a glance at me. It was enough to drive a man to insanity, and yet I lived for it.

It was better to be a bystander in her life, helplessly watching as she found happiness and fell in love with another than to deprive a deserving woman of my heart because I could never give that to someone else when it was still bound to another. I was content to die alone and love her from afar so long as she was happy.

"I'd rather sleep on the floor than with you!" Wednesday's venom matches mine.

I clench my teeth, refusing to let myself laugh. I love her spirit. The fight that burns through Wednesday's blood is instinctual—ingrained in her DNA. But I have to focus on the negative feelings. I need to draw up the memories of Wendy's shaking breath as my brother screwed her in my bed because that is the only way I can stomach being so cruel. "That can be arranged, Darling."

"You're a pig." She rolls her eyes. "Why even bring me to this stupid island if you're going to be an ass, Peter?"

I didn't have a choice.

"Because I can." I fill a canister with water from the pitcher on the counter and grab a pocket knife out of a drawer. I doubt I'll need it. The island is divided. Half mine. Half his. A bargain we set in stone that no one would dare cross, but the living are unpredictable. Even more so after they've died.

I slam the drawer shut and grab my water bottle. I can't be here and look at her any longer. Not when she reeks of Cass. His scent oozes out of her pores. It was subtle at first, but the longer we are together, the stronger it becomes.

He's marked her as his.

I wrinkle my nose as I walk past. "You smell. Take a shower before I get back."

"You're leaving?" The sorrow in Wednesday's tone catches me off guard.

I stop at the door, my hand on the nob and deja vu hits me hard. If I'm not careful, Wednesday and I will make the same mistakes over again and I refuse to let history repeat itself.

"Don't pretend you want me around, Darling." Hate me, I remind myself. She needs to hate me, even if making her do so cuts my heart out. "Besides, I have things to do."

"But I just got here. You said we needed to talk."

"That was last night." When I thought about taking Wednesday home and protecting her from afar. I was reckless in bringing her to Neverland. I forgot how quickly emotions can cloud judgment, which is why I don't hold it against Wednesday that she left with Cass. I backed her into a corner and she reacted. Doesn't mean I like her decisions. "You made your choice."

"What choice, Peter? What are you talking about?"

Something new burns inside me and a fire I'm unfamiliar with climbs my neck. I clench my fists as an overwhelming need to punch something sinks its teeth into me. I vaguely recognize the sensation. It's similar to the feeling I got when her sister, Tyle, was around. Only worse. "I'll be back later."

"What am I supposed to do?"

Not sleep with the first man you find on the island!

"I don't know. Figure it out. You seem more than capable of entertaining yourself," I say, slamming the door behind me.

CHAPTER 15

Peter

I smell him even after I leave the treehouse.

Cass's scent sears my nostrils. It wafts through the trees, carried by the breeze. It surrounds me, poking the fury beneath my skin. I told him to be her friend, not her fuck toy. I wanted him to charm Wednesday and win her heart, not stick his crooked dick where it doesn't belong.

I shout, anger consuming my thoughts and swing at the tree nearest me. My knuckles ache as the trunk cracks, but I feel better.

Until I smell it again.

Cass's Fae mark.

My feet take me to the beach while my mind pelts me with images of what they've done. Memories of Wendy and James merge with the present. Hundreds of living years have passed, and the sting is still just as sharp.

"Hey, Pete. Can we—"

The world fades to black and a high-pitched ring fills my ears. I lose myself and have no idea what I'm doing. When I can see again, both of my hands are around Cass's neck and Xyris and Emmit are trying to pull me off. I shake free of their grips and hold my hands up. I'm good. I won't do it again.

Cass coughs. He rubs the red skin and the sight of my mark on him is satisfying. "What the hell, Peter?"

"You slept with her?" I yell. That feeling climbs my neck again. I want to strangle him, snuff his stupid Faery life out with my bare hands just so he can never touch her again. I take a deep breath and test every bit of restraint I have. Cass is my friend, I remind myself. Not my enemy.

"I did what you told me to do."

"I told you to be her friend. Not fuck her, Cass." I rake my hands through my hair and pull at the roots. His smell is everywhere. In the air. On the sand. On my skin. I run to the water and stick my hands in a wave. I need to get it off before I puke.

"She told me to man up or she'd find someone else. Who did you think she'd wind up with? You?" He waits for me to answer, but I don't. He's right. Wednesday would rather peel her skin off than climb in bed with me last night.

"But you marked her." Like a fucking territorial cat in heat.

"Where's your shadow, Peter?" he asks, changing the topic.

I glare, despite the validity of his question. His presence would explain what I'm feeling, but he's gone, roaming the island. I could always sense his emotions, but they've never felt like my own. He is not angry with Cass. This is all me. "We both know I have no control over where my shadowself goes or what he does."

"You haven't been this pissed off in years. Not since he left you."

Cass is right. I'm feeling things. I drop my shoulders at the realization and a new emotion pushes through. Shame. "Is it just me? Or does anyone else feel different?"

"I cried this morning," Scarlet whispers. Heidi puts her arms around her lover's shoulders. "I woke up and let out all the pain I'd been holding in. It poured out of me. I couldn't stop until every last tear was shed."

"And I felt bad for her," Heidi adds. "I wanted to take her sorrow away, but I was so happy she felt something more than fear. That's when I realized I wasn't angry anymore."

"The island is shifting." Emmit looks at Cass. They talk amongst each other in silent language, which only they understand. Belle taught me how to hear it once. I couldn't understand a word she said, but it sounded like tinkling bells.

"Why are we pretending you're the bad guy?" Aria asks. "What don't we know?"

"Everything." I look at Cass and Emmit. They nod simultaneously. I don't need to hear their words to know what they are saying. It's time everyone knew how they came to the island and what Wednesday means for their future.

CHAPTER 16

Wednesday

Nothing.

There is absolutely nothing useful in this damned treehouse.

The moment Peter left I began searching for something. Anything to use against him or to give me leverage, but I've come up with jackshit. Peter's room is painfully bare. His dresser holds a handful of white shirts, green or khaki shorts, and a few pairs of jeans. All of which are lying on his bedroom floor.

I don't care.

He's made a mess of my life.

I can make a mess in his house.

Peter's bathroom mirrors Cass's, with a large banana leaf shower, toilet, and sink. I try not to think about how the basics of life, like plumbing, work in Neverland. It's not likely there's a septic tank in this tree, and I don't want to know where all the nastiness goes.

I walk back into the hallway and set my hands on my hips. All that's left is my room and the open living space. I doubt the books on Peter's shelf hold any secrets. Judging by the layer of dust on the covers, I don't think he's touched them in a while.

That leaves the kitchen—if the space can even be called that—

and about a dozen cabinets and drawers. The whole wall across from the living room is storage. Not abnormal, except every other aspect that makes a kitchen habitable is missing. The stove. The sink. Hell, there isn't even a refrigerator. My stomach growls, but any hope I had of finding something to eat has died.

I start tearing through the cabinets on one end of the wall and make my way down the line. Everything comes out. Blankets, sheets, and pillowcases are on the bottom. All a crisp, bleached white. A knitted throw blanket and an old crusty bear are in the cabinet next to that. Tufts of fur linger on my fingers as I turn it over. There's a patch on the backside void of fur. I smile as a distant memory I can't place settles into my bones, like a warm cup of coffee. I place the bear back on the blanket and tuck it in for safekeeping. Tossing it across the room and onto the floor feels wrong.

The next cabinet is boring—big bowls for mixing and a few other odds and ends. The same can be said for all the other cabinets. I continue to pull everything out, on principle. Every little inconvenience I can cause Peter is a win in my book. It's not until I reach the top corner of the last cabinet that I search that I find something... peculiar.

My fingers skim across the hardcover of a book. I pull it off the shelf and hop off the counter and back onto the floor. Short people problems. My five-foot-five stature makes me full of fun but vertically challenged most days.

The lettering on the cover and spine is worn. Faded with years of age and devoured by dust. The hard backing separates from the binding as I open it and my soul screams when the book cracks. It's a first-edition publication of *Peter and Wendy* by J. M. Barrie.

I flip through the pages, carefully turning each one. They're as delicate as the petals of a wilted rose. The last thing I want is for one to tear or separate from the binding. I don't give two shits if the damage upsets Peter. Hurting a book this old ravages my feeble teacher heart.

I take it to the wingback chair and cross my legs as I settle onto the cushions. I've read this book a thousand times over, watched the movies... the one with Jeremy Sumpter is my favorite. Read about a dozen retellings, but nothing has come close to the feeling of holding a first-edition print.

All children grow up, except one.

It dawns on me, as I re-read the ancient pages that there are bits of truth in the tale, but most of it is wrong. Peter did grow up, and his lost boys aren't a band of children but a dozen or so wayward misfits, most of which he ignores. I frown as I take in the story, pillaging through each line as if it is the first time I'm reading it. Taking apart each sentence and comparing it to what little I've learned about Neverland in the last twenty-four hours... which isn't much.

"You shouldn't be reading that."

Cass's voice makes me jump. I slam the book shut. A cloud of dust plumes, blooming in the air and tickles my nose until I sneeze, once. Twice. After the third time, my eyes are itchy and my nose is runny.

Cass picks a handkerchief from the pile of linens on the floor and hands it to me. "You good?"

"Yeah." I wipe my eyes and then blow my nose. "Dust allergy. What are you doing here?"

His lips lift into a lopsided smile that makes my stomach flip. He tucks his hands into the pockets of his khaki shorts and shrugs. "Can't a guy miss his girl?"

"You're such a sap." I roll my eyes, but I know he can see the blush on my cheeks.

I don't know how long I've been sitting here. A couple of hours. Maybe? Time is irrelevant when the sky is only various shades of pink, orange, and blue. What I do know is we haven't been apart long enough for Cass to actually miss me.

"If you're catching feelings for me, we need to quit now before things get complicated."

"Life in Neverland is madness, Wens." Cass sits in the seat beside me, a gray accent chair with a lower back and deflated tufts of fabric. "Now that you're here, it'll soon come to an end."

"Does anyone on the island understand you?" I laugh because I have no idea what he just said. It's either a whacked compliment or a threat wrapped in velvet.

"Feel like running away with me?"

"I'm thinking no is the safe answer." The last time I played a game like this, Peter brought me to a beautiful island I can't enjoy because there's no return ticket home. I don't think these people know what sarcasm is, and it would be my luck that Cass would have a one-way ticket to the River Styx. "Although I might change my mind if you can sneak me back home."

Cass reaches forward, brushing his finger against my cheek, and tucks my hair behind my ears. "Your soul burns too bright for the world you were born into."

"I'll take that as a no?"

He shakes his head and beads of water drip off his blonde hair. I can't help but wonder if he went swimming before coming to see me or if he's just sweaty from the island heat.

My mind strays to what Cass could have been doing. Chopping wood shirtless. Playing ball in the sand. Doing pull-ups on a tree branch, toning his already taught muscles. My frustrations with Peter turned me on. That man gets under my skin in the most aggravating ways and sweet Cass will reap the rewards.

"We're going to the mirror pool." Cass's voice seeps into my lust-filled thoughts. I lick my lips. His eyes follow the movement, watching me with the same desire I'm fighting. "I thought you might want to join us."

"Who is we?" There's one person on this island I'd prefer not see, especially if water is involved. I would rather Peter come home to an empty house and trip over the mess, forcing him to deal with it all on his own. I want him pissed off that I messed with his things. I want him wondering if I'm off with Cass. And I want him cursing my name and wishing he'd never brought me to Neverland.

"Not Peter," Cass answers. It must be obvious that I don't like that man because his lips lift into a delicious smirk.

"Okay. Give me a minute to get ready." I want to hide the book from Peter and read some more of it later. Based on Cass's warning not to talk about the tale, I have a feeling it was hidden from Peter. Not by him.

I step over the obstacle course that is Peter's possessions and head to my room. As soon as I'm through the door, I spot my suitcase—a rolling leopard print travel bag, on my bed.

It's a unique pattern. Neon blue is the primary color with black spots. I bought it to piss off Tyle when we were eighteen. It's a one-of-a-kind she had her heart set on. Personally, I hate the damn thing. It's too flashy, but its uniqueness makes it easy to find in an airport.

Or a mythical island.

I hide Peter's book in the top drawer of my dresser and then walk to my bed. I unzip my case and everything from the bachelorette party is still there. My toothbrush. Clothes. EReader. I pull each item out and set it on the bed. My heart squeezes with homesickness. Never in a million years did I think I'd want to return to take-out, Netflix, and the simplicity of my life, but I miss every boring, predictable aspect of it.

Cass's knuckles rasp against the doorframe. "You okay?"

I look over at him, my eReader clutched to my chest, tears in my eyes because its battery is full. When I held it last, it was on its last leg, a mere fifteen percent. Someone charged it for me.

"He went back," I whisper.

"What are you talking about?"

I look at all of my things. Tears fall down my cheeks. I think this is what Peter wanted to tell me last night, that he was going back, that he might have taken me, and I stupidly pushed him away because I was drunk and pissed off. I ruined my chances of going home.

I'm so mad at myself I could scream, but I'm even angrier

with Peter. How could he just let me leave? Why didn't he speak up? If he would have said something, I wouldn't be here.

I hate him.

I hate him so much it hurts.

"Peter went back to Florida without me." I squeeze my eyes shut, desperately trying to stop the flow of tears before they get out of control. "He lied."

"Babe." Warm arms wrap around me.

I bury my face in Cass's chest. It's not often I feel completely helpless. There's always a way out, a next step that changes everything, a bright side. I'm having a hard time finding the silver lining today. I think I've done well to keep level-headed, but this feels like rock bottom.

I need to get home.

After a few shaky breaths, I realize I should stop pushing Cass away. This is what I wanted yesterday. Him under a love-drunk spell. I want him so wrapped up in me his lips loosen. I need him to spill the island's secrets. I don't believe we're in Neverland. Sure, that may be what they call this place, but it doesn't exist. As for the weird sun anomaly... I have an answer for that, too.

Alaska.

Alaska has what's called a polar night. The sun hides from one region for almost sixty days, casting them in darkness. Wherever we are, it must be a fluke area of the world like that. I'll search for the name of this island's phenomena whenever I find cell service again.

As my breaths begin to steady, I notice something odd about my beautiful jailer. I raise my head to look Cass in the eyes. "Can I ask you a question?"

He smiles down at me, perfectly straight teeth bared. "Anything."

"Why can't I hear your heartbeat?"

CHAPTER 17

Wednesday

Dying is the greatest adventure of them all. Peter's words echo in my mind. *Death is unpredictable. Sometimes, people come back... different.*

I pull back and place my hand over my chest, searching for my own heartbeat. It thrashes in my chest, thumping with enough vigor to keep both myself and Cass alive. Each thrum beneath my skin should be steadying, but it only creates more worry. More uncertainty in the line of understanding I've only just crossed.

"I see you've found one of our secrets." Cass's smile falls. He walks to the edge of the bed and sits, disregarding the clothes that cover the mattress. "I hoped to have more time with you before you realized our truths."

"What truths?" I push my suitcase to the headboard and sit beside him. My shirts wrinkle underneath my weight and my shoes topple off the edge but right now, I don't care. Cass takes my hand in his and I notice the warmth radiating off his skin. Something impossibly unnatural for someone without a pulse.

"Neverland is an..." He pauses and his bushy brows push together while he tries to find the right words. "An in-between place. A place where nothing lives or dies."

"That's impossible." Neverland doesn't exist. This is Alaska.

A beautiful, mysterious place where the laws of life are sometimes bent. Not broken. Existence after death, an in-between realm where souls go after they leave the body, that kind of madness doesn't exist.

"Is it?" Cass takes my hand and places it over where his heart should be. There is no drum of life. No rise and fall of his chest. We stay like that for minutes, longer than any person could dare to hold their breath. Even without the steady rhythm of breathing, the heart should be doing something, like getting angry at the lack of oxygen and yelling at the lungs with its fists. But my hand never moves, not once. "Everyone on this island is stuck, Wednesday, somewhere between life and death."

"So, this is purgatory?" My heart beats, I remind myself. It beats, which means I'm alive.

Cass's doesn't.

What does that make him? *No, stop thinking like that, Wednesday.* Cass is lying. He has to be. Oh, god. My thoughts flip, jumping tracks like a train out of control.

Did I sleep with a dead guy?

Am I a necrophile?

"I see your mind spinning." He chuckles and the sound makes me angry. Nothing about what he's telling me is funny. I slept with a corpse last night!

"I'm as alive as you are," he adds, answering my unspoken question. "My body needs food. My lungs need air. Just because my heart doesn't beat doesn't mean I can't feel, Wednesday."

Feeling was never my concern. "Can you die?"

"Yes, but not of old age."

Cass pulls a small knife from his pocket and the blade flips open with the push of a button. He presses the tip to the palm of his hand. Bright red blood seeps out of the small hole, proving that he can be hurt.

He pulls the blade away and holds his hand up. A bead of blood trails down his arm. By the time it drips off his elbow and onto the sheet, the cut has healed.

"I can bleed and bruise, but it's incredibly hard to kill me. Not impossible; I've watched my kind die more times than I'd like, but it's not an easy task."

I take Cass's hand and run my finger over where the cut was. His skin is impossibly smooth, the hole sealed from the inside out in a matter of seconds.

Seeing is believing.

I wish I had closed my eyes. "Is everyone on the island like you?"

"No." He cradles my cheek and forces me to look up at him as he speaks. "Emmit is the same as me. Aria, Xyris, Scarlett, and the rest of The Lost are souls who veered off track on the way to their next life. Unclaimed by the underworld. Forgotten by their own. They are forever stuck, forced to forever experience their last emotion."

"That sounds horrible."

He nods. "Heidi and Scarlett were murdered by Heidi's stepdad because he was closed-minded. The bastard forced her to watch as he tortured Scar. She died in fear, hoping that Heidi could save her. Heidi died fighting."

"That's awful." I think back to when Peter pushed me off the boat. To the fear of missing out on my life. To the pain and pressure on my lungs and body. I wouldn't want to stay like that for all eternity.

He nods. "They're stuck in those feelings, reliving the last moments of their lives. So long as they're here, they'll never find peace."

"And here I thought she just didn't like me," I mumble aloud.

Cass chuckles, but the sound is forced. He's trying to keep his light-hearted, carefree attitude, but I can see how hard it is for him to talk about this. "Trust me, beautiful. You'll know if Heidi doesn't like you."

"So...is Peter?" I swallow hard, not wanting to ask the question. This is a lot to take in and I'm not sure how much more I can swallow.

"He's not one of The Lost, but he's not like Emmit and me either." Cass sighs and scratches the back of his head. "He's...a devotion gone wrong."

I nod, not understanding, but I don't push for more. Cass is as white as a ghost. The golden glow of his skin is gone, muted by the harshness of his truths. It must have been hard to tell me as much as he did.

I lean over, cup the back of his neck, and pull his lips to mine. I kiss him, more for my benefit than his. I'm relieved to feel the flutter of lust pool in my stomach.

Cass breaks our kiss but stays close, his lips a whisper away. "You don't have to pretend, Wednesday. I understand if you don't want to do this anymore."

"This changes nothing. You and I..." My breath hitches. I can't lie and say that we're something because even though I like Cass, there's someone else standing in the way. "We're having fun."

Cass slides his hand under my shirt and kisses me again. His fingers play with my nipple. It puckers, tightening because of his touch.

I fall back onto the bed, and my suitcase is annoyingly in the way. I push it to the ground as Cass tugs at my shorts and panties. They slide to my ankles and I kick them off. He doesn't try to drag out my pleasure this time. Instead, he's quick to free himself and find my entrance.

I don't ask for a condom. We've done it once without, so there is no point. This time, though, I tell him, "I don't want a repeat of last time. If you come inside me again, we're done."

"Yes, my shining star," he says as he pushes into me.

I squeeze my eyes shut and breathe through the discomfort. I'm sore from yesterday, and skipping foreplay has me pretty dry, but with each thrust of his hips, things feel better. I push on his shoulders, wanting a new position, but Cass pins my wrists to the mattress. He tunnels into me, his thrusts rough and claiming.

Last night, I wanted to be punished, but today, I want to feel good. My mind hasn't let go of our conversation or that I could have gone home. It's hard to enjoy the ride. I fake an orgasm to keep Cass's ego from deflating. That seems to be what he was waiting for because he's pulling out and finishing on one of my shirts a few minutes later.

I lay there and stare up at the ceiling. *He has no heartbeat. He should be dead. I fucked a dead guy... again.*

Cass turns onto his side and he rests his cheek against his fist, while those hazel eyes look at me. "Has anyone told you how beautiful you are after sex? Your skin glows with life."

I exhale a laugh, unsure of how else to respond. "I don't think I'll ever get used to how you talk."

"Good." He smiles, and if I weren't already struggling to catch my breath, I would be breathless because this is the type of smile to suck the air from your lungs. "That means I will forever have you in the palm of my hand."

"Easy, killer. I wouldn't go that far." I let Cass thread his fingers with mine and I can't get over how warm his skin is. Without a heartbeat, there is no circulation. What's giving him life if not that? "I like the way you make me feel. That's it. Don't make this more than it is."

Cass rolls on top of me. His legs spread until he's sitting on my lap. He leans over, one hand on either side of my shoulders, and says, "I like that you make me feel, Wednesday. You have no idea how long it's been since I've thought about anything but..." He cuts himself off and presses a quick kiss to my lips. "We need to get dressed."

"Oh? Do we?"

"Yup." Cass climbs off of me and reaches for his shorts. "You're coming with me to the mirror pool. There's something I want to show you."

CHAPTER 18

Wednesday

The grass is soft under my legs, not itchy or wet. I changed out of Tyle's bikini and into my cutout one-piece. It's black with a thin strip of fabric connecting the top to the bottom. It's basically another two-piece, but this one is clean, which makes me happy. I also put on a pair of shorts Cass and I found at the Pirate's Market and paired it with the *ACOTAR* shirt I used as a pajama in the Keys.

I sit on a small knoll that overlooks an open field. Cass, Xyris, and Heidi run around under the cotton candy sky. The sun has shifted, coloring the clouds in deep hues of purple and blue but this is the closest they get to nightfall. Not as bright, yet never fully dark.

Scarlett sets a mason jar filled with lightning bugs beside me. Their butts glow bright and then the light winks out for a heartbeat before lighting again.

"Catching them is half the fun," she whispers, her lips lifting into a small smile.

"If it creeps or crawls, it's not for me," I admit.

I've never liked bugs. As a kid, they gave me nightmares. The only creatures I could stand were butterflies and dragonflies. Eventually, I learned not to scream when a bee flew past me, but it took a lot of willpower. Looking at the lightning bugs, I know they are harmless, but that doesn't stop the urge to run away from making a quick appearance.

"I don't like them either." Scarlet stares at the little jar of bugs. The lid has small, oblong holes in it that look like they were made by the point of a knife. "The lightning bugs." She's quiet, always so hard to hear. I have to strain my ears to catch what she says, even though the world around us is still. "Their glow flickers on and off. It makes me feel... bad."

I think back to my conversation with Cass. *Forever in a state of fear.* I understand now why Scarlett never speaks above a whisper. The fear of being heard by the wrong person, being caught and tortured again for simply existing and loving someone, must always be on her mind. My thoughts wander to what memories the flickering light of the firefly's butt might trigger. I shudder as too many horror movie scenes come to mind. "Then why come?"

Scar's lips lift slightly. Her amber gaze follows Heidi as her partner struggles to catch fireflies without killing them. "Because it makes her happy."

Heidi grunts and curses under her breath. She peeks between her fingers, her brows knit, and she curses again. She jumps in the air and clasps her palms together, repeating her failing attempts to fill her jar.

I look at Scarlett skeptically. "That's happy?"

"Yeah." She laughs. It's barely louder than the whispers I've grown used to, but the sound makes me feel joy. Somewhere beneath all the worry and constant torture of living, Scarlett has happiness. I don't know how long it lasts, but knowing that she isn't solely stuck in a state of fear like Cass described is a relief. "Heidi's got a resting bitch face, but she means well," she adds.

"If you say so."

Silence falls between us. At first, it's nothing more than quiet air, but the longer we sit, the thicker it becomes. I'm sure the tension is in my mind. Scarlett is busy watching her mate grunt and growl while I watch Cass. He effortlessly fills two jars with glowing bugs, laughing and joking with Emmit and Xyris between handfuls.

There's a heaviness in my chest. Questions that burn under my skin, dying to be asked. But how? Where do I even start without raising suspicions? "Have you guys been together long?"

"Long enough to feel like forever, but I love her." Scarlett pulls her knees in and hugs her legs. She rests her chin on her knees. "Even when all I want to do is run."

"I might be overstepping, but that doesn't sound like love."

"I don't expect you to understand. You haven't been around long enough." She meets my gaze. "I like you, Wednesday, but I hope you never find out what I mean."

"You've been here a long time, though. Haven't you?" I hold my breath and hope Scarlett doesn't dig too deep. Heidi would question me and want to know why I'm asking. She's always on edge, understandably. I can't imagine growing up in a world with so much hate that she was murdered for falling in love.

Scarlet sighs. She plucks a blade of grass out of the ground and tears it into tiny pieces. "It feels that way, but I'm not sure. Time isn't linear here. It just...is."

Cass comes over with two glowing jars in his hands. His smile is wide, eyes alight with life. "Are you ladies ready?"

"I still say she needs to catch the damn bugs herself," Heidi growls, her eyes narrowing into slits on me.

"Shut it, Heidi." Xyris spits. "Emmit caught damn near all your lightning bugs. You'd still be out there, killing each one you touch if it weren't for him."

"Whatever." She rolls her eyes.

I stand and brush the dirt off my ass. Cass leans forward, wraps his arm around my waist, and nuzzles his nose against my neck. It tickles and a laugh leaves my lips. I smile against him, relieved my mind isn't stuck on the lack of heartbeat problem. It's hard to make a man want to spill his secrets if touching him makes me want to puke.

"Ugh. Get a room."

"You're just jealous." Cass steps back and drapes an arm over my shoulders.

"Please. I wouldn't touch your sloppy seconds with a ten-foot pole."

A small part of me jumps for joy. They heard our bedroom romp last night, or about it. News is traveling which means if it hasn't already reached Peter's ears, it will.

Before I can open my mouth to spit a rebuttal, Xyris takes me by the elbow and pulls me out of Cass's embrace.

Cass lets me go and I slam into Xyris's hard chest. Xyris looks down at me and I notice that his eyes are the color of an autumn sun: red, orange, and brown. It seems like everyone here has unique irises and I wonder if their color has to do with their deaths because no living person has eyes this vibrant.

"Don't let Heidi get under your skin." Xyris reaches up and tucks my hair behind my ears, using both hands. "There is nothing sloppy about you."

"I don't need you sticking up for me." I step back and clear my throat. "But thanks."

"What did I tell you?" Cass chuckles. "I knew that fucker would try to steal my girl."

"I thought you and Emmit were together," I ask as embarrment colors my cheeks.

"Oh, I'm one hundred and ten percent his." Xyris looks at Emmit and winks. "But we like to add a little spice every now and then. Don't we, baby?"

Emmit shrugs. "When you've been together as long as we have, adding something new from time to time keeps the spark alive."

"And you're okay with this?" I look at Cass. For someone who calls me a shining star and constantly tells me how amazing I am, he doesn't seem bothered by the idea of Xyris trying to sleep with me.

He shrugs. "Who am I to stop you?"

The man who had his dick in me a few hours ago!

"Baby, just because I fucked you doesn't mean you can't explore everything this island has to offer," he says, almost as if he can hear my unspoken thought.

My jaw drops. I don't know what to say. I think I'm in shock.

Cass cups my cheeks. He presses his forehead to mine until he's all I see. "If you want to bring someone else into the bedroom with us, I'll welcome them. If you want to shack up with Captain Fucks Everything Up, too, go for it. I won't punish you for wanting to feel everything Neverland has to offer because feeling is a gift. Live in the now and enjoy what this life has to offer."

"Does the same go for you?" I feel guilty asking. I'm using him, but that doesn't mean I want to catch a disease. If Neverland doesn't have electricity I doubt it has antibiotics.

"No. You're the first partner I've had in years. There is no one on this island I want besides you."

"Get a room," Heidi coughs.

"Come on now, Heidi. Don't be a prude." Xyris elbows her in the side. "We all know how much you love voyeurism."

She flips him off and links arms with Scarlet. They walk across the grassy knoll, paying no mind to the boys and me.

Emmit looks up at the sky. Faint traces of stars permeate through the clouds. Their light is stuck behind the tufts, permanently lost to us. "We need to go."

"Go where?" I ask.

Cass hands me the jar of glowing bugs. "To the best kept secret in all of Neverland."

CHAPTER 19

Wednesday

"No. Absolutely not."

I stand at the mouth of a cave on the side of a mountain they call the Neverpeek. Jagged rocks lay on top of each other, forming a makeshift opening I'm supposed to blindly walk into.

"You're going to miss the best part." Cass has been waiting for me to build up the courage and follow the others inside, but I can't force my legs to move. A cold sweat covers my skin to the point that thinking about stepping inside the mountain makes me physically sick.

"I'm sure it's cool, but I don't know, Cass." I press my back against the stone. Crisp dew permeates through my shirt and grounds my body.

"Trust me," he insists, running his fingers down my arms. I'm sure he's trying to be comforting, but his touch undoes the dew's magic and makes my skin clammy again.

My heart races, the palpitations alarmingly fast, then slow, then fast again. "You're asking a lot for a guy I just met."

"Wednesday, can you honestly tell me we feel like strangers?" Cass ducks to meet my gaze even though I'm trying not to look at him. "Can you say without a shadow of a doubt that you don't feel it in your bones the way I do? This thing between us is stronger than first-time-fuck-lust." He arches his eyebrows. "If that's all you feel we are, I'll hike down to the beach with you and chill there for the rest of the day." He takes my hands and squeezes them. "But if you feel even an inkling more, I'm asking you to take the leap and trust me."

I can't deny there's a sense of familiarity when Cass and I are together. Being with him has the same comforting feeling of walking into my house with a pecan pie candle burning, an ease that hugs us like an easy blanket. He doesn't feel new. He feels old, in the weirdest, most amazing sense of the word.

I glance at the mouth of the cave and notice the downhill incline, new worries creeping in. "What happens if it rains? "

My question is met with a flash of teeth. "It never rains in Neverland."

I swallow hard and nod. Of course, it doesn't. That would require the sky to change and it's always the most annoyingly beautiful shade of pink.

There's a persistent throb behind my left eye, but I step onto the first gray stone. It's wider than me and, if I were to lie across, it would be nearly twice as long. My legs shake, but I force them to take another step and another.

Cass skips ahead and crouches low in front of me. He twists when I get close. His eyes, the same shade as the evergreen's trunks that surround us, shine. "Want a lift?"

"Am I that pathetic?" I don't protest. I trust that he knows every foothold and low-lying arch of this cave. I'd be stupid not to climb onto his back. It's funny, though; the first time we did this feels like a lifetime ago. *How was it just yesterday?*

Cass hums, drawing out the inevitable truth of how painfully unprepared my life has made me.

Did I expect to be stolen away to an island full of gorgeous men?

No. I don't think even the best-read novel could have

prepared me for this, but I wish I had gone hiking at least once before today because I am exhausted. My hands are swollen and tingling, and we haven't done anything but walk.

"You are beautifully innocent." Cass turns his head and kisses the side of my arm. "I prefer you this way. It means I get to play hero for a little bit longer."

"As opposed to what? Being the villain?" I'm joking, but something stirs in my chest. It's a precarious sensation.

Cass chuckles, avoiding the question. We hike deeper into the cave. The stones are slippery and uneven, but as suspected, he knows when to reach out and steady himself. He turns a corner and the little light carrying in from the opening disappears. If not for the glow of the bugs, we'd be walking in darkness.

"Was this your plan all along?" I ask, the hackles on the back of my neck standing on edge. The further we trek, the more I regret not trusting my instincts. I can't shake this feeling of unease. "To earn my trust so you can kill me later?"

"Telling you my plan will ruin the surprise." Cass sets me down and I slip. My Converse were made for sidewalks and basketball courts, not island adventures. He grabs my waist and steadies me. I look over my shoulder and flash a thank you smile.

"Are you sure you're ready for me to spoil my devious plan?" He arches one eyebrow and gives me a smolder that would make Flynn Rider jealous. "Fine," he says in a mocking, pubescent tone. "You're right. I need you to die. But the question is how?"

He rubs his chin and twists invisible beard hair. I stare at him, completely lost for words and the insane fucker winks. I laugh because it's the only thing I know how to do. For a second, I was worried. I almost believed him.

"You're crazy, you know that."

"I've heard it a time or two." Cass tucks his hands into the pockets of his shorts, a cheeky grin on display. We walk, side by side, on (thankfully) level ground, the only sound in the cave our footsteps and my beating heart.

"Hey, Wednesday?" he says, his voice a whisper in the near darkness.

"Hmm?"

"Look up."

Stalactites hang from the roof like teeth reaching down to eat us. It would be terrifying if not for the glow of green and yellow algae decorating each spike like an inverted Christmas tree.

Cass takes his mason jar and twists the lid. His lightning bugs fly free. My first reaction is to recoil and hide, but as I watch them drift toward the glow, they remind me of the night sky. I stare at them in awe of their beauty.

"Open your jar." He nudges me with his elbow.

I twist my lid free and release another slow swarm of twinkling lights.

"I haven't seen stars in almost two hundred years." There's a longing in his voice. "This is the next best thing."

My heart squeezes. I've only been in Neverland for a few nights and already miss the little comforts of home. I hadn't thought about the big things, like how I'll never get a whole night's rest because there will always be light. I'll never make another wish on the first star because there aren't any. How many more little things am I missing that I haven't even realized? What did Cass lose when he became trapped here?

"It's amazing." As the bugs fly higher in the cave, I watch their lights flicker on and off, with no rhyme or reason. It's easy to imagine them as stars in the sky. I connect the dots, creating my own little dipper and north star.

"Where is everyone else?"

"A little further down. There's a pool of water if you're interested in swimming."

A chill rolls through me. I'm not ready to face the water again. "Do you think we could hang out here for a bit? I'm not in the mood for a swim."

"Of course." Cass kisses the side of my head.

We sit in the dirt and lean our backs against a large stone, creating our own constellations and talking about make-believe worlds with monsters, magic, and a lost princess that could save them all.

107

Wednesday

"I see you found your things," Peter snarls when I walk through the door. He's sitting in the corner with an ancient copy of *Pride and Prejudice* in his hands. "Wonder how they got here?"

"I don't know. It's crazy how things just show up in this house. Like the mess on the floor." I smirk at the blankets, pots, and knick-knacks everywhere. "Didn't feel like cleaning it up?"

Peter closes his book, eyes narrowed on me. "Have fun with your boyfriend today?"

"Cass isn't my boyfriend."

"I can smell him on you."

"Sucks for you." I shrug.

Peter is up and out of the chair faster than my brain can follow. His hand touches my shoulde, and he pushes me backward until my back hits the wall. "Careful, Darling. Keep it up and I'll be fighting fire with fire."

"You can try, but I've got to want you for it to work, Peter, and I'd fuck every man on his island before touching you. You repulse me."

He chuckles, that dark sultry gaze dropping down to my chest before finding my face again. "Your nipples disagree."

I slap him because I hate how much I want him. He takes my assault like my hand is nothing more than the breeze caressing his skin.

"Naughty girls get punished, Darling. Are you a naughty girl?" he asks, darkness filling the blue of his irises.

"What are you?" I wonder, not meaning to ask the question aloud.

Peter's lips lift into a wicked smirk. "You think your boyfriend told you everything about Neverland? You're wrong."

Squirm and stand taller. "I know enough."

"Do you?" He unsheathes a knife from the holster at his side. The hand on my shoulder turns and his forearm pushes against my neck. The pressure teeters between thrilling and uncomfortable, but it's the look in his eyes that scares me. The sheer hatred burning through a lusty haze.

"Peter, you're hurting me."

"Did your precious boyfriend tell you how time works?" He runs the blunt edge of the blade down my cheek.

The metal is cold, but that's not why I shiver. "We're in between life and death, day and night."

He cuts my shirt open, slicing the printed mountain in half, then snaps the string holding my bathing suit top up. It falls, leaving me bare before him. Peter takes in the swell of my breasts with his eyes. The hunger in them matches the need ripping through me. Peter holds the knife in his fingers and presses his palm against my chest. "Your heart is racing."

I take a slow breath, noticing his pupils constrict. The truth that I want him as much, if not more than he wants me, is an anchor. It keeps me in this moment and lets me feel the ache inside, instead of remembering that I'm supposed to be a tease making his life miserable.

"Do you know why you feel so much, Darling? It's because your precious human heart is trying to keep pace with the world you live in while existing in mine." He pulls away and slashes the blade across my arm.

"Asshole!" I cover my wound with my hand. Fury rips through any heady thoughts I had and tears pool in my eyes, stinging almost as bad as my arm. "You cut me!"

"Did I?" He smirks and I don't know how I ever found him attractive.

"What do you mean, *did I?*" I show him the wound on my arm, but it's gone. The only indication that I was hurt is the blood on my hand and a barely visible scar. "I... how?"

Peter leans against the counter, stepping on the blankets I threw on the floor. "How long would you say it takes a cut like that to heal in your world?"

"I don't know... maybe a few minutes of pressure for the bleeding to stop and a few days for the scab to be gone."

"Very good, Darling. How long did it take here?"

"Seconds," I whisper.

"A second in our world is a minute in yours. Minutes, hours. Hours, days. You can't trust time." He taps his temple. "It will fuck with your mind. Neverland will twist everything you know about the world, your life, and turn it on its side."

I feel the blood drain from my face. It's been days, does that mean I've been gone for weeks? Months? At this point, if I were to find a way home, would I even have a home to go back to, or would all of my things be sold and my apartment re-rented?

"The only place on the island you're safe is in this tree house. Hate me, if you will, but the Island's magic can't touch you here. Your feelings are real, and your thoughts are safe. Out there." He points at the door. "You're powerless against it."

"I don't believe you."

"Why? Because you like Cass? That's cute. He's not who you think he is. None of them are." Peter tucks his knife back into its holster and pushes off the counter. He heads to the door, ready to leave me alone in this house. Again.

"What does that make you, Peter?" I yell, venom biting every word.

His steps falter. He stands in the middle of the room, shoulders rolled forward. His breaths are slow and controlled to the point they're rhythmical. He doesn't look at me, but I feel the weight of every word as he says, "I'm what you made me be."

CHAPTER 21

Wednesday

Peter was right.

Time isn't linear.

I thought I had figured out day versus night—the sky a brighter blue versus the deep purple wisps that appear later in the day—but not nearly enough time passes in between for it to be the equivalent of the sun falling and the moon rising. The only thing I've consistently counted is the times I've fallen asleep, eight so far, and even that is unreliable. I can't tell the difference between a nap and a night's rest.

The longer I'm on the island, the more I question.

How did The Lost come to Neverland?

Why can't they leave?

What happened to Peter? He never flies or crows like the stories describe. Has he lost his spirit? His magic? Where did it all come from in the first place?

Cass is no help. He dodges my questions with kisses and sex. If he wasn't so good in bed I might be mad, but watching Peter's face burn red whenever we pass makes me care less and less about the unanswered. I'll eventually find what I'm searching for.

One way or another.

But I can't ask Peter anything because he's keeping his distance, which only pisses me off and gives me even more questions. Why bring me to this stupid island if the plan was to ignore me? He made me feel like the only girl in the world when we were in Florida. He set my soul on fire, woke every nerve in my body, just to douse it all in ice water.

Because here I'm nothing.

I can't make sense of it.

And since Cass refuses to let me stay over anymore, I'm forced to sleep under Peter's roof every night, in the bed I woke up on my first night, even though the treehouse is always empty.

Peter makes it a point not to be home when I am. Perhaps his absence is a token of truce. If he spends every evening the way he is tonight, tangled up in Aria's lips, I'm glad he's not around.

Heat climbs my neck as I watch him share a glass of whiskey with her on the other side of the bonfire. Aria takes his crystal tumbler and looks up at him through long lashes. Her lips taste his against the glass.

Peter leans close, whispering into her ear and I remember what his warm breath against my skin felt like. It made me crave those lips. I wanted them to touch me in places I wouldn't dare show in public, but I would have ventured into voyeurism for him. I sigh and stare down at my cup. I hate Peter and secretly wish I could stab him in his sleep, but I can't deny I'm jealous.

Peter is a beautiful man. His good looks are what drew me to him in the first place, but it was those lips that turned my insides to liquid.

"You okay there, beautiful?" Cass wraps his arms around me from behind and pulls me close.

"Just tired." I lean against him. Guilt stabs me in the side again, a reminder that while I enjoy sex with Cass, it's Peter I think about when I come. Most nights, I can push past my thoughts and enjoy the feeling of his body in mine, but tonight, I need a break. "I think I'm gonna call it a night."

"Do you want me to walk you to the tree house?" His voice is a gentle caress against my skin. It's touch unable to break through the barrier I've built tonight.

Watching Peter flaunt his affections with someone else hits harder than I ever could have imagined. I'm angry and hot and on the verge of tears all at once over a man who barely gives me the time of day.

"No. I know the way." I kiss Cass's cheek. If I accept his offer as an escort, I'll be pity fucking him tonight, and he deserves better. "Thanks, though."

I give a slight wave to the others and hop off the picnic table before Cass can try and change my mind. Peter and Aria don't notice my departure. They're engrossed in conversation, shamelessly touching each other out in the open. I want to yank her out of his arms by the hair, and that's not me.

All the more reason to leave.

I follow the worn path from the beach to the treehouses. The first time Cass and I walked through the woods, I didn't notice the pressed-down grass and dirt-covered path we took. Back then, it felt like the forest was closing in on me. The trees dropped their branches low to grab me, they lifted their roots to trip me, and the bugs tried to turn make me back by attacking.

I was an outsider wandering into uncharted lands. Now, I know when to duck and weave. I know which roots seem to rise and how to avoid walking into a floating swarm of no-see ums. I've grown accustomed to the ways of the island. It's accepted me as one of its own and up until this gnawing feeling, I was happy to be one of The Lost it protects.

Cass said everyone here is stuck, forever trapped in their last emotion. If that's true, I don't want to feel like this for all eternity. Full of anger and jealousy. I refuse.

It's time I made a plan to get out of here. No more lingering about. There's nothing useful in Peter's treehouse and Cass hasn't been forthcoming with more information. But how the hell do I get off of a freaking island?

I stop in my tracks. The answer comes to me and I feel stupid for not having thought of it sooner. I need a boat. Not a boat, those will capsize and sink the moment they come across a big wave.

What I need is a ship, and I know just where to find one.

CHAPTER 22

Wednesday

"Stars above, Peter, you scared the shit out of me," I say when I recognize the shadow lingering on a tree. I look around, half expecting him to jump out and scare me. Seems like the sort of thing the twisted blend of storybook Peter and Broody Mcglare would do, but I don't see him.

I cross my arms, irritated by being caught snooping around the far end of the forest and wait for his version of a reprimand. Technically, no one told me I couldn't be here, but Cass has avoided this side of the island ever since our jaunt to the pirate cove and everyone else is either with him or on the beach ever since taking me to the Pirate's Market. I'm thinking there's an unwritten rule of where I can and can't go, which makes the anticipation of what will happen next even worse.

"You can come out now," I tell him, putting my hands on my hips.

The thought that Peter left Aria's side to search for me feeds the jealous bitch in my veins. I fight a smug smile amused that he would leave the comfort of her lips to come find me, especially since I left Cass behind.

Maybe he's hoping to have another run-in? If so, I'm all for it.

Need pools in my stomach. Peter's knife to my neck turned

me on to the point I came within minutes of touching myself the other day. I hope he listens outside my door when I whisper his name, wishing it were his fingers beneath my panties instead of mine.

I can't deny there's something between us, an invisible string connecting my lady bits to him. All of him. His glare. His touch. The sound of his breath against my ear. Even the harshness of his words.

If he wants a repeat of what happened in the treehouse or even to take things a step further, I'm game.

"Peter," I call again.

The shadow shakes his head.

I look more closely at the dense foliage around us and realize Peter's shadow can't be cast the way it is without him standing directly across from it. "Peter isn't here. Is he?"

The shadow shakes his head and I realize there might be some truth to the fabled story. Peter's shadow really did leave him. Maybe that's why he brought me here. Maybe he asked if I was Wendy because he thought that I could reattach it for him.

Stupid man. I could've saved us both a lot of heartache if he had spoken up instead of assuming because I'm not Wendy Darling. I don't know how to sew a shadow to a foot.

"Well, I guess this puts us in a predicament, doesn't it?" I ask the shadow.

He cocks his head to the side and stares at me. I almost laugh at myself for expecting a verbal answer. Still, I talk to him because if the shadow can follow and hear me, I need to know if he's on my side or if he's Peter's snitch.

"I want to keep exploring the woods, but it seems I've been caught. Are you going to tattle on me?"

Shadow crosses, his arms mimicking my stance, and shakes his head.

"Good. Maybe you and I can be friends, unlike your other half."

Friends with Peter isn't an option for so many reasons I can't count them. For one, he literally kidnapped me. That's a deal breaker in itself, but he's too sexy for his own good, and he knows it. The arrogant jerk knew what he was doing by flirting with Aria. He knew I'd fall into his jealous trap and die a miserable death.

Shadow's shoulders rise and fall, as if he's laughing.

I smirk, unamused that he thinks whatever Peter and I've got going on is comical. I'm about to keep walking when it occurs to me that I'm lost. All the trees look the same, to the point that I'm not sure I could even find my way back to the treehouses.

"Hey, Shadow, do you think you can help me? I'm trying to get to the pirate's side of the island."

He shakes his head and viciously waves his arms in an ex-shape, signaling I probably shouldn't go there.

I give him a look, unsure if the shadow can see the *come-on* expression I'm trying to convey or if he just sees my head tilted sideways. "I'm going with or without you. If you're with me, you can make sure I don't get lost along the way. I mean this is Neverland. Isn't it? I'm sure there are carnivorous plants and dangerous animals somewhere on the island. What if I stumble into them because I'm all alone?"

I wait a solid three seconds before marching through the trees again, stepping on broken twigs, listening to them echo in the eternal twilight.

Shadow jumps a couple of trunks ahead of me and waves his arms. I fight my smirk and stop to look at him. He bends over, rests a hand on his knees, and wipes sweat from his brows. We have a stare-off, if that's what staring at something without eyes can be called, and I think I win.

Shadow sands upright and waves for me to follow him in a different direction. One I'm fairly certain doesn't lead me back to the treehouse or the beach.

"See," I tell him, the pride of knowing he wouldn't let me walk into danger evident in my tone. "I knew you and I would be friends."

If Peter were here, he'd probably be rolling his eyes at me, but considering that Shadow has none we walk side-by-side. Him jumping from one tree to the next, and me trying not to trip over fallen branches, upturned roots, or my own feet.

We walk and walk, crossing what feels like half the island together. Shadow doesn't attempt to communicate with me and the closer we get to the cove, the more nervous I get.

Cass and I avoided the pirates the last time we came. Sure, I saw them, but we didn't talk to anyone. The shops we went to were dead inside, and as soon as the one with the large hat got close, we left. I don't know what to expect from these people. I'm hoping they're civilized and not misogynistic jerks with bad hygiene.

I decide to talk to Shadow, even if he doesn't answer, is better than running scenarios in my mind. If he understands what I'm looking for, maybe he can help me find a way home that doesn't require bartering with the pirates.

"Can I ask you a question, Shadow?" He doesn't motion that he hears me, but I keep talking. "Does Peter think I can attach you to him again?"

Shadow laughs, covering his hand with his belly, and dropping his head back. He stops walking for a moment and holds up one finger. I watch him catch his breath and wipe tears I can't see from his eyes. After a breath or two, Shadow shakes his head.

"Damn. There goes that theory," I say aloud. "Do you know why I'm here?"

Shadow shakes his head again.

"I want to go home," I tell him, letting the longing I've buried deep inside slip into my voice. I've held it in so tight, tried to be strong every day that I've been here, and make it seem like I don't care even though I'm impatiently trying to count the days until I can see my family again.

I can almost feel the sadness flow from Shadow, which is ridiculous because shadows can't feel. He reaches out to touch me and I extend my hand. Logically, I know it's impossible, but right now, I feel more alone than I have in my life. I think it's hitting me that if this doesn't work, if I can't find a ship to sail me back to America, I'm going to be on this island for the rest of my life. A life that might be longer and filled with more pain than any existence I could have lived back home.

My fingers touch the darkness that is the shadow's hand, but all I feel is air. His fingers cross into the light. Their dark form turns to dust, disappearing before my eyes. Shadow retracts his hand to the quasi-darkness and holds it up, showing me that he's fine.

I force a smile and nod, relieved that he didn't hurt himself to comfort me, but feel hollow. I start walking again, not in the mood to talk anymore. Shadow leads the way, staying as close to my side as possible without crossing over my own shadow.

The trees around us thin, the forest fading behind us. We step out of the thick and cross a grassy knoll that seems to stretch for an eternity, but I vaguely remember walking it with Cass.

Far ahead, we reach a mountain's edge. Shadow climbs the rock wall. I follow him up, careful to place my hands and feet in the places he does. The ledge we're looking for isn't far, maybe ten feet above us but my arms are screaming when I finally pull myself over the edge. I lay there, my chest tight and out of breath for at least five minutes.

I don't remember the climb being this difficult. Or the walk being so far. I furrow my brows, trying to recall details from the first day I was here and frown when I realize a lot of them are gone. "Neverland makes you forget," I whisper to myself, unable to place where I'd heard it before. A movie, maybe? Or perhaps a book. I shudder at the truth of the words and make a mental note to start writing things down. What if I already found the key to getting home, and I forgot it? What else am I forgetting?

I push myself off the cold stone and smile, relieved, when I recognize the red handprint beside a slim opening in the stone. I poke my head into the crack. It's darker than I recall, but I remember the steps. I counted one hundred and twenty-eight from one end to the other the last time I was here. I touch the wall and dew coats my hand. The opening is slim, barely big enough for one person to cross through sideways, but I had no problem fitting.

I turn sideways, careful not to let my back touch the jagged wall, and search for Peter's shadow. He sits at the ledge of the cave, cross-legged.

"Are you coming?"

Shadow shakes his head.

"Why?"

Shadow raises his hand, like a child making shadow puppets would, and his fingers shift into the shape of a ship.

"You're afraid of boats?"

He shakes his head again. This time, he holds his hands above his head to look like a man with a large hat with a feather on it.

"You don't like pirates."

Shadow nods. Leaving him makes me a little uneasy, but that's why I'm here, to find a captain. "I'll be back soon. Wait for me?"

Shadow shifts back to his Peter-like self and gives me a thumbs-up.

This is it. I take a deep breath hoping my nerves will settle. *One way or another, I'm going home.*

CHAPTER 23

Peter

I t's a struggle not to follow Wednesday when she leaves Cass's side and ventures into the woods. Not to push her against a tree and claim those lips. Not to touch her sun-kissed skin that will forever be a toasted shade of golden brown. Not to trace my fingers down the seam of her tan lines and watch her pretty face twist in pleasure.

Every day I wake, there's a new ripple in my shadow.

A crack in my soul.

I thought I could sit back and let her love another. I thought the years of torture while I stood on the sidelines to let my brother woo the girl I loved, only to lose her on this stupid island, had hardened me.

I was wrong.

My shadow's jealousy burns through me, more potent than my own, his rage a second inferno almost as strong. Our feelings are one when it comes to Wednesday and they're making it hard to stay focused.

The only way to break the island's curse is for her to fall in love. I am not an option. My soul is not my own anymore. Cass was supposed to be her new mate, but it's killing me to wait on the sidelines again. I want her. Even if it means condemning The Lost to eternal purgatory, I have to have her.

I sat back and did nothing the first time fate stole my heart.

I won't let it happen again.

CHAPTER 24

Wednesday

Walking through the cove alone is a different experience than when I came with Cass. With him by my side, there was no sense of danger because we passed through the streets like ghosts. This time, it seems like everyone notices me.

I try not to let the wandering eyes shake me. Pirates are probably like sharks and can smell fear. I hold my head high, exuding false confidence, and read each shop sign. I've passed three saloons, two oddity stores that look to be bursting at the seams with clothes, and a handful of hobby carts.

I decide to take a chance on a saloon called Harper's Edge because I'm sweating. The sky may be the same shade of pinkish blue as it is by the beach, but the sun burns hotter over here. There is no ocean breeze to cool the air even though the cove has a wide mouth and the buildings sit lower than the tree tops.

I thought I attracted attention on the boardwalk, but as I push the swinging doors open, it feels like everyone's eyes are on me, my jean shorts, and my Machine Gun Kelly tee shirt. I'm a fish out of water in my Converse because everyone in the bar wears boots and jeans or khaki pants. The only other girl in the room is behind the bar and even she seems better dressed than I am.

I try not to laugh, my fear getting the best of me, because it looks like I traveled back in time five hundred years to the era of Blackbeard and all his scallywags.

"What can I get yeh," the bartender asks, her accent heavy but indiscernible.

"What do you have?" The only thing I've drank on this island is water and Faery wine and I have a feeling that neither of them are served at this bar.

"Yer new around here, ain't yeh?"

"Is it that obvious?"

"Yeh, love." She laughs and pulls two wooden mugs from beneath the counter. "Yeh got a tongue for the stout stuff, or are yer a weaklin'?"

I'm not a fan of shots and drinks like Jack and Coke make me cringe. I want to enjoy my alcohol, not swallow fire. I also know that this is a test and even if I have to hold my breath to down whatever she gives me, I'll do it. "Surprise me."

The girl chuckles and pulls the cork out of a small barrel, letting its dark liquor pour into the cup. I have a feeling it's gonna taste like fire, but thank her anyway.

"That'll be ten shillings," she says, sliding the cup across a teak countertop.

I stare at her, eyes wide. Money was never an option on the beach. We've eaten and drank and lived on the left side of civilization and so I have nothing to offer. "Oh, I'm sorry, I don't ..."

Someone sets a silver coin on the counter beside me. "I've got her, Melinda."

"Thank you," I say, looking up at pale blue eyes encircled by a thick layer of charcoal. The man's lips lift, revealing two dimples with a thick scar going through one. I blush as I take in the dark stubble on his jaw and the gold hoop in his ear.

"Haven't seen yeh around these parts," he says in an accent that's either English or Scottish or something ending in *-ish*. My knowledge of dialects goes as far as movies and audiobooks and for all I know they are wrong, but this man's voice is *right*.

I'm embarrassed to find him attractive and doubt someone with so much swagger would look twice at me. But those sky-blue eyes trail over my body, stopping briefly on my chest before reaching my face again.

I shiver, goosebumps peppering my skin, and not in a bad way. It reminds me of the way Peter made me feel in Florida, full of excitement and desire with an added familiarity that we've met before, but I would recognize the pirate if we crossed paths in the past, and I'm sure we haven't.

"Seems like I might need to dress better in these parts of the woods." I smile down at the drink I'm too scared to try. What is it with this island and men? Every one of them, down to the hobo-looking one in the corner, is breathtaking. Possibly in need of a shower, but still beautiful. I lean closer to the one beside me, playfully whispering, "Everyone keeps looking at me."

"I assure yeh, Sunshine, it's not because of yer clothes." He holds a finger up and the bartender hands him a mug filled with something yellow and frothy.

"Sunshine?" I ask, enamored with the pet name.

"Aye. Yer beautiful, casting a ray of golden light, but dangerous to anyone who looks too long." He winks and chugs half his drink.

I hide the heat of my cheeks by lifting my cup. The smell of my drink singes my nostrils. Whatever came out of the barrel is going to be hell to swallow. I take a small sip and the alcohol attacks my throat with flames from hell. It's more bitter than black coffee and takes every bit of willpower I have not to spit it out.

He laughs, bellowing out a deep chuckle. "That's precious, Sunshine. Never seen anyone make a face like that while drinking."

"Fuck you." I reach for his drink, convinced it will be better than mine. He lets me steal the rest and I'm relieved when it tastes like butterscotch. I gasp for air, fire still burning my lungs.

"Generally speaking, I like to know the names of the lasses I swap spit with." He flashes me a set of pearly whites and holds out his hand. "The name's James Panton."

"Wednesday." I set my hand in his and he shakes it with a firm grip. "Roberts."

"Well, Ms. Roberts, it is a pleasure to meet you. Would yeh like another round?"

"Of what you're drinking? Sure. But this..." I slide my nearly full cup to the side. "No, thank you."

James chuckles. He takes my mug and tosses the contents back as if it were an oversized shot. He winces as he swallows, but the moment the cup is on the counter again, it's like he just drank water.

Melinda brings us two full glasses of butterscotch beer, then leaves us to tend to the man who's fallen asleep on her table across the room.

"Dance with me," James stands and holds his hand out for me to take.

"There's no music." Even as I protest, I find myself agreeing to the request. The least I can offer is an awkward dance after he bought me two and a half drinks.

"So long as our hearts beat, there is music in our souls." He spins me once, then pulls me close to his chest. We sway, slowly stepping to a melody he hums.

"Are all the pirates as nice as you?"

He smirks and dips me backward. "There is no other like me." We're upright again, my hand in his, resting against his chest. I can feel the slow, steady beat of his heart. "Why? Looking fer new company already."

"I'm sorry. I don't mean to be rude."

"Apology accepted."

James twirls me around the bar floor. We skirt around empty tables and chairs. The eyes that look at us when we draw near avert their gaze, as if they're afraid. I notice but keep the observation to myself, curiosity getting the best of me.

"It's just... I'm in search of a captain."

"Yer in luck. I have a ship." He kisses my hand and we stop dancing.

My heart races from the excitement of maybe finding someone to take me home and being in his arms. We take our seats again and I'm surprised to find our drinks are still cold.

"Where is it yer wanting to go?"

"To Florida."

My answer makes him pause mid-sip. James sets his drink on the bar top and stares at me, his eyes taking me in with more than surface interest. "A journey like that is no easy task."

"I know, and I don't have much to offer."

"I'll make it easy on yeh. Go on a date with me, Sunshine, and I'll take yeh to the moon if that's what yeh want." He takes no time to think about a reply.

I chew on my bottom lip. I'm already in over my head juggling Cass and these unresolved feelings for Peter. I know myself. Give me a few drinks and an evening filled with good conversation and dancing and my lady bits will be begging for a ride.

But I'm turning into the person I swore I wouldn't be.

James sees the hesitation on my face and grins. He takes my hand and presses his lips to my knuckles as he stands. "There's no pressure, but if yeh decide to take me up on my offer all yeh need to do is return to Harper's Edge and I will find you."

"You make this sound easy."

"And yer making a single night with me more than it is. I promise I don't bite, unless yer into that sort of thing."

James winks and I shove his chest. The look he gives me in that moment strikes a chord deep inside. I've seen it before, somewhere, only I can't place when or how.

"Until we meet again."

CHAPTER 25

Wednesday

Navigating back to the treehouse is more challenging than I anticipated, even with the shadow's help. My brain is fuzzy from the butterscotch beer, but I feel good. I hum a melody similar to the one James and I danced to. I think tonight is the most fun I've had since coming to Neverland. Even as I tried to negotiate a way home, the constant blanket of stress I carry when it comes to Peter and Cass was set aside. It was nice.

But as I stare up at the ladder that leads to the spider web of rope bridges, I feel that blanket falling on my shoulders again. The only relief I have is the small sliver of hope that James will honor his word. One date, that may or may not lead to more, and I'll be on a ship sailing far, far away.

I climb the ladder's steps and then crawl across the bridge to Peter's door. This is another thing I can't imagine doing for the rest of my life, crawling like a helpless imp. I stand, my breaths ragged, and open the door.

I couldn't see the lights on from outside.

I didn't know that the treehouse wasn't empty.

I stand in the open door, my jaw dropped, unable to tear my gaze away from Peter's naked body. The hard lines of his muscles, shadowed by ink and hair are beautiful. I swallow hard as my eyes dip lower. There's a bar with a small silver ball on each end going through the head of his dick. I've never felt anything like that inside me before. I stare at him and all his glory, wondering if he's always this big or if he's a grower and there's more to come.

"I'm sorry," I whisper. My cheeks burn red. I step inside, quickly closing the door, and cover my face with my hands.

Peter chuckles and the deep rumble of his voice makes me ache to be touched. I hate how much I still want him. All those anti-hero books I read have ruined me.

"Is Aria around?" I manage to ask. I force myself to find a mental picture of them together on the beach. If I focus on the jealousy I felt, I might be able to make it to my room without soaking my panties.

"Why would she be?"

"I don't know, I just assumed you and her..." I peek through my fingers hoping Peter's disappeared to put clothes on. He stands in front of me, inches away. I flinch involuntarily, and his *thing* touches my leg. The soft head brushes a thin layer of stickiness on my skin and I want to know if he's hard for me or someone else.

"Assuming things can get you in a lot of trouble." Peter grabs my wrists and tugs my arms down. He holds them at my sides. I step back, bumping into the door, but he's still barely a breath away.

"I... I should go to my room."

"Probably." He smirks and I get the feeling I'm in for a ride. "Answer me one question and you're free to go."

Would he keep me here if I don't? Better question: do I want him to? "What?"

Peter leans close, his breath tickling my ear, and whispers, "Is it my name on the tip of your tongue when Cass is inside you or just when you touch yourself?"

I swallow hard, not wanting to admit that his name *is* the one I want to cry out. I enjoy Cass. He makes me feel good, but he doesn't give me *this* feeling, the one where I'm standing on the edge of a cliff about to fall into something I know I'm not ready for.

Peter's hand closes around my throat, his touch gentle yet firm. "Truth or dare?"

I don't respond.

"I dare you to kiss me," he says with a quick lift of his lips.

I can't even blink before his mouth is on mine. I don't fight against his tongue sweeping past my lips because I want it. I fist his hair and pull him closer and our teeth clank. This isn't a sweet kiss full of hope and desires. It's pure lust. A primal need to be satisfied that we're only grazing. I drop my hand between us and wrap my fingers around this shaft. I stroke his thickness, moaning against his mouth because touching him turns me on.

Peter bites my lip and I gasp, the pain sharp but enjoyable. "Truth or dare," he asks again.

"Truth."

He takes a micro-step back and I let him go. "Did you enjoy that?"

"Did you?" Without breaking eye contact, I wipe the beads of pre-come that coat my palm against my shorts.

Peter glances down at the hard thickness poking against my thigh. There's a question hanging in the air I want him to ask. I wait longer than I should before saying, "I'm going to bed."

Peter steps to the side. I won't deny I'm disappointed. Peter is the kind of man mothers warn their daughters to stay away from. The kind that has to be experienced before they can be washed out of their system. I need to cleanse myself of this addiction, strange and unwanted as it may be, and the only way to do that is by giving into it first.

"Darling?" he purrs just before I reach my room.

I grip the doorframe. He once said he could read my expression. Well, I want to keep these feelings to myself. *If* we're going to fuck, it's going to be on my terms, not when he's dangling what I want most on a string, just out of reach.

"Do you believe in love?"

"Why?" I look over my shoulder, expecting a cocky grin, but he stares at me with interest, pure curiosity in his eyes and I can't resist asking, "Are you falling in love with me?"

"You'd be so lucky, darling. If I loved you, the stars would shine and the sun would rise." He doesn't laugh or give me that condescending, breathy chuckle I despise. "You didn't answer my question."

I watch him, waiting for the shoe to drop, but he simply waits. He doesn't move across the room or lift his lips in a smile. He doesn't shift to lean against the door or ruffle his hair. He just stands there. Waiting. "Yes, Peter, I believe in love."

He finally smiles, but the sight tugs at my heart. I've never seen anything so sad. "Good."

CHAPTER 26

Wednesday

Peter's words haunt me.

I don't know why. It was just a question, one that would be normal in any other setting, but it's kept me up all night, tossing and turning, thinking about what it would be like to fall in love again.

Would it make me ache to be touched? Or would that need be satisfied without asking? Would love cause me to be short-tempered and want to smack him whenever I'm around? Would our lips crash together in a heated kiss that makes me weak in the knees every time we feel like fighting?

I roll onto my side and find Shadow sitting on the silhouette of the chair, watching me. His presence is an odd comfort, but the fact that he can't soothe my skin makes me long for touch even more.

"Can he fall in love?" I ask, knowing the question will go unanswered.

"I owe you a truth." Peter's deep rumble carries from the hallway. I push onto my elbows to see him better. He stands, arms crossed in the doorway, his shoulder leaning against the frame. "Is that the question you want to ask?"

My chest rises and falls chaotically as he crosses into my room.

My heart picks up speed with every thump of the heel of his boot take against the wood floor. He grips the footboard of the bed, long, thick fingers curling over the wood.

"Going out?" I don't think I'll ever get used to the sight of Peter's naked body. Dark denim covers his legs and hugs his ass, but his chest is bare and the effect on me is the same.

"Ask me to stay and I won't," Peter's voice carries a hidden question and I have a feeling this moment will change everything between us. He leans closer, his body inching over mine, waiting for me to make the next move.

I swallow hard, unable to tear my gaze from his. I feel that nervous fire igniting inside me again, growing into an all-consuming blaze that demands to be touched.

"Stay," I whisper.

Peter pounces, moving like a predator in the night. He covers me, his body pressing against mine while his fingers thread through my hair and his mouth crashes against mine. His kiss is hungry, demanding, and yet gentle. There's a hesitation in his lips that makes me angry. I hook my legs around Peter's waist and his restraint snaps. Gentle fingers turn rough. He fists my hair and pulls my lips from his so he can sink his teeth into my shoulder. The pain is sharp but wonderful. I close my eyes and arch my back, relishing in how thin the line between pleasure and pain is.

Peter takes the neck of my nightshirt and tugs, ripping it down the center until my chest is exposed. "You're perfect."

He kisses the swell of my breast. Sucks my nipple into his mouth. I stare up at the ceiling, struggling to keep my breaths controlled. He slides his hand under my pajama shorts, finding that perfect, tender spot between my legs and I gasp, already on the brink of coming from his touch.

"Not yet, Darling," he whispers, then sucks the lobe of my ear into his mouth. "You're not allowed to come until I'm inside you. Understand?"

I chew on my bottom lip and nod, unsure of how I'm going to meet his demands. I'm already so close. Forcing myself to hold back is torture, but I try. He kisses the sensitive spot of my neck and presses a second finger inside. "Good girl."

I close my eyes and focus on my breathing, forcing myself to keep a slow, steady rhythm while Peter kisses down my chest, stopping to suck my nipple between his teeth, then continues to make his way south. He pulls his fingers from my folds and yanks my shorts off. I barely have time to take a breath before his mouth is between my legs. He sucks on my clit and I scream his name, unable to stop the sensation running through me. I grip his hair and pull his face closer, desperate to feel more.

"I need you inside me," I say through heavy breaths. "Please, Peter, I can't take much more."

He lifts his face, a wet sticky smile in place, and slides up my body. He fists my hair again and pulls my mouth to his, parting my lips with his tongue. "Do you like the way you taste, Darling?"

I hum against his lips.

"Words, sweetheart."

I barely get the *yes* out before Peter thrusts inside me. There's no slow, gentle teasing. No taking his time and letting me adjust. I cry out, the sound a heady mixture of pleasure and pain as he discovers every inch of me. Just as I'm getting used to him, he flips us. I'm straddling him, bouncing while his hands roam my back, side, and chest.

"Oh, god, Peter, I'm—"

"No," he demands.

Peter grips my hips and slides me off of him and onto the mattress. He flips me onto my stomach and lifts my ass until he's happy with the angle, then sinks into me again. The pleasure is instant. My walls tighten around his length, and I come first, harder than I ever have. Goosebumps pepper my arms as the high passes.

Peter fists my hair and pulls me upright, still keeping a steady pace. "You're so fucking wet," he says against my ear. He drops a hand between our bodies and rubs my clit, pushing my body toward another climax.

"Fuck," I breathe, heat growing inside me.

I'm going to come again. Pressure builds in my center, the need to release, to push greater than anything I've felt before. I give in to the sensation, euphoria claiming my body as my come gushes out of me, coating Peter's dick, balls, and my bed sheets.

"That's right, baby. Come for me." Peter digs his fingers into my hips and pulls me closer to him as he thrusts deeper and harder until his seed coats every inch of my insides.

Far too quickly, Peter pulls out and rolls beside me. He extends one arm and I lie beside him, my head on his chest. We stay there, catching our breaths.

"Do you regret it?" His tone is rough, but I hear the insecurity behind the bravado.

I press my palm to his cheek and turn his face to look at me. "It was perfect."

It was everything I thought fucking with Peter would be like and more. I close my eyes and let myself fall into a new feeling. Peacefulness. A strange calm that makes me feel like I've finally found the person I'm meant to be with.

As I doze off, I don't think about the events that brought us here or how I need to get home. I don't worry about the tomorrows, what this means for Peter and me, or what I will tell Cass... if anything.

I curl into Peter's side, his arm wrapping to hold me close, and fall into the deepest, most restful sleep I've had since coming to Neverland.

CHAPTER 27

Peter

I wake to a banging on the front door. *Thump. Thump. Thump.* I groan and wait, hoping whoever is out front will leave, but they're persistent. They keep pounding until I finally decide to get up.

I slide my arm from underneath Wednesday, careful not to wake her. For a second, I stand there and just look at how beautiful she is. The light rouge of her lips. Her butterfly lashes. The soft curves of her body.

She's perfection.

And she's mine.

The pounding outside continues. I grab a towel from the bathroom and wrap it around my waist. I unlatch the front door lock and yank it open. "What?"

"What the fuck did you do?" Cass asks, his tone laced with equal venom. His eyes narrow on me and the terry cloth at my waist.

"Nothing yet. I was going to take a shower, but you've fucked that up," I quip. I take a breath, not meaning to be short with Cass. It's not his fault I hate him. I pushed him into a relationship with Wednesday. I presented him with the forbidden fruit, hoping he'd take a bite, then hated when he fell under its spell. If

I'm honest, I don't hate Cass. I hate myself for letting Wednesday be with anyone besides me. But he's a better target to lash out at. "What do you mean, *what the fuck did I do?*"

Cass steps to the side and I don't know how I didn't notice the moment the door opened. Darkness fell over Neverland, blanketing our island in deep blue hues accentuated by the moon's glow. I step onto the porch and look up, eyes wide with wonder as I see the stars in the land I call home for the first time in centuries.

"We need to call a meeting," Cass insists. "The Lost are freaking out. They've never seen the island in anything but twilight."

He's right. But I'm not ready to move. I count the constellations and find True North, then spot the second star to the right and grin—Wendy's favorite star in the sky. I don't know if it has a name. I'm sure it does since humans claim everything they can, but Wendy used to call it the wishing star. She sent her deepest desires there and hoped they'd come true. I stare up at it and send a wish of my own. *Forgive me.*

"Peter," Cass huffs.

"Let me get dressed." I grab the edge of the door and meet Cass's gaze. He knows what I've done. I can see it in his eyes but I don't have the courage to voice my actions. Not yet. Soon, everyone will know, but for now, I want this moment between us to be mine. "I'll be out in a minute."

I shut the door, feeling Cass's frustration come through the wall. I cross into the kitchen, grab a frosted glass, and fill it with water. The cold chill does nothing to soothe the fire beneath my skin. It burns like a parasite stretching my soul to make room for his.

I freeze, realizing the sensation, and look behind me.

My shadow is attached, following my every movement. I lift my leg and wave my arm, and he does what I wish without protest. I lean against the counter and stare at it. My thoughts are empty, void of rude interruptions. I kind of miss the intrusions, as odd as it seems. My shadow and I may not have agreed on much, but he was my ally. The only being I could truly trust.

And now he's gone.

I run my hand over my face and take a deep breath. I'm not used to so many feelings kicking up at once. Longing. Sorrow. Worry. And most heavily, love.

I pad back into Wednesday's room. I wonder if she'll realize what's happened. Her precious mind runs a mile a minute, and I've left enough breadcrumbs.

I brush my fingers against her cheek, pushing her wild locks aside, then kiss her skin. She stirs with a half-conscious moan. "I have to step out for a bit."

"Where are you going?" She rolls onto her back, butterfly lashes fluttering, trying to stay open.

"Island bullshit. Go back to sleep. I'll see you when you wake."

"You sure?"

I kiss her lips. She smiles against my mouth and the lasso around my heart tightens. The longer Wednesday is here, the more dangerous it is for her. Now that the Island has shifted, our time together is even shorter than it should be. "Positive. Rest, Darling."

I stand, but she reaches for my hand. "Peter?"

"Yes, love?"

"Tell me the truth, there's something here, isn't there?" She hesitates, and her big brown eyes reach mine. "I'm not imagining it. Right?"

"What we have is more than *something*, Darling. So much more."

CHAPTER 28

Wednesday

I've woken in this bed every day for what feels like a lifetime, but I've never had a reason to smile like I do today. I roll on my side and hug the sheets. They still smell like him and any doubts that last night was a dream are erased.

I need to tell Cass, I think to myself, the quick upturn of my lips falling. He may be all right with sharing me, but I'm not that girl. I don't think Peter would be down for that, either.

I take a quick shower, then put on a fresh set of clothes. The treehouse seems darker, but the shadows don't faze me. Clouds crossing over the sky create a similar darkness. I don't think anything of it until I step outside. The moon, nearly full, smiles down on me and the stars twinkle around the almost round sphere. It's breathtaking. This must be what Peter meant when he said he had to deal with island problems.

I run down to the beach to find him. The glow of a fire greets me through the trees and the sound of eighties music bounces off the leaves. I'm surprised to see The Lost drinking and celebrating as I step out of the brush.

"Wednesday!" Scarlett says loud enough for me to hear her over the music. I'm shocked. This girl barely whispers, and now she's excitedly yelling my name. "You're here."

She hands Heidi her drink and runs over to me, pulling me into a hug. I'm so taken aback I don't know what to do. "Hey, Scar."

"Do you see the moon?" She drops her head back and looks up at the sky. "It's the most glorious thing. Don't you think so?"

"It's something." Probably bad based on what Cass told me about the island. "Have you seen Peter?"

"Don't you mean Cass?" she asks, a twinkle in her eye.

"I don't know if I'm ready—"

"Ready to what, beautiful?" Cass comes up behind me and snakes his arms around my waist.

"Oh, hey." I turn to look at him and he kisses me. My stomach drops. I feel guilty, like I'm doing something wrong even though Peter and I haven't had the conversation about what we are. And we *are* something. I can feel it like I feel the air in my lungs. The question is... what?

I break the kiss before Cass's tongue can try to part my lips and spin in his arms. "I was just saying I don't know if I'm ready for a drink yet. I haven't eaten anything since I got up."

I lick my lips and don't like the sour flavor his left behind.

"We can fix that." Cass takes my hand and guides me to the fire.

I feel eyes on me, but every time I look up, no one seems to be watching us. The Lost are happily dancing or talking with each other.

I take the plate of grilled corn and the roll that Cass hands me and force a smile. I'm being paranoid. No one knows Peter and I slept together, and if they figure it out, then so what? From what Xyris said, The Lost swap partners anyway. Why can't I?

A pit swells in my stomach and, suddenly, I'm not so hungry. Images of Peter fucking the other girls assault my mind. Him railing Aria from behind. Heidi riding his dick while he eats out Scarlett. I force myself to take a bite of bread and struggle to keep it down.

"Are you okay?" Cass takes the plate and touches my forehead with the back of his hand. "You don't look so good."

"I'm fine," I insist, though I'm not sure he believes me. A thin layer of sweat coats my skin. I can't make the pictures go away. Can't stop seeing Scarlett's *O* face in my mind. "A little thirsty."

"Hang tight." Cass steps to the picnic table and fills a cup with a deep red liquid. "Best Faery wine of the season."

I swallow most of the glass in one gulp, half listening to him ramble about cherries and pomegranates. The first wave of euphoria hits within minutes and it silences my thoughts. I finish the glass, finally able to breathe easy, and ask for another.

Cass laughs, his voice a deep, incomprehensible rumble and blurred music. He takes my hand and leads us both to a picnic table. He lifts me onto the table and fills my cup again.

I'm lost in the feeling of electricity buzzing beneath my skin and I feel the blood rushing in my veins. It tingles, like when my foot falls asleep and I wake it without warning, but instead of the sensation being painful, it carries heat to the best parts of my body and turns me on.

Cass says something about regret and I snap my gaze to his.

"Wednesday!" Xyris calls as he and Emmit cross the sand, their lips swollen, hair a tousled mess. "I've got to know something."

"What's that, handsome?" I surprise myself with the compliment but let it go because it is the truth. Xyrs is gorgeous. Everyone I've met on the island is.

"Are you named after the murderous little girl from the nineties?" he asks.

"No." I laugh. "That would have been cool. I was named after hump day because my mom knew I'd grow up to hump a bunch of things."

Emmit bursts out laughing, his head drops back as he howls.

"What's so funny?" Aria asks, walking up with the girls.

"Inside joke. Had to be there." Xyris shrugs in reply.

Heidi flips him the bird, though there's a large grin on her face. I don't think I've ever seen her smile. She's pretty when she's not being a bitch.

"Stars and scars, Cass." Aria giggles. "What did you give her?" She takes my cup and tosses the red stuff on the ground. "No more of that or you'll likely tell us all your dirty secrets."

My eyes go wide, realizing I said that out loud. I look at Heidi, an apology on my lips but she smirks against her glass and rolls her eyes. "No hard feelings, Darling."

"Here." Aria hands me a drink that looks like the stars, clear with glistening bits throughout. "This one is my favorite. It's made with dragonfruit."

"Easy now," Heidi warns. "That shit's like a pissed-off ex-girlfriend, sweet as can be until it's time for something new. Take it slow."

"Oh, look." Aria covers her heart with both hands. "She cares about you."

Heidi flips Aria the same vulgar gesture, but then grins and looks at me side-eyed. "What can I say? The little bitch has grown on me."

I've drank half my glass already. It went down smooth, which is probably why I'm smiling, enjoying the songs on the radio and not caring to explore or probe anyone for information.

"I've got to know," I finally ask. "Why are you using that dinosaur of a radio and not a Bluetooth speaker?"

"No wifi," Aria tips some of her wine into my almost empty cup. "The island is a dead zone. But we have an insane amount of cassette tapes and rechargeable batteries connected to a solar charger."

"The downside of island living," Heidi adds.

"It's not so bad. You get used to the slower way of life," Scarlett chimes in.

"I wish things could stay like this forever," Cass whispers into my ear, his voice full of longing and sadness.

I forgot he was beside me. The wine is good. Too good. My head feels heavy and it's hard to keep my eyes open. I don't know why. I was fine a moment ago, but something feels different. Wrong.

"Cass." I look for him, but he's no longer at my side. I don't know when he left. He was here a second ago. I think. My vision blurs and the world becomes a swirl of lights and colors.

Someone touches my cheek and I hear my name, but the voice sounds far away and worried. Strong hands grip my arms and shake me. I force my eyelids to lift, expecting to see Cass steadying me, but dark eyes meet mine. I shiver as Peter's gaze burns a hole in me. I remember why I like him so much. He's stunningly handsome, even more so than the others.

I reach up and touch his cheek but my hand hits his skin harder than I anticipate. It smacks against his jaw. I wonder if he likes it rough. If next time I should slap him and see if it makes him come harder.

"How much have you drank tonight?" I hear the worry in his voice, but I can't do anything but grin.

"Two small dragon fruits and a red wine that Cass gave her," Scarlet replies. There's a change in the air. A tension I can't place.

"We should go." Peter takes my hands in his. My legs give out as I slide off the table. He catches me before I fall and lifts me effortlessly.

"I don't understand," Aria mumbles. "I cut the wine to an eighth of its potency. It shouldn't have done this to her."

Peter grunts in response.

"I'm sorry," she pleads. He ignores her, carrying me past our friends. "Peter, I'm sorry!"

No one tries to stop him as he takes me into the darkness. I roll into his chest and reach up to touch his cheek. "Don't be mad at her, baby. I'm just a little drunk. I'm all right."

Peter ignores me, the crunch of his boots over fallen twigs the only sound between us.

"Baby?" I ask, a crushing sadness filling me.

"Shhh," he whispers. "You'll be okay. As soon as we get some water in you, you'll be all right." But there's something about the way he says it that makes me nervous.

Somehow, Peter climbs the ladder to his tree house while holding me. He walks us through the front door, up the stairs, back to my room, and lays me in bed. He disappears into the bathroom and returns with a damp rag and a cup of water. He then sets the rag on the back of my neck and insists I drink.

I sit upright and take the glass but as soon as I take the first sip my stomach doesn't feel right. Something inside me flips and the feel-good sensation turns into a world-spinning, thunder-roaring ache. I hold my belly, hoping that the turmoil inside settles. "Oh, god."

There's no time. Liquid pain climbs my throat, dragging a whirlwind of emotions and the wine I drank along for the ride. I race for the bathroom but my legs give out and I puke all over myself and the floor.

CHAPTER 29

Wednesday

"*You're too good to keep.*"

My head spins. Skin hurts. I open my eyes, and there's Peter again, sitting backward on the chair and watching me sleep just like the first night he brought me here. The room is dark, lit only by a lantern on the bedside table.

"Your such a fucking creeper." I groan as I try to sit up but my muscles are too weak. Too tired.

"Eat." He slides a plate of toast over.

I try to laugh but it comes out closer to a whimper.

"What happened? I feel like I walked off a cliff."

"If you do, make sure I'm there."

"Why? So you can catch me." I wink, but he doesn't take the bait. Peter stares at me, a deep-set frown on his lips. I push onto my elbows and touch his hands. "What's wrong?"

"What do you remember about the other night?"

"Not much. Why?"

"You've been out cold for two days. I was worried the wine got the best of you. I thought..." He shakes his head.

"Two days!" I sit up and immediately regret moving so fast. I lay back down and groan. "What the hell was in that...Oh, god." I cover my hand with my mouth and look for something, anything to throw up in.

Peter is ready and waiting with a bucket. I hate that I need him, but I'm grateful for his presence. He fists my hair and holds it out of the way while I hurl, but there's nothing left in my stomach. Yellow bile burns my throat and when it runs out I dry heave a few more times before my body gets the memo to quit. I fall back onto the pillow, more tired than when I woke up.

Peter sets a cold cloth on the back of my neck. He holds a cup with a straw in front of me. "Rinse your mouth out."

I swish the cold water around and spit into the bucket, then do it again before swallowing a small amount.

"You need to eat, Wednesday. You're too weak." Peter picks pieces of the toast apart and holds it in front of me. "Please."

I'm scared to put anything in my stomach, but I eat it anyway. "If you wanted to get me in bed again, all you had to do was ask," I tease, trying to lighten the mood.

Peter smiles and wipes my hair from my face. "Another time, Darling." He pinches off another bite and feeds it to me.

"Promise?" I groan, my stomach cramping again and I roll on my side to face him. I look at the darkness floating in the blue of his irises, then close my eyes.

"I'll fuck you until the bed breaks if that's what you want." He strokes my head, pushing my hair away from my face. I feel so drained. It's getting harder to stay awake. "But you've got to stay awake, Darling, don't give in."

"Do you believe in soulmates, Peter?" My eyes drift closed, the dark void of sleep calling to me. "Because I feel complete when I'm with you."

"Darling, don't do that." Peter taps my cheek. He sounds so far away, his touch so light I can barely feel it. "Wake up, Wednesday. Come on. Stay with me." His voice breaks and it's the last sound I hear before letting myself drift back into nothingness.

CHAPTER 30

Wednesday

Thunder cracks in the sky.

Flashes of yellow light flicker through the room, cutting through the darkness. I don't know how long I've been awake, lying here, waiting for my voice, my legs, any part of me to listen to my brain. It's a terrifying feeling, being trapped in your own body, your mind awake and full of life while the rest of you is listless.

Little by little, the spell on my limbs lifts. My toes wiggle. My fingers open and close. Rain cascades down the window and each rumble in the night brings life to my body again. I'm not sure how long it takes. Time seems to move on its own, crawling by, but eventually, I'm able to sit up. My arms feel like lead, heavy and awkward to move. My legs as impossible to wield as Thor's hammer.

Step by tremulous step, I cross the room. Fire burns in my lungs. Something so simple as walking twenty feet shouldn't be so exhausting, but I'm drained. I collapse against the doorframe, half ready to give up, and fall to the floor.

Peter's eyes lock on mine the moment I break through the shadows veiling my room, his face a mix of shock and terror. He shuts his book and jumps out of the chair to be at my side. "What... what are you doing?"

Peter ducks under my arm and holds me by my waist. His scent—the same rich mix of earth and sage—fills my veins. It takes me back to a day that feels like a lifetime ago when he filled me as thoroughly as his cologne does.

He practically carries me to a nearby chair, my legs barely working, and helps me find a comfortable position. He kneels in front of me and his deep blue eyes search my face. The longer he stares, the more I don't like what I see in return. His lips press together into a tight frown and his eyebrows pull together. "You shouldn't be walking around so soon. You'll drain yourself."

"I didn't want to lie there anymore." My voice cracks from lack of use. I sound like a woman who smokes a pack a day—raspy and nothing like myself.

"How long have you been awake?"

That's the question of the day. How long did I lay there motionless, unable to control my body or scream out for help? My room was dark when I finally found the strength to open my eyes, leaving one vast stretch of nothingness for another. I didn't dream while I rested, or if I did, I can't remember. "A while."

Peter's frown deepens. "I wanted to be there when you came around again. I'm sorry I wasn't."

"Was I asleep long?" I feel like I know the answer. I wouldn't be this sore if I had simply slept for an evening. Something happened and I need Peter to tell me what.

"You should eat something," he deflects. "Build your strength up again."

My stomach cramps at the mention of food. The pain spreads from below my belly button around to my back, violently alerting me that it's hungry.

I nod, tired again, and close my eyes as Peter walks to the kitchenette behind me. Cabinets open and close as he gathers his items. I focus on my breathing but my chest is heavy. I force my lungs to take in air and then let it out over and over again, each breath feeling like a papercut on my chest. Existing shouldn't be this painful.

Peter brushes his fingers down the side of my arm, his touch gentle, as if he were caressing the petals of a rose. I open my eyes and smile. Peter looks down at me with worried eyes but returns the gesture. He lowers to his knees, a small brown cup in his hands, and sits on his heels.

"Careful, the tea is hot." He hands me the cup and places his hands over mine to help me lift it to my lips, tilting it slowly. The liquid is pleasantly warm, sweetened with honey and of lavender. It soothes the cracks in my throat and makes swallowing an easy task instead of a chore.

"Thank you," I rasp, feeling a little more like myself after a few sips.

"Hang on." Peter brings both our hands to my lap and rests the cup on my legs. He gets up and practically runs to the kitchen to grab a small cardboard box. "Cass brought these by this morning."

Peter reveals two blueberry muffins and sets them on a wooden plate. He finds his place in front of me again, takes my cup, and sets the muffins in their place on my lap.

"He'll probably be back once the rain stops to check on you again." Peter's lips lift into a sad smile. "I...uh... didn't feel right telling him about us while you were out. He still thinks he has a future with you." Peter hesitates and I can see the worry in his eyes again. "Does he, Darling?"

"I don't feel right," I confess. I'm not trying to avoid the question, but something inside me isn't as it was before. It's hard to pinpoint what is different. My arms and legs aren't as heavy, but it's not a physical change that's weighing on me. It's something else. A heaviness on my heart, a pinpoint hole in my soul.

"You gave Death a run for his money. I'd be surprised if he let you get away unscathed." Peter doesn't look at me as he tears the muffin into pieces and feeds it to me. I think he's trying to be playful and show me the side of him I glimpsed so long ago, but there's a dark cloud hovering over us. His glee feels forced.

"You scared me, Wednesday." Peter swallows hard and bloodshot eyes meet mine. They're glossy, filled with tears he refuses to release. He closes his eyes again and lets out a shaky breath. "You were in and out of consciousness for a week. I thought I was going to lose you."

"I don't understand." I press the palm of my hand to my forehead. A dull ache pools behind my eyes. How could a week have passed? It doesn't seem possible. "The last thing I remember is sitting by the bonfire."

I cup Peter's cheeks and lift his face until he has to look at me. The man who's only ever shown me confidence is lost. He's a shell of the person I've grown to hate. A broken boy on his knees. "I'm okay," I whisper.

He shakes his head. "I don't know that you are, Wednesday."

Hearing my name on his lips is jarring. Peter has only ever called me Darling, but it's his words that make me shiver. I can say the words all day long, but he's right. Something is missing. I can't explain what or how I know, but there's a void where that piece once was.

I lean down and kiss Peter's lips. He doesn't let me linger. His arms wrap around my waist and he holds me the way I'd expect him to if this were goodbye. Tears pool in my eyes and slowly run down my cheeks as I realize he thought we wouldn't see each other again. The severity of how close I was to dying again shakes me to the core.

This whole time, I wanted nothing more than to leave Neverland, but now, I can't imagine saying goodbye.

CHAPTER 31

Wednesday

Days pass, the sun rising and falling more times than I care to count, but with each change of the sky I grow stronger. Able to walk further and stay awake longer. Dying twice–or coming close to it–took more out of me than I thought possible, but I'm still here.

Neverland will have to try harder if it wants me as one of The Lost.

I haven't seen Cass yet. I've been awake for days, yet he and the others keep missing me, or so Peter says. He claims they've stopped by while I've been sleeping, but I don't buy it. I've been awake for what I think is a week and haven't napped once. I think they're hiding something.

Especially Cass.

I doubt Peter would tell him we slept together while I've been recovering. His default mode may be dick-head, but he's not heartless. Cass is his friend. Besides, he would have told me if that conversation happened. Something else is going on and I want to know what.

I sit beside the window, one of Peter's books in my hand, waiting for him to return. His library is more versed than I initially thought. While it's mostly classics, there are a few shelves that make me grin, specifically the cheesy romance novels with Fabio-like men on the covers.

I'm on my second novel and the stories themselves haven't been bad so far. If I ever make it home, I'm going to raid my mother's books. She's been dying for me to read some author with the last name Ward, but I couldn't get past the covers. I smirk and turn the page of my book. I bet she's a smut reader from way back.

My ears recognize the creak of the hinges on the front door. I dog-ear my page and close the book. Looking at the shadows outside, if I were to guess, I'd say it's almost noon. It's still weird to see the sun rise and fall in Neverland. We haven't talked about what caused the change. Thinking about it now, Peter's danced around a lot of my questions the past few days.

"Hello, Darling." He heads straight to the kitchen and begins to make us lunch. He unpacks a loaf of bread, tomatoes, cucumbers, as well as a handful of other things grown in the garden.

I walk to the kitchen and lean my arms on the counter. I like watching Peter work, watching the way his muscles flex. Even the simplest movements, like making an avocado sandwich, are beautiful because of him. "What have you been up to today?"

"The girls found another creature today. A duck-like bird with feathers of orange and purple coloring mixed within the usual brown and white. It's extraordinary." He slides the plate between us and takes one-half of the sandwich. "I haven't seen one since I first came to the island."

"When was that, Peter?" I pry, trying to learn something about him. I've been an open book, answering every stupid thing he's asked while I've been stonewalled. "You don't talk about the past."

"Because it's better left there."

"Right." I drop my half-eaten sandwich on the plate and leave him in the kitchen. I've had enough. We haven't talked about what *this* is, but fuck buddies don't play house. If that's all we were, he would be eating my ass right now, not my sandwich. I walk to my room and slip on my shoes.

"Where are you going?" he asks when I open the door.

"Anywhere but here." I hesitate when I reach the wooden bridge. I haven't crossed one of these on my own in days. My legs shake, but I need to make it to one of the other treehouses, or any other treehouse on this stupid web, to reach a ladder. I don't know where I'm going from there. I don't care either. I just need to get away from Peter.

Step by terrifying step, I cross the first bridge. Peter follows, staying annoyingly close, barely a step behind, spotting my every move. I glance behind me. His hands are out, ready to catch me if I fall. I want to be mad. I'm trying to get away from him, but I'm glad he's there.

"Look at you." Peter beams when we're on the ground. "Conquering your fears."

My heart is racing, but I feel good. Do I want to do that again? No, but at least I know I can make it on my own. "I didn't need your help back there."

"I know, but as long as your heart is beating, I will be there whether you need me or not."

"And what if it doesn't? What happens then, Peter? Will I become one of The Lost, forever stuck on this island?"

I don't want the answer. I've come too close to dying too many times. It occurs to me that in both instances, he was there. It pisses me off as I realize he could have been finishing what he started the other day. All of this was always his fault; everything I've been through, both good and bad, has been because he dragged me here.

"What will you do when you finally kill me? That's why you brought me to Neverland, isn't it? To finish what you started."

"Wednesday." Peter's eyes widen in shock. His head shakes back and forth, but I'm not sure I believe it's anything more than a show. "I may have pushed you off that boat in Florida, but you were never in danger of dying." He reaches for me, but I pull away. I can't stand the thought of him touching me right now.

"You're lying."

Peter's brows draw together. He's quiet, likely trying to come up with another lie, but I'm not falling for his tricks anymore. I was stupid to trust him so blindly.

Maybe Peter didn't want me dead this time, but he certainly wanted me away from Cass. *Damn that jealous prick. His plan worked.*

I glance around, looking for somewhere to stomp off to. I don't care if I'm being childish. But he'll follow me everywhere I go. *Almost everywhere.*

"I can prove it," Peter says, his voice jumping with emotion. "I can prove I never wanted to hurt you."

"How?"

"I need you to trust me. One more time." He drops to his knees and hugs my legs. "Please," he begs. "If you truly believe I want you dead after this, I promise I'll take you home."

"Today." It's not a question. I refuse to stay a minute longer than I have to. If Peter won't honor his word, there's a pirate in the cove waiting for me. Fucking him is no different than when I slept with Cass. I'll spread my legs one more time if it means getting home and away from this beautiful psychopath.

He nods. "Today."

"Fine. What do you need me to do?"

CHAPTER 32

Wednesday

"How much further?" I pant as we climb over a set of boulders somewhere in the heart of the island.

"Almost there, Darling." He's told me the same un-reassuring sentence four times in the last... I don't know how many minutes. It lost its conviction a while ago.

My muscles protest every movement, strained from being contorted into positions they've never seen before. My hands are sweaty, fingers swollen and tingly. My chest burns and lactic acid seeping into each breath.

I hear the sound of rushing water before I see it. Panic slices through me. He doesn't honestly think I'm going to swim with him again. Does he?

Peter ducks under a thick branch and continues up the terrain. I follow, two feet behind in case I need a running start. Eventually, the thicket thins into a clearing that opens up to the sky. He strides to the edge of the cliff and stares down at the water cascading along the side of the mountain as it falls in beautiful shades of white and blue.

I follow him but keep a safe distance. The view is glorious, unlike anything I've ever seen, but I don't know what it has to do with Peter's truths.

Peter climbs the boulders to our left and sits on the highest one's edge. He lets his legs hang over, then says, "Tell me about Neverland."

"What do you mean?" I inch closer. The spray of the waterfall blowing upward in the breeze is refreshing. I sit beside him, my stupid heart silencing the cynic in me that warns me that I'm in danger...again.

"I'm not an idiot, Darling. I know you found the book." He stares off at the horizon. From here, we can see the forest cascading down the mountain to the beach and the endless ocean around us. "Tell me what you think you know about me and my island."

"Neverland is a place where you don't grow up," I tell him the story I learned as a child, about pirates who waged a war with him for no reason, and the children he stole in the middle of the night. I talk about Tinkerbell and how her pixie dust mixed with happy thoughts makes everyone fly. My smile grows with each word. I love the tale, probably more than Tyle claims to. For her, it was something else to take, but for me, it is a story of infinite possibilities.

Peter is quiet as I finish my tale and he's got that far-away look again. The one that makes me wonder which memory he's lost in. "I fell in love with Wendy the moment I met her. She was beautiful, and kind, and... just..." He shakes his head. "More."

His lips lift into a sad smile. "But she was betrothed to my brother, James, so I had to let her go."

I touch his arm, knowing how much it hurts to lose someone you love to a sibling. I wonder if James was like Tyle and stole Wendy maliciously, or if it was beyond his control. "I'm sorry."

"My father knew I loved Wendy and he still gave her to him. Wendy was a good wife. She was faithful even when I wished I could convince her otherwise." He lays back on the grass and tucks an arm behind his head. "She used to tell their boys, Michael and John, stories of an island filled with magic and adventure. She was a wonderful storyteller."

"You named the island Neverland because of her. Didn't you?"

He nods. "James thought it would be fun to charter a ship and search for her mysterious island. He planned to take the boys to any ol' piece of land and give them an adventure, but a storm came out of nowhere and our ship fell into a whirlpool. I don't know what happened after that. All I know is we woke up on the shore: James, Wendy, some of the crew, and I. Everyone else was lost at sea."

"Oh, Peter." I can't imagine the pain he must have felt losing his nephews. I lost a cat once, Blue, and it destroyed me. He was my person, the other half of me for seven years of my life. My family didn't understand the pain it caused, but I felt like I had lost a piece of myself. I can't imagine what losing a child you love feels like.

"The shit thing is, this island was everything Wendy described. The boys would have loved it. Especially the Faeries."

"Tinkerbell."

"Bell was one of the three on the island and the most underestimated. She was beautiful and free-spirited, but evil and she was infatuated with James from the moment she saw him." Peter turns his head to look at me. He reaches out and touches one of my curls. "The Fae aren't capable of love. They are obsessive and compulsive and will do anything to get what they want. Which is how we got ourselves into the mess we're in."

"Tink tried to kill Wendy. Didn't she?"

He twists my locks between one finger and the next. "I made a deal with the Fae to save her life. My soul for hers, under the premise that I thought we would be together, but they took her away."

"Back to the land of the living."

"I always knew you were smart." Peter stands. He walks to the edge of the rock and tucks his hands in his pockets. "I didn't realize what I'd done when I made that deal. It's my fault The

Lost are trapped in Neverland. I didn't know the Fae would take every soul they touched. I thought they just wanted mine."

"It doesn't make sense." I touch his elbow. He looks down at my hand, then up at me. "How is their eternal damnation your fault? You didn't bring Wendy and the boys here." Unlike me.

"It doesn't matter." He threads his fingers through my hair and touches his forehead to mine. "All that matters is that you're here. You *are* Wendy. Her soul brought back to life, reunited with mine. That's why this bond between us is so strong. You were only ever meant to be with me, Wednesday. You're my soulmate in every sense of the word."

I arch my back to put space between us. "Peter, that's crazy. You can't honestly think I'm your dead sister-in-law."

"Oh, Darling, but you are. It's why I'd never risk your life. It's too valuable. Your return to Neverland means the curse is breaking. The souls can go home and we can be together again."

"I don't believe you. Take me home, Peter. You promised you would." I look up into his eyes and emotion clogs my throat. "Please."

"My Darling." Peter wraps his fingers around my neck and pulls my mouth to his. He kisses me, and even though I want to fight it, my body melts into his. It falls under his spell and my lips part right as he shoves me off the ledge.

CHAPTER 33

Wednesday

I *'m going to kill him!*

I don't bother screaming. I'm too mad. I should have known he would do something twisted. After all, he is Peter Pan, the conniving trickster the stories are based on, if I believe him.

I do believe him.

I believe everything he said, down to the notion that he never meant to put my life in danger. Just like I know he wasn't the one to poison me on the beach. The revelation is almost as startling as realizing I'm no longer being assaulted by wind. Strong arms hold me tight against a warm body. I close my eyes and let his scent fill my lungs. I'm still pissed, but as we float to the ground with the elegance of a feather, I'm no longer afraid.

Peter sets me on my feet and steps back, apologetically lifting his lips. He tucks his hands in his pockets and shrugs. "I'm sorry."

"You idiot!" I smack him. He takes my hit, his eyes steadily on me, filled with regret. There's a red mark on his cheek, but it's not enough. I'm still pissed, filled with adrenaline from falling, so I shove his chest. "You could have killed me. Again."

"But I didn't."

"Is that supposed to make everything better?" Livid, I draw

back to hit him again. He raises his arms defensively and his hands close around my wrists, restraining but not hurting me. "Take me home, Peter. You promised you would."

His face blanches as the fear that his trick might not have worked sinks in. I wish it hadn't.

"No," he says, his voice steady with authority.

"Fuck you, Peter." I yank my arms and he lets me go freely. I walk away from him with no clear direction as to where I am or where I'm going.

A thread in my chest tightens. Peter may be my soulmate, and I may have loved him in another life, but he doesn't deserve my love now. I hope this wasn't how he treated Wendy, because if so, I'm ashamed of my past self.

"Wednesday," he pleads, running after me. "I love you. I fell in love with you the moment I laid eyes on you, both in this lifetime and the last. Please...just..."

"No!" I spin on my heels to face him. Peter stops where he is, giving me some semblance of space but it's not enough. "You cut me."

I watch his gaze roam over my body, looking for a wound he can't see. My pain is every bit as physical as it is emotional, but the source runs deep.

I place my hand over my heart, anger burning into tears I don't want to shed. "In here. I trusted you time and time again, and all you do is break that trust. I believe you when you say we're soulmates, and I believe that you don't want me dead, but you have a lot to learn about what it means to love someone. This..." I gesture to the island and everything that's conspired between us. "This isn't love. It's an obsession."

My words hit their target.

Peter lets me go without trying to stop or follow me.

I walk to the side of Neverpeek and follow the mountain's jagged terrain. I need space to sort through my emotions.

I feel too much.

Falling in love with Peter took a lifetime I don't remember

living and yet the ache to be with him is as strong as if the experiences were my own. I need time to decide what I want to do with these feelings somewhere I won't be badgered by The Lost, stalked by Peter, or guilted by Cass.

I find a familiar rock formation and feel relief. I know one place Peter or his Shadow won't go. Someplace that'll buy me time with someone I should probably see.

Wednesday

"Another round," I tell the man behind the bar.

He narrows his eyes on me but refills my cup for the third time. I don't have money to pay, and I think he suspects, but this is the same bar I stumbled into last week. James found me then and swore all I had to do was step back into Harper's Edge and he'd find me again.

I'm counting on him to keep his word.

And to pay my tab.

The brown liquid I ordered burns as it goes down my throat. It's not as potent as the stuff James bought me last time or as fast-acting as the Faery wine, but it's good. With each cup it stings less and I'm able to push aside my conversation with Peter that much more.

I take a swallow, then hold the mug in both hands, my thoughts torn. My goal this whole time has been to go home and Peter has kept that from happening.

Although if I'm being honest, my original plan didn't work out like I'd hoped. I won't deny that I enjoyed sleeping with Cass and didn't give finding a way home my all, but Peter is one hundred percent to blame for my current stalemate.

My thoughts teeter again, and I'm back to the same internal

debate. Every time I decide to leave, there's a tug on the string that wraps around my heart. As crazy as it sounds, a small part of me doesn't want to say goodbye.

People spend their whole lives searching for the person they're meant to be with, and I can't deny that I've found mine. I can't help but wonder if I'll regret walking away without giving us a fair chance. By Peter's wonky time logic, I've been missing for months. What harm could come from staying a few more days?

There's also the nagging thought of *would he even let me go?* I'd almost bet that he would track me down again. The thought, or perhaps the alcohol, lifts my lips. I would love to see him court me in my world.

I sit on my stool before the bar and think about what dating Peter would be like. We could share so many firsts. I could take him to my favorite restaurant and show him what a movie theater is. We could stroll through the parks and he could call to the birds. I bet they'd swoop down to hear his song because he *is* Peter Pan.

I take another sip of my drink, half wondering how it's nearly empty but not caring enough to dwell on it.

"You're a sight for sore eyes." Cass slides onto the stool next to me and taps the bar top. A cup, twin to mine, is set before him, the same frothy brown drink inside.

"Eyes work two ways, mister." I point my fingers at my eyes and then his. I hold my serious face as long as possible, but a hiccup ruins it.

Cass grins and I remember that was the first thing I noticed about him, gorgeous body aside. He was always so happy, truly, deeply, happy. I draw my brows together at his smile because it doesn't seem genuine today.

"I tried to see you. We all did." He turns to face me and crosses his ankle over his knee. "Peter wouldn't let anyone in."

"Oh." That sounds like my Peter. So controlling. "And here I thought you didn't like me anymore."

I reach over and squeeze Cass's arm. He covers my hand with his, his touch colder than I remember. "I told you, beautiful, you shine too bright for this world. I could never gaze upon you with anything but wonder."

"Awwe. There's my riddler again." I suck in a breath. My bladder screams at me that it has to pee. It does that when I drink. Gives me no notice before sending those annoying warning tingles to my belly. "I've got to find a bathroom."

He points to the corner of the bar. "I'll be here when you get back."

I tap his shoulder as I pass and run across the room. I make it to the toilet with just enough time to pull down my shorts. Peeing feels like heaven, the second-best feeling to an orgasm. I stare at myself in the mirror as I wash my hands. I have to tell Cass about me and Peter. If I were to leave Neverland tomorrow, my secret would haunt me, and I don't like living with ghosts.

"I'm back," I say as I slide onto my stool again.

Cass is on his second cup and mine, though it was barely empty, has been refilled. I thank him and cheer our glasses together. I don't think I've ever seen Cass have more than one drink in the time we've been together. I nurse my glass as he finishes his and asks for a third.

"Are you okay?"

"Oh, beautiful, I'm far from it." He frowns and stares at the cream-colored froth. "Can I ask you a question?"

"Sure. What do you want to know?"

"Why him?"

I don't feel so good anymore. The alcohol I've drank turns to lead in my stomach. "I wanted to tell you."

Cass's lips quirk into a heartbroken smile. He nods and I think the question is based on suspicion more than knowledge. "I had a plan, you know. One I worked on for the equivalent of centuries if I were to live in your world."

"To do what?"

"To take my home back." He drops his head. There's so much disappointment and longing in his tone.

I feel every word because I know what that pain is like. I want to go home so bad it hurts. I reach out and touch his arm.

A sharp pain pushes behind my eye, like a migraine hitting. I blink it back and try to comfort my friend. I'd like to think that, despite the way we ended, we are friends. "I'm sorry, Cass. Is there anything I can do?"

"Oh, beautiful. You've already done enough." His face lifts into a smirk that makes my skin crawl. "More than you realize, actually. I never stood a chance against Pan until you came."

"You," I whisper, my eyes widening in disbelief as what he said sinks in. I let my guard down and gave myself to Cass on so many levels, to the point that I would have trusted him with my life. It's a slap in the face. "It was you."

I pull my hand back and the movement sends the room spinning. I haven't drank enough to be feeling this disoriented. Something is wrong with me, again, and I already know he's the reason.

"I don't know how you survived the hemlock I laced your drink with, but I'm glad you did."

I press my palm to my head and try to keep the throb pulsating behind my eyes under control. It's horrible, making me light and sound sensitive.

"Turns out, Pan's magic is weaker when you're alive." Cass brushes his fingers across my cheek. I flinch, or try to, but my reaction is delayed and not as impactful as I'd hoped. "The funny thing about magic is it's tied to your life. The more you use, the quicker it depletes you. Unless, of course, you're Peter. His powers were always a mystery to me. His shadow could do whatever it wanted and it never affected him. Until you. You tied Peter's magic to him and all I need to do was wear him down. Neverland was supposed to be mine. Now it will be."

"Get away from me, Cass."

"You'll be singing a different tune when the nightshade kicks in. In large doses, it's fatal, but the amount I gave you should only knock you out." He leans close and I can smell the magic on him.

I never knew what the scent was before, but I understand now: another truth that I didn't realize I needed.

"Do you think Peter will cross the galaxies to find you?" He pauses, letting me process that I'm going to be taken somewhere against my will. Again. "I hope he does."

I stand and try to run away, but my legs are shaky. Cass doesn't bother to follow as I try to flee. He watches, knowing my time is running out.

Unable to fully control myself, I bump into a table and spill someone's drink. "Sorry."

Their face has a halo of light around it. Everything is blurry and getting harder to see. My body harder to control.

Firm hands grab my shoulders. I look up, unable to recognize the face, their features blobs of black and tan and red, but I recognize his scent—a familiar hint of earth, sage, and bad decisions. As much as I hate that I'm forced to trust him, I'm glad he's here.

"What happened?" Peter 's voice drips with concern. His hands shake and I wonder if it's his body twitching or mine. I hope it's mine because I feel the air around us trembling.

"Help me."

SECOND
STAR
TO THE
RIGHT

SECOND
STAR
TO THE
RIGHT

CHAPTER 1

Peter

Wednesday's body hangs lifeless in my trembling arms, her head lax, falling backward, her limbs limp. The last words she whispered before passing out were, *"Help me,"* and it takes every ounce of willpower I have not to let my shadow take over.

I feel him under my skin, slithering like a snake, begging to be set free. My body physically cages him in and he riots against the binding, his magic pushing against my bones.

If I knew how, I would release him into the world again. Sharing our body is dreadfully unpleasant. In the realm of the living, we don't have a choice. My soul is forced to return to his former self.

A simple shadow.

A mirrored version of myself with no ability to move on his own and no voice to be heard.

I'm not a fan of silence. I like hearing my other half, especially when his thoughts are baleful.

"Let me hurt them," he shouts and I'm surprised to hear him again. *"I'll kill everyone that touched our Darling."* Shadow's rage tangling with my own creates a dangerous cocktail.

I want to rip the throat out of the person who hurt our

Wednesday Darling. I want them to suffer. I want their heart to beg for release. I want to feel each beat until it finally stops, and then I want Shadow's magic to bring them back to life just so I can do it all again.

I want to avenge our Darling, but killing everyone on this side of the Island to find the sorry bastard isn't in the cards.

Not yet.

Shadow's impatience sends a burst of energy from my chest. The shockwave ripples through the air with enough force to blow napkins off the table and rock a wind chime.

I search the room, my eyes taking in every detail with a speed and clarity I don't usually possess.

Shadow's power rolls beneath my skin like a wave in the ocean. I can touch it and manipulate it, but he wields its true potential. He's connected to the Island in ways I can only dream of. It bends to his will and feeds off of his emotions. Even now, the clouds outside of the bar darken in the sky. Thunder rolls above us and I can feel the shift in the room's air, just like I would if I were to stand outside.

Lighting cracks somewhere overhead. A flash of yellow flickers in the gradually darkening bar. The room is empty, except for the drunk passed out in the corner and the shaky barmaid. At first glance, nothing looks amiss, but it doesn't take me long to notice four glasses on the countertop.

Two filled nearly to the top.

Two empty.

Sitting side by side in pairs.

Shadow's voice screams in my ears to burn down the bar and torture the maid until she squeals like a pig. I'm inclined to listen, but the featherlight woman in my arms keeps me somewhat grounded.

Still... someone did this to my Darling, again, and when we find out who it is, they will pay.

"I see you've met my date," my brother's voice croons from the doorway.

My shadow lurches at James with the intent to smother his lungs with darknes. Dark mist drifts toward my brother like a cloud of fog in the night, but it only stretches an arm's length away.

Shadow is tethered to me and his anger is a seething heat that overpowers my senses. I feel his desire to tear James to shreds and, while I am not my brother's biggest fan, he is still my brother.

My flesh and blood.

More than the bonds that tie me to the Lost.

The only living family I have left.

James's boots carry a heavy thud as he crosses the room. Our bartender visibly relaxes in his presence and I try not to laugh. Now that Shadow and I are bonded, I think I could strike James down with a bolt of lightning, should I choose.

And that's where the problem lies.

Most days, I don't want him to suffer.

My brother may have chosen to side with the Fae, but he doesn't hold their powers. He's still human, with an unbeating heart and a soul that can be saved. The day he sacrifices that, it's game over. I will have lost him.

"Your date?" I echo.

Shadow thrashes like a ship trapped in a glass bottle during a hurricane. Gusts of wind rattle the windows. Wooden shutters slam against the siding, and innocent people holler at each other outside on the street to find safety.

Shadow doesn't like the thought of Wednesday being in the same room as James, let alone his date. I don't either.

James's brows pull together and he frowns. He drinks in my Darling with his eyes, thirstily lapping every inch of her lifeless body. "What did you do to her?"

Wednesday shudders and gasps for air. Her lungs wheeze, struggling against whatever coils around her bones like a snake. I shift her in my arms and steady her head against my shoulder. I hear her heart rhythmically beating in her chest, but with each second that passes it weakens. Her life force disappears, like the sands in an hourglass, reminding me that time is precious and being wasted.

Still, I hold my composure. Appearances are everything. If James knows what the Darling means to me, to all of us, he'll tell his Fae bride. Wednesday will never have a chance at life if Belle knows she exists.

"I was about to ask you the same question."

"Don't be coy with me, brother," he snaps. "I just got here."

"Right, and I'm supposed to believe that's not your drink over there."

"It's not," James growls, his tone final. So much like our father.

A violent shudder rips through Wednesday. I hold her tighter, unable to breathe as I wait for the convulsions to pass. Seconds turn into a painful minute, and her seizure shows no signs of stopping.

Shadow grows weary. His nervousness turns my stomach. Another minute passes. Shadow's dark presence stops reaching for James and wraps around Wednesday like a blanket. He steadies her heart and slows her breathing. After what feels like a lifetime, her body calms, but she still doesn't wake.

"You're wasting time, Peter. Time she doesn't have!" Shadow yells at me.

He's right, but the adrenaline I felt when I walked into the bar is wearing off. I *need* Wednesday to be okay. Not because she's the key to breaking the curse or because she's Wendy's reincarnation. I need her to survive whatever this is because if she dies it will be my fault.

If I hadn't listened to Shadow, if I hadd just left her alone, she wouldn't be dying.

James grabs my elbow and tries to shift Wednesday out of my arms and into his. "I'll be taking it from here."

"Over my dead body." I jerk free of his grasp. Anger pours out of me in waves again; this time, it's just as much mine as it is the dark beast's. Shadow's darkness shoves James back a few steps, then wraps around Wednesday again. My brother's balance falters, but that small win does nothing to ease my fury.

"That can be arranged." James grins and the wickedness in his expression chills my bones.

I shoulder past and ignore his last comment. I don't want to fight my brother tonight. I can't guarantee Shadow will let him live this time, not when our Darling's life is on the line. But that doesn't mean I wouldn't put a dagger through his heart if it means Wednesday will live.

James follows me through the saloon's swinging doors and yells, "Peter!"

"*Ignore him,*" Shadow urges, but I can't.

My brother sounds worried, an emotion I can say he never showed when Wendy's life hung in the balance. I turn to face him, unsure if the delay is a trap, but he genuinely looks concerned.

"Is she okay?" he asks.

I let out a heavy breath, two things coming to light at once. One, James knows Wednesday. The how is irrelevant; our Island is small, and I know she sometimes wandered. I let her because Shadow was always close enough to keep our Darling out of danger.

What concerns me, though, is how well they might know each other. How deep do my brother's feelings run for the other half of my soul? I close my eyes and swallow the sting of the past as it creeps up my throat.

The second thing I know at this moment is that James would hesitate if he had to kill her. What I don't know is for how long. How far will his defiance be tolerated before Belle forces his hand?

"I don't know," I admit. "But she will be."

I push off the ground, not wasting another minute, and shoot into the sky. I don't think about how James has never seen me fly or what the pirates will assume. My thoughts are on Wednesday.

Only Wednesday.

The sun begins its descent into slumber, twilight rising to prepare us for night. I know the direction I'm headed, like I know my shadow. To the second star, soaring until the magic of night ripples through the air and the sun crosses into the other realm. By sea or by sky, that's when the veil between our world and hers is thin enough to pass through.

It kills me that I have to do it this way, but I'm keeping my promise.

It's time to take my Darling home.

CHAPTER 2

Wednesday

I never considered how a single moment could change my life.

One decision, so seemingly insignificant at the time, has the power to affect everything.

As I lay here, unable to move, trapped in never-ending darkness, I try to pinpoint the moment my life veered off course. Most might say it was when I took a drink from a handsome stranger at a bar—who I think might have stalked me before that day—and then tried to kill me. But I could argue that my downward spiral began on January eighteenth.

That's the day I skipped my afternoon workout and came home early to find my twin sister and my then-boyfriend fucking on my brand-new couch. Who knows, maybe if I hadn't caught them, it would have been a one-time hookup and I would be blissfully unaware, cooking him a vegan dinner while he played video games on the leather sectional that I later dragged down to the alley from our third-floor apartment and set fire to.

Believe me when I say it was more therapeutic than the rebound dick I chased in the following weeks.

Or maybe I need to look further, all the way back to high school, to the first day of Biology when Kenny Dean Admire sat down next to me. There were still half a dozen open seats in the room, including one next to my sister, Tyle, but Kenny chose to sit with me. It was the first time I was put before my sister, and I was ecstatic.

Thinking back to that day, I can still feel those nervous butterflies springing to life. The excitement every time we locked eyes. The lust from something as simple as our fingers brushing against each other. It was magical.

If only I had the foresight to lie and say that I had a lab partner or maybe even agree to work together so long as we kept all of our interactions flirt-free, I wouldn't be in the situation I'm in.

Oddly enough, though, if I ignore the fact that I don't know where in Neverland I am, and that the two gorgeous men I trusted and gave myself to tried to kill me in their own wicked way, and that I've possibly been kidnapped twice in the last three weeks, I don't hate Neverland like I did when I first got here.

If given the choice, I'd do everything exactly the same because it brought me to Peter.

He's my fairytale come true.

The other half of my heart I never wanted until I knew what missing him would feel like.

He's a dick who has done everything wrong, but he's my dick, and as much as I want to fight the pull I feel to be with him, I can't. Wendy Darling, my past self, loved Peter. She was his soulmate, which makes him mine, too.

How?

I don't know. Logic rarely plays a part when the heart is involved and for me, that rings true. I can hate Peter. I can be so angry with him that I want to wring his neck, but when it comes down to the bare bones of how I feel there's no denying that a big part of me loves him, even though I wish I wouldn't.

A faint beeping carries into my thoughts. At first, I didn't notice it, but the sound continues until it becomes something I can't ignore. It echoes melodically in the dark, then beeps again. Louder this time. Again and again. And then there's a whoosh.

Beep. Beep. Whoosh.

Beep. Beep. Whoosh.

There's a tingle somewhere in the darkness, and I vaguely remember that I have arms. It seems silly, but I've been floating for what feels like forever with nothing but my thoughts to anchor me in the sea of night. My body is abstract, disconnected from my mind. Or maybe it's the other way around. I'm not sure. Just like I'm unsure if this is what unconsciousness feels like in the land of the living.

Dying and bright white lights seem to be synonymous with where I come from, but no one asks about the unconscious or the people in comas.

I wonder if this is what it's like for them? A never-ending night that stretches on like the sea, surrounded by nothing but memories and thoughts of what could have been until the world comes back into focus? If so, why does no one talk about it? Why don't we acknowledge the place between life and death? I have no doubt that's where I am.

In between.

The sensation in my arms grows stronger. It's pinprick-like but not uncomfortable, and then, without warning, I feel heavy. My whole body tingles and it aches from immobility. I try to move some part of me, any part, but nothing happens. I'm conscious enough to know I can move but not enough to make it happen.

If I could sigh, I would, but even my lungs don't follow orders yet. I remember this from the last time I was drugged. Waiting for my body and my mind to connect is torture, but at least this go around I know what to expect as I wake.

Except for that sound.

Beep. Beep. Whoosh.

I don't know what that is.

A cold breath of air pushes through my nose. It doesn't fill my lungs, but I'm not struggling to breathe, either. It's an odd feeling. One that makes me want to take in more air, and so I try, but my next breath is a mix of natural warmth and damp coolness.

It reminds me of the forever frost that coats the inside surfaces of all the cups in the Treehouse web. The thin layer of ice defies all logic, but I've seen it with my own eyes, and I've touched it with my two hands, so I know it exists. Just like I know without a shadow of a doubt that Neverland is real, Fairies—or Fae as they like to be called—can't be trusted, and magic is all around us.

Another cold breath pushes into my lungs and strangely enough, it makes me think of Cass. I was with him when I first felt the touch of Neverland's magic and it is because of him that I'm stuck in the between.

A twisted thought chills my bones. One I never considered before, but when you're trapped in your mind there's nothing to do but think, and this one thought has me on edge the longer it sits.

The air in Neverland was only ever comfortable near the treehouses. There the cups were coated with forever frost, making our drinks cool and refreshing. When I drank with James, everything was at room temperature. Not uncomfortably warm, but not cold either.

Except for the drink I shared with Cass.

I only took a few sips, but now as I think back to it, my glass was chilled.

What if Cass is behind the frost? I know nothing about him, not really. Not the things that count.

Ugh, I have so many unanswered questions!

If Peter Pan is real and his shadow is a living entity separate from his body, why couldn't Jack Frost or some version of him be real, too?

Another question to add to my ever-growing list. I worry I'll be stuck like this and never get to ask Peter, but then that tingling sensation spreads to my toes and I remind myself I just have to wait.

CHAPTER 3

Peter

Days have passed.

Days of arguing with incompetent doctors.

Days of sitting in a painfully uncomfortable chair, watching machines breathe life into the other half of me.

The doctors don't do much. Shadow and I see them twice a day. Once in the morning. Once after the sun has set. They look at the numbers on the machines that beep and whoosh and tell us it'll be soon, but they never say when soon is.

I don't think they know.

The nurses are more helpful. They check on our Darling every few hours, making sure she's as comfortable as possible. Sometimes they turn her body to prevent something called bedsores. It's painful to watch as her limbs fall lifelessly in the direction gravity pulls. If not for the ability to hear her heart and the annoying beeps from machines that never cease, it would be easy to confuse her as one of the dead.

"*This is taking too long,*" my shadow urges. He's restless. His magic hums under my skin like the tingle of a foot unexpectedly waking from sleep. I hadn't noticed the discomfort in Neverland, but here the pain worsens each day we wait for our Darling to wake.

"And what would you have me do?" I think to my shadow. He hears me as clearly as if I were to have spoken the words out loud. Just as I hear his grunt of frustration. He wants to use magic on her, but I'm worried about the effects it'll have in this world. Not just to our Darling, but to us too.

This realm is angry with our presence. She tolerated us when our visits were short, but as one day drags into the next, she takes from me. I'm tired. A kind of tiredness that rivals the pull of darkness and I'm afraid to close my eyes. I'm not certain this realm will let me open them again if I do.

"Find our Darling in the darkness. She's lost between the worlds and the longer she's there the harder it is to come back!"

I feel his fear. Neverland is a broken bridge between death and the afterlife. Most souls make it to their destination, but some—those with unusual trauma—get stuck all on their own. Others are stolen on their way to the afterlife. A problem my shadow has been battling for more lifetimes than we should be allowed to live.

But Wednesday is somewhere else.

A dark maze between the realm of the living and the dead. I only know it exists because it's where Shadow was created. I don't remember it, and I don't know how to navigate within its confines, which is why I'm hesitant to enter its clutches.

"We're wasting time!" he growls.

I don't disagree. Time may move faster in the realm of the living than it does in Neverland, but it feels slower. Back home, before the magic shifted, a day was measured by the clouds. Orange and pink hues meant our day had begun. When they shifted to bright blues and deep purples, we had passed into the evening. We had no hours to count. No minutes that crawled away. No second hand that ticked and ticked. The days came and went, but here—in this room that smells of chemicals and death —time is torturous.

"It's too dangerous," I caution. We would have to put my body to sleep somewhere and hope that I could find that realm. Hope I can locate her. Then pray that I can bring us both back.

The plan relies too heavily on magic. Shadow may be willing to risk what little we have left on the endeavor, but I'd rather reserve our magic for a surefire save.

Shadow riots inside me. He pushes and fights to break free, but in this world, he's lucky to be more than a dark mirror forever stuck at my side.

He kicks and my leg jerks in response. *"You're scared because you're weak."*

I am.

Shadow's ability to control me, even for the slightest of moments, is proof. At this point, I don't know how to remedy my weakness. I feed my body the food this world provides and nourish it with the water they steal from the land, but it's never enough. No matter what I do, the pull to close my eyes and fall into the dark abyss is too strong. "Your point is moot."

"Let me heal you, Peter. Once you're strong, you can save her."

"At what cost?" Magic comes with a price and the cost of using it in this realm is steep. The day we brought Wednesday to Neverland a plane crashed. Most would find that tragedy purely coincidental, but the ten souls who lost their lives washed up in Neverland. They became prisoners of the Island and I think it is because of what Shadow and I did. "Whose life will be lost to extend ours?"

"I won't take to the point of death. You're not that weak yet, but you will be if we don't do something now!"

I pick at a straw wrapper and tear it into tiny pieces. "Save your magic for our Darling. She may need it more than me."

"I can't heal her if you're dead, Peter! I can't exist in this world without you. If you die, I die."

"I'm not dying," I whisper the words out loud but I don't believe them. One look in the mirror and I can see the toll this realm is taking on my body. It won't be long before I deteriorate into the dust I'm meant to be.

"Yet."

The machine that beeps in rhythm with our Darling's heart

makes a new noise. A faster beep and then two slow ones. Then another faster one.

I don't get my hopes up. Twice now she's stirred and not woken, but Shadow is anxious. He fights my resolve to stay in the chair. I forfeit the battle, not willing to waste my energy on him, and stand by Wednesday's side. She groans and turns her head from one side of the pillow to the other.

Hope moves me to sit on the edge of her bed and grab her hand. It's a painful emotion. My stomach thrashes like a ship in the sea, and my heart races at the speed of a hummingbird's wings. I hate the sensation but cling to it all the same. "Darling? Can you hear me?"

Wednesday's eyes flutter open, but they're hollow. She stares up at the ceiling, her body awake, but her essence far, far away. She's soulless. A living beast touched by death. That hope I felt falls into a puddle on the floor. People aren't meant to return from Neverland. When they do, they come back broken.

"*Darling*?" Shadow says, his voice carrying out of my mouth. He refuses to accept that we gave Wednesday the same fate as Wendy. He takes her hand and sends a surge of magic from me to her.

My head spins the moment his magic leaves my body, but I feel it tug at something in the ether. It fights with forces I can't see, pulling at the woven fibers in my body. Whatever Shadow's magic wants feels like acid in my veins. I take a shallow breath, unable to close my eyes because Shadow is still watching Wednesday for signs of life. Still holding onto her with doleful desperation.

Wednesday sucks in a sharp breath. Her body shudders as it comes back to consciousness. She looks around and, this time, there's a warmth to her brown eyes. Her head tilts to the side and she finally sees me. The color drains from her already pale face, but then her lips lift into the most beautiful smile I've ever seen. "You're here."

I'm so relieved I almost laugh at the ridiculous thought that I would be anywhere beyond her bedside. I hated the minutes we were apart and made them as few as possible because I refuse to let Wednesday wake up alone this time, questioning her sanity and wondering where I am. No, I will stay here until she wakes or this realm claims me.

"Did you think I wouldn't be?"

CHAPTER 4

Wednesday

Bright white lights push their way through my eyelids. It's uncomfortable and yet I can't shy away from it, even as brown and yellow spots cloud my vision. With every beep and whoosh that permeates the darkness, the blotches over my eyes clear away. I recognize the sound somewhere deep in my mind, but the memory is blurry.

Beep. Beep. Whoosh.

My throat is dry to the point it burns when I try to swallow. I blink some more and white ceiling tiles take form. They're large, twelve-by-twelve squares, with specks of gray sprinkled throughout like stars in a hazy sky. The thought of being outside on an overcast day is comforting, but I'm nowhere near the outdoors. I'm in a small room that smells like bleach and latex, with too bright of lights and that incessant sound.

Beep. Beep. Whoosh.

Out of the corner of my eye, I see an IV stand. A clear bag hangs from it, tubes draped loosely, finding a home in the beeping monitor and then connecting to a venous catheter in my hand. It hits me that I'm in a hospital, and for a split second, I can't remember why that realization feels odd.

"Darling."

I turn my head to the sound of his voice, desperately hoping I didn't imagine it. Peter sits on the edge of my bed, cloaked in shadow. His hand holds mine and while I should be concerned that I can't feel his touch, I stare at him, shocked by what I see.

Peter looks nothing like the man I last saw in Neverland. Dark circles hang under bloodshot eyes. His cheeks are hollow, the skin clinging onto them in a way that reminds me of the dead. His dark hair is unkempt, oily, and possibly thinner. He's aged ten years in the time I've been here, and even though he looks days away from meeting the Grim Reaper himself, my heart races at the sight of him.

"You're here," I say, unsure of if the man I'm looking at is *my* Peter or something else.

He squeezes my hand and a faint tingle radiates from his touch. "Did you think I wouldn't be?"

Tears I can't control swell in my eyes. They fall down my cheeks in slow, steady streams. I can't explain the feelings I'm hit with. There are too many layers on top of each other, but crying feels good.

"Oh, Darling." Peter pulls me into his chest and holds me.

Weeks of frustration, grief, and fear pour out of me. My tears are silent but powerful, touching parts of my soul that needed a release from the weight it had been carrying in Neverland.

"I'm sorry," I whisper as I wipe my eyes. "I don't know where that came from."

"Never apologize for the feelings your beating heart carries." Peter touches my cheek. His hand is cold and calloused, more so than I remember. "Only the living can feel so fully. I'm jealous."

The blues of his eyes darken and black wisps of magic pouring into them. I know now what that darkness is. I remember everything from Neverland and even things from beyond, Wendy's memories. Gifts from when he pushed me off the Neverpeek mountain.

"Hello, Shadow," I whisper, cupping Peter's cheek. His lips twitch upwards and then pull down into a frown. The darkness I glimpsed fades away and I'm met with the same worrisome blues I've grown so fond of. "Are you okay?"

Peter takes my wrist and pulls my hand from his face. He looks at me with an intensity that makes me think he's searching my soul for lingering damage. "The question is, are you? I didn't think it was possible to fear for you more than I did in Neverland, but you've proven me wrong." He laughs, but the sound is forced.

I find the remote to my hospital bed and press the button to sit upright. The muscles of my back ache in protest. They've been still too long, angry from the time in this bed and likely the journey from Neverland home.

A shuddering thought crosses my mind. Peter killed me to bring me to his home. I don't want to know what he did to bring me back to mine.

"Tell me what's going on. Where are we?" I start with those questions because the one I'm dying to ask scares me. In nearly every story I've read the use of magic has consequences. I imagine Peter's magic does too, which could be why he looks like shit. I need to know if I've taken something from him or someone else in Neverland, but I don't think I can handle the answer if it is yes.

"We're at a hospital in Fort Lauderdale."

"Why here?"

"Because I was..." Peter's eye twitches. He grunts then corrects himself to say, "We were worried you wouldn't make it any further. Someone did a number on you again, Darling. Any chance you know who it was this time?"

"How is it possible both of you are in there?" I whisper, meaning to keep the question to myself but, like usual, I have a problem keeping my thoughts secret when Peter is involved. He draws my truths out of me without trying, and I unwillingly give them to him.

"It's not easy," Peter says, his voice huskier than usual. For a fraction of a second, the darkness clouds his irises again, but then that deep blue pushes through and Peter is solely himself again.

I watch him, waiting for a deeper explanation or answers to

the questions he knows I'm thinking. *When did Shadow re-attach himself? How does his magic work in this world? What is it like to feel Shadow under his skin?*

Peter responds to my silent questions with a distant stare. He's here physically, but his mind is elsewhere.

I shift under the blanket and feel the stubble on my legs catch on the fibers. I pull them closer and run my hand across my shin. I fight a frown at the sensation. My legs aren't just stubbly, they've turned into a forest. I hate to think about what the rest of my body is like. I press my arms to my sides so that Peter can't see the hair that's probably in my pits and let my gaze sweep across the room.

My room is private, which is nice, not shared with a thin curtain to separate me and a stranger. The bed takes up most of the space, but I seem to be in a corner. My window is roughly five feet from me, in a narrowing passage, with a chair seated awkwardly between us. I have a bathroom to my right, presumably with a shower, and the door to my room is straight ahead. I can see the corner of the nurse's station and the rolling computers they take from room to room, but not the nurses themselves. All things considered, I'd say it's pretty private. A blessing since talk of Neverland would probably land me in the psych ward.

"Do you know where my clothes are?" I ask since that's one of the things I don't see. My shoes are nowhere in sight either. I'm hoping there's a closet in the bathroom that my stuff is stored in.

"Why?"

His question irritates me, but I try to keep my frustrations to myself. There's a lot Peter doesn't understand about this world, like money. As shitty as it is to say, he can stiff a bartender a few dollars on a drink. They'll be pissed, but no one will ruin his credit over it. Hospitals require names, birthdays, and Social Security numbers. Everything we can't honestly provide because red flags might go off about me. For all I know, my name is tagged as a missing person. As soon as someone realizes I'm awake, the cops could be called, and I don't know how to answer the questions of where I've been, who took me, or whatever else they might ask. "Because we need to get out of here."

"We're not going anywhere until the doctors are certain you're okay." Peter shifts in his seat. His leg spasms, kicking outward and striking the edge of my bed. Something is going on with him. The longer we're here, the more likely it is someone will notice, and that could be just as problematic.

"I'm fine. Honest." I wrap the blanket around my waist and scoot to the edge of the bed. Peter's at my side the instant my feet hit the linoleum tiles. My legs wobble beneath me, but I stay upright. There's a tugging sensation between my legs and I see a piss bag hanging off the side of the bed, connected to me by a catheter tube. I groan, embarrassed, and grab that along with my IV stand and head toward the bathroom. "But we need to get out of here. I doubt I have insurance anymore and I can't afford the bill attached to my stay."

"Everything is paid for," Peter insists. He wraps one arm around my waist and tries to usher me back into bed. "Sit down and stop worrying."

I don't sit. Instead, I poke my head through the bathroom door of my room. I was right about the shower being in there, but not about the closet. My clothes and shoes aren't anywhere to be seen.

My heart races with anxiety and the *beep beep beep* of the machines race with it. I need a shower and to put something on that doesn't expose my ass to the world, and right now neither is an option.

"How, Peter? Every day we're here costs tens of thousands of dollars. Do you have that kind of money?"

"Yes," he says flatly.

Peter curls his fingers over mine, and this time, I let him lead me back to the bed. He stands before me, and seeing how loose his clothes are on his body tugs at my heartstrings. He's wasting away and I don't know why. I wish he'd tell me what's going on, but like all the other questions I've ever asked my inquiry is ignored.

"I have an account overseas set up that anyone can access so long as they know the PIN."

"Sounds like a good way to get robbed," I mumble.

"Maybe, but I change the number every time I call for access. It's never the same number twice. If someone is smart enough to hack it, they deserve the spoils, but I promise there's more than enough in there for the both of us." He unhooks my piss bag from the IV stand and attaches it to the side of my bed. "Money isn't an object. Whatever you need, Darling, it's covered."

I need a lot of things, mostly in the form of answers, but I get the feeling that Peter isn't going to give those to me. He never does. He's skilled in the art of avoidance and redirection. In another life, he would have made a good lawyer. Or maybe a car salesman. "Can I ask you for a favor?"

"You could ask for my life and I'd give it to you, Darling."

There's a heaviness to his words that makes me think he's telling the truth. He looks so thin, so frail, I can't help but worry that's exactly what he's done.

"Can you run to the store and get me some clothes, and maybe a razor and some shampoo and soap? I want to leave this place as soon as possible, but I can't do that if I look and smell like an ape."

"I can if you promise to let the doctors look you over while I'm gone."

I'm positive the hospital staff has seen every inch of me more than once. I doubt another exam will make a difference, but if that's what it takes to get out of here, so be it. I call that an easy compromise.

"Okay, Peter. It's a deal."

CHAPTER 5

Wednesday

Ayoung brunette pokes her head into the room within minutes of Peter stepping out of the room. Her big brown eyes widen when they settle on me. I give a small wave because what the hell else am I supposed to do?

"Oh!" the woman says quietly. She stares at me for less than a half-second, but it's enough to tell me that she didn't expect to meet my gaze. She doesn't wave back. Instead, she yells, "Doctor!"

The nurse hurries to my bedside and pushes buttons on the monitors that are tethered to me by stickers, a finger clamp, and a cuff. Squiggly lines appear on a small screen, then shift into new frozen lines. She pushes another button that brings the machine to life again and then it makes more beeping noises.

A few moments later, a man in a long white coat enters the room. His dark hair is slicked back, and his face is clean-shaven, but it's worn with little wrinkles. The tells of long nights with too little sleep and too much coffee. He sits beside my legs, on the bed, with a kind smile on his face that says *I'm your friend, Wednesday. Trust me.*

I'm not sure I can trust anyone in this world, let alone this hospital, but I smile back and hope it tells a convincing tale. *I am nobody worth worrying over. I am fine. Let me go on with my boring, completely normal life, and you'll never see me or my deteriorating friend again.*

I don't think the doctor believes my face. He picks up the chart hanging on the edge of my footboard and then flips through the pages. I doubt he's reading the words. My chart is an inch thick and he's done with it in less than a minute.

"Hello, dear. My name is Dr. Hall," he says, handing my file to the nurse. They exchange a silent conversation, using only a few glances, before he turns to me again. "Can you tell me your name?"

"Wednesday." My voice cracks and there couldn't have been a worse time for it to happen. My doctor lifts an eyebrow, losing faith in my *I'm fine* act.

The nurse hands me a small cup of water. I smile appreciatively and take a sip. The cold liquid is a shock at first. Ice clanks in the cup and I have to remind myself that the cups here aren't lined with forever frost.

I'm hit with an unexpected sadness that I'm no longer in Neverland. That place never felt like home, but now that I've left it, there's an ache in my chest to return. It takes a few seconds for me to get my bearings, but when I do, I try to convince Dr. Hall that I'm okay again.

"Roberts. My name is Wednesday Roberts."

He nods to the nurse and she scribbles something in my manila chart. I've always hated that about doctors. They write or type things about you, and you never see what is written. For all I know, the woman is playing a game of hangman and Dr. Hall's just signaled her a letter using their secret code. I could be billed for a fucking game of hangman and I would be none the wiser.

The nurse's badge holder twists on the lanyard around her neck. I can see her identification card and her name. Carmen Right. A pretty, used-to-be brunette who has on more makeup than Target carries. She's a walking TikTok filter. She is beautiful, but I have a hard time trusting a woman who feels she needs to hide herself behind a pound of makeup. Does that make me a judgmental bitch? Probably, but if I'm going to risk spilling any of my secrets, I need to know who it is that I'm talking to. I've seen some crazy videos where people look one way when they wake up and transform into a totally different person after an hour in the bathroom.

"Can you tell me what day it is?" Dr. Hall asks, and I'm embarrassed when I can't. I shake my head, so he prompts," What about the month?" When I don't answer, he tries, "Year?"

I let out a shaky breath. Tears of frustration prick my eyes because I don't know.

I don't know how long I was in Neverland or how long I've been lying in this bed. I don't know if my sister went through with the wedding or if our parents were so torn up about my disappearance that it was postponed. I don't know if my goldfish, Rocko, is still swimming happily or if he died from a dirty tank and neglect.

I.

Don't.

Know.

Anything.

I almost wish my lack of knowledge is from memory loss because that would be expected, but it's not. It's because my favorite fairytale came to life.

Unlike Wendy, who willingly flew into the night sky, I was forcefully taken. In a span of weeks, Neverland sucked my life away like it was a black hole. It made me forget things that were a part of everyday existence. At one point, I even forgot I wanted to leave because that's what Neverland does.

It makes you forget.

But I remember everything that happened there and I can't talk about any of it.

"Short-term memory issues are normal, Mrs. Roberts," Dr. Hall assures me. He pats my leg, like I'm a little kid and the sensation is anything but reassuring. I feel patronized and a little uncomfortable.

"You have what's called anticholinergic toxic syndrome. Confusion is an expected side effect. A few more CCs of saline and you'll start to feel like yourself again." He squeezes my knee and my hackles stand on edge. I don't like him touching me, but I'm sure the act is meant to be comforting, so I let it go. He stands, nonchalantly adding, "You were lucky. The poison used to drug you isn't something we've seen at this hospital. We almost couldn't figure out what it was."

"What was it?"

Dr. Hall writes something in my chart, then nods to Nurse Carmen. She steps up on instinct, as if responding to a conversation I wasn't privy to.

"I'm just gonna check your blood pressure, sweetie." She takes my left arm and slides it into a blood pressure cuff. It hugs my skin, creating enough pressure to make me wince, then releases with a beep. I understand the cuff's purpose, but I've always hated them. They remind me of being bound, unable to move. Something I've never personally experienced, but I've read enough books for my thoughts to stray to the dark corners of my mind. I don't think it's something I'd like.

My numbers appear on the small screen and Dr. Hall smirks approvingly. He scribbles what is probably unreadable nonsense on the papers in my file, then hands the nurse my chart again.

"We're gonna keep you another night or two for observation," he says as if I didn't ask him a question a few minutes ago. He clicks his pen and then tucks it into his jacket pocket. "I'm sure everything will be fine, but I want to be safe."

"If it's all the same, I'd like to be discharged," I tell him, irritated at having been ignored, but I'm picking my battles. Another day here is another handful of hundred dollar bills in his pocket. Dr. Hall is probably looking at me and seeing neon green dollar signs.

Too bad for him, I'm broke.

Dr. Hall and Nurse Carmen exchange glances. I don't like the look on their faces. I have the nagging feeling that his wanting me to stay might go beyond earning a paycheck. They're hiding something, which is bullshit because whatever it is, it's about me. I have a right to know.

I stare at them, waiting patiently for that look to turn into words, but no one speaks up. It's a reminder of the harshness of this world I'd forgotten about.

The only person who will look out for me is me. As soon as they leave, I'm going to read through my chart and find out what they're hiding because I get the feeling they won't tell me.

After a brief moment, Dr. Hall flashes a toothy grin and says, "How about we run some labs? As soon as those numbers come back, I'll sign the release."

"I don't want—" I don't bother finishing.

Dr. Hall leaves the room before I can ask him anything else, and I'm drawn back to a moment when I was a kid. Even for routine appointments, the doctors came and went in less than five minutes. It didn't matter that I had to sit in the waiting room for what felt like ages. I felt like they believed their time was more important than mine, and that same feeling rings true now.

Nurses, on the other hand, are never rushed. They take their time. They are the soldiers in the medical war, making sure each casualty is taken care of with utmost care. They are unappreciated heroes.

"He means well," Nurse Carmen says with an apologetic grin. She adjusts the tubes in my IV machine and fluffs my pillows. "He's just a little brash sometimes."

"Why are we running another round of labs if everything is fine?" I ask her, hoping she will give me a straight answer and not some medical jargon I'll have to decode once I have a phone again —another item to add to the ever-growing list of things I need.

"Your husband said you were at a nightclub when you started acting funny. He thought someone had spiked your drink."

My husband?

Did I miss something major while I was out cold?

I glance down at my left hand and a certain finger is bare. The relief I feel is instant. I used to dream about the day I got married, and an unspoken goal of that day was to remember it. If I'm going to financially and emotionally tie myself to someone, I'd like to think that person and I would have lots of good memories together, that day being the best of them all.

I can't say Tyle feels the same. She's made it known her only plans on her wedding day was to look pretty and get shitfaced. You'd think she'd want to cherish the moment. After all, she must have been desperately in love with Kenny to steal him away. But no.

The bite of jealousy still stings, not because I want Kenny back. I'd rather let Cass kill me a thousand times over, in new brutally painful ways, than get back with that man. What hurts is that Peter's unconventional family—minus one...there's always one—is more loyal to him than my own sister is to me.

My twin sister.

And that hurts worse than any death I might face.

My relief of not having a wedding that I've forgotten twists into something darker, dancing on the brink of disappointment. I don't know if my feelings are turning or if these are latent emotions tied to Wendy's memories.

Apparently, I'm her soul reincarnated. I thought Peter was crazy, but when he pushed me off of Neverpeek Mountain its magic opened my eyes to more truths than I was ready to accept.

That being one of them.

Ready or not, I know it's true. When I look at Peter, I feel her longing. It's cold and full of sorrow, but then my own desire to feel his touch ignites a fire in my veins that only grows when it finds Wendy's gasoline. It's confusing as hell, especially when she loved him so deeply and I teeter on the line between lust and hate.

A flash of a memory I know isn't mine sparks in my mind. Peter stands on the sidewalk beside a brick building and an iron gate. He smiles at me—Wendy—and my heart soars. He tucks unmarked hands into the pockets of tweed pants and stares at me. I walk closer, taking in the subtle muscles outlined beneath cream-colored sleeves. His shirt is buttoned nearly to the neck, but it's open enough to reveal skin as pristine as a new canvas. He leans closer to say something, but I can't hear his voice. Whatever it is, my cheeks flush with delight.

I blink and the memory disappears. I'm back in the too-bright room that smells like bleach, lying on an uncomfortable bed in nothing but a paper-thin gown, staring at a woman I'm not sure I can trust.

"He doesn't wear a ring," Nurse Carmen adds as she tops my water cup with ice. "But he's shot down every girl who's hit on him with a cheesy line about you meaning more to him than life itself." She looks at me with adoration, then sighs. "He must really love you."

Peter's definition of love is borderline obsession. He shows kindness in his own ways and knows how to satisfy me physically, but he has no boundaries.

Obviously.

Most relationships don't start with potential stalking and kidnapping. Despite it all, Nurse Carmen is right. Peter does love me in the only twisted way he knows how.

"You didn't answer my question." I change the topic. Love isn't something I'm ready to commit myself to. Peter and I have a lot to learn about each other first and I'm going to need a ton of groveling after everything he's put me through before I even begin to consider opening myself up to those feelings.

Nurse Carmen glances at the open door to my room. She can feel Peter's presence even though she doesn't realize what the feeling means. He emits a dark tingle that creeps up your spine, exciting fear and lust all at once. It's because of the magic flowing through Peter's veins that we can feel him as he draws nearer.

Nurse Carmen visibly tenses. I'm sure she's worried about answering my question and assumes this sensation is fear of getting in trouble, but I feel it, too.

I reach out and touch her hand. She's so much warmer than The Lost. Their skin has a chill I'd grown so used to, I've forgotten it isn't normal.

Nurse Carmen sits on the edge of my bed and looks at me with worried eyes. "The doctors don't want to say anything because it's too soon to tell, but there may be side effects from the poison. Your labs are reading fine and the last two ultra—"

"Leave," Peter orders. The chill from his presence settles into my skin, his deep growl raising the tiny hairs on my arms. The way he stares at Nurse Carmen makes me shiver, and I'm not even the recipient of his fury.

She opens her mouth to argue until Peter's darkness cloaks the room. The veil is thin, unnoticeable to anyone who doesn't know what they're looking for, but there's a new heaviness in the air that squeezes my chest. I struggle to breathe even with machines pumping air through my nose. I can't imagine what it must feel like for my nurse.

She looks at me briefly, an unspoken apology in her eyes. Her fingers hastily wrap around the metal clip that attaches my chart to my bed. She takes the papers that detail what the doctors put me through, hugs them to her chest, and then leaves.

As soon as she's gone, Shadow's magic recedes. The weight in the room lifts, and I can take an easy breath again.

I push myself out of bed, not caring that my ass is exposed or that I look like I've been through three rounds with a broken hair-brush and lost.

I'm pissed.

That nurse was about to tell me what Dr. Hall wouldn't and Peter and Shadow's high and mighty attitude ruined everything. Now I've got to find a way to steal my chart or convince someone else to let me in the loop because I doubt that woman will come back in here ever again.

Peter tosses three plastic bags on the bed, hopefully with some clothes and toiletries.

I set my hands on my hips, ready to light into him, but once he turns his gaze to me I lose the ability to think. Dark matter fills his irises, only leaving the thinnest ring of deep sea blue at the edges. It lingers, devouring more and more of the royal blue in his eyes until there isn't any left.

"Shadow?"

CHAPTER 6

Wednesday

The Shadow I met in Neverland was of the playful kind, with an air of mystery to him. His magic seemed to have an extra layer of depth that sometimes made me shiver, but I was never afraid of its abysm.

He'd walk through the woods, sometimes as if he were a part of it, and the Island's shadows would reach out to touch his darkness. The animals came to him as if he was their friend while the Lost disregarded him as nothing more than Peter's silent other half.

To me, Shadow was someone I could talk to no matter the subject. He knew the secrets I refused to tell Peter, listened to my questions and answered as many as a silent man could. My body may have belonged to the King of Neverland, but my mind and heart were Shadow's.

I can easily say he was my best friend in Neverland, but there's something different about him here. A primal instinct deep in my mind urges me to run far away even though my body won't listen. My heart races in my chest, wildly throwing my senses out of whack. I could cry and puke all at once from nervousness if only my body would give in to its urges.

"I prefer Pan," he drawls. Unlike Peter, who sounds American with a slight hint of something else, Shadow has strong under-tones of the same mysterious *ish* James's voice carries. An alluring accent as sweet as the Devil's candy. Addicting and potentially lethal. "But I do like the way Shadow sounds rolling off those pretty lips."

Fear wraps itself around me like a noose. I can't control the tears that pool in my eyes or the way my body trembles. I can't make my voice steady or my heart stop racing. I can barely keep myself from cowering, but I manage to stand upright and pretend to be brave when I ask, "What happened to Peter?"

Pan—the only reason I'm not calling him Shadow is because this version of my friend makes the name feel dirty—ambles around the room, looking at everything as if it's the first time. Perhaps it is. He doesn't try to hide his disgust at what he sees. It's written on his face in the way his lips turn down and his brows bunch together.

"Peter and I don't belong in this world, Darling. The longer we're here, the more your realm will try to reclaim us." He drops into the oversized chair in the corner of the room, sitting sideways so that his legs hang over one armrest and his back reclines against the other. He threads his fingers together behind his head, acting as if my world trying to kill him is table talk at tea time. "Your precious Peter would have let us turn to dust in this death castle if it meant staying by your side until you woke."

"Doesn't sound like you feel the same." My legs threaten not to support me any longer. I lean against the plastic footboard of my bed, shielding my exposed backside from him and the nurses in the hallway. I don't know what Pan means by *turn to dust*, but the way Peter's body was withering away I'm thinking sarcasm and metaphors for something less cryptic might be out the door.

"I reap death, Darling, not succumb to it."

A new wave of goosebumps roll over my skin. I believe, without a shadow of a doubt, that Pan has killed things in Never-land. Possibly people, too. If he has—and I'd be willing to bet the answer is yes—there's a good chance he might have been the cata-lyst that brought The Lost to Neverland.

Hell, he could have been the reason I was taken there, too.

The thought is dizzying. I grip the edge of the footboard and try to act like the nagging thought that Pan might have targeted me doesn't bring me to my knees.

If there was a prize for the unluckiest woman, I'm pretty sure I'd be the winner. My ex-boyfriend is a cheater. My rebound a kidnapper. My fuck buddy a murderous backstabber. And now this...

My best friend is a manipulator with stalker tendencies.

Watching Pan control Peter like a puppeteer pulling strings on his marionette, existing as one person and not two bound together, sparks the idea that everything that has happened to me could be Pan's fault doesn't seem as far-fetched as it should.

My chest aches and the *beep beep beeping* of my heart monitor lets everyone within earshot know that I'm freaking out. I hope I'm wrong.

"Death castle?" I ask, my mind reeling.

A new thought, that Shadow could have used Peter's body to kill me, crosses my mind. That would make him my kidnapper, not Peter. Heat climbs my neck to my ears. I clench my teeth and try not to lose my shit. Shadow made me feel like I could trust him. He tricked me!

"Seems fitting," he says casually. "Castles employ people to do their bidding. Cooking. Cleaning. Execution." He flicks his wrist, gesturing to the hospital and the walls that confine us. "This facility has multiple people to aid in the deaths of those it ensnares. It's genius for its generation. No one suspects what's going on."

"The doctors don't kill people here!" I snap. The venom in my tone has nothing to do with defending the staff. My shock turns into anger, and I'm so mad at Pan that I could cry. "They save them."

"Are you sure about that, Darling? I could feast on the souls on this floor alone and the people you call doctors would bring me more without even blinking." Pan stares at me, those dark irises daring me to ask the next question.

I'm not sure of anything, Pan. Thanks for asking. "I'm gonna take a shower."

Pan's jaw tics. I think he's mad I didn't lead us down the rabbit hole of questions like he wanted, and that has me biting back a grin. I hope the feeling festers under his skin and brings Peter back to the forefront. I can't stand to look into Pan's dark eyes and question every interaction we've had over the past few weeks.

"Make it quick. We need to leave within the hour."

I laugh, baffled at how out of touch he is with reality. I want to leave this place just as badly, but the reality of what I want and his unrealistic timeline is that we're going to be here for a while.

"Nothing in a hospital happens in less than an hour. There's paperwork that needs to be filled out and bills that need to be paid, and that's only for discharge. If Dr. Hall gets the labs he wants, we have to wait for the phlebotomist to come to the room, draw my blood, and then take it down to the lab, where we wait for the results to be put into the computer. At some point before the end of Dr. Hall's twelve-hour shift, he'll look at them and tell us what's going on. And then we might begin the discharge process."

Pan grunts, his gaze laser-focusing on my face. He stands effortlessly, where I would struggle to get out of the awkward position, and grabs the bags he purchased. He shoves them to my chest and glowers. "I will happily kill everyone in this building if that's what it takes, but I promise you, we will be outside of this death castle before the sun dips beneath the horizon. Mark my words."

"You wouldn't."

"I would." Pan leans closer. His breath caresses my cheek as he whispers, "I'm nothing like your precious Peter, Darling. He is the clouds in the sky and the water in the sea. I'm the darkness brought on by the storm and the monster hiding beneath the surface."

The balloon in my chest deflates. I feel like I'm falling, tumbling down the side of an emotional mountain. Sure, I'm angry, but that heat is taking a backseat to the hurt I feel.

I thought Shadow was my friend.

I thought he cared about me.

"Why are you being such a jerk?"

Pan grunts and drops back into the oversized chair. "Go take your shower, Darling. The clock's ticking."

I bite my lip to keep it from trembling and grab the bags he brought me. I look straight ahead, refusing to make eye contact or look down. Any shift and the tears will fall. I don't want him to see me cry.

I slide the bathroom door closed and lean against it. My mind tries to process that I'm home and that Peter is gone, but it circles back to how heartless Pan is and drowns in the hurt.

My throat burns when I try to swallow. I'm losing the fight with myself to stay ahead of these feelings. I'm about to reach for the shower curtain when Pan's deep voice carries through the paper-thin walls.

It's a gruff whisper, but I hear him clearly when he says, "Because you'll never love me, Darling. The best I can hope for is hate."

CHAPTER 7

Wednesday

I liked the web of treehouses Peter and the Lost lived in.

The tiny, one and two-bedroom wooden houses are high off the ground, keeping us from predators and, amazingly, from bugs. Their kitchens are small, without modern amenities like a refrigerator or microwave, but their bathrooms have the usual toilet, shower, and sink.

I never asked where their running water came from or where the black and gray water went when discarded. I chalked all of that, and the lack of saturation on the ground, up to the magic of Neverland, and let it be.

But hot water, warm enough to soothe the tired muscles of the body and turn my skin red without causing a burn, doesn't exist there.

Neverland's showers are summertime pool warm.

Comfortable, but not satisfying.

This is a level of heaven the living take for granted.

I don't know how long I've been under the shower's spray. I let the water pressure beat down on me until the air is thick with steam. When my chest aches with each inhale and I'm coughing more than breathing, I shut the water off.

I didn't grab a towel before stepping into the shower because there's a stack of them on the rack above the toilet, which is only an arm's length away. The whole bathroom, sink included, is maybe six feet from wall to wall. It's small by the standards of what I used to live in but comparable to the treehouse bathrooms —an unexpected comfort.

I cover my face with my hands and give myself another second to process. I'm having a hard time wrapping my brain around the fact that Peter brought me home. I'm nowhere close to my family or the city he took me from, but I'm back in the real world and less than a day's drive from being in my bed again.

I'm eager to see my parents, which feels silly to be excited about. Before Neverland, I'd go months without seeing them and sometimes weeks without calling. I let the day-to-day grind of life steal the five minutes it takes to pick up the phone. Maybe it's because I knew I could always call or could go see them. I didn't mind letting the days slip by because there was always tomorrow.

In Neverland, I had no way to tell my family I was okay. There was no electricity or cell service. I couldn't even write a letter because there wasn't a postal service to deliver it. My family was left wondering what happened to me for days, maybe even weeks.

I could call them now, but I think the shock might be too much. Besides, I don't want to just hear my mom's voice. I want to hold her because I know both of us are going to be blubbering messes. Hell, my sister may have even grown a heart throughout all of this. I'm not holding my breath, but I'm not gonna lie; I'd be pretty happy if she cried too.

I pull the shower curtain back and metal rings slide across the rod. I cringe at the sound. It echoes in the small space and makes my ears hurt. Neverland's showers were exposed. Nothing separated the falling water from the toilet or the sink. It was an open area without division, and don't ask me how, but there was never water all over the floor.

"Towel?" Peter—I mean Pan—asks.

I know the man before me isn't Peter because his eyes lack the blue I've grown used to seeing, but my heart and Wendy's emotions struggle with the differentiation. The pull to give in to him is as strong as ever, maybe even more so now that I know we are soulmates. I ache to feel his hands run down the curves of my body, even though my mind protests the desire. But Pan isn't the man I've unwillingly given my heart to.

He's something else.

Something I'm not sure I can trust.

Pan leans against the edge of the sink, long legs stretched out, almost touching the side of the shower-tub-combo. Thick tattooed fingers hold my terrycloth. The semi-translucent ink is new. Peter's sleeve of twisting artwork stopped at his wrists, but Pan has the sketch of a realistic eye on his left hand and symbols over his knuckles surrounded by wisps of smoke.

Pan doesn't shy away from looking at my naked body. His eyes roll over my curves, slowly tasting me with each shift of his gaze.

I cover my tits and lady bits the best I can with my hands. He may look like the other half of my soul, but he is not Peter. He has not earned the privilege to see my body, though I can't help feeling aroused by the way he's looking at me.

"What the hell, Pan?" The new name feels weird on my tongue. If he hadn't turned Shadow into something provocative, I'd still call him that to his face.

I should save that name for when he's inside me.

No! Stop it, Wednesday. You are not allowed to fuck the crazy shadow man. This is where I draw the line. Two psycho kinda-not-boyfriends are enough.

Pan holds the towel out, a devilish grin on his face, waiting for me to take the terrycloth. I swear, if he can hear my thoughts, I'm going to strangle him.

"Relax, Darling. It's not like I haven't seen you naked before."

I groan and snatch the towel from his hand. I wrap it around myself, not bothering to dry off, and then cross my arms. "So, you've been spying on me."

He laughs, but it sounds nothing like Peter's light-hearted vibrato. The deep chuckle burns a hole in my heart. It's a reminder that Pan is a separate person and that Peter might be somewhere trapped in his mind. "Look around, Darling. What do you see?"

A psycho.

A creep I don't trust.

A murderous stalker who played the part of my friend to manipulate my emotions, hoping I'd never discover the truth.

"I don't know. A bathroom."

"Exactly. You only see what's staring you in the face, but everything in this room casts a shadow. It's there whether you notice it or not."

He motions for me to look at the small spaces. I hate to admit it, but he's right. The sink, toilet, shower rack, hell, even the toilet paper on the roll has a shadow. I guess I've always known where there was light a shadow existed, but I never equated any of that to him.

"Except for you." I twist the water from my hair, pretending to be uninterested in what Pan says, then let it fall over my shoulders again. Truthfully, it scares me that he has no shadow in this world. I don't know what it means for Peter or our future. If we even have one.

Do I want one?

I can't think about that yet. Peter and I can't begin to figure out what we are if one—or both of us—get hauled off by the police. "I thought you said we were in a hurry."

"We are."

I lift my eyebrows, silently hinting for him to give me privacy. It's clear he won't leave on his own, so I erase all possibilities of anything happening between us. Knowing Peter, that's what he would be waiting for. I can't imagine Pan's motives would be different. "Then get out so I can get dressed!"

Pan stands but doesn't leave. He comes closer, popping the bubble that is my personal space, and steps into the shower. I take a step back and realize there's nowhere to go. My bare shoulders press against the shower wall, and my damp towel clings to my skin. I cringe. The thought of the germs that might be on the tiles gross me out, but what other option do I have?

Pan grabs my wrists and pins them above my head. I struggle against his hold until my arms decide they don't belong to me anymore. I want them to pull and fight, I want my legs to kick him in the nuts, and I want to thrash like a wild animal until Pan gives me back my personal space, but all I can do is stand there and glare.

The worst part, he knows it.

Pan leans closer until his cheek touches mine. A surge of lust races through me. I close my eyes and fight the need I feel. I subconsciously lean into Peter's body, wishing with all my might that he would come back to me.

Pan's breath tickles my ear when he whispers. "I've only ever seen you through Peter's eyes. Touched you through the sensations met by his skin. I will take all the time I want, Darling, because you are a beauty that needs to be appreciated. I can feel your hesitation and taste your fear, but you're just as much mine as you are his."

I swallow the lump in my throat. There's a tingle deep in my stomach. I don't want to want Shadow. He's not Peter, and yet there's a new slickness between my legs.

Pan drops my arms and steps back, out of the shower. The air between us lightens and a weight on my chest lifts. "You have ten minutes to get dressed before I walk out those doors."

"What happens if I'm not ready?" I call after him.

Pan stops in the doorway. He grips both sides of the frame, his back muscles flexing beneath his shirt. "Then I'll pick your ass up and carry you." He looks over his shoulder, that wicked grin in place. I hate how my heart flutters and how my skin aches to touch him. Most of all, I hate that Pan knows how much I crave him. He knows I can't control my physical reaction to his body and I think he likes it. "Best put your clothes on quickly, Darling. I'd hate to kill anyone who looks at what's mine."

CHAPTER 8

Wednesday

I don't know how he did it, but Pan has my discharge release in hand by the time I finish getting dressed and blow-drying my hair. I put my clothes on as soon as the bathroom door closes, but then take my time to style my hair. A hair brush can only do so much when sea salt and wind factor into your daily routine. Ponytails and braids became my go-to style, but here all I have to worry about is humidity. I don't have tools like a curling iron or a straightener, but a lot can be done with a round brush and blow dryer.

I look in the mirror, pleased with my appearance, then open the door. Pan stands outside, glowering, but he doesn't toss me over his shoulder or carry me out of the hospital like a brute. He grabs my things and hastily shoves them in a leather duffle back and he *does* carry down the hallway.

"Excuse me," the hospital's security guard says as we near the exit on the ground floor.

I hold my breath, bracing myself for Pan's backlash. We've made it this far without confrontation and paid the bill without throwing chairs. Walked past a dozen doctors and nurses without so much as a death threat. We were so close...

Pan turns and smiles at the man. "How can I help you?"

"You dropped this." The man sheepishly holds a pair of black underwear that must have fallen out of my bag.

I blush and snatch the undergarments, embarrassed. "Thanks."

"Good looking out." Pan salutes the guard with two fingers. The man nods in acceptance and we continue out the doors. I side-eye him every step of the way, unable to figure out where the personality change is coming from. How did he go from a murderous psycho to a cordial member of society?

As soon as we're outside, Pan snatches the panties from my hands and tosses them into a nearby trash can. "You won't be wearing anything another man has touched."

There he is. I roll my eyes. "Possessive much?"

"Yes," he states flatly.

I cross my arms and keep my mouth shut the whole walk to the parking garage. It's only across the street, but it's long enough to get my point across that I'm not happy. In the bedroom being dominant is a turn-on, but I'm not for someone telling me what I can and can't do beyond my sex life.

I watch Pan as we cross the street, scrutinizing everything from the way he walks to how his jaw clenches every time he looks at me.

There's something different about him. Physically, he looks better. His cheeks are fuller, his skin less pasty, and he's filling out his clothes again. But the change runs deeper than what Pan looks like. The air of mystery that surrounded him when we met down in the Keys is coming back. I want him to look at me and talk to me, and not because I like the guy. There's a string wrapped around something inside me that makes my chest physically hurt if I don't have his attention.

The feeling reeks of Shadow's magic. Thanks to the Neverpeek, I recognize the sensation is more than hormonal desire. I also know that the change comes with consequences. Pan is sacrificing *something* for Peter to get better.

I try not to think about what the price for Peter's health might be as we climb three flights of steps. Someone—Peter or Pan, not sure who—parked their car on the top floor of the building. My legs cry out with each step. They haven't worked this hard in a long time. Lactic acid pools in my muscles. They burn and ache, and even though I'm in pain, I can't make my mind stop replaying Cass's last words. *Peter's magic is tied to his life.*

The more he uses it the quicker it kills him. Pan is not high on my list of people right now, but if healing Peter means killing himself, I have to stop him. One life isn't more valuable than the other.

"How are you doing it?" I ask when we reach the rooftop of the parking garage. There's one car parked in the center of the floor. That's it. And a singular camera hangs outside the stairwell door, but it's old and unlikely to have audio. I don't worry about anyone hearing our conversation.

"I need you to be more specific, Darling. I've done a lot of things in the last twenty-four hours." Pan pulls a ring of keys from his pocket and twirls them around his finger.

"How are you healing him? And why isn't he back yet if you are?"

Pan stops walking and presses a button on his key fob. Head-lights from the silver sports car flash.

"Peter is resting," he says after a pregnant pause. "His body grows stronger, but he is weak. Whether he knows it or not, he needs this recharge because the moment we cross into Neverland, I'll be kicked out of this body and he won't get another chance to heal."

I reach for Pan's arm. It's the first time I've touched him since I woke up. My stomach jumps, and my nervousness makes me giddy. His skin is warmer than I expected. Peter's hands were as cold as ice though the rest of his body was a touch warmer. Here he almost feels life-like.

Pan looks down at my hand, surprise dancing in his eyes. I touch his cheek, feeling the familiar tug of emotions I'm not ready to accept. I need time to process Wendy's emotions and determine where I stand. Peter is not Pan. Both men betrayed me but both men hurt me. And even though they are separate people, I worry about them both the same.

"What is healing Peter doing to you?"

"Nothing," he says far too quickly.

I chew on my lip and gauge how much knowledge I'm willing to share. Peter liked to dance around the truth like he was afraid of what might happen once I knew things. Pan seems to be the opposite. I think he wants me to understand his world and my place in it.

I hesitate for a heartbeat, then decide to see if he can validate some of what Cass told me.

"I know the magic is tied to your life and using it is risky. Probably even more so in this world. I want Peter to get better, but not if it means losing you in the process. You are my friend, Shadow. Despite everything you've done, I need you to be okay too." As soon as the words leave my lips, I realize I mean them. I don't want Pan to hurt, even if I am pissed at him.

Pan swallows hard. For a split second, I think I've broken through his jerkface facade and found my friend again but the softness I saw in his eyes vanishes. Pan's features harden again and the air around us drops ten degrees.

"You don't know the first thing about magic." He turns away and walks toward the headlights that flashed. "The sun will be setting soon. We need to get going."

"Then teach me!"

Pan ignores my plea and pops the trunk of a sports car open. He drops my bag in the back and slams it shut.

"Where'd the car come from?" I ask. I don't know what it is. I'm not a car person. Besides knowing that it's silver, two-door, has the Corvette logo, and costs more than I used to make in a year, I'm clueless as to what it is.

"Peter bought it." Pan walks around the passenger side and tosses the keys at me. "For you. Hope you can drive a stick."

"Nope."

I toss the keys back and Pan catches them with one hand. I don't want the car. It's too flashy, and if Peter had mentioned anything to me in the ten seconds I got to see him, I would have said as much. "Guess you'll have to take it back."

"Not likely." The headlights flash again when he unlocks the car. He walks to the driver's side and slides into the seat. He starts the car and pushes a button to put the top down. It latches into a secret compartment behind the seats, disappearing as if it never existed.

I don't know why, but I'm nervous. Maybe it has everything to do with the stream of thoughts warning me to be wary of Pan, or maybe it has something to do with the fact that I have no idea where he plans to take me. He's not bound to the promise Peter made to bring me home. He's not bound to anything beyond existing within Peter's body.

Pan turns the radio lower and looks at me with arched brows. "Any day now, Darling."

"No." My voice is a whisper lost in the night, but he hears it.

I think he chuckles darkly, but it's hard to tell over the sound of the engine. Pan unclicks his seat belt and gets out of the car.

"I'm torn, Darling," he says, walking around the front of the vehicle. "I'd hoped you would make this easy and follow directions, but I'm glad you're not."

The fingers on my right hand twitch. I look down at the spasming muscles and try to take control again, but Pan's magic wraps around them like a thin glove. My arm bends at the elbow. I watch my hand flex without command and my wrist twists to show the back of my hand first, and then my palm.

"You like that. Don't you? Controlling me."

This time, I hear the sound that vibrates in Pan's chest. "You have no idea what I'd like to do with you, but it's no fun if it's not consensual."

My cheeks heat. He wants to fuck me. I can work with that. Everything that happens to my body is my choice. I chose to manipulate Cass, even if it was done poorly. I chose to sleep with Peter. Now, I'm choosing to use my body to get answers.

I lean against Pan's side and press my chest into his arm. Not the smoothest of moves, but it'll get the job done. "I'll happily get in if you tell me where we're going."

Pan's brows bunch together. "I thought that was obvious. I'm taking you to your family."

"Oh." Maybe he is tied to Peter's promise after all.

"But first." Pan slides his hand to the back of my neck. His fingers lace through my roots, gripping and pulling my face upwards. I look into those eyes, curious to see if there is a trace of blue, but all I see is my reflection in the darkness. "You and I are going out to eat."

"Why?"

"Because you want answers and I may never get the chance to be with you again. It's your choice how far we take our relationship, Darling." He drops a singular kiss to the nape of my neck.

I suck in an audible breath. Pan's lips are a drug sweeter than anything this world offers. A taste isn't enough. All they do is tease my body and make me want more. "I promise to let you know my limits; if you promise to tell me everything Peter wouldn't."

Pan steps out of my personal space and opens the passenger door for me. "You won't like what you hear."

"You don't know that." I slip into the seat. It's lower than I expected and I almost fall into it, but Pan is ready to help me get situated with a steadying hand.

"I do, Darling." He closes my door and looks down at the ground as he rounds the car again. I can't hear what he says next, but I can read his lips when he adds, "I really do."

CHAPTER 9

Wednesday

I stare out the window as Pan drives us through town. The engine purrs angrily when traffic halts us to a stop. His foot is lead, wanting to race down alleyways and around cars, but the traffic lights every ten feet stop us every time.

I think Neverland altered my brain chemistry because I find it odd how so many people can co-exist without interacting. Strangers walk past each other, ignoring the presence of the person next to them. They talk on their phones and drive in their cars, and not one person bothers to smile at anyone else.

In Neverland, the Lost are always a part of each other's lives. As for the pirates... well, I don't know how close they are, but they would nod and smile at everyone they walked past. I miss that feeling of familiarity. Even in the cove, where I only knew James, I felt safe. I could roam freely without fear of being harmed because I was friends with him and the pirates were his allies.

In my realm, everyone is your enemy. No one trusts their fellow man, especially the ones who are suffering, and I find that heartbreaking.

Pan pulls the car up to a valet stand at a side entrance of the mall. I didn't know malls offered valet services. The one we have in my hometown is half-dead with more empty stores than people who shop. I'm guessing this mall is busier with a richer clientele than the one I'm used to.

"Good morning, Miss," a young kid says as he opens my door. He holds a hand out to assist me out of Pan's tiny death trap, then trades a claim ticket for the keys.

"Don't talk to her," Pan growls. He wraps his hand around my waist and ushers me into the mall.

Once we're inside, I step out of his hold and stop near the entryway. I cross my arms and shift my weight to one hand. "We need to talk."

"Is that so?" Pan shifts to face me.

"You've got to stop being such a jerk." I drop my arms and point behind us. "That man was just doing his job."

"I highly doubt his job included flirting with you."

"He was being nice!"

"He was trying to take what is mine!" Pan booms.

A few passersby stop walking to look at us, but no one says anything about the outburst. They look at us, eyes wide, probably judging Pan for yelling and me for allowing the conversation to happen. It makes me anxious to know that people are looking at us even as the shoppers keep walking.

"I don't belong to you," I whisper, my voice holding all the strength I can muster. "I am a person, not a possession. Either you start treating me like someone you care about and not something you own, or I'm done. Done with you. Done with Peter. Done with Neverland."

The words feel like acid in my mouth. My heart breaks and falls to pieces at my feet. I haven't had time to sort through my feelings and decide what I want from Peter. A friend. A lover. Something more that spans the galaxies and defies time. Cutting the cord on whatever we are feels like selling myself short of something that could be amazing, but I refuse to be in a toxic relationship.

Pan's eyes soften. He sighs, his shoulders rolling forward slightly. "I'm sorry."

"You're not forgiven, but I accept the apology." It's more than Peter ever gave me for all his wrongdoings.

Pan's lips lift slightly. The armor around him falls for a moment and I think I see the shadow I befriended on the Island again. He holds out his hand. "Walk with me?"

I take it and this moment feels like a glitch in time. This is what new couples did when I was in the ninth grade. They'd stroll through the mall on a Friday night holding hands and killing time for the sake of it. Back then, no one my age had a job or money. The guy I liked used to save his lunch money to take me to a movie and I would get twenty dollars from my parents to buy us dinner.

I have no clue what day of the week it is, and Pan supposedly has more money than I'll ever know what to do with, but this feeling—holding hands and window shopping—is nostalgic. It makes me giddy.

"Let's go into this one." Pan reaches for the handle of one of the shop doors. The big-name stores have roll-up doors that are open all day, but a few of the more expensive shops have glass doors. This is one of those stores. The kind of place I would never step foot in because a shirt is probably a hundred dollars and I can't even afford a sock.

"Are you sure?" I hesitate. Pan holds the door open for me, patiently waiting for my mini panic attack to subside. He said not to worry about money, but I do. I have none, and throwing away God knows how much on an outfit stresses me out. "I don't need anything this fancy. I'm sure Malley's or Sunningdales will have a nice dress I can wear for dinner."

"They might, but I already rented out the store."

My jaw drops. He did not. Tell me he did not! I look around and sure enough, there isn't anyone inside. Only two ladies stand behind the counter, practiced smiles in place, waiting for us to come in.

"Shadow," I whisper because I don't know what else to say. The gesture is painfully sweet and a little bit creepy.

"I don't want to hear another word." He sets his hand on the small of my back and escorts me inside. "Let me spoil you. It's the least I can do."

"Hello, Mr. Darling," The brunette with bright red lips says when we step inside. "I have the rack you requested ready in the dressing area. Mindy will serve your refreshments and we will both be here should you or your wife need assistance."

"Thank you," he says flatly. "But we'll be just fine."

I follow him to the back of the store where the fitting rooms are. The rooms are set up like a bridal shop, with each section having its own viewing area and a mini stage.

We walk to the furthest dressing bay and Pan gestures to a rack of dresses. Gowns both long and short, sequined and feathered, hang in order of color. I run my fingers over the hangers and stop at a green one that catches my eye. I check the tag and almost choke on air when I see how expensive it is.

"I can't." I look up at him with pleading eyes. "These are too expensive."

"Darling." He takes my cheeks in his hands and dips his head until our foreheads meet.

Time slows when we touch. Nothing matters except the way he makes me feel. I'm spiraling out of control, but have never felt safer in my life. This man will be both my savior and my undoing.

"I'd buy you the world if it meant more time with you." His husky voice vibrates my center. The way I'm feeling, it's hard not to believe in instant love. I wonder if this is how he feels, torn between what is logical and what is *us*. "Don't deny me the satisfaction of seeing you happy."

Damn this man and his ability to make me remember what living feels like. Life was easier when I existed in the moments between lust and hate. "I'll make you a deal," I finally say. "For each dress I try on, you've got to answer a question."

"Done," he says without hesitation.

I finger through the hangers and pull out a couple of dresses that catch my eye. "Real answers. None of those twisted half-truths Peter likes to give when I ask questions."

"I wouldn't dare." He takes the dresses from me. "Let me help."

I allow it because I think a part of Pan is hardwired to be chivalrous. He and Peter grew up in a different time, when in an age where men opened doors and women were cherished. He sets the dresses on the hanging hooks for me.

"Thank you."

"I'll be right out here." He tips an invisible hat and walks back into the viewing area.

I close the door and start stripping. I step out of my jeans and grab the first dress off the hanger. It's a flowy, red thing with feathers falling from the waist in cascading lengths down to my heels. It's hideous, but every dress is an answer given. I'll try on the whole damn store if that's what it takes.

I hold it and my girls with one arm and reach for the door. "Can you help me with the zipper?"

Pan stands. His eyes run over my curves as he comes near. He smirks, liking what he sees. There is no mirror in the dressing room. I'm forced to step onto the small stage to see myself. I face the wall of glass but don't look at myself. My gaze is fixed on Pan, watching his expression as his hands roll up my back.

I bite my lip and fight another rush of desire. My body craves him like it craves chocolate during red-week. All I get are tastes, snack-size fixes from his touch that aren't nearly enough to satiate me.

Pan's fingers trail down my arms once the dress is secure. Static bounces between our bodies, torturing me. He's close and yet too far away at the same time.

"Anything you want to ask me, Darling?"

Right. Questions. That's the whole reason I agreed to try on this stupid dress. I clear my throat and turn to face him. "What are you?"

"Starting with the heavy stuff." He chuckles lightly, but the way he stands, the stiffness in his arm as he runs a hand through his hair, tells me he's on edge. "One day, I just existed. I could feel the Island. I could communicate with it, just like I could communicate with Peter." He shrugs and tucks his hands into his pockets. "Been here ever since. Next dress?"

I nod and he undoes the zipper. I hold the fabric to my chest and return to the fitting room. I close the door and let the gown fall to my feet. My back presses against the cold surface of the wall. It tethers me to this room and this moment. I squeeze my eyes shut and wrestle to keep my emotions in check, but it's a losing battle.

I'm struggling with sorrow. I can't imagine how hard it must be not to remember where you came from or who your parents are. What it must have been like to be alone when he came into existence. Tears pool in my eyes for him. They fall down my cheeks when I blink, carrying sympathetic sorrow. I wipe them away and grab the next dress.

"If I wanted to go back to Neverland, how would I do that?" I ask through the closed door.

"You want to come back?"

I walk out again, holding another dress to my chest. I didn't like this one on the rack and hate it even more now that I see myself in it.

Pan grins and shrugs. "Want me to zip that one?"

"No. The yellow washes me out." I turn on my heels and hastily go back to the fitting room. I don't know what's wrong with me. I've always had big emotions, but they're magnified today. I feel everything so much more intensely than I ever have. Even drunk me doesn't compare to this. *Did I come back broken?"* I don't know yet, but if I did, is it possible?"

"When the sun meets the horizon the path between our worlds is open."

"For how long?"

"That's another question. Do you have another dress on yet?"

I shimmy into a strapless shimmery number that squishes my

girls and open the door. This dress is pretty, but it hugs too tight. My back will be hurting after a few hours. Plus, the way I bloat after eating, I'll look three months pregnant in this number. "Happy?"

"Depends on where in the world you are. As soon as day turns to night the portal closes." He looks over the off-the-shoulder dress. "I like this one. The green makes your eyes pop."

"That doesn't make sense. The sun was still in the sky when Peter pushed me off the boat."

"That's because you were in the Bermuda Triangle. It has wormholes strewn throughout it. Twilight, lightning storms, waterspouts, or any anomaly it deems fitting can open a passage into our world, but it's not consistent. Unless you possess Neverland magic, which Peter did, the living can't cross through. You have to die at the exact right moment to *possibly* find yourself in Neverland."

"Your magic makes no sense!" I say, frustrated. I change out of the strapless and slip on a deep blue number. The color reminds me of Peter's eyes. Dark with shimmery bits. As soon as it's on, I know it's the one.

I walk into the viewing area and Pan's face lights up. He looks at me as if it's the first time we've ever met, like our past and Peter and Wendy's never happened.

I meet his gaze in the mirror. "What do you think?

He pushes off the wall and stands behind me. One hand splays across my belly, pulling me into him. The other wraps around my neck. He tilts my face with his thumb. My heart hammers and my body hums, desperate for more of this man's touch.

That tug in my chest, the string that wrapped itself around my heart when Peter and I first met adds a new loop, tightening its hold. I have to remind myself that the man who holds me is not Peter. He's something else, but at this moment, my soul no longer feels as if it's been split in two. For the first time since Peter has come into my life, I feel whole again.

"You're the most beautiful star I've ever seen, Wednesday."

A smile tugs at my lips. I don't know why I expected something simple like *you look nice* to come out of his mouth. Nothing about my life has been simple since meeting this man.

Pan's head dips to the crook of my neck and presses the gentlest of kisses to my skin. I suck in a breath, surprised by how much it makes me wish his fingers would press tighter and pull my lips to his.

He doesn't hear my silent plea. I get that singular kiss, and then he steps away. Cold air fills the spaces where his body was and I find myself wishing I was in his arms again.

"Keep the dress on. We'll pay for it, then find some more suitable shoes."

I look down at my bare feet and wiggle my toes. "What's wrong with my Converse?"

Pan drops to one knee and picks up my sneaker. I slide my foot out, reverse Cinderella style, and he unties the laces for me. "These don't show the world how beautiful your legs are." He helps me out of my other shoe and ties them together by the laces. "But if your sneakers make you feel beautiful, then we will find a pair that matches better."

It's not that my shoes make me feel beautiful. I'm just comfortable in them. They're the security blanket in my life. Something I know won't let me down. I can run if I need to. I can walk without wobbling or falling. They make me feel like me. So far, they're the only thing since coming back that does.

"I have one more question... for now."

Pan frowns. "I have a feeling I'm not going to like this one."

"Why me? I know you said I'm Wendy's soul come back to life, but why now? Just... why?"

Pan sighs heavily and turns away from me. He ambles around the room, touching the dresses and fingering the jewelry. Doing anything but looking at me. "I've dreamed of you before I knew what dreaming was. Before I even knew what I was. My world was shades of gray seen through my own eyes but experienced by the hands of someone else. I spent years wrestling with the emotions Peter so freely gave up and learning what my place in the world was. I thought I'd found it as a guiding force keeping Neverland and its creatures safe from the Fae."

I sit on the armrest of one of the viewing chairs. I sense that out of everything I've asked, this is the hardest question to answer. "Is that what you do? Keep the Island safe?"

Pan nods, finally looking at me. "It was until you came into existence. Somewhere across the galaxies, your soul resurfaced. I felt it the moment you took your first breath, a painful longing pulling me away from my home. I searched for what felt like a lifetime before I finally found you. You were a child, maybe eight years old, when I first saw you through the window. You were playing with your sister, pretending to be princesses." He touches his chest, a far-off look on his face, and smiles. "Something inside me bloomed that day. I knew you were my other half, but you were so little. I knew from Peter's memories how important it was to let you grow up. So, I returned to Neverland but never for long. I came back every Neverland night knowing time would carry on in my absence. When you were finally old enough to make the trip with me, you'd fallen in love."

I shake my head. The only person I've ever loved was Kenny. I went on dates and had boyfriends, but none of them made me feel the way Kenny did. And he couldn't make me feel the way Peter and Pan do. "How is it possible to fall in love with someone if we're soul mates?"

"Love is a powerful magic in itself. It heals just as much as it hurts. Your heart can experience it as many times as your life allows, but your soul is only ever destined for one."

"What would have happened if Kenny and I had gotten married?"

A shadow falls over Pan's face. He shrugs. "I'm not sure. Lived a happy life, I guess, but I think a part of you would have always hoped for more. More attention. More compassion. Just... more. I left you alone because you were happy. I stayed as nothing more than a shadow in the distance, keeping a periodic eye on you, making sure you were okay."

"Until I wasn't."

He nods. "I think you can figure out the rest."

"Don't you think it's weird you've stalked me since I was a kid?"

"Only if you think it's weird that some part of you feels happier and more complete right now than you have all your life."

He's got me.

I wish it weren't true, but Pan is right.

He strides across the room and takes my hands in his. He looks down at me, pleading for forgiveness and understanding with his eyes. "I know our time is limited, just like I know you may never forgive me for what I've done, but I will do everything in my power to make it up to you."

Pan can never make it up to me. I'll never get back the days stolen or the time lost with my family. The best he can hope for is acceptance and for us to move past it. Sometimes, I think I'm ready to let go of all the hate and anger. Other times, I want to drown in it because it keeps me level-headed. "Who took me? You or Peter?"

"We both did. I couldn't have brought you over if it wasn't something he wanted, but it was my idea."

I nod, unsure of how to process that. Both men are guilty. Just like both of them stole different parts of my heart. I pull Pan in for a hug. I think we both need one right now.

He was right; I didn't like the answers he gave me.

The truth is never easy to hear, especially when it hurts, but I'm glad I got it.

CHAPTER 10

Wednesday

I don't feel good.

I don't know whether it's nerves or motion sickness from being in a car so low to the ground the past hour, but my stomach turns inside itself.

It hasn't been happy since Pan and I had pizza in the food court of the mall. I guess it could be the food, too. Everything we ate in Neverland was grown there. We didn't add chemical preservatives or red dye number *whatever* to enhance the taste.

I don't think a few weeks of whole foods can change the way my stomach processes food, but I guess it could be possible.

Pan pulls in front of the restaurant's valet stand. The lady running the car service ignores me and heads straight to him. I don't blame her. Pan is gorgeous. Somehow, his muscles are more defined here than they were in Neverland, and there are new tattoos on his body that were never on Peter's. The magic used to heal Peter is transforming their body into something that is purely Pan's.

Pan hands the valet woman his keys without so much as tossing a passing glance her way and rounds the front of the car. He opens my door and holds out his hand for me to grab. "Darling."

Sparks fly under my skin from where his hand holds mine. I feel guilty being attracted to him. Pan may look like Peter, but he's a different man. A beast made of magic, a shadow that fills the spaces inside me I didn't know were hollow until he touched them.

"I feel silly," I say sheepishly, looking down at myself.

We spent over two hours at the mall shopping for shoes and jewelry to go with the dress. Pan found me a pair of royal blue Converse and even though I insisted we keep searching for shoes that better matched the dress, he bought them. They sit in the trunk along with a pair of strappy stilettos I liked—but can't walk in—and a pair of *Disney* Princess pajamas he caught me looking at.

I thought we were done shopping after Pan picked out a white gold teardrop necklace and a pair of dangly earrings that matched, but we weren't. He took me to the spa—an actual freaking spa where they put you in a cotton robe and serve champagne— to have my hair styled and my makeup done. The ladies there plucked, rubbed, and did my makeup better than I could ever dream of, keeping my face subtle yet stylish. Everything felt amazing, but I don't look like me.

At least, not any version he's ever seen.

"You look beautiful." Pan is dressed equally as nice in a deep blue button-down shirt that matches my tea-length dress. It hugs his arms and chest, showing off enough dips and divots that anyone who dares to stare is teased by what could be underneath.

I know what Peter's body looked like underneath his clothes. Every curve was hard, but every edge was soft. His muscles were made by his way of life. Defined but not bulging. His ink carefully placed to accentuate his beauty. Looking at Pan, I can't help but wonder what new artwork might be hidden beneath that shirt.

My cheeks flush. I'm hot, even with an ocean breeze blowing from behind the building. Our reservations are at some five-star restaurant in the Horizon Hotel. I've never heard of either place, but *my date* swears they have the best Filet and lobster in the country.

Pan kisses my knuckles and then intertwines his fingers with mine. We walk through the hotel lobby and are quickly seated on a private terrace overlooking the water.

Within seconds of getting comfortable, our waitress appears. "Good evening, folks. My name is Molly and I'll be your server tonight. Can I start you off with something to drink?"

"Whiskey and coke," Pan drawls.

It's hard not to smile. I remember the day we met—well, Peter and I—and how he was doing his best to pretend I didn't exist while watching a football game. He sipped on a whiskey and ordered one again on the glass-bottom boat tour. It gives me hope that Peter is somewhere in there, fighting to get back to me. I miss him.

"And for you, Miss?"

"Just water, please."

The girl hurries away to get our drinks. Pan reads over the menu. He periodically mutters about what's offered, but I'm not paying attention. I stare at the vast span of darkness beyond the shoreline and listen to the waves crash along the sand. A knot forms in my chest. It sounds like home and it hits me how much I miss Neverland.

I miss the way the wind blows through the trees.

I miss the fireflies floating in jars. Their lights bright enough to guide my way but not overpower the stars in the sky.

I miss the smell of burning cedar and the tacky eighties music the Lost played through an ancient stereo.

I miss my friends.

Most of all, I miss being free, which is ridiculous because I felt trapped the whole time I was there.

But since coming back, nothing feels right, not even my own skin. It's too tight. Breathing hurts. Eating is uncomfortable. And my head has a light throb that won't go away. Emotionally, I'm up and down more than a yo-yo and I don't know whether I want to fuck Pan or stab him. It's exhausting.

Pan touches my cheek. I jerk out of my thoughts and look into his eyes. They're still dark, without any hints of blue, but there are wisps of charcoal gray in them that bleed into specks of gold and light brown.

He tucks a strand of hair meant to lie loose on my cheek behind my ear. "What's running through that pretty little mind of yours, Darling?"

I sigh and try to focus on the menu in front of me. The words are blurry. I close my eyes, take a deep breath, and then open them again. They focus on the letters, and even though I can read the menu, nothing looks appealing. "Nothing important."

"On the contrary, if it's bothering you so much as to worry your mind, I'd say it's rather important. Tell me."

"I just miss it. That's all."

"What?"

"Neverland." I peek up over the plastic-covered paper. A question hangs on the tip of Pan's tongue, but I'm in no mood to give answers. So, I ask one instead. "Do you know what you want to eat?"

Pan's lips lift into a delicious smirk. I can practically hear what he's thinking. My cheeks heat as I tell him. "I'm not on the menu."

His eyes light up, delighted that I know what he wants. I might want it, too, but for the time being, I'll keep that tidbit secret. "Perhaps for dessert, then."

～

"Can I get you anything else?" Molly asks as she collects our plates. "Dessert, maybe?"

"I don't think your chef offers what I'm craving." Pan winks at me and that damn rush of heat floods my cheeks again.

"Try me," our waitress replies eagerly. "We're very accommodating."

Pan pulls his debit card from his wallet and holds it in the air. "Not interested, but thanks."

Molly takes his card to her kiosk and is back with the slip for him to sign minutes later. Pan tips her generously, then stands and pulls my chair out for me. It's hard not to like him when he's like this. Men aren't chivalrous anymore. Sure, women may get the occasional opened door, but all the other customs are gone.

"Do you want to go for a walk along the beach?" he asks.

"I wouldn't mind seeing the ocean." I let him lead me to the steps that descend to the beach. I hold onto the railing and look up at the sky. The moon is large, just shy of full and the stars twinkle brightly around it.

"You see that star?" he asks, pointing up at the blanket of darkness. "Second one to the right of the moon. Wendy used to call that the wishing star."

"Did you know her?" I stop on the second to last stair and find the wishing star in the sky. *Make a wish,* the little voice in my mind whispers, but I don't know what to ask for. I have too many needs. There's not enough magic in all of the worlds to grant me everything I want, and no wish is greater than the other. Instead, I settle on something temporary and easy to satisfy. *I wish to have no regrets about tonight.*

"No, not personally, but the few times Peter and I came together I could see her through his eyes." Pan taps his temple. "You'd be surprised at how detailed his memories are."

Silence fills the air between us. I like it so much better than the honking of horns on the road or the clamor of background music every building we've gone into. The sounds in Neverland were intentional, if anything at all. It was peaceful living in serene calmness until choosing to stimulate the mind. Standing out here, under the stars, listening to the tide roll in, I finally feel like I can relax a little.

"Are you ready for that walk?"

"Are you going to drown me again?" I side-eye him, half joking and completely serious at the same time.

Pan chuckles. He drapes his arm over my shoulder and descends down the final steps of the staircase. I go with him because I want to believe he is the same Shadow I knew on the Island. I want to trust that he won't hurt me.

"I was wondering how long it would take for you to figure out it was me who pushed you off the boat and not your precious Peter. He hated my plan. We argued for hours about how to bring you to Neverland."

"He once said he was trying to figure out what to do with me."

Pan stops to pick a shell out of the sand. He walks to the water's edge and rinses it off. "He was trying to convince me that we could bring you to Neverland alive."

"And you decided murder was the best route?"

Pan holds the bright red cockle up for me to see. He proudly slips his treasure into his pocket and begins searching through the sand again. "Are you ever going to let that go?"

I walk beside him, deciding to participate in the shell hunt. Looking for brightly colored or oddly shaped treasures is easier than looking at Pan. "Probably not, but if it makes you feel better, I'm not angry. I still don't trust you, but I'm glad you brought me there. It was a magical experience."

I bend down and pick up a piece of sea glass. The round edges are smooth, except for one corner where the ocean hadn't finished buffing away the harshness of its past life. It cuts my finger. I curse under my breath and stick it in my mouth.

Pan perks up immediately and drops the shell he was looking at. "Are you all right?"

"I'm fine." I pull my finger out of my mouth and show him the little wound. There is no blood seeping from the hole, even after my saliva dries from the skin. "See? Nothing to worry about."

But I am worried. I should be bleeding, even just a little. We keep walking, but I'm done picking up shells. The next time I look at my finger, the wound is gone. No cut. No scar. No sign that I was ever injured to begin with. The longer we walk, the more it bothers me.

What if I really did come back wrong?

What if I was never meant to return from Neverland and I'm some sort of living dead now?

My stomach twists at the thought, threatening to bring back the biscuits and chowder I ate. I bump into Pan's chest and look at him curiously. I must be losing my mind. He wasn't in front of me. He was to my side, off to the right, walking in the water.

Wasn't he?

"Don't lie to me this time, Darling." Pan tucks his thumb under my chin and drags my gaze to his face. "What's bothering you?"

"Am I like the Lost now?" My voice cracks. I'm about to cry again and I feel stupid for not being able to control myself. These tears are going to be the death of me.

Pan takes my hand and sets it over my chest. I feel my heart racing beneath my breasts. Each *thump thump* vibrates through me until I feel my pulse in my wrists and neck. He looks me in the eye as he says, "You are nothing like the Lost, or Cass, or even Peter and myself. You are living and breathing. You are growing. You've got a life inside you more precious than you'll ever realize."

"Take me back with you," I say suddenly. "I don't want to be here anymore. I just want to go home to Neverland."

Pan sighs heavily and pulls me into a hug. "I wish I could, Darling, but I can't. You need to be here because you can die. This is the safest place for you until I figure out who wants to hurt you."

I nuzzle into his chest. I don't want to be left behind. I want to stay in Pan's arms, which scares me more than living in either realm. "Does Peter agree?"

"It was his idea."

I yawn. I don't know why I'm so tired. I was fine a minute ago, but now all I want to do is close my eyes.

Pan lifts me into his arms. I curl into his body, pleased at how even though our stance has changed, we fit like cut glass. He carries us back toward the hotel and at some point, I fall asleep. I don't dream of Peter or the adventures I had in Neverland. I dream of Shadow, the dark creature in Peter's human form, and I'm not ashamed to admit I like the things he does to me.

CHAPTER 11

Wednesday

I jolt awake.

Bright light filters into the room. My heart races as I wait for my eyes to adjust. For a moment, I forget that I'm back on Earth and fear Cass has me. I'm not afraid of myself. I'm scared for Peter and the twisted plan Cass has for him.

My fingers grasp at the sheets beneath me. Within seconds, I can see my room, and the tension in my chest eases. I remember that I'm back in my world, heading to see my family, with a man who confuses me.

I push the crisp cotton sheets aside and step out of bed. My dress is still on, zipped up in the back, and my panties and strapless bra are in place. All I'm missing are my shoes, and even they are waiting for me on the floor of the bed.

"Pan?" I call out, walking toward the bathroom.

He pushes open the door dividing my room from the one adjacent. "I'm here, Darling." He leans against the door frame and tucks his hands into the pockets of his gray shorts. "Did you sleep well?"

My throat goes dry at the sight of him shirtless. He's stunning, more so than my dreams had imagined. The tattoos Peter had inked onto his skin are darker, filled with shaded details that are new to the art. Peter's pleasantly sculpted body now looks like it's been carved from marble, the soft edges hard and sharp corners deadly. I itch to run my fingers down those abs. I want to know if they're as firm as they look or if somehow our bodies are still molded to fit together. My sides are squishy, not hard, and my abs are hidden under a layer of love and pizza. Does a man with a body like that eat pizza?

"Um...what are you doing over there?"

"I figured you'd like some privacy. Can't win brownie points if you wake up with a man you don't remember going to bed with."

"Right." I look down at the ground. My ears are probably as red as a rose. I'm so embarrassed I fell asleep on the beach. "I'm sorry about last night. I don't know what happened to me."

"Love." Pan takes my hand in his and kisses the part of my palm that's beneath my thumb. The sensation shoots down my core and to my center, the feeling intoxicating. "You had a long day. I was selfish for not letting you rest sooner."

"I'm not a napping girl."

"Maybe not, but your body has gone through many changes since coming home. You need time to adjust." His lips slide down and press against my wrist. "To heal." He kisses up my arm. "To grow." Paving a path of lust until I'm breathless and his mouth is on my collarbone. "Sometimes your body just needs things you aren't ready for."

My body needs him.

It longs to feel his thick length inside me. It wants to know how Pan moves compared to Peter, and I feel so guilty pining for another man.

The Lost share lovers, but this isn't Neverland and Peter and I have never ventured down that road. What would he think if I slept with Pan?

Can this be called cheating if I'm not sampling a different dick, just a new driver?

"I'm," I say breathlessly. I close my eyes and fall into the feeling of bliss coming from his hands as they caress the sides of my arms. "I'm going to take a shower."

Pan's fingers find the zipper of my dress. He slides the little metal piece down my spine until it hits the stopper. I shiver, and he kisses the soft spot on my neck again. "No one is stopping you."

I turn to face him and look deep into his eyes. It would be easy to walk away. I could thank him and disappear into the shower, then use the water's spray to satisfy the need pooling inside me.

But I don't want to.

I slide one dress strap off my shoulder and then the other. The shiny blue fabric falls to my feet. Pan watches me, his eyes never leaving my face, even as I reach behind my back and unclasp my bra. "What if I want you to stop me?"

Pan doesn't hesitate. He wraps his hand around the back of my neck and pulls me into him. He kisses me like a man starved and I'm his last meal. Savoring. Devouring every ounce I give him.

I drag my nails down his spine. I want to hurt him so he can feel all the pain he's caused me, and then I want him saying my name the moment that pain shifts into pleasure.

I break the kiss, my chest heaving, and look into his dark eyes. All I see is lust. All I feel is desire. "Your move, Shadow."

Pan smirks, accepting my challenge. He grips my thighs and lifts me into the air. I wrap my legs around him. He drops us onto the bed and kisses me again, his hands moving with skilled desire to my lace panties. He rips the lace effortlessly and tosses it on the ground.

"I want to taste you." Pan presses my legs open. His tongue dives between my folds, licking and lapping, flicking and teasing my center.

I claw at the bedsheets, my back arching because I'm so painfully close to coming. My world spins and I'm not thinking about Peter or what Pan might be doing differently or better. I'm not thinking at all. I can't. All I can do is enjoy the ride.

Pan stops right as I'm on the edge and bites the inside of my thigh.

"Please," I beg. The build-up is so intense it's painful. I *need* some part of him inside me. Preferably his dick, but I'll settle for his fingers if that's all he'll let me have.

Pan presses fevered kisses on my leg. His fingers dig into my hips. His grip is bruising, but I want the pain. It teeters me that much closer to my release. "Please what, Darling?"

I grab Pan's hair and pull him to look at me. "Fuck me. I asked once. Now I'm telling you. Fuck me, Pan."

"As you wish." He pulls me to the edge of the bed and kisses me. I taste myself on his lips and my sweet musk makes me even wetter.

Pan drops his shorts and aligns himself with my center. He pushes inside with a deep, big thrust. I thread my fingers through the back of Pan's hair and take hold. I don't want his mouth leaving mine. I don't want to look into his eyes and feel guilty for loving this.

I just want to *feel*.

Pan eases in and out, giving me time to adjust. I moan, a sigh of pleasure releasing some of the tension inside me. He takes that as an admission that I'm ready and thrusts deeper, harder, finding a steady rhythm. It hurts a little, but I like it when he hurts me. I like how good the pain feels.

I let Pan control my body and mold me to his liking. He pushes deeper and I cry out, unable to keep the intensity of the pleasure to myself. His fingers curl around my neck and he pulls me upright, letting gravity control the pressure, and grabs my wrists. He presses them to my lower back and holds both wrists in one hand, making sure he's the only reason I'm upright.

"Say my name, Darling," his husky voice whispers.

I can't. I'm so close to coming. I'm scared that if I do anything besides enjoy the ride I'll miss the wave.

Pan adds a little more pressure to my neck and it sends me

over the edge. A rush of pleasure ripples through me. I shake in his arms and cry out, "Shadow, god, Shadow!"

He arches me upright when I stop trembling and kisses me near my ear. "Good girl."

I'm catching my breath, my body already tingling with anticipation of more, when Pan pushes me downward. With my face pressed into the mattress, he thrusts harder, his balls slapping against me, and I'm coming again when his warmth spills inside. My body hums, happily accepting its penance.

Pan pulls out and kisses the space between the dimples on my back. "Thank you."

I slide onto my belly and rest my head on my arms. That was the hardest, best orgasm I've ever had, but it took a lot out of me. I'm tired again and might just take a nap after my shower. "For what?"

Pan chuckles lightly, then walks deeper into the room. He starts the shower, warms the water, and then comes to my side again. "Let's get you cleaned up."

I force my body upright and take the towel Pan has waiting for me. It's not a pretty sight, holding it between my legs as I walk to the bathroom, but it's better than all the little Pans dripping onto the floor and stepping on sticky cum covered carpet later.

I step into the shower and pull the curtain closed. Pan opens it a second later.

"What are you doing?"

He cups my cheeks, his lips finding mine, and steps in with me. He turns us so the water falls onto his broad shoulders and doesn't spray in my face while we kiss. I love the way our bodies feel together, how mine hums in delight, and his seems like it's made for me.

He smiles when he breaks the kiss and the sight is more beautiful than it should be. "Enjoying every minute I can get."

Wednesday

I'm sore, but it's such an amazing feeling. I let the shower's water fall across my back and close my eyes. I can still feel Pan's hands on my skin. The way they caress my body, touching my tender places with utmost care. So much touching, and petting, and licking. My lips lift into a grin, my heart racing thinking about all the ways he's claimed my body this morning.

The only reason I'm alone in the shower this time is because my stomach growled when Pan was eating me out.

The water turns cold and I laugh because I didn't know that was possible at a hotel. I guess when you've taken as many showers as I have this morning, it was bound to run out. I hate the cold and shut the water off the moment I shiver.

We have only one dry towel left on the rack. I wrap myself in it and come back out into the main space of my room. I grab a washcloth—the only other option that's not come covered—and dry the wet ends of my hair.

"Pan?" I call out. My room is empty, but that doesn't mean he isn't nearby. I pull open the door that divides our rooms and peek inside. I don't see him, so I call his name again. "Pan?"

The key reader on my door beeps right before it opens.

My skin tingles, feeling his magic before he walks into the

room. The man smiles when he sees me and electricity bounces between us. Tattoos peek out from beneath the sleeves of his Nirvana t-shirt and stretch to his knuckles. Jeans cover his lower half and shiny black boots hide his toes. He's got a punk rock meets sex god look going on this morning. If I were wearing panties, they'd be ruined, soaked with need.

"Where'd you go?"

"We missed breakfast, and the little store next to the check-in counter was pretty bare, but I got us some only slightly expired chips, a bag of half-melted chocolate candies, and a Sprite. Not my favorite soda, but it was that or diet." He sets it all on the bed.

"You didn't have to get me anything." I grab the chips and try one. They don't taste stale, so I eat a few more.

Pan twists the top off the Sprite and takes a drink. "You need your energy, Darling." He tries a chocolate, then wrinkles his nose in distaste. "We still have two hours until check out and I'm not done with you."

I laugh. "Please don't tell me you're one of those people who hate—" My stomach rumbles. I cut myself off when a cold sweat covers my skin.

"Darling?"

Bile crawls up my throat. I only get a few seconds' warning before the chips come back up. I grab the little trash can beside the built-in desk and wretch into it.

"You okay?" Pan rubs circles on my back.

I groan and mumble *uh-huh* at the same time. My mouth tastes terrible and my head hurts, but overall I feel fine. "Yeah. That was weird."

Pan reaches for the soda and offers it to me. I feel bad taking it because it's all we have to drink, but we don't have any toothbrushes or toothpaste, and the hotel didn't leave those as complimentary items on the bathroom counter.

"Are you sure?"

"It's all yours, beautiful." He sits on the edge of the bed and watches me with hawk-like intensity. "Are you sure you're okay? Do you want to lie down for a little while?"

"I'm fine," I say semi-convincingly. Now that my stomach is empty, I honestly feel better. Maybe even a little hungry again...for something different. "I think the chips might have gone bad. Once I get some real food in my stomach I should be okay."

Pan eyes me skeptically. He questions if I'm being honest, and I wonder if this weird stomach bug is something I caught from the hospital or the lingering effects of whatever poison Cass gave me. There's no telling what it could have been made from. Neverland has some crazy plants I've never heard of.

Pan grabs what's left of my panties off the floor and picks up the rest of my clothes from the other side of the room.

"What are you doing?"

"Well, we need to get some food in you." He takes all of our dirty towels and tosses them into the bathroom. After doing a quick sweep of my room and collecting the few things I have, he walks through the adjoining door to his room.

"We might as well get on the road, too," he says loudly. I hear a zipper being pulled. There's some shuffling in his room and then the zipper is pulled again. He comes back into my half of our joined space and hands me a pair of jean shorts. "Put these on."

"Okay," I say slowly.

The dark fabric looks a little big. I check the tag and they're a size up from what I usually wear. I don't say anything. Peter—or Pan, whoever did the shopping—got everything else right so far. These were probably the only pair close to my size and in typical man fashion, he probably just assumed they'd fit. I thank him and slip them on. Shockingly, they fit. I tuck the front of my oversized shirt in and grab my shoes.

"Where do you want to eat?" he asks while I'm getting them on.

I think about it as I tie the laces. What's something I haven't eaten in a while? Something I could never get in Neverland and crave now that I'm back.

"K. Kreme donuts!" Those sound delightful right now. The warm, soft dough, covered in glaze that's sickeningly sweet would be divine. My mouth waters in anticipation, but I don't just want donuts. I want something to go with them. I just can't figure out what it is. Finally, it comes to me. "And Chinese."

Pan's eyebrows push together and he looks at me like I've got two heads. "You mean you want Chinese for breakfast and donuts for dessert?"

"No." I laugh. "Together. I think it would taste amazing together."

He hitches my duffle over his shoulder, unconvinced but takes my hand. "Whatever you say, Darling."

I don't get K. Kreme donuts.

The closest shop was forty-five minutes away. Too far for my rumbling stomach. I settled on the sugar-coated donuts the Chinese Buffet served instead. It isn't what I want per se, but it does the trick.

Pan refuses to try my bourbon tofu lo mein and donuts. Whatever. More for me, and man, do I eat.

My food pooch is so big that I have to unbutton my shorts once we got back in the car, but the bloating is worth every bite.

Since leaving the restaurant two hours ago, all Pan and I have done is sit in traffic. It's horrible. We're stuck, practically crawling on the highway doing fifteen miles per hour. At this rate, it's going to take us years to get to the Florida-Georgia line.

"I got you something." Pan reaches into the backseat and pulls out a brown paper bag.

Inside is a book I've seen but haven't read yet. I know the author, though. She writes about billionaire jerks and the badass babes who tame them.

"This novel is about a guy who fucks things up with his mate. Like royally fucks up. Way worse than Peter and I have."

I arch my eyebrows at him and flip the book over to read the blurb. "I highly doubt that. Whatever this guy, Vic, did to Millie is going to be forgiven because it's fiction. Their storyline is written that way."

"So is ours. We're written in the stars, Darling. Our fates sealed before you were born."

"You're such a nerd." I playfully punch him in the shoulder and then open up to the first page.

Pan chuckles. He grabs my hand and links our fingers together, holding it while he holds the car's shifter. "Just wait. One day, you'll stop fighting fate, and when that day comes, you'll have Neverland shaking in its boots."

CHAPTER 13

Wednesday

I must have fallen asleep at some point because the sun has set and Pan has parked in front of my parents' house. How he knows where they live is beyond me, but I don't think to ask. He knows a lot about my past. It's not shocking that my address is one of those things.

My heart is racing so fast it's hard to focus on anything but my childhood home. Mom and Dad painted while I was gone, changing the exterior from shades of sand to gray and black and re-tiling the roof to match. It almost looks like a different house, but our mailbox is still the same messed-up birdhouse I made in the third grade. I was so excited to have cut the wood during STEM class and build something. I didn't care that the birds hated it.

Until I did.

They never came. Not one. They wouldn't even fly near it. Dad must have noticed how much it hurt because he converted it into a mailbox a few weeks later. He cut a door for the front and added vinyl lettering. Horrible lettering that I hand cut because I thought using a machine or buying pre-cut letters was lame. Our last name, Roberts, was barely legible, but Mom and Dad kept it that way anyway.

My lips twitch at the memory of how mad Mom was when Dad anchored it in front of the house. She wanted something bold and chunky so they'd stop getting their neighbor's mail, and Dad gave her a handcrafted box with artistic flair. The *O* is missing, but Mom kept it just the same. If she hadn't, I'm not sure I'd have the courage to be here.

"Do you want me to go with you?"

I shake my head. This is something I need to do by myself.

I'm nervous.

I know everyone will be happy to have me home, but I can't begin to imagine the pain I've caused. It turns my stomach to try. "No. This is going to be awkward enough. Showing up with my boyfriend will make things worse."

Pan's smile reaches his eyes and it's one of the brightest I've seen either he or Peter do. It makes me warm and fuzzy inside and a little horny. If I wasn't semi-freaking out about seeing my family, I'd probably do something stupid like give him head in front of their house.

"Boyfriend?"

"Don't make a big deal out of it." I grab the door handle to get out, but Pan stops me.

"Wait." He summons his shadow magic. It seeps out of his pores like a dark mist and gathers in his palm. I watch, mesmerized. I don't think I've seen him use magic before, not like this. He takes my hand and some of the darkness slips inside me. Its cold touch twists under my skin and wraps around my arm. Dark pigment tattoos my wrist until it looks like someone has drawn a charm bracelet on me with a single pendant.

A marigold flower.

He kisses my knuckles and the darkness he wields dissipates around him. The bracelet he conjured stays on my skin, it's touch cold but not uncomfortable. "Now I will always be with you. All you have to do is call for me and I will find you."

"Why does this sound like you're leaving?" I think I might die if Pan abandons me today. I need him, not right at this moment, but in my life. My heart races and I begin to panic. I guess deep down, I knew he'd have to go back to Neverland; I just thought I had more time.

I'm not ready.

I don't want to say goodbye.

"Darling." Pan reaches up and touches my cheek. I lean into his hand and let a tear fall. I don't care about hiding them anymore. It's energy wasted since they seem to come whenever they choose. He wipes the droplet away with his thumb. "I am leaving, but not today. I will be out here the whole time, just in case you need me, waiting for the chance to be the hero of your story."

He tilts his head, signaling that it's time.

I spend the whole walk—all three minutes—trying to convince myself that turning around and running back to Pan's car is a bad idea. I owe it to my parents to let them know I'm alive and unharmed, but seeing them again is probably the scariest thing I've ever done.

I raise my fist and knock on the door and my pulse vibrates through my body with each passing second. Maybe this was a bad idea. They're going to have questions I can't answer without lying.

I suck at lying.

I forget half of what I say, get tangled up in the details, and ruin the whole thing. The few times I tried lying back in high school blew up in my face. It was better just to tell the truth.

I take a step backward, ready to retreat, when the front door opens.

Kenny's laugh carries over his shoulder. He's still looking at whoever is inside and hasn't turned to see who's on his doorstep, but his laughter cuts off when he sees me.

My ex barely looks like himself anymore. He's got a beard now, full and red, hanging past his chin. He's thicker around the middle, but I guess that's what comfort does. The thought warms my heart because it means he's happy. My sister is (hopefully) happy too. Despite what we've been through, that's all I've ever wanted for her.

"Hi," I say, my voice just above a whisper.

The color drains from his face as if it's just now sinking in that I'm standing on the porch. Maybe he thought I was a ghost, or maybe that my coming home was a crazy dream. Whatever the case, he doesn't let me in.

Time ticks awkwardly by. Seconds turn into a minute and he's still just standing there. The hand at his side shakes. His other grips the edge of the door so tightly his knuckles are white.

"You're cooling the whole freakin' neighborhood, Kenny." Tyle's voice carries across the house and out to us. She sounds tired and a little frustrated. One hundred percent my sister when she wasn't putting on a show to be the most popular girl in town.

"What's gotten into—" She freezes like Kenny did for a half second and then lets out a scream that steals the air from her lungs.

Tyle pulls me into her chest and hugs me, her big belly pressing against my stomach. "I knew it," she whispers. "No one believed me, but I knew you were alive. I could feel it in my bones that you were okay."

Tyle hasn't hugged me since before college, back when we used to pose for pictures and pretend we were best friends. Our relationship was a relationshit most days, but it was important to our parents that we got along. So, for their sake, we tried when family was around. I hug her back, unable to stop myself from crying again.

"You're so big!" I say through a laugh, looking down at her giant belly.

Tyle laughs, too. She touches her bump and looks down at it with pride. "I've got three weeks left on this little guy."

She sniffles as a tear falls down her cheek. She tries to wipe it away before I notice, but I see it and damn if it doesn't make me feel good. My sister missed me. Pride swells in my chest, then twists into something terrifying. I glance at Kenny, who stares at us, open-mouthed, and look at the tiny details of his face. At the little creases around his eyes. At the size of his belly, round from beer and comfort. He's bigger than any man should be after three weeks of being married. And it's impossible for Tyle to be this far along. *How long was I gone?*

"His sister is in the living room sleeping," she adds.

Sister? I struggle to keep myself from hyperventilating. I look over my shoulder for Pan's car, but it's nowhere to be seen. My hand instinctively goes to my wrist and brushes over my new tattoo. The skin where he marked me is colder than the rest of my wrist and for some reason, I find that comforting.

A calm wave washes over me. Pan said he wouldn't leave. He's just a thought away if I need him.

Tyle links her arm with mine and brings me into the house. It smells like cinnamon and homemade biscuits. Mom used to make the best cinnamon twists for us after school. My heart soars at the thought of her somewhere inside, continuing the tradition for Tyle's daughter after all these years.

"Kenny!" She raises her eyebrows and he seems to snap out of the trance he was in. "Close the door."

"Right." He peers out at the street, then shuts the door and locks it. "Sorry."

"Come into the kitchen." Tyle wipes her eyes and guides me through my childhood home.

Mom made some upgrades. Our fireplace has had a facelift, turning from an old brown to a chic white with a new mantel, and the wallpaper that used to line the space behind the couch is gone. She replaced our burlap-looking curtains with plantation shutters and added a new throw rug over the wood floors. All of these updates were needed, but because I wasn't around when they were done, the place feels less like the home I grew up in and more like a stranger's house.

Tyle opens the door to one of the downstairs bedrooms and puts her finger over her lips to tell me to be quiet. A tiny human sleeps in a crib, her thumb in her mouth, dark brown hair widely spread over the pillow-less mattress.

"This is Wanda," Tyle whispers. "Your niece."

I creep closer to the crib and touch the railing as I look over. She's beautiful, a near-perfect clone of her mother when she was little. "How old is she?"

"Almost three."

Three?

Tyle waves me on so we can let the girl sleep. She leaves the door cracked as we exit and wordlessly walks down the hall to the kitchen. My stomach churns inside itself again. I was gone for three years, maybe longer, depending on how quickly they got pregnant. I feel like I'm going to be sick.

I sit on a stool near the kitchen island in the center of the room. Tyle busies herself, pouring glasses of tea and fetching pretzels from the pantry and a bowl of guacamole from the fridge. I grab a pretzel in hopes that it'll settle the angry sea in my stomach. I dip it in the guac, but the smell makes me throw up in my mouth. I wrap that one in a napkin and eat a plain pretzel instead.

"Oh! I started at a new doctor's office, too," she adds, filling me in on the details of her life I missed out on. "Well, it's not new per se. Just new to me. Since I'm so far along and going to be out on maternity leave, they put me on the telehealth calls. I really like them. The other doctors hate when they have those shifts, so I might see if I can do that full-time and work from home after Weston is born."

"Where's Mom and Dad?" I blurt. I love my sister and have semi-enjoyed hearing about how much has happened in the last few years, but the anticipation of seeing my parents is eating me alive.

Tyle bites her lip. She looks beside me, to Kenny, and then lets out a heavy breath. "They died, Wednesday. About a month after you went missing."

That knot of anticipation I've been wrestling with falls to my feet.

The room tilts on its side and spins. Tyle tries to tell me about the accident, but I can't make my mind move past the fact that they're gone. They died, worrying and wondering if I was okay. What's worse, they were on their way to meet another rescue team to look for me. It was my fault. If I had come back sooner, or fought harder to make it toward the surface after going overboard, or hadn't been so hellbent on making Tyle jealous at her bachelorette party, they'd still be here.

A heavy silence fills the room and the air has shifts to darker tones. I feel it linger between us. Tyle takes the nearly empty pitcher of tea off the counter and dumps what's left in the sink. She grabs some new tea bags from a cabinet above the stove and busies herself with the task of making a new batch. I mindlessly nibble on pretzels and simply force myself to do something besides think about Mom and Dad.

"Where the fuck have you been, Wednesday?" Kenny growls, asking the question I've feared most.

A pretzel lodges itself in my throat. I cough and reach for my glass of tea. Tyle won't look at me. She stares at her hands, watching her fingers twist the hem of her shirt. I can see she wants the answer, but is scared of what I might say.

"That's not an easy question." I laugh nervously and feel terrible as soon as the sound leaves my lips.

"Yes, it is." He grips the back of my stool and turns the bench seat to make me face him. "The Coast Guard searched for you for three days, but they found nothing. No trace of your body. Not a stitch of your clothing. Nothing to indicate you were ever on that boat. Tyle felt responsible because she didn't realize you were missing until they disembarked. Everyone, and I mean everyone, was a mess."

The little vein beside his eye bulges. He's angry, but I get the feeling there's more. Things he's been bottling up that have been waiting to come out and I'm the catalyst.

"You can't just show up on our doorstep like it never happened with a bullshit excuse that the answer is complicated.

We need answers!" He exhales a breath, his voice growing louder. "I need answers!"

Wanda cries from the other room. Tyle scowls, her head shaking in disappointment. She looks at me, pleading with her eyes for me to stay. "I'll be right back."

Kenny doesn't acknowledge that she's left the room. He boxes me in, one hand on the back of my chair, the other on the counter, and glares at me, waiting for an answer.

My heart races and I blurt, "I don't know where I was, okay!"

Not exactly a lie. If someone were to give me a map, I wouldn't be able to show them where Neverland is. I couldn't tell them how I got there or how I got home. All I can do is give him tiny truths because no one would believe me if I gave them anything else.

"I was drugged and on some remote Island. I didn't know how long I was there until Tyle showed me Wanda. That's when I realized it's been years. Years of my life were stolen in a place where I never saw the sun or the moon, just glimpses of a twilight sky. I had no phone, no television. Hell, I barely had running water, and when I did, it was never hot. I ate things I've never heard of before, hoping they weren't drugged, turned out some of it was— and prayed nothing happened to me while I was unconscious."

"Wednesday..." he stutters. "I...I'm..."

"Want to know how I got back? I woke up three days ago at a hospital in Fort Lauderdale, brought in by a guy who said he found me passed out in a bar. Is that what you wanted to hear, Kenny? Do you feel better?"

Kenny stands upright, giving me back my personal space, but it's too late. Every emotion I felt when I left home comes to the surface. Every fight, every struggle, every betrayal sits on my chest. I slam my cup on the counter and excuse myself. I run to the downstairs bathroom, silently thanking the stars that Tyle didn't remodel it into something crazy, like a wine cellar, and shut myself inside.

My breaths come in erratic spurts. I can't make them steady or make myself stop shaking. Tears run down my cheeks like a faucet left wide open and I hate how much I've cried since coming home. Everything I said was true, but I wasn't prepared for how much the truth would hurt.

I thought Cass was my friend. I let him have a piece of me that I can never get back. It bonded us, even though he knew we didn't have a future. It was obvious to everyone that I had eyes for Peter, but Cass made it seem like he didn't care. He made me feel like I was special when really, he was using me even more than I was using him. I was his twisted ticket home, and he was going to cash it in, even if it meant killing me.

Someone knocks on the door. I wipe my eyes, not wanting to face anyone, but knowing it's inevitable. I don't know who I expected to see. I think I hoped Tyle was lying and that Mom would be there with open arms to pull me into a hug. And maybe I thought it might be my sister ready to tell me that her husband was a dick and that it didn't matter where I was, she was just happy to have me home.

I don't get either of them. Kenny steps into the small space as soon as the door is open, forcing me back a bit. He closes us in the bathroom together. I tense, ready to defend myself if I have to, then relax. I'm not in Neverland anymore. I can trust the people in this house.

No one here wants to hurt me.

"Wednesday." He reaches for my arm.

I flinch back, unsure of why. Kenny has never laid an ill hand on me. The pain he caused was purely emotional, but I can't control the fear. Cass damaged me. He fucked with my mind and I hadn't realized it until this moment. "Stay back." The words automatically come from my mouth.

Kenny looks at me, pale-faced. He steps back and holds his hands up, but it's too late. The bathroom door kicks open, little splinters of wood flying through the air. I jump, startled by the sound but feel Pan's presence before I see him.

Kenny turns around, fuming at the dark-haired devil that broke into his home. "Who the fuck are you?"

Pan takes one look at my tear-stained face and shoves my ex to the side. My sister's husband grabs onto the sink as he falls and somehow dislodges it from the wall. Water sprays out of the pipes. It covers the walls and falls down onto us like a midday rain.

"Come here, Darling."

I don't hesitate and throw myself into Pan's arms. I can't describe the relief I feel having him hold me but the pain of explaining what I went through and reliving each memory in my mind eases to a dull throb. Now, I'm exhausted and, thankfully, out of tears.

Pan, somehow able to read me, senses my fatigue. He lifts me into his arms and cradles me against his chest. He smells like Peter, like cedar and spice, but with modern-day soap too. And if I close my eyes, I can still find traces of Neverland—woods and magic. "Do you want to stay, Darling?"

I rest my cheek on his shoulder. He understands that I'm ready. I thought I could handle coming home, and maybe if Mom and Dad were here it would have been different, but I can't stay. It hurts too much. I need to grieve their deaths without judgmental eyes watching me, or pitying me. I can't do that here. "Take me home, Shadow."

Kenny begins to stir on the floor. Pan sees it at the same time I do and we seem to have the same thought. It's time to go.

Pan carries me even though I can walk, and I don't fight him on it. I feel safe in his arms. Nothing can touch me so long as we're together. I chastise myself because less than twenty-four hours ago, I didn't trust Pan. Now, he's the only person in this world that I do.

Tyle steps out of Wanda's room, her eyes wide with fear when she sees me being carried out of her house. "Wednesday?"

Pan walks past her, ignoring my freaked-out sister, and takes us out the door. Kenny runs after me. He tries to grab Pan by the arm, but he doesn't know he's picking a fight with a creature from another world. He doesn't stand a chance.

Pan turns and swings on instinct, effortlessly carrying me with one arm and fighting my ex. Tyle screams from the doorway when his fist collides with Kenny's face. Wanda cries in her arms. Everything is falling apart and I'm helpless to do anything but let it happen.

"Put her down," Kenny demands, rushing Pan again.

Pan throws another punch and his fist hits Kenny square in the jaw. My brother-in-law falls to the ground, nose bloodied, lip busted, and this time, he stays there.

"I know you," Tyle says, her voice hardening. She steps off the front porch more certain the longer she stares. "You're him. The guy from the boat." She sets Wanda on the floor, ignoring her cries, and runs after Pan. She beats her fists against his back and claws at his shirt as he carries me to the car.

"No!" she screams. "You're not taking her again. You're not taking the only family I have left."

Guilt gnaws at my insides, but I'm paralyzed both physically and emotionally. I hide my face, ashamed that I'm not standing up to my demons and telling Pan to let me stay, but the truth is I don't want to.

I don't want to look my sister in the eye and see the resentment.

I don't want to walk around my parents' house, haunted by their ghosts.

I don't want to see Kenny live out his happy-ever-after while mine is postponed due to circumstances that stretch beyond this world.

All I want to do is leave.

Leave my sister.

Leave my childhood home.

And go back to Neverland.

Wednesday

I stare out the window as we drive away.

The world moves past us in a blur of colors, but I don't care enough to look at where we're going. I just want to leave.

My heart cracks open with each mile we drive and the guilt swallows me whole. My parents are dead. They never got to meet Wanda and will never see their newest grandchild, Weston. They'll never meet Peter or Pan. I won't get to walk down the aisle with my father or have one last dance with him. I don't even know if he was there for Tyle on her big day.

Our car stops moving and I focus my gaze on the landscape in front of me, actually making the effort to see where we are. An acre of bright green grass decorated with thousands of marble and slate headstones awaits. My heart pounds in my chest and a cold sweat breaks out across my skin. Pan opens my door and a vice squeezes my chest. I can't take a deep breath. I try and try and each bit of air my lungs grasp is smaller and smaller.

"Darling." Pan grabs my arms. "Easy, love, you're getting yourself worked up."

I can't hear what he says. The sound of my heartbeat in my

ears drowns everything else out. The light around him starbursts. I'm shaking and hyperventilating and...*oh my god, my parents are dead*!

"Darling?" Pan cups my cheeks. I look up at him, but all I see are silhouettes cast in shadow. He feels so far away and the tunnel to make my way to him is narrowing. I think I might puke or pass out or...

Pan kisses me and everything goes quiet.

I close my eyes and let him take me away from the darkness, let the layers of the world pull back until all that's left is him. Pan's lips pull me out of my mind and back to him, where nothing matters but us.

"Found you," he whispers, pulling away. I look into his eyes and almost cry when I see one is blue. I have both Peter and Pan, the two halves of my soul together again. Even though it only lasts a moment, that one second feels like home.

The blue iris is swallowed by darkness and I'm left with Pan. The strange shadow man I wanted to hate, but somehow ended up falling for. I'd laugh if I weren't on the verge of crying again. If I were planning to stay in this realm, I think therapy might be good for me. I've fallen too hard, too fast, for men I have no business being with too many times.

"Are you all right, Darling?"

My gaze drifts past my dark-haired savior to the entrance of the cemetery. I assume this is where my parents are. How Pan knows is beyond me, but I don't want to ask. I'd rather assume his magic led us here than go down the darker paths my mind strays toward.

"You need to see them. It'll help."

I shake my head. I can't go there, not if I want to hold on to the paper-thin shred of strength I have left. Seeing their names in the granite would be the straw that breaks me. "Take me away from here, Shadow."

Pan sits on his heels, the name I've only used a few times,

cutting deep. I feel his sorrow as deeply as I feel my own. I look down at the tattooed bracelet on my wrist and finally understand its purpose. It's not just a mark to remind me of him, it links us, broadcasting my emotions and possibly even my thoughts. Pan felt my fear in the bathroom at Tyle's house, which is why he barged in to save me.

He didn't know what was wrong. All he knew was I needed him.

And he came.

"Where should we go, Darling?"

"Neverland. I don't want to be here anymore."

"Shh, you don't mean that."

"I do! I can't have my only family be Tyle!" The car closes in on me again and it feels smaller and smaller the longer I sit. Pan instinctively takes my hand and helps me out of it. He pulls me into his arms and a fresh wave of overwhelming sadness has me burying my face in his chest. "You don't know what it's like to have a sister like her."

He threads his fingers through my hair, running them from my scalp to the ends, trying to soothe me. "I know that she has never fought for you before today. Her attempt was pathetic, but it was something."

He uses his magic to draw my eyes upwards. I hate that he's seen so many tears running down my face in such a short amount of time. I've never been this person, someone who cries at the slightest of things and emotionally spirals out of control. Tyle was dramatic enough for the both of us and I always thought she was stupid for feeling so deeply. I understand now that she couldn't help herself. These feelings are literally exploding out of me. I don't want to be this pathetic, emotional disaster, but I can't make the tears stop. They're just there, doing their thing, as steadily and consistently as my beating heart.

"Give her a chance. You're all she has now, too."

"She has Kenny," I mumble bitterly.

Pan chuckles, the sound light as air, and kisses my forehead. He shifts my body to be under his arms and we start walking. I bristle until we go in a different direction, toward the sidewalk and not the gravestones.

He takes me to an ice cream store two blocks away. The bell over the door rings when we step inside. A woman comes out from around the corner and greets us with a smile. "Afternoon. What can I get you lovely folks?"

I scan the menu. Everything looks delicious and it hits me that it's been years since I had ice cream, not weeks. I've been dairy-sensitive since I was a kid. It tears up my stomach if I have too much, but a little here and there never hurt too bad. I chew on my lip and weigh my options. There's so much I want, but destroying a public bathroom or, worse, the small one of a hotel room would be mortifying. "Can I get your dairy-free vanilla in a small cup?"

"Sure." She lifts the glass door, encasing all the flavors up, and scoops a large sphere of ice cream into a paper cup. "Do you want to mix anything in it?"

"I can do that?" There only used to be one ice cream store, a chain-type place, that did customized mix-ins. I perk up and look at my topping options. "I want to add cookie dough pieces and caramel drizzle."

The woman makes my ice cream and hands it over. I take a bite and it's like an orgasm in my mouth. I forgot how amazing ice cream tasted. I can't even tell it's dairy-free.

"And for you, sir?"

"Vanilla."

"Do you want to add any toppings?"

"Nope." Pan looks at me and winks. "It's my favorite flavor."

I choke on a lump of cookie dough. My gaze jumps to Pan's eyes, hoping to get a glimpse of deep blue again. There's not even a speck within the shades of gray and black, but there is a lot more brown. He has a ring of gold surrounding the darkness that wasn't there before.

Pan pays for our treat with a credit card and then hands it to me. "Here"

"What's this for?"

"You're going to need money while I'm gone. Spend whatever you need. There's enough to last ten lifetimes."

I spoon a scoop of ice cream into my mouth and shake my head. "I don't want it."

He tucks the card into my back pocket and grins. "Who says you have a choice?"

I roll my eyes. Yesterday, I would have been angry with him for trying to control the situation. Today, I feel no ill will through the bond. Every threat, even those made with the straightest of faces, was playful. I don't think Pan knows how to tease, but I can tell this is his way of trying.

We walk down the sidewalk and look at displays in the shop windows. We don't buy anything, but it's fun to look at anyway. Eventually, we reach the end of the little plaza and head back toward the car. I toss my empty ice cream cup in a nearby trash and let the silence fill the gaps between us. Pan doesn't seem to notice, but my mind is racing. The closer we get to the cemetery, the heavier this weight feels.

"I mean what I said, I want to go back." I steal a glance at Pan from the corner of my eye. He doesn't look at me. I'm glad. I don't think I could tell him what I'm going through if he did. "I don't feel right being here. My skin aches and my chest feels hollow. The only time I don't feel out of place is when I'm with you and you're leaving."

Pan sighs, letting out a heavy breath. "I can't bring you back, Darling, not until it's safe."

I bite my bottom lip, struggling with what to do. Peter blatantly asked me if I knew who was behind my poisonings and I didn't say anything. I'm scared Pan will be angry with me for keeping a secret. His brows furrow and I realize I'm sending some big emotions through our bond. He waits patiently for me to explain the fear and nervousness. I take another minute, trying to build my confidence, and say, "What if I could help?"

"The only way you could help is if you know who wants you dead." He laughs humorously, as if that notion is impossible, but as the silence thickens again, his smile falls. He knows I'm hiding something. I can feel his curiosity. "Is there something you're not telling me?"

"Yes…"

"Wednesday!"

"I'm sorry, but I haven't decided if I could live with his blood on my hands."

"He tried to kill you. Twice!" Pan runs his fingers through his hair and stares up at the sky. He's angry, so terribly angry, but trying to calm himself so he doesn't blow up at me.

"He had a good reason," I say sheepishly. Trying to justify what Cass did to me is like trying to explain the logic of a revenge murderer. I may sympathize with what brought him to that place of desperation, but it doesn't absolve his actions. Cass needs to be taught a lesson. I just don't want that lesson to cost him his life.

"Being Belle's huntsman isn't a good enough reason."

Wait, who? "Belle? Like Tinkerbelle?"

Pan nods. "Tinkerbelle is the single worst thing to happen to Neverland. She is behind ninety percent of my problems."

"And the other ten percent?" The *thump, thump, thump* of my heart tells me I already know the answer. It's me. I'm the second-largest problem in his life. Always fretting if I'm safe. Always wondering if our relationship's damage runs deeper than our lust can heal. In the silence that stretches between us, I meet his gaze and his truths are all over his face.

The worry.

The regret.

The love.

"I'll let you know once you tell me who hurt you. It will save a lot of time and unnecessary pain if you'd just tell me which pirate she has under her thumb."

It never occurred to me that Peter would venture into the Cove to hunt for my attacker. It should have because he won't look at the Lost. They're his friends. His family. He'll never see the betrayal coming. "It was Cass."

"That motherfucker." Pan turns to a nearby tree and slams his fist into it. The trunk splits down the center from the base of its branches all the way to the roots, allowing warm light to spill through the newfound opening. He curses under his breath about balancing nature, then holds his hands to the broken bark. His dark magic surrounds the tree to heal it. It only takes seconds to fix what he broke, but once the shadows thin and return to him, Pan looks miserable, almost as bad as Peter did in the hospital and he sways on his feet.

I reach out to steady him, scared he's going to fall out. "Are you okay?"

"Don't touch me!" Pan jumps back before I can comfort him.

My heart shatters because I don't understand what I did wrong. Sure, I kept a secret for a few hours, but does that justify the surge of anger and him retreating like this? I feel as if Pan has cut me deeper than Peter ever did. A strangled sound leaves my throat as I try to breathe and hold back my pain.

Pan sees me struggling and curses under his breath. "Damn it, Darling. I'm sorry," he says with a sigh. "It's not you. This is all me. If you touch me I could hurt you and that's the last thing I want to do."

"How? You touch me all the time."

"I'm what the Fae call a Reaper. It's my job to keep the balance between life and death. Right now, I'm emotional and weak from healing the tree. I don't know if I can control myself and touching you isn't worth the risk."

I chose to focus on the life part of what he says, not the death. I can't think about how many people he may have killed being a Reaper or how many lives he probably took in the hospital when he mentioned feasting on the souls the doctors could bring him. I don't want to think of him as something dark or evil. So, I choose not to. "You keep the Island alive."

"And as many souls on it as I can. There, my power is endless, but here...every breath I take fights my purpose. To survive here with you I have to take years from others' lives. Years they'll never know are missing, but are gone nonetheless."

"And you do that by touch."

He nods. "A bump here. The brush of a hand there. Little by little, I keep myself alive, conscious of what I'm taking because I never let myself get weak enough to lose control."

"Peter didn't..."

Pan shakes his head. "He wouldn't let me feed our body. When he blacked out, I walked through the hospital searching for those who were in the most pain, the people who were ready to move on but whose families wouldn't let go and took what was left of their lives until I was strong enough to control the hunger. The thing that made me..." Pan looks out at the gravestones. "That monster is death himself. A creature created for the sole purpose of ending lives."

I look at him incredulously. "Are you saying the god of death, Hades, made you?"

"I'm saying that the thing that made me, as well as many others, can be found throughout your history. Their names change with each culture, but their purpose remains true. The Grim Reaper, Hades, Osiris, and Odin were all of Fae descent. Each of them was a reaper who fed off the living to have immortality."

"So, something came and took my parents from me? Something like you?" I'm angry again. If there is a monster living in this town, stealing the lives of innocent people just to prolong its own, I want it dead. I want to hunt it down and kill it myself for taking away the people I love.

"Your parent's accident was tragic, but a Reaper did not cause it. What a Reaper did was come and ease their suffering. They created a calmness in their minds and helped them pass into the next life."

"And stole the years they should have had left."

"Yes."

"I think I'm going to be sick."

"Would you rather they suffered? Slipped into a coma, kept alive by machines for years while stuck in the between, waiting for a death that might not come?"

I think about my time lost in the between. It was cold and empty of any signs of life. There was no way to tell time or determine how many days were lost. It was an endless prison where I was stuck in my mind, reliving every moment, both good and bad, over and over again until I regained consciousness. "No. I guess not."

"Our job isn't easy, but we are helping people. Not hurting them."

I feel a little better knowing someone was there to take their pain away, but the sting of their passing is still fresh. It's hard to separate my anger for the creature that stole their final breath from Pan. They are the same species. The same type of monster. "So, you've never stolen years from someone who wasn't dying?"

Pan lets the silence hang between us as he walks to the car and leans against the hood. "No."

Well, that wasn't very clear. I need to know if the man whose dick was inside me this morning is a good person or not. I moved past the murderous aspect of our relationship because it was only my life, but if he's taken others...others who had many healthy years left with no natural cause for it to be shortened...I don't think I could let that go "No you haven't or no you have?"

Anger simmers in the tether that binds us. I don't think it's directed toward me. I don't know how I know; an instinctual feeling, I guess. Whoever it is toward, it's lethal. "No, I have."

"What the fuck?" I yell! I can't believe it. He's a killer. A cold-blooded killer. "Pan!"

"No!" He's up and in my face with a swiftness only Neverland's magic can create. Darkness clouds his aura, seeping from his skin in a thin mist. Pan is so close his breath heats my cheeks, but he doesn't touch me. "Do you remember Mr. Banefield?"

"The man who used to live across the street from us? He died of a heart attack." I rear back, shocked. I always thought it was weird a thirty-four-year-old man could die that young. When we went to the funeral his family was as surprised, too. They said he was in perfect health, never even had a cavity. "Was that you?"

"Yes."

Gods damn it. Of course, it was. He literally told me he'd been a shadow in my life since I was a kid. He needs human life to exist. I just don't understand, "Why him?"

"Because he was obsessed with you!" Pan roars. "That man had pictures of you and your sister in his room. Hundreds of them. He would watch you play and…" Pan growls deep in his throat, his eyes darkening even more than I thought possible. "He was a bad man with bad intentions. I killed him because he wanted to hurt you, just like I killed others I found who were like him."

Fucking hell, Pan.

If that's true, how can I hate you for saving me? Can I really crucify you for helping to rid the world of pedophiles and creeps? I guess with him life isn't just black and white. It's shades of gray and everything in between.

"I don't care if you hate me. Your world is a better place without that twisted fuck. Now, if you'll excuse me, I need to feed." He tosses me the keys from his pocket. I catch them, barely, and stare at the ring.

Panic festers under my skin. I can't drive a stick shift. I need him for so much more than just to drive a car, but, frankly, I really do need him for that. "Where are you going?"

"I don't know." He tucks his hands into his pockets and heads back to the plaza we'd just left.

"Where am I supposed to go?" I call after him. I hope he can feel the desperation I'm drowning in through our bond. He can't abandon me, not here. Take me to a hotel or someplace safe, then let me go.

Don't.

Just.

Leave.

Pan stops walking, his shoulders slumping forward. He feels it. I know he does, but it's not enough to bring him back. "Doesn't matter. As long as your heart is beating, I'll find you. Perks of being soulmates, Darling. It might take a while, but we'll end up together one way or another."

CHAPTER 15

Wednesday

I pace the floor of my newly rented hotel room. My thumbnail is chewed down to nearly nothing. Every time I stick it in my mouth and search for more to bite, my finger stings, aching in protest, but I can't help it.

I'm stressing, freaking the fuck out, because Pan has no idea where I am.

I got the closest hotel within walking distance to his car—that I may have left parked in the cemetery—but I'm still worried we're too far away from each other. I don't know how this shadow bond works or how strong our tether is. Can he feel my worry if he's down the street? Across town? On the other side of the world?

How about in a different realm?

I open the door, hoping to see him walking down the hallway to me, but there's no one out there. The ugly green carpet doesn't even have a discarded dinner tray. It's completely empty. My anxiety creeps higher and higher. My hands already won't stop shaking, and it's only been a few hours.

How am I supposed to survive when he leaves me behind?

I don't know why I'm so worked up. Pan's disappearance should be at the bottom of the list of things my brain can be hyper-focusing on. If I was to be thinking of him at all, it should be how he's out there robbing people of precious years.

I wonder if they can feel when he takes from them. Do they become tired and fall asleep? Do they get a headache and take medicine to alleviate the ache? Or is the process painless to where the affected don't even notice?

I flip the security lock so the door stays propped open, close it as much as the lock allows, and then fall onto the bed. I try to think about something else, anything else, but my mind is restless. After staring at the ceiling for ten minutes, I give up and take a shower to pass the time.

Standing under the water, and letting it fall over my head and down my face, I can almost imagine I'm back in my bathroom at the treehouse. It makes it easier to pretend I'm in Neverland again like this, waiting for Peter to come home after a long day of searching for newly resurrected magical creatures. I hated how he would leave me alone for hours, but I loved when he would come back to me.

"Thinking of me?"

Fear has my fist shooting out on instinct. The moment my hand collides with skin, my brain recognizes Pan's voice. It hits me again how much Cass has fucked with my mind. I hadn't realized how traumatized I was until Kenny tried to touch me. Mix my near assault on Pan into the equation, and it's safe to say I've got some shit to work through.

"Oh, my god, Pan. I'm so sorry."

"Relax, Darling. Didn't even hurt." He tilts his chin upwards to show me the nonexistent red mark from my attack. His skin is flawless. Absolutely perfect.

I punch him in the shoulder—on purpose this time—and cross my arms. "Where have you been? I was worried about you."

"I had some business to take care of."

"You mean lives to steal." I shut the water off and shiver. I hate the cold. My body isn't built for it. My nipples pucker and I love how Pan's gaze darts down to my chest, though I'll never tell him. I grab a towel and begin drying myself, starting with the girls. "Do you feel better now? Less murderous."

"I feel something." Pan rips the towel from me and throws it on the floor. My hands shoot above my head all on their own and press against the wall. My feet spread a little more than hip-width apart. He smirks approvingly. "Want to find out what that is?"

Pan knows what my answer will be. He drops to his knees, hands settling on my hips, and dips between my legs. "You have no idea how hard it was not to touch you when you were in Neverland. The fact that you couldn't be mine made me crave you even more than I already do. But to feel your worry through our bond." He kisses the inside of my thigh. "Your desire. It's more than I can bear."

Pan finds my center and sucks my folds into his mouth. His tongue is fire against my skin and I melt into the warmth. He eats me, feverishly working to bring me to my knees while magically keeping me upright. I try to fight against the sensation. For some reason, my body's response is to pull away. The fact that I can't intensifies everything.

"I'm still mad at you," I say through heavy breaths. Pan kisses the inside of my thigh again. He presses two fingers inside me, and if it weren't for his magical bond holding me upright, I'd be a puddle on the floor.

"I'm sorry," he says, his voice dropping to a husky growl. "Forgive me?"

I forgave him the moment he walked through the door. I think the ease I felt earlier had nothing to do with my shower and everything to do with our souls finding each other again. The world could fall to pieces around Pan, and I'd feel safe and completely satiated with life because he creates a level of comfort inside me that's incomparable. My only complaint would be that I haven't had enough time to enjoy him—a fixable problem with an easy solution.

"Yes," I pant, riding the rush of my climax. I'm putty in this man's hands and he knows it. Hell, he could probably blink in my direction and my panties would be wet.

Pan peppers kisses along my side up to the swell of my breasts. He then sucks my nipple in his mouth, playing with it, licking it while teasing the other one between his fingers.

"Shadow." I thread my fingers through his hair and pull his mouth off my chest. I need to feel him. His hands aren't enough and his mouth only leaves me hungry. I physically ache inside and there is only one way to alleviate the pain.

Pan's smile is feral, his thoughts not far from mine. "Tell me what you want, Darling," he says, looking into my eyes. His black irises are more honey brown than any other color, and I can't figure out why, but at this moment, I can't bring myself to care. I don't feel bad craving Shadow anymore because Peter is within him somewhere. When I have one, I will always have the other.

My Peter Pan.

"I want you," I tell him truthfully. "Always." I kiss him, just enough to leave him hungry. I want him to feel the same desire I'm drowning in, and not because it's traveling through our bond. "And forever." Another chaste kiss.

Pan grabs my thighs and lifts me, a deep growl vibrating low in his throat. My legs wrap around him and the spell on my limbs breaks. My hands can't find his body fast enough. I touch every inch of him, committing the hard edges of his body to memory because I know this is our goodbye. Something in him is changing. I can see it just as much as I can feel it. I know he can't stay.

But I don't want him to go.

Pan unbuckles his belt with one hand while effortlessly holding me against the tiles with the other. His pants fall to his feet and I don't hesitate to make him mine or ask for a condom. I'm ready. I want to feel every inch of him without a barrier between us.

Pan grants my wish, lowering me onto him and pushing inside me in such a way he's both forceful and tender all at once. The way he moves, the way his lips hunger for my body, this is more than fucking. He's claiming me and I'm not ashamed to admit that I am his.

Forever his.

And he is mine.

Pan grips the back of my neck and uses gravity to drive himself deeper. I cry out his name, *Pan, Pan, Pan* as my back grinds into the wall, filled with more pleasure than should be inhumanly possible.

"God, Wednesday," he says. I kiss his shoulders, his neck, anything I can reach. My moans of pleasure echo in the small space and I almost don't hear him when he whispers, "I love you." He kisses my neck and I shiver, possibly from the words more than the touch. "I love you so much it hurts."

My body comes alive with tingles at his admission and I come again. Pan finishes inside me shortly after my release. He holds my body against his chest, probably coming down from our mingled waves of emotions. I fold around him until he grows tired of holding me and sets me on my feet.

"I mean it." Pan tugs his shirt off and reaches to restart the water. "I do. I love you and not because you're my soulmate, or Wendy's reincarnation, or because Peter wants me to. I love you because of who you are." He pulls me into his chest and looks down into my eyes. "I love your beautiful soul. Your willingness to forgive. Your patience. I love you for your ability to simply be you."

"Thank you." I don't want to say it back, not like this, in some dingy hotel shower post sex.

I know it's silly, but I always hoped for some grand gesture like you see in the movies. Kenny is the only other man to say those words to me and the first time they left his lips he was drunk. He didn't remember saying them the next day, or maybe he did and regretted it. When he finally coherently said those three little words, the romanticism of the experience was lost.

Pan takes a step back, realizing I'm not going to return the sentiment, and washes himself. He hands me a towel once we're done cleaning up and I hate the tension builds between us as the night carries on. Even as we lay in bed, pretending to be a normal couple and watching a movie, I can hear the *tick tick tick* of time slipping away.

Pan glances out the window, a frown tugging at his lips, then tries to focus on the television again, but he's a man divided.

"What's wrong?"

"I don't know." Pan sighs and walks to the window. He draws the curtains and stares up at the night sky. "But something isn't right in Neverland. It's calling to me."

"You should go."

Pan looks over his shoulder at me, his face a mix of emotions. "You're right, I should. Doesn't mean I want to, though." He grabs my hand and draws me into him, kissing me so tenderly and with such love that I don't know how to respond. My heart breaks because this truly is our kiss goodbye.

Tears well in my eyes when we break away. "I need you to know why I didn't say it back."

Pan's gaze softens when he looks at me. I wish the love I see eased the pain of goodbye but, if anything, it makes the sting worse because I know leaving is just as hard for him as it is for me.

Maybe even harder.

"You don't need to say anything. I know what's in your heart." He runs his thumb over my dark tattoo. "Remember?"

I nod and swallow the lump in my throat. "Okay. Good, but you need to know I won't say it until you come back. I'm holding those words in my heart so you don't forget me."

"Darling." He holds me in his arms. "I could never forget you." I relish in his warmth and the way his magic wraps around me like a blanket. The cold feels like dewdrops on a spring day. Beautiful. A little annoying. But magical.

"Will you see me off?"

I shake my head and nuzzle into his chest. "That's probably a bad idea. When it comes to the moment you actually fly away, I can't promise I won't beg and plead for you to stay."

"I would. In a heartbeat."

"I know, and I can't ask that from you. The Lost might be in danger. They might need you." I step out of his arms and sit on the bed, my back to the door. I know that if I watch him go, I'll follow. The chord that links us together will pull tight and I won't be able to stop myself from trying to make him stay. "Go. At the very least, you have Cass to deal with."

Pans face hardens. "Yes. Him." He glances out the window again. His jaw ticks with frustration at whatever is pulling him away. He's silent, fighting a war within himself.

"If I don't go now..." He lets the sentence trail off. I understand what he's not saying.

I stand again and kiss him on the cheek. Pan reaches for me, to pull me into him once more, but I dodge the embrace. It's time to cut the cord and let him go. Besides, it's only for a few days. I can survive a few days on my own. I lived for years without him in my life. This won't be easy, but it will be doable.

I walk to the bathroom and shut myself in it. I slide down the door and bury my face in my hands. I don't need to look into the room to know the moment Pan leaves. I feel his departure as an anxiety attack wraps itself around me. My heart thuds in my chest as my soul fights to chase after its other half.

This ache is unlike any pain I've ever felt. It runs deeper than the hurt from losing my parents or the bite of betrayal love has repeatedly given me. The pain twists itself around my spine, seeping venom into my blood until the world is nothing but shades of gray.

Something inside my chest snaps and the pain is as real as if my bones were breaking. I scramble to the mirror and lift my shirt. Every movement, every breath is excruciating. I don't see any marks in my chest or back. There is no sign of physical damage to my body.

But it hurts. So. Bad.

I open the bathroom door and make my way to the bed. The room has the beautiful scent of earth, sage, and morning dew. The perfect mixture of both Peter and Pan. I lay on the mattress and hug Pan's pillow to my chest and my finger brushes against the tattoo he left me with.

I wonder where in the night sky he is and if he's crossed into Neverland yet. I hope he can't feel how much it hurts to be left behind, even though I know it had to be done. I don't know how far our bond stretches, but I hope he's out of reach.

I don't want him to know what it feels like to have a broken heart.

CHAPTER 16

Pan

Leaving Wednesday is the hardest thing I've ever done.

My darkness fights to stay with her. It pulls, kicks, and claws at the threads of her realm. It pleads with my body, doing everything in its power to return to my other half. I wonder if this is what it felt like for Peter when his soul split from his body and became me.

Agony.

I soar through the sky, fighting the urge to turn back with every star I pass. The only thing that keeps me going is knowing I'll be back for her in a day. Two tops.

Cass is no match for me. His powers are weak from lying dormant all these years. All I have to do is find his ass and he'll be dust in the wind, and then I can bring our Darling back.

My heart hangs heavy when the bridge between Neverland and Wednesday's world comes into view. The moment I cross into Neverland, I'll never feel her again. Her lips will belong to my other half and I'll be in the backseat watching them live out their lives together, forced to feel their emotions secondhand, like a reader and their favorite book.

It will be torture.

But I'd rather be an active bystander in their lives than nothing at all.

"Get ready, old friend," I say to Peter as the veil between our world and hers draws nearer.

I hesitate for a moment to take the last breath I'll breathe. Once I cross over, I won't just be losing the chance to be with Wednesday, I won't be human anymore. I'll never smell the crisp scent of ocean air or taste the cold sweetness of ice cream. I'll never feel the fullness of air in my lungs or the warmth of another hand in mine.

The temptation to abandon Neverland and be selfish is almost as strong as my desire to stay with Wednesday. I could easily do it, live out the rest of her life in Peter's body, saving souls from suffering.

A scream breaks through the barrier between our worlds. I react, the pull to save whoever is in need jarring me out of my selfish indulgences. I soar through the bridge, prepared to be sent back into darkness and kicked out of this body, but I stay in control.

"Peter?" I think to him. I flex the fingers on his hands, waiting for him to take over, but his resistance doesn't come.

My mind is my own. Empty. Void of any traces of my other half.

"Peter!" I demand as I soar above the clouds.

He's quiet and that makes me worry. He should have regained control. I've never lived in his body for this long after crossing over. I draw my magic inside myself and search for a sign of life, but there's nothing. Peter is gone.

A cannonball shoots up at me from a ship below. The force of air whooshing by me throws me off balance. I tumble in the air, narrowly missing a flock of seagulls. I find my footing after a handful of somersaults and soar higher into the thicker tufts of cloud.

"Come down, little brother. We need to have a chat!" James yells from below.

I call to the sea, wanting to make waves for the old codfish. I would love to see his boat topple over and for him to be drenched like the rat he is. I hate the man. I would have killed him off years ago, but he's the only being on this island that Peter has shown attachment to.

I don't know why.

All James has done is aid Belle in destroying Neverland. He's hunted souls for her to feed on, growing her powers in the process. He is the singular reason why that bitch is alive, and she's the reason Peter's Wendy died.

"Peter!" James yells. The boom of another cannon sounds and a ball whooshes past me on the right.

I clear my throat and test a few words, trying to muster a dialect that resembles my other half. "You expect me to play nice when you're trying to kill me, brother? That's bad form if I say so myself."

He shoots another round and misses by a mile. If I didn't know the man, I'd say he was missing me on purpose. "Where's the girl, Peter?"

I fly down and land on his ship. "If you kill me, you'll never know," I taunt. Even if he leaves me alive, I'll never tell him. I'd rather die than aid in that crazy bitch's plan to rule Neverland. She'll suck the Island's magic dry and turn our home into a wasteland.

"I don't want to kill you," James says beneath his breath.

I see the conflict on his face. It's puzzling because I've never noticed it before. He blindly follows Belle's orders, but today he's at war with himself. *Odd*.

"You'd have been dead long ago if that were the case." He laughs humorously, but his shoulders fall forward. The man looks tired, a feeling I've never personally experienced until this weekend with Wednesday. I sympathize—another new emotion for me—and sit on the forecastle railing. James climbs the steps from the deck to be beside me. "I have no choice but to try, brother."

"That Fae bitch's claws run deep?"

"You have no idea." He turns his head and I can see bite marks along his neck. Reapers steal time, but the rest of the Fae steal lives. They need the blood of the living to stay young. A few drops will satisfy their thirst, but most are wicked and kill for the fun of it, spilling enough to live for years, tasting as many souls as possible.

"She's safe."

"She'll never be safe," he says solemnly.

I don't waste my breath arguing. Belle will never have our Darling. I'll die before even a drop of her blood is spilled.

James's shoulders slump forward. He's a defeated man. Broken. Trapped in a meaningless existence. I growl, not liking these new revelations. In my eyes, James has always been an enemy, but to Peter, his brother is kin to a victim. I don't like it. Makes it harder to want to see him dead.

The smells of ash and cedar tickle my nose. I search the horizon for the origin. Neverland burns as large plumes of smoke rise into the air. How did I miss that when I flew in? More importantly, why can't I feel the Island crying out to me?

"She'll burn the Island to ash looking for her." James pulls a sword from his sheath and hands it to me.

I have no need for weapons. The Island and my magic have always been more than enough, but a strange tickling sensation in the back of my mind urges me to take it. I do, without a word of thanks, and shoot up into the sky. I fly toward the treehouses and to the souls I've kept hidden all of these years, pleading to the gods I'm not too late.

My home is on fire. Bright red flames lick each house that Peter built. My hands may not have physically twisted each branch and mudded each wall, but I feel ownership of it.

Our reservoir that holds the dirty water from our bathrooms is dry. I reach for the clouds, calling to the sky to put the fire out, but it doesn't respond. Like the ocean that ignored my calls to rock James' boat, the Island isn't listening.

I groan, frustrated, because I don't know how to stop the flames from taking over. I grab fistfuls of dirt and throw them on a nearby lick of fire but it does nothing. I snap a few fronds of an unburnt palm and fly to the water. I dunk them and then drop them on a roof, hoping it will make even the slightest of differences, but all it does is create more smoke.

I cough and a memory deep in Peter's mind tickles my consciousness. Smoke inhalation is just as deadly as fire. It hits me that my souls, the Lost, could be trapped inside somewhere, dying.

I fly to the nearest treehouse, not caring about how I now have a body that can burn, and make my way to the porch. Heat sears my flesh, but I fight through the pain and kick in the door. The walls are orange with fire lights. Dark smoke fills the air, trapped inside by a ceiling that hasn't yet collapsed.

"Xyris," I call out while walking from room to room, searching his house for any sign of life. My relief that it's empty is short-lived. The roof falls into in the bedroom. Pieces of the floorboard break away and fall to the ground. His house is collapsing, taking everything he owns with it. I feel sorry for the loss of his treasure, but grateful his life isn't among them.

I use the opening in the roof to fly out of the hut, ignoring the burn of the flames as they lick my arms and legs. I fly to the next house and comb through it as thoroughly as I did the first. I search for my friends and then move on to another once I'm convinced the house is clear. One by one, I double-check that my friends are safe.

The last treehouse is the worst. The fire's flames are so hot they're blue. I shouldn't go in it; Peter's body is already blistering, but I can't shake the guilt already festering about not searching *every* treehouse. I fly around it twice, searching for a way inside that won't lead to my own death. There's a window on the back half engulfed in flames, where the fire is only shades of red.

I raise my arm to protect my face and break through the glass. The air turns to steam in my lungs. I can barely see, let alone breathe, but still manage to call out. "Hello? Is anyone there?"

Smoke surrounds me. I crouch low to the floor. Everything is shadowed or burnt. I can't see shit, but I do my best to make my way through the house. I find Aria huddled on the shower floor. The fire somehow hasn't touched her, but it's close.

"Aria?" I shake her shoulders and tap her cheek, but her eyes won't open.

Something falls in the other room. If I had to guess, I'd say it was either part of the ceiling or the floor. Whatever the case, it's not good.

I lift Aria's unconscious body into my arms and the pressure of her skin against mine has my knees buckling. Peter's body is teetering on the brink of exhaustion. It smells of charred clothes and burnt hair. His pants have caught fire, melted in places, and sticks to his legs. His shirt is a barely there thread, holding on by microfibers. But every bit of pain we suffer is worth it because knowing that our family is safe is all that matters. Aria's death would have been on my conscience if I hadn't searched for her. I couldn't live with that. I don't know why the Island is rejecting me, but it's still my job to keep it and the people we love safe.

I look around at what's left of her treehouse. There's no clear exit, and every second I stand here searching for a way out, the fire grows bigger. Smoke fills my lungs and this body doesn't like it. I cough and cough. Unable to free myself from the dark noose that's wrapped around me. Spots cloud my vision. Peter's body can't take much more, and I can't reach my magic to heal him.

I run toward the nearest wall and leap. I turn my back to it, so I go through the flames first and shield Aria as best as possible. I feel each bite of the fire and the razor-sharp sting of wood as it splinters into me. I feel the air try to lick my wounds and fail to lift us out of danger as we fall onto the ember-covered ground.

I land first, taking the brunt of the fall. The wind is knocked from my lungs and, for a brief moment, I wonder if this is what it feels like to die. The pain of doing something as simple as catching my breath ravages every neuron inside me, but I don't let it take control. I roll onto my side and force my legs to carry us away from the flames. I fall to my knees the moment it's safe and lay Aria on the ground.

I touch her blistered cheeks, terrified that I'm too late. I hate when people die. The curse of the Reaper is to see what their lives should have been. Absorbing their years is to absorb their future. Each life I've taken weighs on me. Their shadow lives haunt my dreams. It's why I chose to stay in Neverland. Here I have the power to ward off death, but I can't give life.

"Aria!" I cry out. She doesn't respond.

I place my ear to her chest and by the grace of the gods and all the stars in the sky, it beats. The sound is quieter than a breeze passing through a meadow, but it's there. I beg my powers to wrap around Aria and heal her body. The dark shadows I carry don't respond. They stretch, just out of reach, to where I can see them but aren't close enough to wield.

I beat my fists against the ground. Frustrated. Pissed that Peter won't return. It's his fault my powers are fading. I'm not meant to exist like this. I rummage through Peter's memories, searching for a sign of what to do, until I find an ancient lesson on CPR.

I watch the scene play out like a movie in my mind. The details are as crisp as if they were played on the television in Wednesday's hotel room. I pinch Aria's nose and breathe clean air into her lungs, then press on her chest, grasping at strands of hope that I can push the smoke out of her body.

I breathe and push, and breathe and push, refusing to accept that I've failed.

Aria gasps. Her eyes fly open and she coughs. I roll her onto her side and pat her back, helping to clear her lungs and the relief I feel can't be described.

Aria sits upright. Her breaths are shallow and labored but her lungs move on their own. She looks at me, eyes wide.

"Peter?" she says and the fear in her voice would have sent me to my knees if I wasn't already on the ground.

Something falls over my face. I'm pushed forward, onto my stomach, and then everything goes dark.

THE
ISLAND
OF THE
LOST

THE
ISLAND
OF THE
LOST

I left this world brokenhearted.

With wounds held together by bandages and duct tape.

I was dying inside, trying to put the pieces of my life back together. Unsure of up from down. Dreading spending each night alone because the memories of my sister and my ex-boyfriend's betrayal haunted me.

It's funny how the cuts on my heart, that I thought would never heal, are barely scars now.

How time, as unreliable as it may be, can mend all wounds.

Well, most.

The pain I feel now runs deeper than anything I've ever felt. I live another life every time I close my eyes. I feel Wendy's love for Peter and James as if it were my own, blurring the lines of everything I know. But walking in her footsteps each night is better than existing in this purgatory because there I get to see Peter.

I get to touch him in their stolen moments.

I get to hear his voice whispering to me in the dark.

And I get to feel her guilt for loving one brother more than the other.

CHAPTER 1

Wednesday

I t's been days.

Days of waiting and hoping for Pan to come back to me.

Days of having takeout delivered because I didn't want to miss the moment he returned.

Days that drag on, minutes feeling like hours, and he still hasn't come back to me.

I look at yesterday's pizza box, still sitting on the table with a half-eaten slice inside, a war wages inside of me. On one hand, I should eat something because I skipped breakfast. What little of the plain cheese slice I tried to eat last night is all I've had in the last twelve hours. On the other hand, my nerves are so shot, I've barely been able to keep anything down.

Is it worth it to eat if I know I'm just going to throw it up later?

I roll onto my side and hold Pan's pillow to my chest, wishing it was him. Wendy Darling's emotions have twisted with mine, pushing away the anger and fear I clung to while in Neverland. I shouldn't let her feelings consume me. I would be better off hating both Peter and Pan for turning my life upside down. I *should* be thanking them for bringing me back to the life I begged and plotted to return to.

Instead, I'm drowning in depression, missing a man I never wanted to love, and desperate to return to a world no one believes exists.

I hold the pillow tighter, fully understanding why Wendy Darling donned a pen name and twisted her stories into the beloved fairy tale. She would have been put in an insane asylum had she told her truths any other way.

I've wondered more than once if talking to someone about what I went through might help ease the pain of missing the other half of my soul. At the very least, it would help me sort through how I feel and what I want. I might even figure out how to separate all things Wendy from my everyday existence and only draw on her experiences when I'm ready.

But the only person who knows I'm not dead is my sister, Tyle, and she is the last person I want to see.

Her life is perfect.

I huff out a laugh that is swallowed by a sob. Of course, it is. Tyle got everything I wanted in life, right down to our childhood home, while I'm stuck pining over an impossibility.

I bury my face in what's left of Pan's scent. Thanks to my breath, the cotton smells more like stale pizza than him, but it still has a hint of earth and magic. Soon, though, even that will be gone.

And then I'll have nothing.

A new wave of sadness has me crying again. I've given up trying to control my tears, let alone stop them. Centuries of longing flow through me, and every time I close my eyes, I let in a little more pain. Watching Wendy live her life, feeling it as if I'm experiencing it all myself, is torture. Yet, I willingly put myself through that pain because living in her reality while I dream is better than existing on my own.

A *rap, rap, rapping* on the door has my heart skipping a beat. No one should be knocking. I have the *do not disturb* sign on the door specifically to avoid human contact, and there isn't a soul alive who knows where I am.

Except for my Peter Pan.

Oh my gosh!

I wipe my eyes, excited and hopeful that Pan has returned. Or maybe it's Peter. I don't know who I want to see more. They're the same man, yet different all at once. Pan will likely barge into the room and take me in a hungry kiss. Peter will probably tuck his hands into his pockets and give me that lazy grin of his. Both will have me on my back within minutes of returning, and while I'd rather see them at the same time, having either one would send me over the moon. I love them both separately and equally and would be happy to see either.

But if I had to choose...

Hell, I'm not sure I could.

I run my fingers through my hair and try to make myself look somewhat decent. I should have taken a shower and I'm kicking myself for not thinking to be ready for when the other half of my soul returned, but there's no time now.

I hurry to the sink, put on some deodorant, then brush my teeth for all of thirty seconds. My mouth feels cleaner and minty, and while I'm too gross for sex (I need to shave pretty much every inch of my body), I don't feel like a cavewoman anymore.

He knocks again.

"I'm coming!" I yell. My heart races with each step and my stomach lurches. I'm so excited I could puke, but I try to hold it back. That would ruin our reunion. Although even if I did, we'd probably laugh about it later.

A small arrow of fear strikes my bubble of excitement because three days is just a few hours in Neverland. I doubt Peter has found Cass yet, but if he's here, that means one of two things. Something terrible has happened or it's safe enough for me to return.

I'm praying it's the latter because being in this world again is torture. Time moves too slow, forcing me to feel more than I ever thought possible.

I reach for the chain on the door. My fingers fumble, the

connection between them and my brain broken, like a song on a fuzzy radio station. Bits of what I want them to do eventually break through the static and I finally slide the chain, twist the latch on the door, and tug it open.

My heart falls to the floor so hard that I have to bite my tongue until it bleeds to keep my tears at bay.

It's not him.

Of course, it's not.

"Thank God. You're here!" Tyle throws her arms around me and pulls me into a hug. She then cradles my cheeks in her hands, looking at me like she's scared I'll disappear the moment she closes her eyes.

"How did you find me?"

Tyle drops her hands and we awkwardly stand in the hallway until it hits me that she's waiting to be invited in. I step to the side and open the door wider. Her nose wrinkles once she's inside. I sniff the air. It has a mild sour smell, so I don't judge her for the face she makes, even though I know she's judging more than just the room.

"Someone left a note a few days ago stating you were here, in this room, and to come get you." She lifts the pizza lid. A fly scurries out, and I'm glad I decided to skip lunch. "I thought it was a joke. Kenny had told Kierra that you'd come back the other day, she went to a dark place after you died, and I thought the note might have been her way of coping with an old wound. But it was eating at me. So, I came." She pokes her head into the bathroom and relaxes when she realizes it's empty. "Where is Peter?"

"You remember his name?" I ask, surprised. Tyle used to go through boys so quickly that she'd name them all *handsome* so she wouldn't call her new toy by the old toy's name. The fact that Peter's name stuck after knowing him for less than ten minutes is shy of a miracle.

"How could I forget? Peter has haunted me ever since I met him. It took me a minute to match his face when I saw him at the house, but there was no mistaking who he was once I did." She lets the part about him being the man who took me hang in the air. I don't finish the statement for her and desperately hope she doesn't ask.

"He left," I say as impassively as possible. She won't understand that every minute he's gone, I die a little inside. Hell, I don't even fully understand. All I know is that I feel like a ghost in this world without my Peter Pan.

Tyle takes a hard look at me and frowns. "You're sad about that?"

I shrug, not having a good explanation. "It's complicated. You wouldn't understand."

"I understand perfectly, Wednesday. It's called Stockholm syndrome. You were held captive by him for years and you fell in love. It's perfectly normal, but that doesn't make it okay." She reaches out and touches my arm. "I can help you through this."

I jerk free of her touch, horrified. She doesn't know anything. Peter Pan didn't hold me prisoner. He was my friend. He saved me more times than any man should need to. She's wrong! "I don't need help, Tyle. I'm fine."

I turn my back to her, walk back to the bed, fall into the heap of blankets, and grab Pan's pillow again. I close my eyes and wish for sleep, desperate to see Peter's face again.

"This place is a dump, Wens." Tyle tries to shift the conversation, and that tone, the one laced with judgment and disappointment, comes out of hiding.

"Why are you here, Tyle?" I don't look at her. I don't want to see her glowing with love as she grows her baby. Yes, I'm still bitter. Just because I don't love my ex—or want him anymore— doesn't mean I can't still be angry.

Family is supposed to be forever.

They are supposed to be the people you can always count on.

My family isn't in this room. They're back in Neverland because those people are more loyal to me than my own blood.

"I was worried about you." The bed dips as Tyle sits beside me. She pushes the blankets back until I have no choice but to look at her. Dark bags peek through her concealer. She looks tired and years older as her makeup folds into the fine lines of her face. "When that man took you again..." She bites her lip and shakes her head. "I thought I'd lost you."

"Stop." I push up onto one arm and glare at my sister. "Stop pretending that you care about me. You don't. You haven't since the seventh grade when you woke up and decided that we weren't twins anymore."

"Wednesday." Tyle swallows hard and closes her eyes. I give her a minute, although I'm unsure why, and wait for her to compose herself again. "I'm sorry."

"Sorry can't change the past." I get up and start cleaning my mess because I don't know what else to do. I can't just sit here and pretend that singular word erases years of trauma, because it doesn't.

"I know." She sighs, taking the empty bag of chips from my hand and carelessly dropping it to the floor. "But damn it, Wednesday, you're all I have. We have to stick together."

"What about Kenny?" I raise my eyebrows, curious about her response.

"Things with Kenny are complicated. We got married because of Wanda, but we don't love each other. He's been cheating on me since before the wedding." Tyle drops into the chair, unconcerned about crushing my only clothes.

"Sucks, doesn't it?" I cross my arms, wanting to hold on to my anger, but as I watch my sister wither from the strong woman who didn't care about anyone but herself to a broken shell of that person, I can't stay mad.

"You know what they say." She forces a smile and tries to sound playful, but I can hear the tears on the brink of breaking free. "What goes around comes around." She sniffles and then stretches her smile wider. "Enough about me. What are you doing, Wednesday? Why are you in this hellhole? This place reeks, and, no offense, you look like shit."

The look Tyle gives me warms my heart because if Mom could

see her, she'd be proud. Tyle has mastered the *I'm disappointed but still love you* face.

I'm not sure what to say. Outside of what I did a few minutes ago, I haven't made any effort to brush my hair, put on makeup, or even find matching clothes since Pan left. All I've done is sit here and cry.

And wait and cry.

And eat and cry.

And then throw up because I'm so upset and anxious and ready for him to come back that I can't keep anything down.

But if Tyle is here because Pan sent her, I can't help but fear he knew that he'd be gone more than a few days. The color drains from my face when it hits me that he may never return. Pan planned for my sister to find me because he knew I wouldn't leave this room. Ten lifetimes of money sits in his account and I would have spent half of it wasting the years away.

Just. Waiting.

The shred of hope I have that he'll return shatters. I bury my face in his pillow again, overwhelmed with a new round of tears. Tyle shifts and holds me in her arms. She can't begin to understand my pain, and still, she keeps me in her embrace, trying to ease the ache.

"Wednesday." Her voice cracks as she fights her own wave of emotion. "Come home."

"I don't have a home."

"Yes, you do. Your home is with Kenny and Wanda and me. We've missed you." She pulls back and looks me in the eyes. "We love you."

I lean against the side of the bed and curl my knees into my chest, wrapping my arms around them. I don't know if I can be in that house without Mom. It hurts too much.

Tyle sits beside me and touches my back. "It doesn't have to be forever," she adds, reading my mind. "Just until we get you settled, sort out the whole death certificate thing, and get a job.

You're welcome to stay as long as you want, but I know you won't."

I laugh humorously at the thought of living with my sister and her husband. The three of us under the same roof, playing house, sounds like a nightmare.

"How have you been paying for this?" Tyle asks, looking around the room again.

"Peter left me some money." I pause, tempted to keep everything Peter and Pan related to myself, but I need help moving and probably selling the car. So, I add, "And a car."

"He gave you a car?" she asks, eyebrows arched.

I nod and laugh when I say, "I don't know how to drive it. It's a stick."

"Oh, honey, once you learn how to work a stick, it comes naturally," my sister says with too much enthusiasm, trying to cheer me up. She wiggles her eyebrows and I can't help but laugh with her. It feels so good not to be in constant competition with each other.

Neverland years aside, I can't remember the last time we sat together and got along without pretending.

"Please, Wednesday, even if it's just for a few days, you need to get out of this place. It smells like puke in here." She wrinkles her nose again.

That's because I can't keep anything down.

I let my head fall against the mattress and stare at the popcorn ceiling. As much as I don't want to be around Kenny or in that house, I don't want to be alone. Heartbreak is harder when you're alone. "I don't know."

"Okay. No pressure, we can talk about where you'll live later." She holds up her hands in mock surrender. "What about lunch then?"

"Huh?"

"Lunch. Let me take you to the mall. We'll go shopping and get something to eat. My treat."

I'm about to tell her no when my stomach cramps. I touch my

belly, feeling its angry rumbles. I'm still not used to all the additives this world puts into its food. I throw up half of what I eat, which is why I've mostly had chips the last two days. Something about the grease and the salt mixes with me. It's the only thing I can keep down but I probably should put something besides crap in my stomach. And I really do need some more clothes.

"Fine," I concede. "Let me take a shower and get ready."

"Oh, thank God."

"What?"

"I didn't want to say anything, but you smell terrible." She grins, teasing and telling the truth all at once.

I grab a pillow that isn't Pan's and chuck it at Tyle as I pass the bed. I don't forget the years of bullshit she's put me through, or how I still hate her, but a small part of me is glad Tyle showed up.

With her here, I'm not alone.

CHAPTER 2

Wednesday

"**O**h! Try this one on." Tyle tosses another pair of pants over the fitting room door.

I've gone up three sizes since Pan left.

I shouldn't be surprised. All I've done is lay around and let carbs cling to my hips, but it still stings. I know we're in that wave of life where all bodies are beautiful and skinny isn't the only way to be anymore, but I can't unprogram my grandmother's words from whispering in my ear.

Never above a size three. Sorry, Grams. I was a solid five before I left this world. Now, I'll be lucky if I can squeeze into an eight.

"Don't stress." Tyle tries to comfort me, but it's a hard pill to swallow. "I don't even look at the numbers anymore. Every designer is different, so they aren't universal. A seven in this store could be a four in the next."

I shimmy out of the jeans and tug my shorts back on. Even they feel tight today. I sigh, fold the pants I don't want, and rehang the shirts and dresses back on their original hangers. "I'm done."

"Are you sure?" Tyle asks when I open the door, holding two more flowing dresses draped over her arms. Neither of which looks like anything I would pick for myself. "We could try a different store."

I shake my head. "I don't want you spending any more money on me."

"I don't mind." Her eyes go wide as a new idea comes to mind. "I know! We can get our toes done. I haven't seen mine in—"

"Tyle!" I cut her off. Today has been great, but I've done more walking in the last three hours than I have since leaving Neverland. My feet are killing me and the veins in my hands are swelling. I have to wiggle my fingers to keep the skin from pulling too tight and hurting. "Thank you, but no. I'm ready to go."

"Where?" she asks, worry weighing heavily in her tone. "You can't go back to that ratty motel, Wednesday. You'll catch a disease."

"I'll figure it out."

"How? You don't have a job to pay for anything. Heck, according to the government, you're dead! Red flags will fly if you try to get a place and they have to run your social."

I hang the clothes I don't want on the return rack and grab my bags. Tyle's bought me five outfits: three dresses, a bathing suit, some pajamas, and a pair of flip-flops. A part of me feels bad. This is money she should be spending on the new baby and, if Peter's account is as flush as he described, I can more than pay for the things I need.

But I know the moment I say his name or mention anything that has to do with him, Tyle's sweet side will vanish. She'll either turn into a crazed mother-hen again or the switch will flip to bitch because I refuse to let her talk shit about him. It's easier to keep my secrets and enjoy this happy, loving side of my sister than it is to rock the boat.

"One night," I concede. "I'll give you one night, but I swear, Tyle, if Kenny does anything even remotely shady, I'm cutting his balls off."

She laughs, assuming I'm joking. "Relax. You have nothing to worry about. Kenny will behave."

"How do you know?"

"Because you're not his type anymore." Her smile falls for a fraction of a second, letting slip the hurt she tries to hide from the world, but then is back in place bigger and brighter than before.

I touch my chest and drop my jaw in fake despair. "I'm crushed. How ever will I survive?"

"The same way I've been." Tyle links her arm with mine and grins. "By eating your weight in ice cream every chance you get."

***

I clench my teeth and push the bowl of ice cream away. My stomach has tied itself into a ball of knots. Milk wasn't something we used in Neverland. I don't think I can handle the dairy anymore.

"What's wrong?" Tyle asks.

"I don't feel good." I lay my head on the cold countertop and ground myself to the sensation. It feels good against my clammy skin.

"Again? You didn't feel good after lunch either."

"The food wasn't so processed where I came from," I admit. We haven't gotten into the details of where I was. I think Tyle is afraid to ask, but she knows, at its core, I was in a different world. Except she thinks that phrase is a metaphor and not a hard truth.

"Please don't be mad, Wens," Tyle says hesitantly. She chews on her bottom lip, a habit we both have when nervous, and asks, "But, is there any chance you could be pregnant?"

"No," I say without hesitation and laugh. "Definitely not."

"It's just you're food sensitive and your clothes don't fit and if I'm being honest, your belly is a little distended."

"Believe me. It's not possible."

"When was your period?"

"I..." I try to remember, but it was before Neverland. About two weeks before we went to the Keys. Three years ago. How do I explain that? "I'm not sure. A few weeks ago, I guess. It's not like I could keep track of the days."

Tyle leaves the kitchen and walks down the hall, then comes back with a piss test in her hand. "Humor me."

"Why do you have that?"

"It's an extra from when we found out about Wyatt. After the second positive test, I didn't see the point in wasting any more." She grabs my shoulders and low-key lifts me off the barstool. "Go. If you just had it a few weeks ago, then there's nothing to worry about."

"Seriously, Tyle. This is stupid."

She sticks the test down my shirt, loosely tucking it between the girls. "Stupid or not, it will make me feel better."

It might make her feel better, but my insides are squirming. The likelihood of me being pregnant is less than one percent, but there's still a chance. One I'm not ready to confront. "You're not gonna let this go. Are you?"

"Nope."

"Fine." I groan and set off down the hall to the bathroom. Someone has fixed the sink. You'd never know Pan destroyed the room just a few days ago. I almost wonder if Kenny's face has healed, but then decide I don't care.

I prep myself to pee on the test and my heart foolishly races. If we were in the real world, I would be nervous. Between my boys and Cass, I've had enough semen inside me to get a nun pregnant by immaculate conception. But Cass said he couldn't get me knocked up. It's physically impossible. Both him and Peter's swimmers are dead, and by default, that means Pan's are too.

Plus, I have the implant in my arm.

My bladder relieves itself the moment I'm seated on the toilet and ready. Peeing on demand has never been a problem for me. The skill has come in handy more than once with the random drug tests my job used to do. Though I never would have thought it would be useful for something like this.

I cap the end of the stick and set it on the counter while I pull up my pants. I turn to flush and the blinking screen of the digital test catches my eyes. The world around me stills into one long moment. Disbelief has me questioning the validity of the test. I had the results in less than a minute. That and the test almost nine months old. It could be wrong.

It has to be wrong.

But as I read the results over and over again, I know it is right.

I'm pregnant.

CHAPTER 3

Wednesday

"Wens?" Tyle softly knocks on the door, her knuckles echoing through the silence. "Are you okay in there?"

I hug my knees to my chest and bury my face in my arms. I don't know how many minutes have passed. I've been in here long enough for my eyes to run out of tears and my heart to stop hurting, but not long enough to numb the ache of emptiness inside me.

The nurse in Fort Lauderdale knew I was pregnant.

That's what she was hesitant to tell me, and the only reason I can think of why that information would have been withheld is because Pan knew and had asked them not to say anything.

He knew I had a baby in my belly, and he still left.

"I'm fine," I manage to say, my voice trembling.

Tyle's tone is heavy with concern as she tries to coax me out of the bathroom, but I'm not going anywhere. "You don't sound fine, Wens. I'm coming in."

The door creeps open. Tyle pokes her head in first. I raise my bloodshot eyes over my arms and look at a speck of dirt on the tiles by her feet. She moves closer, her voice barely a whisper, "You are. Aren't you?"

I can't meet her gaze. Instead, I curl further into myself, hiding my face in my arms again. It's confirmation enough, but if Tyle needs more the test is still on the counter, happily blinking *Pregnant* for the world to see.

Tyle grunts and groans as she slides down the wall, but she manages to sit beside me on the floor. Her warm arms wrap around me, offering fragile, unexpected solace. We sit together, neither one of us saying anything as a new wave of tears runs its course. "Whatever you decide, Wens, I support you."

My throat feels raw, every syllable an effort to utter, but I manage to ask, "What?"

"There are options," she says as gently as she can, but her words hang heavy in the air. "You don't have to keep it."

I sit upright, disgusted that Tyle would suggest I give away my child. Peter's child. Or is it Pan's? Stars above, I hope it's not Cass's baby. All three of them came inside me within days of each other. Granted, it's been a few weeks since I slept with Cass, but I don't know where I was in my cycle when I fucked him.

I'm either growing a half-fairy or a zombie. I'd laugh if the prospect wasn't so depressing. I don't know what this child is or what it might be able to do and I am the only person in this world who could care for it.

Besides, if it were discovered that my baby could fly or freeze things or do any of the possible gifts it could get from its father, it would be studied and experimented on. Its life would be nothing but pokes and prods, blood draws and scans, and tests upon tests. I refuse to let that happen.

Gathering my strength, I raise my head and meet Tyle's gaze. She needs to understand, even if I can't put into words what I need to say. "I'm keeping it."

"Wednesday." She sighs. "Keeping the child of your kidnapper could be emotionally damaging."

"And giving it away would be worse." I look at my sister, silently begging her to understand without giving my reasons. I can't explain, but she's a mom. She has to understand how hard it would be to carry Wyatt for nine months and then never see him again.

"We're going to need a nanny to take care of all of these babies." She leans in and nudges me with her shoulder.

"Or a dog named Nanna," I tease. Tyle's brows knit together. The reference went so far over her head that I don't even bother trying to explain. "Never mind."

Tyle tries to push herself to her feet, but her big belly gets in the way. I stand before she can roll onto her side with the intent of getting on her hands and knees, and offer her a helping hand. I stumble back a step at the awkwardness of her weight, and we both laugh.

"I'll need to sell Peter's car," I say, the heaviness of reality crashing down upon me.

Tyle's eyebrows shoot up in surprise. "That's right! I forgot he left you a car."

I nod. "And a little money. Not a lot," I lie, "but enough to get me on my feet again."

"Where is it? What is it?" Tyle whispers as we make our way back to the living room. She pokes her head into Wanda's room and peeks in at her. She smiles, reassured that her daughter is sleeping soundly, and closes the door again. "Do you have the title? Kenny can pick it up from... where is it?"

"The cemetery."

"Seriously? He left you at Mom and Dad's all alone!" Tyle shakes her head, her hatred for Peter growing with every new sentence I say. "I swear if I ever see that man again, I'm going to kill him."

I try to downplay the situation to reassure her. "It's fine, really." But deep down, the hurt of being abandoned in this world lingers like an open wound. "And I don't know about the title. Is there a way to see who he registered it to without raising any red flags?"

Tyle chews on her bottom lip and stares off into space for a minute. Her gaze snaps back to mine a second later, a mischievous grin dancing on her lips. "Maybe. I have a friend at a dealership who might be able to work some magic. I'll give him a call."

Tyle pushes off the couch and heads toward the kitchen where her phone is. I watch her hobble, wondering if I'll get that big or if this baby is going to grow faster having been conceived in Neverland. I set my hands on my belly and look down.

Peter was wrong. The greatest adventure of my life won't be dying. It will be raising our baby (I refuse to believe it could be Cass's).

I smile at my non-existent pudge, imagining what motherhood could be like when a cool breeze sweeps through the room, sending shivers down my spine. I reach for the blanket laid across the cushions behind me when I hear the softest whisper in my mind.

"Hello, Darling."

CHAPTER 4

Pan

Someone kicks me in the side, causing a sharp pain to ripple through my body. The ache lingers, refusing to fade away, despite the Island's usual reach to mend the broken. Seconds pass and my magic doesn't heal me. It should have. Just like it should have called to the sky for rain and the ocean for waves. Yet, its power eludes me. I can feel the pulsating energy as it stirs beneath the earth, vibrating with an almost taunting presence. I can taste the metallicness in the air, but I can't make any of it listen to my pleas.

A voice slices through the silence, etching itself like a scar in my mind. "I thought the great Peter Panning would be more difficult to capture." I recognize it without needing to see the face to know whom it belongs to. Belle—Cass and Emmit's sister—kicks me in the side again and says, "Pity."

The rough burlap sack over my head is abruptly ripped away, revealing a dimly lit room. My eyes take a moment to adjust to the pale glow of fireflies in lanterns, but I recognize where I am as. I'm in a holding room deep within one of the caverns beneath the stone castle carved into the mountainside. One of the many forgotten dungeons the Fae King used to keep.

Peter's friends, the Lost—Aria, Heidi, Emmit, and Xyris—

hang in iron shackles from their wrists alongside me, their uncon-scious forms swaying slightly. The only one awake is Emmit. His head moves in the slightest, warning me. I don't know what the warning is for, but whatever it is, I'm not supposed to do it.

"Tell me, Peter." Belle's voice echoes in the barren space while her footsteps click ominously. She remains hidden in the dark, her presence felt rather than seen. "Are we going to do this the easy way or the hard way? I do so hope you make things difficult. I haven't had any fun in ages."

Belle finally steps into the dim light wearing a glittering green floor-length gown. The woman looks ready for a ball, not a torture session, but that is Belle. Her vanity is her greatest weak-ness, aside from her hunger.

I force a grin and try my hardest to sound like my other half. It's been so long since Peter has seen Belle. I doubt she'll notice the difference between my eyes and his, but she'll recognize my voice. I sound too much like James.

I was cursed with the parts of Peter that he didn't want, including anything that tied him to his old life. Like his accent. And most of his memories. "Good to see you, Belle. You don't look a day over two hundred."

Belle studies me. I've only had a voice for a few days. Trying to hide my natural accent is difficult but not impossible. *But do I sound like Peter?*

Her lack of response makes me nervous. I blow Belle a kiss and her nose wrinkles. She looks at me like I'm a dog who just shit on her shoes and then dragged all of my crap on the train of her dress. She schools her face to seem impassive, but I can see the rage pooling beneath the surface. Good. That's something I can work with.

"Where's the girl?" Belle demands, her tone laced with impa-tience. I feel a small sense of relief, but I don't let it linger. I'm on a ticking time bomb, the fuse growing shorter the longer we're in each other's presence. My only hope is that Belle's lack of patience will make her careless.

"You have a room full of pretty girls. Which one would you prefer?" I reply, feigning innocence. There is only one woman worthy of Belle's time, The Darling, and she will never have her.

With a swift motion, Belle's open hand lands a stinging slap across my face. "Please play games with me, Peter," she says, fury bleeding into her sarcasm. "I want so badly to make you bleed."

I press my lips together and swallow a knot of nervousness. My heart ticks faster. The moment she tastes my blood, she'll know I'm not Peter. She will drain me, mercilessly, for the mere pleasure of it and absorb what's left of my magic into her veins.

But that's not the worst part. When a Fae drinks the blood of another, they gain access to their memories, though it's the last drop that holds a person's greatest secret. Belle would bleed me dry for that drop alone because it would lead her to Wednesday.

I can't let that happen.

"Do it, Belle. I dare you," I challenge, my voice trembling slightly. "Cut my skin. Taste my flesh because without my shadow it will be ash in your mouth. It will take back every year you've stolen and you'll be nothing but dust in the wind."

"Liar!" she screams. She grips my chin between her fingers and tries to compel me into telling the truth, but she's weak. Her magic wraps around my words, but they aren't strong enough to rip them from my lips.

I bite down on my tongue until I taste iron, then lick my lips, purposely staining them red. I pray she doesn't call my bluff, but this is something Peter would do. "Want to find out?"

Belle huffs in frustration and shoves my forehead. My skull cracks against the stone. Pain—a feeling I'm not used to and have only felt secondhand—wraps around my head and shoots down my spine. It's intense and dizzying, but I laugh because that's what Peter would do, too. He'd poke the bear over and over until she lost her temper. Before the Darling arrived, everything was a game to him.

One he always had to win.

"Your blood may be no good to me, but I have a buffet of

souls to choose from. Where should I start, Peter?" Belle walks past our friends, dragging her nails across each one's cheek, spilling blood as she makes a turn around the room. "Which pathetic little half-mortal do you love most?"

"Leave them alone, Tinkerbell!" Emmit roars. He pulls against the iron cuff. The metal sizzles as it sears another layer of his skin away. I know it hurts, it has to, but Emmit hides the pain behind a mask of indifference. "They aren't a part of this."

"Sweet baby brother," she coos, her words laced with false affection as she turns her attention to him. "Don't you understand? I'm doing all this for us."

"Liar!" he growls. "You've only ever thought about yourself. This has nothing to do with me."

"Do you know what our father had planned for you? He was going to ship you off to war. He wanted you dead." She touches her chest, giving an Emmy-worthy show of practiced care that he sees straight through. "I saved you."

"You killed him. You killed everyone."

"I did it for you," Belle claims. Her voice cracks and I might've believed her if I didn't know better. But I do know better. Just like I know about the souls she bleeds to feed her thirst and how the more vital the memory, the stronger her magic is. I know that her borrowed power lasts days, sometimes less, before it wanes and she's forced to feed again.

"You killed them to be queen. You don't care about me. You never have," Emmit counters, a vicious smirk curling his lips. "Too bad the Island saw through your bullshit and picked someone else to rule."

Belle smacks him and her nail slashes across his cheek, leaving a deep gash that seeps crimson. "Now look what you've made me do," she mutters, a mixture of irritation and disappointment clouding her face. Belle heaves a sigh and strides over to Heidi, unchaining her and dragging her by the wrist toward Emmit. "Drink," she commands. "Once you taste the power their memories hold, you'll be so much stronger."

"No."

Belle cuts Heidi's wrist with her thumbnail. Blood wells up and leaks down her pale skin. "Your body won't heal itself without help anymore. Drink!"

"No!"

"Why not?" Belle demands.

"Because she's my friend," Emmit says defiantly. "I won't do it. I won't be like you."

"Put her life to use or waste it. I don't care. Either way, she dies," Belle coldly retorts. She slides her thumbnail across Heidi's neck, slitting the artery that feeds the brain, then drops the body. Blood leaks out of our friend at an inhuman speed, a puddle of deep red stains the dirt and seeps into her clothes.

"Stop this, Belle! Stop her bleeding," Emmit pleads, desperation creeping into his voice. He pulls at the cuffs again. They've rubbed his skin raw, down to the muscle. If he doesn't stop, they'll eat through his hand.

Belle pretends to consider for a moment, feigning kindness. She shakes her shoulders and a shower of golden dust fills the air. She catches a handful of it and tosses it at Emmit. He stops writhing, his body frozen in place, save for the movement of his eyes.

"I think I'd rather have you watch her die," she remarks, a sinister edge to her voice. "All you had to do was take one little taste. You could have healed her the moment your strength returned, but you chose to let her rot. What happens next is on you."

She steps forward and cups his cheeks in her hands, ducking down to meet him at eye level. "I am not your enemy, little brother. One day, you'll see that."

Belle's attention shifts back to me. "As for you," she declares. She walks to each of the Lost and tosses her golden dust on them, ensuring that time cannot touch their motionless forms. "Every day you delay, another one of your friends will die." She stands before me, her gaze locking with mine.

I clench my teeth, refusing to break eye contact. We've found ourselves in another game, one I'd happily lose to kick her in the stomach if I weren't pretending to be someone else.

Now would be a good time to come back, Peter. My thoughts are torn between chastising him for abandoning us and all the ways I'm going to kill this bitch when I get free.

"I will drain every last drop of their blood. I will extract their souls, and I will obliterate any chance of them having a life beyond this one," Belle threatens, a wicked smile playing on her lips. "I've been generous by allowing you to keep your pets." She pauses and smirks. "Did you think I didn't know? I know everything, Peter. I've kept my word to your brother all these years, but the Darling changes everything."

"What did my brother promise you?"

"You have... seven friends, correct?" Belle's voice drips with malice. "Will you let them all die? Or perhaps just this one? The choice, Peter, is yours."

"Belle!" I shout, my voice filled with a mixture of desperation and defiance. "What deal did James make?"

She chuckles wickedly and turns the corner, leaving me alone with nothing but my thoughts.

James

"What are you going to tell her?" Smee asks, her voice laden with worry. She nervously twists the tassel on her shirt, wrapping it around her finger repeatedly. "It's been almost a week and there haven't been any new souls in the Neversea. That's never happened."

"I know." We've combed the dark blue waters for hours this morning, searching for even one soul passing through. There weren't any. Just like there weren't any the day before. Or the one before that. If I'm counting correctly, there hasn't been a new soul since Peter left with the Darling girl. A fact that hasn't stopped rolling around my mind since she left.

"Belle could start feeding off us again."

"I know."

"I don't want to give her another piece of me, Cap," Smee continues, her voice trembling. Fear and sorrow mingle in her words, while panic pushes its way to the forefront of her emotions. "I can't let her feed on me again. We can't give her the others, either. She's—"

"Smee!" I yell, and my voice reverberates in the ship's cabin.

She flinches. I pinch the bridge of my nose and close my eyes. Raising my voice was a mistake I already regret, but I had no choice. I know Smee's traumas and make a conscious effort to avoid triggering her. Yet, today, I've failed.

Releasing a deep breath, I look at my friend. Smee tries her best to hold herself together, but her resolve is crumbling. Her pain is my fault, a weight that does not sit easy on my chest. I step forward and pull her into my arms. "I'm sorry."

Smee nestles her face against my chest, her breathing uneven and ragged. She hates crying. Another trauma from another life she's lived. Pain is funny like that. It scars the soul in ways the living can't imagine and resurfaces whenever it pleases.

"I promise," I assure her, my voice steady. "Nothing is going to happen to yeh."

She looks up at me, her eyes reddened by tears she doesn't want to shed. "What about the others, Cap?"

I cup her cheeks and press my forehead to hers. Neverland is the bridge between life and death, and my ship has become the Ferry that takes souls to the afterlife. Most willingly embark on the journey, content with the lives they've lived and ready forf the afterlife, but every so often I find a soul who is tormented and not ready to move on.

I offer them a chance to work through their demons and a safe space where they have all the time in the world to process whatever is holding them back from transitioning into the afterlife.

For a cost.

A memory.

One they have no say in losing.

I don't reveal the full extent of the consequences or how painful it is to let go of something that defines their very being. Or the agony they'll endure when Belle sinks her teeth into them to extract it. But I do promise it will only happen once.

A promise I will do anything to keep.

I brush away the long strands of auburn hair that have fallen over Smee's eyes. "She won't touch them. I'll take care of it."

"How?"

Her doubt is unnerving, but I try to reassure her. I recognized long ago that this woman was going to be the metaphorical death of me. Her smart mouth. Those pretty brown eyes. That unwavering trust and dedication. She offered me something no one in my life ever had, true dedication. So, I made her my first mate.

"I'm scared, Cap." She tugs at the lapels of my coat, trying to get closer, but there's barely enough room for the air between us.

I force myself to remain patient and not patronizing. I remember what it felt like to be afraid. The sensation was lost to me until the other day when I saw Wednesday unconscious in Peter's arms.

Watching him fly away with her damn near broke me, but I had to let them go. Getting her out of Neverland was the only thing that could save her but that doesn't mean a single day hasn't gone by where I haven't lost sleep, wondering if she's okay.

"Do yeh trust me?" I arch back and duck to find Smee's eyes.

She nods, her conviction clear. "With my life."

"Good." I kiss her hairline and step away. The sun is nearly at its peak in the sky. I can't stay much longer or I'll be late. Belle hates it when I'm late. I grab my sword off the center table and my hat from the hook. "I'll be back."

"Where are you going?" Smee follows me to the deck but doesn't cross the ramp to the dock. She's terrified of the Island and for good reason. Belle isn't the only bloodthirsty monster within our woods.

"To talk to the devil herself."

***

I hear the clink of heels echoing off the stone walls before I see her. Belle is beautiful, dressed in a glittering dress spun from the silk of butterfly wings, but all the Fae are a gift to the eyes. Or so I've been told.

Today, her long blonde hair is pulled into a bun at the top of her head, tied with a vine of green leaves and delicate yellow flowers. Tonight's gown reveals the scars of her past. She wears them with pride, unbothered by the two long marks that run from the center of each shoulder blade to the middle of her exposed back.

The skin there is a tender shade of pink and raw, the edges around her scars bruised purple as if her wings had just been ripped from her flesh. But she lost them ages ago in the war against her people. Her father, the late King, ripped them off of her himself, robbing her of ancestral magic.

It's why Belle needs the memories of the dead. She draws on forbidden blood magic to keep herself in power, but the balance only lasts as long as Neverland's current king reigns.

Peter.

"You're late." Belle sneers, striding past me without sparing a passing glance, heading toward her chambers.

I follow, obedient as always. Forever playing my part to keep those I care about an arm's length from danger. "I'm sorry, my queen."

Belle pushes open the door to her room. Her fingers reach for the thin straps of her dress as she steps inside the door closes and I quickly lock it to make sure we won't be any interrupted. Per her usual orders. Even though her soldiers are mindless drones, and have never even thought to look in on what we do, no matter how loud she makes me scream.

Belle glances back, her brows furrowing with disdain. "Why are your clothes still on?"

"We have a problem," I confess.

"That we do," she purrs, running her fingernails down my chest. With practiced ease, she unbuttons my pants and wraps her hand around me. "Your cock isn't inside me yet."

This is the moment when I usually close my eyes and mentally transport myself somewhere else, with anyone but her.

A lifetime ago, I found Belle feasting on Harper, one of the few survivors from the original shipwreck. She tore into him, ravaging his body like a starved animal, then began hunting for the next soul to feast on. I panicked. It was my fault we were trapped on the Island. My fault the crew and my kids died. I didn't want any more blood on my hands. So I struck a deal with her, offering anything she wanted as long as she swore off killing my kind.

I didn't know what making a deal with the Fae would cost or how every word is twisted in their favor. I thought I offered her myself in place of the survivors. I thought she would feed on me and leave the rest alone.

I didn't specify how long she needed to stay away from the others, so in her mind, she didn't break her word. The last crew member died two days later. The only souls left were me, Peter, and Wendy. I refused to let her have them, so I found her someone else to feed on. The first Lost I ferried to the Island.

"There are no new souls in Neverland."

Belle stops rubbing my length and meets my gaze. "What do you mean there are no new souls?"

I find her stare and hold it. She sees my boldness as bravery when really, I just don't give a fuck anymore. "We've circled the Island and found no one."

Belle crosses the room and grabs a silk robe to cover herself with. "No one willing to stay?"

"No. I mean not a single soul in the waters. There isn't anyone to ferry into the next life."

"That's impossible." She chews on her thumbnail and paces the room. The skinny heels of her shoes and the beating of my heart in my ears are the only sounds until she finally asks, "How long?"

"A week."

"Why didn't you tell me this sooner?" she demands, her voice brimming with anger.

"I needed to be certain. I didn't want to raise any alarms if the gods hadn't changed the path to the afterlife to avoid the Island, but it seems they have."

"The gods aren't the problem. Neverland is. It's shifting." She pauses, contemplating what could be the cause. "Something has changed."

I tuck myself back into my pants, grateful not to have to perform tonight. I don't take pleasure in satisfying Belle. Her tastes are rougher than mine, although my skin seems to have hardened over the years. Her nails draw less blood each time she digs them into my back and I heal faster. The past few times, I've even made it to the cove and put my shirt on without ruining it.

"It's that girl." She sneers.

"Who?" I ask, hoping she doesn't know about Wednesday, but Belle knows everything. The Island whispers to her, just like it does to Peter.

Her glare turns sinister as she changes the topic. "You know the deal, James. I need to feed."

I nod and pull my shirt over my head, my body forever at her beck and call. That was the deal. This is what I thought she wanted all those years ago.

Belle positions herself behind me, her fingers gripping my shoulders. "Your memories are always the tastiest." She presses her lips to the side of my neck. "Anything you'd like to forget?"

"I don't care. Just do it," I reply, my tone heavy with resignation.

Belle sinks her teeth into my neck and a searing pain spreads through my body like poison in water. She swallows mouthful after mouthful of my blood, searching for a memory worth taking. For the others, they have no control. She latches onto the most precious parts of their past, the core memories that shaped them because those are the strongest. She rips that part of their life away even as the body fights to hold on. It's a painful tug of war that usually ends when the soul has collapsed at her feet, too weak to fight any longer.

It's then that I collect them and take them to the Inn, where the lost soul is nursed back to health, but they aren't the same. They sense the void, the absence of something vital, and the unknown gnaws at their consciousness.

But because I've sacrificed myself more than any other being on the Island. I know how to shield the important parts of myself.

I give Belle a memory from my childhood. One that feels important but has no true meaning. I feel the moment it leaves me. Ice coats my insides, turning my blood cold. She sucks away the last Christmas I had before my mother passed. Thousands of wounds, cut by invisible knives, slice me to release the memory as another part of my soul dies, and then Belle releases me. She steps back, wipes her mouth with her thumb, and licks that finger.

"Such sweet sorrow." She hands me a towel to press against my wound. "I wish you would fight me, though. The memories are so much sweeter when the souls refuse to give up their past."

I hold the cloth to the bite mark. It will be healed in a few hours, but I'd rather not ruin my shirt while waiting for the hole to close. "I gave up fighting yeh decades ago. Why start now?"

"This won't last more than a few days, James. Your memories are the sweetest because I uncover another layer under your thick skin, but they don't satisfy me the way fresh meat does. I'll need more blood. Soon."

"I understand."

"We have a whole island of souls. If you can't find me new ones, I expect you to bring a pirate to me next time."

"Understood." I grab my shirt off the floor and turn to leave, but Belle slows my movements. She's strongest after a feed, not needing her dust to sway the hand of time.

"Where do you think you're going?" She tisks. "I haven't had my way with you yet."

CHAPTER 6

James

My shirt clings to my back, drenched and saturated with blood. I abandoned any hope of salvaging it nearly an hour ago when the bloodsuckers emerged from their hiding places within the Neverwoods. The mutated mosquitoes swarmed me the moment I ventured out of Belle's mountainside castle. They still hover, occasionally attempting to latch onto my skin, but their teeth can't break the cotton fabric.

I lean against the wall and hide in the shadows of Shelly's Seafood Shack. I should have regained my strength or, at the very least, stopped bleeding by now. I reach up and touch the bite mark and there's a squishing sound when my fingers meet the raw skin. Dark spots float in my vision. I should eat something, maybe even rest, but not here.

I whistle once, knowing Smee is somewhere on the deck, watching, waiting for my return. She hates coming into the Cove and does everything she can not to step foot on our grounds, but that whistle is our safe word. Spelled long ago to travel any lengths. It's not something either of us uses lightly. I close my eyes, too tired to keep them open and wait.

"Stars in the sky." Smee touches my cheek, waking me from a slumber I didn't realize I'd fallen into. "What did she do to you?"

"Nothing I can't handle," I say as confidently as I can muster, but even I don't believe my words. I'm weak. Belle took more than I realized, possibly even more than she intended.

Smee grabs me by the arms and pulls me upright. I must have slid down the wall when I passed out because I don't remember shifting off my feet. The shooting pain in my back feels like a blade reopening the wounds, and I clench my teeth to keep from cursing and release the tension with a grunt.

"Bullshit." Smee ducks under my arm and attempts to support my weight. "I've never so much as seen you come back with a scratch."

"And I've never seen yeh set foot on the mainland."

She rolls her eyes and ignores how big of a deal her being here for me is. "What happened?"

"I don't want anyone to see me," I mutter. I am the leader of these lands—the embodiment of strength in the eyes of the pirates. If I'm viewed as weak or unable to care for our crew, the Cove could turn to chaos. Not because they would overthrow my reign but because the Island could.

"I'll deal with anyone who tries to cause problems," Smee says.

We make good time to the boat. If anyone caught sight of us, they remained hidden in the shadows and, for now, kept their mouths shut. We limp our way to my quarters on the ship, each step more arduous than the last.

I'm tired.

So, unnaturally, tired. All I want to do is close my eyes and...

"Hey!" Smee taps my cheeks. "You can't sleep, Cap. Not yet." She hurries to the other side of the room, pours me a glass of scotch, and grabs a wooden peg. "Drink this and then bite down."

I swallow the alcohol in one gulp. It burns, but that's a fire I enjoy. I take the peg before the Scotch and fear can settle in my stomach and put it between my teeth. Smee tears my shirt at the collar until the fabric hangs off my shoulder. She sucks in a breath, taking in the claw marks and bite wound. There's only been a handful of times where I've needed her help after a visit with Belle. Based on her silence, I sense this might be the messiest aftermath to date.

"This is gonna hurt."

"Just do it," I grit.

Smee threads a needle and then pokes the end through my severed skin. I bite down hard on the peg and grip the side of the couch. This hurts more than when Belle stuck her teeth in me. Smee threads in and out, pulling the hole shut as she goes.

"Almost done," she says, leaving out the second half of her sentence. *With this one.*

Eight stitches and my shoulder is mended. Another twelve in various places along my spine and my back has finally ceased to bleed.

"This isn't right," Smee says as she helps me into a clean shirt once I'm bandaged. "I've never seen anyone bleed this much. Not in Neverland."

"The Island is changing." My hands shake as I pour myself another glass of scotch. I should probably go down to the Galley and eat, but numbing the pain seems more appealing.

"Is that possible?"

"It's Neverland," I say halfheartedly. I swallow the liquid; its burn is a dull warmth compared to the searing pain from my stitches. "Anything is possible."

Smee chews on her bottom lip and loses herself in her thoughts. She's only been with me for the last decade or so, but that's longer than all the rest. There's so much to this island I wish I could show her, but the stronger Belle gets, the more dangerous it is to venture outside of our cove.

"Could explain why the tides have changed."

"What did yeh say?" I ask, unsure if I heard her right whilst setting my glass on the counter.

Smee hitches her thumb over her shoulder and looks at me, puzzled. "The tide. It's going out."

Adrenaline has me pushing through the pain and hobbling

out to the deck to look over the rail. Far-off waves push the water onto our shoreline, but with each new rush, the water doesn't touch the sand where it last kissed.

Smee is right. The tide has shifted for the first time since I set foot in Neverland.

"Smee," I say excitedly. "Ready the sails."

"Where are we going?" She follows me, probably convinced I'm crazy, yet she still rings the bell to signal the crew. They'll all be here soon, ready to take the old girl out to sea again.

I hurry back to my quarters and pull out my maps. I've drawn every inch of the Island and the waters surrounding it. I've sailed to the horizon, only to be cast out to the other side of my map, but today will be different. I can feel it in my bones.

"James?" she asks cautiously. "There aren't any souls in the water. We already looked today."

"We aren't looking for souls." I roll the papers and tuck them under my arm. Time is ticking away. Each second is precious and every one lost could mean the difference between making it there or not. I look at my crew, eight sailors who have sworn themselves to me. I smile, proud of the men and women I've come to call my friends, then meet Smee's gaze. "We're going to fetch ourselves a Darling."

CHAPTER 7

Pan

I've watched and waited for Heidi to show signs of life, but there's nothing. We've had injuries in Neverland before, bad ones that would have killed the soul if it were anywhere else. The worst was when Scarlett almost beheaded Emmit last summer, but even his wounds healed. In a matter of minutes, he was back to his old self, laughing and calling himself Nearly Headless Em.

There was never any doubt that he'd be okay because the wound stopped bleeding and the skin stitched itself back together almost as soon as the blade passed through. The longest we've ever waited for someone to heal was five minutes, and that was stressful. But this, watching the life fade from someone both Peter and I care about, is excruciating.

"She's not healing? Why isn't she healing?" I plead, my voice quivering with fear.

This was Emmit's island before it became ours. He should know its rules better than any of us. I want him to tell me that Belle's dust is delaying the healing process and that once it wears off, Heidi will be fine. She'll wake up pissed with a minor headache, but she'll be okay.

But the longer it takes him to answer me, the less likely that feels.

Emmit's gaze remains fixed on Heidi's body lifelessly sprawled on the cold dungeon floor, surrounded by a pool of her blood. His silence feels like a weight pushing a truth I don't want to swallow down my throat.

I've witnessed horrible things as Neverland's Shadow, but I've never seen anyone die.

"Belle was wrong, you know," Emmit mutters. "I wouldn't have been able to save her. That's not how my gift works."

There are only three fairies left on the Island—Belle, Cass, and Emmit. Cass was never shy about his powers. He was happy to add touches of Forever Frost all around our little compound to make things more comfortable for the Lost.

I learned about Belle's ability to manipulate time while I was in shadow form, witnessing the extent of her cruelty firsthand as she used her dust to drag out the suffering of her victims. But Emmit has never used or even hinted at his gifts.

Peter never asked what he could do, and up until now, I've never been able to. "Why would she say it then? What can you do?"

Emmit shakes his head, his gaze falling to the ground. "It doesn't matter."

A heavy silence hangs between us, pregnant with questions I sense he doesn't want to answer, but I am not Peter. I won't push my curiosities aside for the sake of making others comfortable. If Emmit can do something to save The Lost or if he can help us out of this mess, I need to know what that is.

"How long will her dust last?" I ask, trying to steady my voice to sound like Peter's, but it shakes. The Island is changing. It's not listening to me anymore, and it's hurting the souls it used to protect.

I'm scared of what else it might do to them. Better yet, to me.

"Depends on how strong she is. This time freeze could last a few hours or a few days."

Days.

The notion brings a mix of relief and fear. Days would grant me time to strategize and plan to escape, but it would also keep me separated from Wednesday for longer than planned. I initially thought I would only be gone for a few weeks in her time, but now it seems like it might stretch to months. Stars above, I hope it's not years. However long it takes, she will despise me, thinking I abandoned her, but at least she'll be safe.

"You're not Peter," Emmit says, his voice barely a whisper. It's a statement, not a question.

I consider lying, but the gravity of our situation demands honesty. "Was I that obvious?"

"No, Belle would have devoured you if she knew." Emmit presses, urgency lacing his words. "Where is he?"

"I don't know," I admit, and that singular truth scares me more than any other I have to offer.

"What do you mean, you don't know? What happened out there?"

"Peter was dying. The mortal realm was reclaiming his spirit and he was too scared to leave Wednesday. He passed out in the hospital and I took over to give him a chance to rest. I thought crossing into Neverland would put him back in charge and kicked me out of his body. That's what usually happens, but he never came back. I can't even hear him."

"This isn't good."

"I know."

Emmit shakes his head. "I don't think you do. You were the one in command when you crossed into Neverland. Right?"

"Yeah. So?"

"There can only be one reigning king and you're not him," Emmit emphasizes, his words hitting me like a sudden blow. He clenches his hands again, tugging at the chains relentlessly.

"Emmit! What is going on?" I whisper yell. I don't know if Belle has guards that would tell her what they overhear or if the room is spelled to carry our voices across her castle. I shouldn't risk anyone listening to our conversation, but I need answers.

"By the laws of our land, you killed the king, which means the Island will choose a new ruler. Everything we know about Neverland is about to change," Emmit explains.

"I didn't kill him. I'm right here."

"Exactly. You," Emmit points out, his finger jabbing toward me. "Not Peter."

CHAPTER 8

Wednesday

I let out a piercing scream, the pain ripping through me, unbearable and relentless. A small part of me wishes I listened to Tyle and went to the hospital to deliver, but I couldn't risk it. My pregnancy may have been normal, easy even compared to what I expected, but there's still a chance this baby could be born different.

"I can see the head!" Tyle says excitedly. "One more push, Wednesday. You can do this."

I shake my head, tears mingling with sweat as another contraction seizes my body. The pain spreads from my lower back, down my legs, and wraps around my chest. I can't breathe, can't think beyond the building pressure.

"Push!" Tyle yells.

"Now!" Peter's voice echoes in my ear. He's been a constant throughout my pregnancy, a whisper in my mind, an intangible presence. A figment of longing my imagination conjured to ease the sting of being abandoned.

I scream once more, summoning every ounce of strength I have left, as pins and needles crawl up my spine, overwhelming every sensation until the pressure suddenly releases, leaving me breathless. I collapse onto the air mattress we blew up on the living room floor, an exhausted, sweaty mess.

"It's a girl," Tyle says, moving closer to my side.

I struggle to prop myself up on my trembling arms and gaze at the tiny bundle of blonde hair wrapped in a terry-cloth towel. She's beautiful.

She's blonde.

Oh, fuck. I sink back onto the air mattress and silent tears stream down my cheeks as I realize what that means.

"Hey," Tyle coos, attempting to console me. "It's ok. You don't have to see her. I have a friend in child services who could—"

"No!" I wipe my eyes and pull myself together. Today is a good day, a happy day.

I hold out my hands and Tyle carefully places the baby girl in my trembling arms. "I just needed a minute."

"Does she look like him?" My sister asks softly.

"Who?"

"Peter."

"No," I say solemnly, although I wish my baby girl did. "The baby isn't his."

Tyle's eyes widen with shock. "There were others? You had to—"

"No," I interject flatly. "I chose to be with Cass."

"So, you're relieved?" she asks, confused. I get it. Everything that happened in Neverland is confusing, and she barely knows half of it. "Those are happy tears?"

"Yeah, Tyle," I lie. "I'm happy."

"What are you going to call her?"

I hesitate. I toyed with so many names, but none of them felt right. Waverly. Willow. Wendeline. Now that I see her, I understand why they were wrong.

"Mira," I say confidently. That name was never on my radar, but it came to me the moment I laid eyes on her. "Because she's my little miracle."

***

I sit in my old room and watch Mira sleep. Tyle converted it into a playroom for the kids after I refused to move in. We both agreed that the three of us—her, Kenny, and me— under one roof would be a recipe for disaster.

Instead, we transformed the detached garage into a one-bedroom suite for me and Mira. I'm close enough to help with the kids but far enough away to have some privacy. It's worked out well, especially since Tyle went back to work in the office last month.

But I reluctantly agreed to sleep in my old room for the next few nights. Tyle insists I should be close in case I need an extra pair of hands, but I think she just misses the new baby smell. Wanda is walking and talking, ready to conquer the world, while Wyatt is crawling, eager to chase after her.

I place my hand on Mira's chest, a surge of terror coursing through me along with the irrational fear she'll stop breathing. Her heart beats steadily beneath my touch as my hand rises and falls in rhythm with her breaths. I stare at her in awe, still struggling to believe that I brought such a beautiful thing into this world. Despite partly belonging to Cass, she's perfect.

"You should eat," my sister's voice drifts from the doorway.

"I don't want to leave her," I say without looking away.

"I get it; being a new mom is scary." Tyle takes me by the hand and pulls me out of the rocking chair. "But you've got to take care of yourself, too, Mama. Mira isn't going anywhere. The kitchen is just downstairs and you can watch her on the video monitor while you're there."

I don't want to leave. Something in me aches at the thought of walking away, even just for a few minutes, but Tyle is right. Mira is settled. Safe. And I am hungry.

I follow Tyle downstairs. As soon as we're in the kitchen she pulls out all the fixings to make me a sandwich. She goes through

Mom's motions, cutting off the edges and sectioning it into quarters. Just like she does for her kids. Something I plan to do for my own daughter.

How crazy is that? I have a child.

"What made you decide against the traditional W?" Tyle asks, pulling me from the comfort of my thoughts.

"An M is an upside-down W. I figured it was close enough."

Tyle laughs, then picks the sugary bits off of the blueberry muffin she bought for breakfast this morning. "And here I thought I would be the rebellious one."

A sudden chill sends a shiver down my spine. I wait for the familiar whisper that usually accompanies the sensation, but my mind remains eerily silent.

"You okay?" Tyle asks, concern etched on her face.

"Yeah, I've just got a weird feeling," I say as a sense of unease settles over me. "I'm going to check on Mira."

"Wens, she's fine," Tyle reassures me, adjusting the monitor to face me. "See?"

"*Hurry*!" Peter's voice shouts in my ears.

I jump off the barstool, startled to have heard him so clearly, and sprint up the stairs. My heart pounds in my chest as Peter continues to yell, *"Faster, Darling! Run!"*

I skid to a stop in the doorway as a figure bends over Mira's bassinet. I know him, even without seeing his face. That Jack Frost blonde hair. The chill that follows wherever he goes. The heart-racing excitement drenched in fear.

"You did well, Darling." Cass turns toward me, cradling Mira in his arms. "She's beautiful."

"Give me back my daughter," I seethe.

"Our daughter," he corrects, a hint of menace in his voice.

"Cass," I warn, my voice trembling. I never thought I'd see him again. I didn't even know he could leave the Island. But I try to be strong for Mira. Scared or not, I'll do anything to keep her safe. "I swear to the stars, I'll kill you if you don't hand her over."

"Your threats are useless, whereas mine…" He pauses, barely looking at me, and ice spreads like spider webs across the floor.

"What do you want?"

"Nothing you can give me, but her…" Cass looks down at my daughter and their resemblance is uncanny. "She can give me the world."

"Cass." I step forward, determination burning in my eyes. I don't know what he has planned but, knowing him, it can't be good.

"Say goodbye to Mommy, Mira."

"Cass!" I lunge at him, but instead of colliding with a body, I pass through a burst of snow and crash into the bassinet.

I push through the swirling flakes, scattering them across the floor, searching for a portal or a marker of some sort—anything that can lead me back to Neverland.

"Wens?" Tyle's voice fills the room. She freezes in the doorway, her eyes widening as she takes in the ice and snow invading her home in the middle of May. "What's happening?"

"He took her!" I say frantically. Tears fill my eyes as I realize that I can't follow them to Neverland. I'm stranded in this world, alone again, while my daughter is with a monster.

"Who?"

"Cass."

"The man you said was her father?" Tyle tries to put the pieces together, but she doesn't have enough clues to make everything line up. I left so much out of my story, too many details about where I was and with whom.

I don't have the strength to explain. I'm physically exhausted from giving birth, in pain from my fall, and emotionally in shock. I nod because right now, that's all I can do.

"Where'd they go?"

"To Neverland."

"You can't be serious," Tyle says in disbelief. "Is that what they called the place they took you to? That's so fucked up."

She starts rattling on about trauma and triggers, and I vaguely hear her mention something about calling the cops, but I'm only half listening.

Pan said he and Peter argued for hours about how to bring me to Neverland, which means it's possible to get there without dying. I decide right then that I don't care what I have to do or how long it takes; I'm going to get my daughter back.

"Thank you, officers. We'll be in touch." Kenny closes the front door and rejoins Tyle and me in the living room. She's holding Wyatt close, rocking him to keep him quiet. Silently basking in relief that he wasn't the child stolen.

I hold a cup of tea in my hands. It's gone cold waiting for me to take a sip. I don't like it cold. The cold brings me back to the nursery and to the frost that has yet to melt on the wooden floors. The cops called it a scientific bio-weapon. They said I was lucky it didn't touch me. They couldn't be more right and wrong if I spelled it out for them.

"Your description was really helpful," Tyle says, trying to reassure me, but nothing she says will ease the ache in my chest. "I bet they'll have a sketch drawn up lickety-split. Cass's face will be all over the news by sundown."

It won't make a difference. The cops could post Cass's face on every billboard across the globe and no one would find him.

"Wens?" Kenny gingerly touches my arm. I jump in my seat, startled by how cold his hand is, and spill the tea all over their couch cushion and my leg.

"Sorry," I say, frantically searching for a napkin to soak up the liquid before it stains the upholstery.

Kenny drops to his knees before me and takes my hand. He sets my cup on the coffee table beside us and looks me in the eyes. "It's going to be okay."

I force a tight-lipped smile and nod. "I know."

"It's nearly dark," Tyle says. "Is anyone hungry?"

I look out the window. She's right. It's twilight. The only time when the veil between my world and theirs is thin enough to pass through.

I push Kenny aside and run upstairs to my old room. It's the same disheveled mess, only worse now that the cops have trampled through and I drop to the ground and touch the ice trails. They've etched themselves into the wood like burn marks. I crawl on my hands and knees, searching for anything that might be different. Waiting for Peter to speak up and guide me home, but he's been eerily quiet since Mira left. I can't even feel his presence anymore.

"Wednesday?" Tyle asks cautiously. "What are you doing?"

"Looking?"

"For what?" she asks, probably thinking I've lost my mind.

I sit back on my legs, frustrated. "I don't know, a clue. Something that could tell me where he's gone or might go. Anything, really."

"Sweetie, there's nothing here."

"I know," I say reluctantly.

"And there's nothing you can do right now," she adds.

I know that, too, but I don't want to admit it because saying that out loud feels like giving up.

"Unless you can tell the police more details about the Island you lived on or something about Cass's past that could help track him down, you just need to sit tight."

"I don't know anything about his past, but I do know a little about Peter's," I say, an idea forming. "Tyle, I need your passport."

"What?" She looks at me, startled, then shakes her head. "No! Why?"

"Peter mentioned having family in London. I could go there and find them."

"Do you realize how crazy that sounds?"

"Yes, but I have to try, Tyle. It's the only lead I have." England is where the Peter Pan stories originated. There's bound to be something tangible I can grab onto there. Wendy's original journals. A paper trail of Peter's estate and what happened to it. Or maybe I can find the bank holding all of Peter's money and find out how he's been contacting them. I might not have a solid plan yet, but I know I'll learn something there. I just know it.

"No."

"Tyle!" I shout, frustrated and on the brink of tears.

"No! I'm not going to support you running away to chase after that man. Peter's not the one who stole your baby. He can't help you."

"You don't know that!"

"Neither do you!"

"I'm going," I say, my voice firm. "Either you give me your passport, or I'll find someone to forge me one."

"Here." Kenny steps into the room, holding a little blue booklet.

"Kenny!" Tyle yells. "What the hell?"

"You can't mamma-bear her, Tyle. It won't work. Either support Wednesday and have a relationship when she comes back, or fight her tooth and nail and lose her forever."

"I don't want you to leave." She takes the passport from her husband and hands it to me.

"I know, but I have to go." I pull her in for a hug. This feels like the beginning of goodbye and I'm surprised at how much I don't want to go. Tyle became an unexpected anchor in my life, but I can't stay. "You'd cross oceans for Wanda and Wyatt, wouldn't you?"

"In a heartbeat," she says without hesitation.

"Well, that's what I'm going to do. I don't care how long it takes; I'm finding my daughter."

"Okay. Just promise me you won't disappear again. I can't lose you twice."

I force another smile. My heart breaks because if I find a way to Neverland, I can't guarantee I'll be able to come back. But Tyle doesn't need to suffer through that pain just yet. I'll call her every day and reassure her of how grateful I am for her these past few months. I'll make sure she knows she's loved and that, no matter what, I'll never forget her. I agree to her promise because today I can keep it.

Tomorrow...

I make no promises about what the future holds.

CHAPTER 10

James

A large wave crashes over the bow of the Jolly Roger. The Neversea is angry, trying to hold us back, but we've come further than we ever have before. I hold the helm with both hands while the winds and waves try to force me to return to the Island.

Smee hangs onto the railing as she climbs the steps to meet me on the quarterdeck. Another wave washes over the side, drenching her, nearly dragging her to the trenches of the Neversea, but she hangs tight. The boat rocks to the other side, affording her a brief moment to reach me before it tips the other way, and we're soaked again.

"Yeh should be below deck," I tell her. Sea water drops off my hair and into my eyes. I wipe it away quickly, only able to fight the ocean with one hand for so long. "It isn't safe up here."

"I don't think she can take much more of this," Smee says, ignoring my request.

"She's a good ship. She'll be fine." I hope.

I built the Jolly Roger from scraps of Mariner, the first ship I sailed to Neverland. Pieces of her floated to shore, as well as remnants of other boats the Neversea claimed. It took a few years and a lot of trial and error, but she's held strong since her maiden voyage.

I wince as seawater washes over the deck, this time from behind. The salty spray clings to my shirt, probably staining it red as it saturates my bandages.

Belle's marks are closed thanks to Smee's quick work with a needle, but the skin is still sore. My cuts haven't healed like they ought to have, and the bite mark on my neck is festering. The dark purple veins around the wound and her poison has spread in the last three days from a tight-knit circle into tendrils reaching down my back and over my shoulder. I can't worry about what will happen if they reach my heart. Right now, the goal is to make it out of this storm alive. And then find Wednesday.

"Cap?" Smee asks wearily. She points to a dark mass in the water. "What is that?"

"The gates of hell," I say, half-teasing, but it's precisely what I'm looking for. I spin the wheel, banking us hard to the left and straight toward the mouth of the beast.

The ocean fights to keep us away from the portal to the realm of the living. She throws us from side to side, begging us to turn around, but we can't go back. Not until we have the Darling.

Smee loses her footing and slides across the deck. My heart lurches because I can't help her. We'll lose control of the ship if I do. I watch, terrified that my first mate will go over, but she grabs onto the taffrail just in time.

"Get below deck," I order once Smee is on her feet again.

That was too close a call. Our code dictates we care for the crew over the sailor. If someone falls over, they're gone. Plus, once a soul is pulled from the Neversea, it can't go back. The deep waters will eat through them like acid. There are minutes, if that, to save them, but if rescuing one means damning the rest...

Well, everyone here knows the risk of coming aboard.

"No," Smee states firmly.

"That wasn't a request."

"I'm not going anywhere, James."

"Stubborn ass woman!" I fire off, half-teasing. She is stubborn, but I wouldn't have her any other way.

"Ungrateful scallywag!" she spits back, grinning. "What's the plan?"

"We're going to sail into the whirlpool and hope to come out the other side."

Smee looks to the darkened water, thrashing with whitecaps, then back to me. My plan is as, if not more, reckless as it sounds. "Seriously?"

"If yeh've got a better way to cross between realms, I'm all ears."

"Fucking hell." Smee grabs a nearby dock rope and wraps it around her waist. "If we die, I'm finding your ass in the next life and killing you."

"Duly noted. Now hang on!"

The ship groans as we slide into the vortex. Something cracks and lightning thunders from above. Dark clouds in a once-blue sky begin to rain down on us, sending another warning that I stupidly ignored the first time I crossed into these waters. This time, I know what it means. Sink or swim, ride or die, our world is about to change.

"Get ready to hold yehr breath!" I yell over the sound of lightning and rushing water. I don't know if Smee hears me, but I take in a big gulp of air just as the ship falls into the center of the whirlpool and we're surrounded by water.

CHAPTER 11

Pan

Scarlett's screams echo in the damp dungeon. She's the first to wake from Belle's time spell. I have a feeling Belle let her dust wear off so I can see my friend's suffering before being forced to watch another die.

I still have hope the Island will heal Heidi's wounds, but that hope is fleeting. Her skin lost its golden hue, possibly two days ago. That guess comes from the timeline of when Emmit and I got our last meal. If you could call crackers and a slice of ham a meal, but it's better than fully starving. Belle has fed and watered us just enough to keep our bodies from shutting down so she can drag out our pain.

"Scar," Emmit says in a tone meant to calm her. "Look at me, not Heidi."

Scarlett's cries turn frantic. She sags against the wall, her arms stretching tight as she turns into a useless bundle of emotions. Emmit tries his best to soothe her, but the girl needs a hug—something neither of us can provide.

"Scarlett!" I say, my voice booming through the room.

She looks at me, eyes wide because Peter never yells, but her cries have temporarily ceased. I've shocked her enough to derail her train of thought. It's time to put her to use and make a break for it.

Emmit's face pinches together as his head moves from side to side in a warning. A tinkling sound rings in my ears. A language I haven't heard in ages but recognize—the voice of the Fae.

Act like Peter, he cautions. *Not his shadow.*

"We don't have long before the others wake or Belle comes back," I warn, trying my hardest not to scare her. Scarlett is like a baby deer, curious but skittish. One wrong move and the thread she's holding onto will snap.

"Belle?" Scarlett asks, her eyes widening with the realization that we aren't playing a game. Peter liked to play games, never this dark or cruel, but the Lost partook in some twisted games nonetheless.

"I need you to pull yourself together," I say slowly. "Your chains, can you get your hands out of them?"

"What?"

"Goddamn it, woman, your wrists!" I take a breath and summon every bit of strength I have left not to shout. I let the air out slowly, then use my most placating voice to say, "You're so tiny. Do you think you can slip out of the chains?"

Scarlett twists and tugs against her bindings. Her arms move, but not enough. The metal cuffs are smaller than her knuckles. They won't slip past. "I can't."

"What if you break your thumbs? Maybe if you dislocate the bones, your hand will be small enough to slip free." Logic to save our lives. But fear and pain can alter the brain, and Scarlett is in shock, not survival mode.

"What! No!" Scar shakes her head. "What's gotten into you?"

"It's not a bad idea," Emmit mumbles. "I can't heal him," he adds, meeting Scarlett's gaze. "But I can heal you. It'll only hurt for a few minutes."

"Have you two lost your minds?"

"There's a reason you're awake and the others aren't," I lie, but half suspect the admission to be true. Every move Belle makes is calculated. We are pawns in her game and she'll wipe us off the board if we're not smart and careful. "When Belle realizes you're no longer asleep, she'll come for you next."

Scarlett looks from me to Emmit. Her eyes are wide and wet with new tears. "You think she'll kill me?"

I swear to the stars and gods and Fae and every other deity out there, if this woman asks me another pointless question, I might just kill her myself. "Yes, Scar. Belle's a little mad and using all of you as leverage to try and force me to tell her where Wednesday is."

"So, tell her!" Scarlett squeals.

"She'll still kill us," Emmit adds, bringing home my point. "Just because she can. You escaping and setting us free is our best chance at surviving right now. Not what you want to hear, but it's true."

A new sob leaves Scarlett's lips. She wastes precious minutes working through her emotions, and we have no choice except to wait and hope Belle doesn't walk in to make her next kill.

Scarlett sniffles and looks at Emmit. Her face is red and blotchy, her eyes glassy pools of grief. Her breaths come in shallow gasps, but her words are steady. "You're sure you can fix me?"

Emmit nods. "The first hand is going to be the most painful. Try not to scream. The second should go faster because you can snap the bones out of place. Once you're free, come straight to me."

"Okay," Scarlett whispers.

For the first time since I left Wednesday, I have a shred of hope we might escape. Not the panicked kind that clung to Heidi, but a pure wishful chance. But hope is a tricky devil. It skews one's perspective, diverting focus from reality to an improbability.

Scarlet tugs and tries her best to slip free. Her skin pulls as it drags against the metal bindings. She bites her lip to keep from crying out, but her wrist isn't moving, not the way it should. She can't manipulate the bones enough on her own.

I reach for my powers, even though they haven't listened to

me since I arrived, and beg for the Island to free her by any means possible. I wait and hope for the sensation of the Neverland's magic to fill me, but I'm hollow inside. Void of the only feeling I've truly ever known.

Peter has disappeared and the Island has abandoned me.

Despite being surrounded by friends, I am alone for the first time in my life.

"It's okay," I tell her as the reality that this is where our lives ends sinks in. "You did your best."

Scarlett nods her head, unable to speak. I'm sure she's in pain, and the realization that Belle will be coming for her soon is probably hitting home.

I drop my head and close my eyes. I'm tired. This body is fading, even with the food Belle feeds us. I'm not sure how much longer it will last.

I think of Wednesday and smile at how big she must be. I wonder if she's had the child yet and if it's a boy or a girl. I bet she hates me for leaving without saying a word about its existence. If I had, I wouldn't have been able to leave her behind. I needed to pretend the baby wasn't there and hope to be back in time for either Peter or me to be by her side for it's birth.

But I've failed her.

And the little one.

"Ow," Scarlett mumbles and there's a new clanking sound. I open my eyes, and she's rubbing her hip with her hand.

I stare at the fallen shackles in disbelief. The Island listened. Please tell me it heard me and actually listened! "How did you get free?"

"I don't know. They just popped open. What now?"

I'm so excited I could fly, but my happy thoughts aren't enough to lift me off my feet. Still, I have hope again. Neverland may have stripped me bare of my magic, but she hasn't left me to die.

"They're simple locks," Emmit directs. "A twist and latch, but no key is needed. They're meant for the Fae, not mortal souls."

Scarlett goes to him first and just as he said, all she needs to do is twist a small knob and flip the latch for him to be set free.

Emmit's wrists look terrible, red and blistered from the metal burns, but he takes Scarlett's hands in his and starts muttering under his breath.

"Thank you," she says when he lets her go.

Emmit nods, but he looks weaker, aged at least another two or three years, too. "Help Peter, then release the others. I'll find us a way out of here."

Scarlett hurriedly unlatches my bindings. My arms ache, finally released from the awkward position, but it's a good ache. I grab Emmit by the elbow as he passes. He stops and looks at me, but the spark in his eyes is fading.

"Are you okay?" I ask.

"Nothing comes free." He holds up his hand and there are new marks on his wrist. "When I heal someone, I take on their injuries. To save Heidi would have meant killing myself. I loved her, but her life wasn't worth sacrificing mine for."

I nod, understanding, and let him go. The only person in all the worlds I'd die for is the Darling, and that's only if it were a last resort.

It takes a few feeble minutes to free Xyris and Aria from their shackles. I help lower them to the floor. Belle's dust hasn't worn off yet, but I have a feeling it will soon.

Aria's skin is in worse shape than Emmit's. Burn marks cover her arms and back. The charred black skin is angry, and her wrists have rubbed themselves nearly to the bone. She's going to be in a lot of pain when she wakes up.

"I found a way out," Emmit says, coming back into the room. "But we don't have a lot of time."

He picks Xyris up, cradling him in his arms while I reach for Aria. I'm careful with how I hold her. Even the slightest touch pulls away the paper-thin skin around her burns.

"What about Heidi?" Scarlett asks. Her gaze bounces from Emmit to me as we have a silent conversation.

"I can't carry both of them and keep Aria's skin intact, and you're too weak," I say to Emmit, the language of the Fae coming back to me. I'm not sure if I'm getting everything right, but he seems to follow what I'm trying to say.

I could try...

Don't, Emmit. You need to save your strength. Peter would understand if we have to sacrifice one to save the group.

He chuckles lightly but I don't think Scarlett hears it. *You sound like a pirate.*

That's possibly the worst insult I've ever been given. They're loyaless souls, blindly following a *Captain* who knowingly feeds their memories to Belle to save his own skin. James is spineless and has zero regard for the hell he's put Neverland through.

As much as I hate the man, I try to sound like James when I tell Scarlett, "Heidi is literally dead weight. We have to leave her."

Scarlett's mouth falls open. Abandoning one of his own is something Peter would never say. He'd find a way to save everyone, even if it meant sacrificing himself. "We can't! I won't."

"You're not strong enough to carry her and we can't." I lift Aria slightly in case Scarlett needs the reminder that my hands are already full. Her living friend needs me. Her dead one is already gone.

"If it helps, Heidi didn't feel anything when she died," Emmit adds. "We'll do a remembrance for her when it's safe, but you need to make a choice, Scar. Stay behind and die, too, or let her go and live."

Scarlett bites her bottom lip. Tears well in her eyes again, and I get it; it's hard to say goodbye. "This feels wrong."

"I know," I agree, "but staying here won't bring Heidi back. All it does is put you in danger and she wouldn't want that."

Scarlett sniffles and tries to hold in her tears. She's breaking, we all are, but doing her best to stay strong. "Is it wrong that I want to make Belle pay for what she did? Does that make me a bad person?"

"I'm not the right person to ask," I admit. If I could access my magic, I'd have struck Belle dead with a lightning bolt the moment she touched one of the Lost. The Island delivered them to Peter to keep their memories safe from Belle. I don't know why, but I'm sure it had its reasons. They were to be protected at all costs, and I lost one.

The weight of my failure feels like a knife in my lungs.

Maybe the Island took my magic as punishment. I left Neverland when it needed me most. Because of me, the Lost were unprotected.

"Why not?" she asks, but I don't answer.

Emmit saves me from answering and leads us down a dark corridor. There are no lights to guide us. The deeper we go, we can't see what's coming or what's been left behind. There's only the sound of our breaths and the pitter-patter of our steps.

Scarlett's question plays on a loop in my mind. Is it wrong to want payback for Heidi's death? No, I don't think it is. Why?

Because I intend to kill the bitch, and her brother, too.

CHAPTER 12

Wednesday

I see her sometimes, late at night when the stars fade into day and the alcohol is deep in my veins. Mira's beautiful face, with her thin blonde hair, peacefully sleeping in a wood-carved cradle. It's not often, only around the full moon when the veil between her world and mine is thin, but I look forward to the visions. Those nights, as hard as they may be, are better than the ones where I have nothing but my thoughts and dreamless sleep.

I poke at the ice cubes in my drink with a straw and wonder if she'll look any different tonight. I can always find something, a subtle change that marks her growth. A child's infancy is precious. Babies change so quickly that it's hard to appreciate the tiny milestones, like turning their heads. She's done that twice now, which tells me my original concept of Neverland time wasn't too far off.

My baby girl is approximately three weeks old.

Three Neverland weeks, the equivalent of nearly three years in this stupid world.

I'd give anything to be with Mira and have tried everything shy of killing myself to find her. My biggest hesitation is that doing so might not take me to her. I can't risk Cass being the only parent she knows. I am a firm believer that circumstance greatly influences a child. If all Mira knows are lies and deceit, she doesn't stand a chance at becoming the good-hearted person I know she's meant to be.

If I knew dying would take me to her, I'd do it in a heartbeat, but until I have guaranteed passage into Neverland, I'm not ready going that route.

I sip on my soda and wait for the night to slip away. There's no point in drinking just yet. I have to find that happy line between wasted and functional, or else I'll fall asleep and miss my chance to see her. I only get three nights a month.

Three precious nights I refuse to waste.

Tyle thinks I've lost my mind and maybe she's right. Maybe I dream of Mira because I can't let her go. And maybe the few times I've thought I've heard Peter's voice since she left were nothing but a symptom of insanity. If it is, I'm not ready to give up my craziness.

"Can I buy you a drink?" a deep voice asks.

I smile against my straw and glance at the man who's made himself comfortable to my right. He's handsome, with dark skin as smooth as chocolate and amber eyes. His wide smile is welcoming, but I know what he wants.

The answer I've yet to decide is, do I want it too? Will he be the one to finally fill the void Peter Pan left or will he be just another body to pass the time?

"Sure. I'll take a Scotch and soda," I say to the bartender.

"A woman with refined taste. I'm intrigued."

"Are you now?" I push my virgin drink aside and thank the bartender as he slides the mixed drink in front of me. The first sip is bitter. The bartender used the cheap shit, but I don't mind. It hits hard and fast. Exactly what I need if I'm going to make it through the night.

I tune my new friend out as he talks, not even catching this man's name, but I let him continue. I smile and nod when appropriate. I even manage to pitch into the conversation with small tidbits of nothing.

"I bet you would," I say when he mentions how he'd love to get to know me better.

I smile and talk and flirt until I've had enough drinks to where I feel sorry enough for myself to ask, "So, is this your plan? To sit here and buy me drinks all night, or will you ever make a move?"

"What did you have in mind?"

I toss back the last half of my cocktail—my fourth in less than an hour—and grab the man by the hand. I lead him to the back of the building where the bathrooms are.

It's almost midnight. I don't have time for hotel rooms and foreplay. I don't want to cuddle after the deed is done and fall asleep in his arms. I just want a good, hard fuck to feel halfway normal for five minutes.

"Move," I say to the lady at the front of the bathroom line.

"Fuck you! I have to pee!" she retorts. I don't blame her for being angry, but I've got a small window to feel good before my night takes me home. A few more drinks and a walk by the river after last call, and I'll finally get to see my baby girl.

Until then, I've got an emptiness inside me to try to fill and time to kill.

"Piss in a corner." I open my clutch, pull out a hundred-dollar bill, and shove it at her. "Then go buy yourself a new pair of panties."

I push forward as soon as the door opens, before the woman in line can skirt past, and lock both me and my new friend inside. I grab him by the waist of his pants as he says, "Fuck, that was hot."

I don't care to talk and make quick work with his belt to drop his pants. I fist his cock with my hand and pump his long, thick length. The guy drops his head and presses his lips to my neck while I mentally prepare myself to be stretched and stuffed. It's gonna hurt, but I welcome the pain. It reminds me that I'm alive and that I can feel something more than emptiness.

Mr. Big Dick slides his hand up my thigh to my center. He

pushes my panties aside and dips one finger inside me. I wish I could say it feels good, but he's not who I want, so it just...feels.

"Don't tease me, baby," I pant, faking a breathless moan. "I want to feel you." Men like it when I tell them what I want, and this one caves at my whispers.

"You got it, sugar." He lifts me by the hips, onto the edge of the sink, and drives inside of me with one harsh push.

I wasn't ready. I cry out, the heat of accommodating someone so big almost too much to bear, and Mr. Big Dick takes it as a sign of endearment. He thrusts deeper. Harder.

I drop my head back against the mirror and stare at the drawn-on drop ceiling tiles. Eventually, this should start to feel good, but the dry friction and the sheer size of this man is a wickedly uncomfortable combination. Until it does, I fake breathless pants of pleasure.

"Seriously?" James's voice seeps into my thoughts. "Come now, Sunshine. Yeh can do better than this. Can't yeh?"

I almost smile at the familiarity. James sounds so real, so much like the man I met at the Cove. He's been a constant in Wendy's memories and she's pushed him into my dreams almost as much as she's pushed Peter. I never expected to miss a man I barely know, but I feel just as tied to her husband as I do Peter Pan. This living two lives, both mine and re-living hers, is confusing.

I roll my head to the side and gasp when I see pale blues encircled by a layer of charcoal looking at me. James's midnight black hair is longer, falling into his eyes, but when he smiles those same two dimples come out of hiding and warmth fills my belly. He's not dressed in a flowing white shirt or loose black pants like he was at Harper's Edge. He blends into this world, wearing dark skinny jeans and an ash-colored Henley.

I've never seen James outside of my dreams before. Not even in my reckless days, when I thought channeling Bella from *New Moon* would bring Peter's voice back after he left me. It's always been Mira, and occasionally, I get to sneak a glance at Cass when he's with her. Watching them in that twilight hour is like peering through a window.

They're so close, yet painfully far.

A tear slides down my cheek as I stare up at the ceiling tiles again. Maybe my sister is right. Maybe all of this is in my head and I *am* losing my shit.

The thrusting stops and Mr. Big Dick pulls out of me. I wait for him to tell me how he wants my body next, but in the span of a heartbeat there's a crashing sound. I open my eyes and find him lying unconscious on the dirty bathroom floor, his pants and boxers at his knees, the singular stall door still swinging and clanging against its lock.

James steps into my line of sight, blocking my view of Mr. Big Dick. He plants his hands on either side of the sink I'm perched on, boxing me in. He smells like cedar and the sea and the scent tugs at a memory. I'm not sure if it's mine or Wendy's but longing fills my chest. I reach for his cheek, half expecting my hand to go through his face like a mirage, but I touch skin. Warm, scruffy skin.

"This wasn't how I hoped to find yeh again, Sunshine." His frown is deep. I'd feel bad if he were truly here, embarrassed even, but he's not. My mind has either created an imaginary friend or blurred the face of someone who could look like James and is torturing me. "What are yeh doing?"

I shrug, still unconvinced I'm not having some weird drunken hallucination. "Trying to feel something."

"Right," he says as if he understands the gaping hole living has left.

The real James might. I've watched through Wendy's eyes as she drifted away from her marriage and pulled toward Peter. I felt her heartbreak as James fought for their relationship, even though he knew she was unfaithful. It's hard being able to relate to both sides of the story because both we're victims of circumstance. Neither one of us is destined for happiness.

"How's that working out for yeh?"

I shrug again. Clearly, it's not going so well. I'm having conversations with am imaginary man in public, my pseudo-date is passed out on the floor, and I haven't orgasmed in years.

Life is great.

James comes closer and brushes his nose along my jaw. My heart races as the warmth in my chest drifts lower. "I can make yeh feel again, Sunshine," he whispers, his breath hot against my ear. "All yeh have to do is ask."

Right. Just ask my imaginary ex-whatever to stick me with his non-existent dick because that's going to make me feel normal again. Wendy's memories filter into my conscious thoughts. For a moment, I'm her again—like I am in my dreams—tied to James's bed naked. He dips between our legs and the rush of pleasure she feels has me blushing.

Fingers trail along my jawline and pillow my bottom lip. The past fades away and for a heartbeat, I consider asking. What's the worst that can happen? I fall that much further down this rabbit hole of hell? I fuck yet another man in this dirty bathroom? Mr. Big Dick couldn't hit it right. Who knows, maybe this guy—if he's real—can. *Stars, I really am losing my mind.*

"Please."

"Say it, Sunshine." James's voice is a low growl that awakens something deep inside me. Anxiousness mixes with excitement and it has my resolve bending. "I've waited a long time to hear those words."

"Fuck me, James." Stars above, I hope this isn't some fucked up hallucination. If it is, though, I might have to buy stock in whatever kind of scotch that was. I'd drink it every night if I could.

James takes my chin between his thumb and forefinger and tilts my head. "As yeh wish."

James

Finding the Darling was harder than I expected.

This world is bigger than I remembered. The streets are louder, the cities busier, and the magic it once held is damn near gone. Days passed, sailing along the coastlines, before I finally felt the same pull that sucked me into Harper's Edge weeks ago. The extraordinary thread that ties our past and the present together.

Peter thinks he and the Darling are soul mates, and that may be true, but she chose me in that life and the one before and was meant to in every life after had we not been sucked into Neverland. That's the beauty of rebirth. When a soul moves onto the next stage of their life, they find their way to their lovers once again.

So long as the Darling and I exist in the same realm I will always find her, love her, and then give her the choice of who she wants to be with.

However, discovering her in the dirty bathroom of a tavern being fucked by a man who has no business sticking his dick inside my Darling was not a part of the plan. But even the best-laid plans have hiccups.

"Fuck me, James," she whispers, her voice trembling.

A smirk tugs at my lips because I've waited too many years for my Darling to return. Her soul may love my brother, but this woman is unsure of what she wants. All she knows is that without us, she is incomplete.

But tonight, she'll learn what it means to feel whole again.

I pinch Wednesday's chin between my fingers and pull her lips to mine. She holds back, probably unsure if this is what she truly desires. I give her time to decide, but I know what will happen. The moment she opens herself up to the idea of us, this world will find a spark of magic it lost long ago.

Wednesday's tongue pushes into my mouth and a jolt of energy courses through me. The air ripples around us in a way that would make me nervous if we were back on the Island but here the magic in the room has everything to do with us and nothing to do with Neverland.

Wednesday grabs me by the shirt and pulls me closer. She feels it too, this hum of life. I know she does. Her legs wrap around my waist and I lift her off the dirty counter. I don't need the help of the sink to support her. She's light as air in my arms.

Darling's fingers touch everything they can reach. My hair. Neck. Back. Her kisses are hungry, like she's been starved of life and I'll happily give her mine if that's what she needs.

Her nails brush over the stitches on my back and my muscles tighten as a ripple of pain fights the heat she emits. I ignore the discomfort and support Wednesday with one arm while my other hand finds my belt and I drop my pants.

"Are yeh sure about this, Sunshine?" Reckless isn't usually my brand of woman.

Neither is intoxicated nor brokenhearted, but this is my Darling. My *wife*. Something my brother and everyone else who toyed with Wednesday seems to have forgotten. For better or worse. In life and beyond death. We belong to each other.

"Please," she whimpers and that's all it takes for my hesitations to crumble.

I drop her onto my shaft, careful not to hurt the woman while her hands search for a part of me to grab onto. She pulls my mouth to her and kisses me again, panting between breaths, begging, "More, please, more."

I back her against the wall and angle myself to drive deeper. She melts into me. If I'm not careful, I'll come soon, and I can't have that until I know my Darling is satisfied.

I rip the front of Darling's dress and drop my lips to her shoulder. Wednesday's back arches and, like a memory come to life, I feel her come undone. When I'm sure she's satisfied, I pull out, set her on her feet, and finish in my hand.

I've already had children and lost them. There is no pain comparable to the feeling, not even death, which is why I won't risk conceiving again. Not even with my Darling. I watch Wednesday in the mirror as I clean myself up. She stands, unmoved from her spot on the wall, eyes closed.

"Yeh okay over there, Sunshine?"

She smiles, still lost in whatever thought has captured her mind, and says, "Yeah. Best I've been in years." She sniffles, then looks down at her feet and wipes her eyes. "If only this were real."

I dry my washed hands on my pants and cross in front of her. She's so tiny, even in heels. She barely reaches my chin. I crouch to be at eye level and try to read what's going on. Wednesday looks older. Tired. So much like the woman I met in the cove, but different too. "How long has it been since yeh left Neverland?"

Wednesday's eyes snap open as her head tilts to the side like she's finally breaking through the fog and seeing me for the first time. "You know about Neverland?"

"Answer me, beautiful. How long?"

"Three years."

Fuck. I run my hands through my hair and push the strands back. It's longer than I like, but the damned things grow faster in this world than they do in mine. I could cut it tonight and by tomorrow it would be in my eyes again. That should have been my first clue that time doesn't run parallel to Neverland. It skips days. Hours. Weeks.

No wonder the Darling looks so lost.

"Why are you here?" Wednesday asks as if she doesn't trust her own eyes.

I don't blame her. I can't begin to imagine the hell she's been through living on these lands. All the more reason to bring her home.

Wednesday tries to cover herself, but the torn dress and her lack of bra leave her chest out there for the world to see. I pull my shirt over my head and hand it to her. Can't have everyone looking at what's mine while we make our way to the ship.

"I owe yeh a voyage, love. Thought yeh could use a ride back home."

Wednesday's eyes dart to her date, still out cold from the bit of dust I stole from Belle on the floor. "What about him?"

I walk over and tuck the man's cock back into his pants. Despite trying to claim what was never his, he's done me no wrong and doesn't deserve to be shamed by being left exposed. I check his pulse to make sure I didn't hit him with too much magic and am satisfied when I feel the slow beat steadily quickening beneath my fingertips.

"He'll wake before sunrise." I pause, giving her time to process, then add, "Yeh should cover yehself."

"Oh." She pulls my forgotten shirt over her head. It falls to her thighs, nearly as long as her dress. Her gaze drifts to the mark on my shoulder and the deep purple trails that have spread like veins across my skin. "Are you going to be okay?"

In truth? I'm not sure, but Bell's poison and my well-being aren't something worth troubling the Darling with. We have enough on our plates navigating to the ship tonight and the voyage back to Neverland tomorrow won't be easy.

I force a grin and extend my hand, which she quickly takes. It feels good having her close again. Almost like old times. Too bad I know it can't last. "With yeh by my side, Sunshine, I've never been better."

CHAPTER 14

James

"Stop," Wednesday gasps, her voice strained. "I can't go any further." She doubles over, her hands bracing against her knees. Shallow, rapid breaths do little to alleviate the burning sensation in her chest.

We've walked ten blocks tonight, across the street and along the waterway. We're close to Father's old building. The names of the roads may have changed, and the structures are different, but the river stays the same, as does the bridge. The four walls I slaved in may not be here anymore, but I'd know their location all the same.

Wednesday's gaze finds a spot of land that, decades ago, had a bench overlooking the channel. She stares at it, almost puzzled, and I wonder if she remembers all the afternoons we spent having lunch there. It was our thing, every Thursday at noon. A ritual Wendy started once Father announced our arranged engagement, a way for us to get to know each other.

I learned she was allergic to peanut butter and hated chocolate. Her favorite fruit was strawberries and she favored cats over dogs because of their independence. She'd rather have her hair up in a ponytail than down, but feared her hairline would recede. She hated makeup, but her mother would chastise her for leaving the house without it, so she wore as little as possible. And how her favorite flower was the carnation. Yellow. Not pink.

As for Wendy, she learned every secret I ever had.

"We've got only about a mile to go."

"A mile?" Wednesday's eyes widen in disbelief. She stands straight and tries to look commanding, but her shoulders round forward and her face falls. She's exhausted. Rightly so after the night I've given her. "You're asking a lot of a drunk girl in heels."

Perhaps I am. This world doesn't lend itself to walking. Cars crowd the roads and planes dirty up the skies. In Neverland, we walk or sail. A two-mile trek is nothing more than time spent on the journey, but I get the feeling that walking more than a block is unusual in this world. The Darling's shoes are less than ideal, too. I imagine traveling on a three-inch spike would be difficult, which could be why she's steadily gotten slower. If I were alone, I'd have been back to the boat by now.

"Put yeh arms around me," I order. Time is ticking away. We need to set sail before the sun rises if we're to make it to the tip of the Triangle by daybreak tomorrow. If we miss the full moon, we'll have to wait another month for the portal to open again. I'm not sure Neverland has that much time left. The pirates need me and the Lost...

They have Peter, although I get the feeling that if he left the Darling here this long, something is amiss.

Wednesday obeys and lets me lift her into my arms without questioning or complaining. The stitches on my back stretch as the muscles bend to adjust to her weight. The sensation isn't pleasant, but it's not the worst pain I've felt as of late, either.

"You're hurt," she says, careful not to touch Belle's bite mark. "You shouldn't be carrying me."

"Yehr as light as air. I'll be fine." I'm not exaggerating. She's like paper in my arms. Thin and fragile.

This world has not been kind to the Darling and I want to know why. I want to understand what she's been through the last few years and why she was so damn reckless at that bar. If she truly thinks I'm a memory brought to life in the night, then someone needs to have a talk with her about boundaries. Life is meant to be lived, with a nominal amount of danger thrown into the mix, not risked for moments of pleasure or memories lost in a black void.

"You know they make this thing called a car," she says as we near the bridge. "We can easily get a ride to wherever it is you want to go."

"I'm not meant to be in the world, Sunshine, or any of its contraptions." Also, the motorwagons look a lot different than the last time I saw, let alone rode in, one. I don't like how they entrap their passengers. Yeh can't feel the air on yehr cheeks or smell the spring blooms as yeh drive by. They shut yeh away from the world and that's not a vessel I want to be trapped in.

"Wish I could say the same," she mumbles. Her sorrow is heartbreaking. She stares into the night, falling into her mind again. I can see I'm losing her, and I'm not ready to let go.

"Peter was right to bring yeh to this world but wrong to leave yeh on yehr own, which is why I'm taking yeh home."

She hums once in agreement, but I'm not sure my words are getting through. It's ok, though. Everything will be alright once she wakes in the morning and realizes I'm here for her.

I hold Wednesday a little tighter, hoping she can sense how grateful I am to have found her, even if having her this close is a bitter pill. The last time I had Wendy in my arms like this was on our wedding night. I carried her from the car to our hotel room. We laughed as I struggled to climb three flights of stairs, then fell into each other for the rest of the evening once I made it to our room. Tonight seems to have unwound itself backward, starting with sex and ending in my arms, but I don't mind. I thought Belle had stolen these memories from me. To have the Darling in my arms again is a gift I won't question.

Wednesday rests her head against my chest and closes her eyes. Her breaths are deep and steady. Peaceful. "I wish that were true. It's going to hurt when you leave."

"What hurts yeh, Sunshine?"

"Feeling hollow again." Her words grow softer as she drifts off to sleep, "I thought I'd see Mira tonight, but this is nice, too."

"Who's Mira?" I ask, but Wednesday is out cold. I let her sleep. Reckoning that I'll find that answer in the morning. We have a long journey ahead of us tonight and an even bigger one tomorrow.

~

"That her?" Smee asks, her eyebrows arching, seemingly unimpressed by the tiny unconscious woman in my arms. Or perhaps it's how Wednesday is wearing my shirt and I'm tending to her in a way I have no other.

I step into the rowboat waiting for us on the River Thames and settle myself in the seat, careful not to wake Wednesday. Smee shoves us off the bank and then grabs the oars. She rows us, knowing good and well that I wouldn't bring just any mortal back to the ship.

"I hope she was worth it," Smee adds, and I can't help but note the jealousy in her tone.

Smee and I have never been anything more than captain and first mate. There may have been a few longing stares on both ends, but my body has been Belle's for what feels like an eternity, while my heart has only ever belonged to my wife. There's never been room for anyone else. "She is."

Smee rows silently to the ship. This is one thing I've always appreciated about her. She doesn't feel the need to fill the quiet spaces with drivel. If she speaks it's purposeful, occasionally thoughtful, but never for the sake of simply making noise. "Your bite mark looks like shit. Why didn't you tell me the poison was spreading?"

I glance down at the deep purple marks on my chest. The veins have spread to my arm and nearly reach my elbow. If not for the festering hole, it could pass for a terrible tattoo of a jellyfish. Oddly enough, the tentacles stretching toward my heart aren't as vibrant as they once were. Their length stretches across my chest, but instead of being a deep maroon, they've faded to a soft purple. "It wasn't high on my priorities. Getting the Darling was."

Her brows wrinkle with disapproval. "You've never tried to find her before. Why now?"

"The Island changed when she arrived and it changed again when she left." I didn't notice it at first. The shifts were subtle. Birds in the sky. Bugs in the air—pretty ones, not just the blood-suckers. Things that lay sleeping woke, but the biggest change was the sun. It rose for the first time since we arrived in Neverland and that had *everything* to do with Wednesday. I'm not sure how or why just yet, but I'll figure it out. "I think the Darling might be the key to breaking Belle's timelock on Neverland. I haven't healed yet, which means her dust is weakening."

Smee leans forward, letting the oars rest in their holders. I can see the worry in her eyes. She would have made a good wife and mother to someone had death not selfishly stolen her. Too bad for him, I wanted her, too. "If Belle's dust weakens and your wounds don't heal, you'll die, Cap."

"Good. I'm ready." The tide carries us the last few feet to the port side of the Jolly Roger. Our tiny boat bumps into it and the force is enough to jolt us around a bit. I wonder briefly if this is what it feels like for the souls we pull out of the Neversea. My experience was different. My choice given before I knew what I'd condemned us to.

"You don't mean that." Smee grabs the faded netting hanging over the taffrail of the boat and whistles. Someone from the crew drops a rope ladder over the side. We could have climbed the net, but life is hard enough. Why not do things the easy way when given the chance? "How are we going to get her on the ship? You can't carry her and climb."

"Yehr the brains, Smee. I trust yeh can figure something out." The easiest way would be to hoist Wednesday and me up when we raise the rowboat, but Smee needs to figure that out on her own.

If Belle's poison keeps spreading, the Jolly Roger will need a new captain, and Smee is the only one I'd leave her to.

Smee groans loudly, making her point that I would be lost without her, then smiles. "No chance the Darling can fly, can she?"

Perhaps. There's no telling what gifts the Island graced her with or how far their powers stretch, but until I know for sure what the Darling is capable of I'm keeping all my suspicions to myself. "I think Peter solely holds that card."

"Of course, he does. Your brother is never around when we need him," she grumbles as one of our deckhands lowers the cables down to connect the raft.

"Yeh know why he can't be a part of anything we do." The Fae are tricky. Bargains are never what they seem. There's always more hiding beneath the surface, twists and sacrifices one can never predict. I didn't ask enough questions the day I met Belle. I blindly made a bargain to keep those I loved safe. It took Wendy from this world. It created an unmendable rift with Peter and left me with no one but the Fae bitch herself until she needed new souls and the cove was created.

"You're right. I do." Smee clasps the claw hook around the loop and secures the boat. I smile, pleased she came to the same conclusion I did about the rowboat. I knew she would.

"But does he?" she continues. "Or any of the souls on the Island for that matter? The pirates think he's a monster that's in bed with the Fae, trying to keep them from moving on to the next life. The Lost think you're a heathen, stealing souls for your own diabolical needs. Why not tell everyone the truth and about what you're doing?"

"Yeh know why." Because it's my fault we were all trapped in Neverland. I chartered the ship. I broke course to follow the whispers of legend. I damned us all.

"When are you going to let your guilt go?" Smee steps off the boat and grabs the ladder. She whistles again and the crew hoists Wednesday and me up. "No one in their right mind would have believed the legend to be true. You sought an adventure to excite your boys and woo your wife. Did it go wrong? Yeah, but you don't have to keep punishing yourself."

That's where Smee's wrong. It was my fault. I knew to avoid the Triangle, just like I knew the vortex at its center would take us someplace magical.

I just didn't know everything it would cost me.

Wednesday

My head is killing me, so much so that the pounding wakes me from the deepest sleep I've had in a long time. I don't want to open my eyes. I already know the sun will be mean and the world will be punishing because I let myself fall too deeply down the rabbit hole last night. Even lying still, gravity isn't my friend. My stomach rolls from side to side and I don't know if I'm kicking myself for not eating dinner or grateful.

Last night was something else. Wendy's memories have always been vivid, to the point where sometimes they're all I have of Peter to hold onto, whereas mine from Neverland are broken. I spent so much time angry with him that I don't have many good ones to look back on. As for Shadow, he gave me two nights to remember. Two amazing nights filled with answers and orgasms, but it's not enough to justify the kind of broken heart he left. If it weren't for Wendy and the way her past mingles with the present, I might have moved on by now.

Loving a ghost is painful, improbable, and lonely.

But loving the man Wendy knew, and feeling those moments so fully, it's as if I lived them myself, and that complicates things.

Especially when she loved two men with her whole heart. Each in a different way and for different reasons, but it was still love.

Which brings me back to last night.

What the hell was that?

I've had some wildly amazing sex dreams that left me sweaty and panting when I woke, but I've never been intimate with someone and seen another man's face. Out of all my Neverland lovers, I thought it would be Peter since he and I have actually had sex before. To see James was crazy. Unexpected.

But fuck, it felt good.

I don't know if I was drugged or just drunk, but to feel something besides emptiness again was worth waking up on the right side of the Grim Reaper's hangover-blade.

"Pretend all you want," an unfamiliar female voice says, "but I know you're awake."

A surge of panic has me hoping that I didn't let that man bring me back to his place. Logically, he had to have, unless we invited a third person into my bed that I don't recall. Stars above, if this is his wife I think I might cry. I know what it feels like to have your man betray your trust. I never want to be that source of pain for another woman.

The first thing I see when I open my eyes is wood planking, running laterally along the wall. I push myself up, noticing how it surrounds the room and how little decorative elements there are. The space is the size of an average bedroom, but there is no dresser or TV. No closet or noticeable bathroom. There's only the bed, large enough to comfortably fit three, and a chest at its foot.

And the girl.

Can't forget her.

"I see why Cap likes you." She frowns disapprovingly. "You're pretty, but I'm not convinced you were worth the hassle."

"Cap?" I ask, trying to figure out what the nickname could be short for and come up with nothing. Maybe it's short for some ethnic name that matches his heritage. Last night's lover was

African... I think. Or maybe Hattian. Am I a terrible person for not knowing?

"Hmm. Not too bright, though," she says more to herself than me.

"Look, I don't know who you are, but if you're his wife, then I am so sorry. I didn't know about you and wouldn't have slept with Cap if I did," I insist, my guilt eating away at me. Have I really sunk so low as to become this person? The fear that Tyle is right—that I need to move on and stop blindly searching for a lead that will never come—knocks the wind out of me.

I don't want to give up.

I'm not ready to move on.

But letting my morals slide to try and fill an endless void isn't something I'm okay with. Living my life out of a suitcase and chasing ghosts isn't healthy either. I know I have to make a change. I'm just not ready.

"Quit giving the girl a hard time, will yeh, Smee?"

That voice. I recognize it the second James opens his mouth. I look past the girl, Smee, and jump out of bed as soon as I see him. He welcomes me, wrapping his arms around my waist, and pulls me in for a suffocating hug.

I breathe him in, relishing the thick scent of seawater and pine. I never thought I'd see anyone from Neverland again, especially James. I pull back and touch his face, just to be sure I'm not imagining him. His day-old whiskers are rough on my hands, but the coarseness reminds me that he's real.

"You're here," I say in disbelief.

"Aye. I am."

It hits me then that last night wasn't a crazy dream or warped hallucination. I slept with two men last night, one being the brother of the other half of my soul. *Oh, my stars. Peter is going to kill me!*

I jump out of James's arms and use his shirt to cover myself. I feel terrible. How could I? How could he?

"Smee, I think yeh should leave," he says to the girl.

She crosses her arms and gives him a Cheshire grin. "I don't know, Cap. This is starting to get good." James narrows his eyes at her and she groans. "Fine. I'll go see what Cook's got going for breakfast."

Smee walks past us, chuckling under her breath. She looks at me with those judgy eyes and my belly twists. I get the feeling that she knows exactly what I let James do to me last night, and I don't think she's happy about it.

Smee closes the door to the cabin and I snap my hand up to smack James across the face. He catches my wrist, one lip lifting in bemusement.

"Careful, Sunshine. Yehr going start a game I'm not certain yeh want to play yet."

I jerk my hand back so unbelievably angry with him. And myself. And turned on. Why am I turned on? My center tingles with anticipation. My needy vag wants him. Hell, I want him and I can't explain why. I bite my lip, whispering to Wendy's feelings to go away, but it appears that she wants him to.

"Why are you here?" I ask, unsure if I should push him out the door or push my way back into his arms.

Wendy was a confused woman, forced to choose one man over the other, never fully satisfied with either. I don't know how. Peter was gentle and eager to satisfy me, not caring about himself. Pan was wild, desperate to feel what he never could.

But James, he was something else.

"I promised yeh a voyage." His gaze skirts the walls of the cabin for a moment, then finds me again. "Seeing as yeh found yehr way to Florida on yehr own, I thought a return expedition might make up for my shortcomings."

His comings were anything but short, if I remember correctly.

Stars above, I'm such a slut. But I don't care.

I grab James by the back of the neck and pull him to me. He is ready, waiting for my invitation, and doesn't hold back the second it comes. He rips open the shirt I'm wearing and finds my chest.

His fingers touch, and kneed, and pinch and by the stars, it feels good. He guides me backward until my knees find the edge of the bed and our kiss breaks as I fall onto it.

I watch James as he pulls his shirt off, too consumed by the vision in front of me to feel guilty. He's beautiful. His body is corded with more muscle than both Peter's or Pan's. Dark marks stretch from a wound on his neck across his chest and down his arm. They fold into the dips and grooves of his body, looking like they belong, but something about them feels wrong. I don't get to ask what they are because James pulls my legs open and dips his head between them.

My panties are an afterthought and must have been lost last night because I don't know where they are. I gasp the moment his tongue meets my folds and reach for the sheets. My instinct is to pull away and fight the pleasure I desperately crave but James holds me there until I'm shaking with a release that feels so good it coats the bed.

He licks his lips, hungrily looking for more of my juices, and kisses my inner thigh.

I want more.

Need more.

I curl those long dark locks around my fingers and push his head back between my legs. He chuckles and the vibration of his laugh is intoxicating. I should feel guilty face-fucking my ex-lover's brother, but his tongue and his fingers feel too good for me to care. I come again, although I'm not sure how it's possible because every man I've been with since Mira's birth has fallen short, yet here James is bringing me to my knees twice within minutes.

He kisses my inner thigh once more as I lay on his bed, my heart racing, gasping for air.

"Now that I've had my breakfast," he says coyly, "we should probably head downstairs for yours."

James's thick length taunts me through his trousers. There's no way I'm letting him out of this room like that. Everyone will know what we've done if they don't already.

And I don't like the way that Smee woman looks at him.

"What I want isn't downstairs." I roll onto my knees and grab James's hips. He raises an eyebrow at me as I unfasten his pants, but he doesn't stop me. He's not a gentleman like Cass, wanting to preserve my virtue or whatever. James lets me take what I want without question, and what I want is to choke on his dick.

I fist his shaft and pump it a few times to get it ready. I like the way it feels, his skin to mine. A glistening bead of precum stares me down and I've never wanted to taste someone's cock as much as I want his. I lick the head, relishing the sweet tanginess of his pre-seed, then swallow as much of him as my throat can handle. I take almost half of him before my swallow reflex kicks in.

Not gag. I don't have one of those.

James grabs me by the hair and guides me to a pace that suits him. I bob up and down, slurping and sucking, anxiously waiting for the moment I can taste him. My nipples pebble again, my body wanting more. He senses my desire and pulls my hair harder. I grab James's balls and apply pressure to that sweet spot near his taint. He wants to play dirty, I can, too.

"Godsdamn yeh, woman," he groans a moment before filling my mouth.

I suck every last drop out of him, happy to have provided even an ounce of the pleasure he gave me.

And then feel like a horrible person again. The fucking whiplash is brutal. Guilt gnaws at my conscience as his taste lingers on my tongue. I can't do that again, no matter how good it felt. It's wrong and disrespectful to Peter, not that I've seen or heard from him in three years...

Does he even have a say in my life anymore?

Stop it, Wednesday! Morals. You have those. Remember?

"What just happened?" I ask, trying to piece together the bits I understand...which isn't much.

"It's called oral. Do we need the sex talk, Sunshine?" James teases as he pulls up his pants.

"Not what I meant." I look for the shirt I wore last night and find it in a heap by the bed, buttons scattered across the floor. It's going to be about as useful as my dress.

James, the perceptive one that he is, opens the trunk at the foot of the bed and tosses a pair of sweatpants and a baggy tee at me. "Ah. Yeh want to know why whenever we're in a room it's like lightning in a bottle."

"Not exactly how I'd put it, but yeah."

"Yehr my wife," he says as if that's all the answer I need.

I strip out of what's left of my clothes and step into his. A drawstring keeps the pants from falling off my waist, but the shirt swallows me. I feel like I'm back in college, wearing Kenny's clothes after a wild night. All I'm missing is some cold pizza, a walk of no shame, and a hangover.

I hold up my left hand and teasingly wiggle my fingers. "Where's my ring, honey?"

James bends over the trunk again and rummages through it. I watch him, fascinated by the muscles of his back. Curious about the scars and stitches. Desperate too…

For stars' sake, Wednesday! Get it together!

"If it's a ring yeh want." He holds up a diamond the size of my thumbnail. It's beautiful and sparkling, set on a white gold band, and literally the ring I have always dreamed of. "Then it's a ring yeh'll get."

My heart races. I feel like a kid on Christmas looking at all the presents, anxious to open them and start playing. Until the logical side of my mind slaps me upside the head. That is probably Wendy's ring. Not mine. And even if it was meant for me, I'm not ready for whatever it is James has to offer.

I take a step back and shake both my hands. James is too much, and moving way too fast. I've literally met the man what… three times? Two of those times in the past twenty-four hours. "Easy, killer. I was kidding. "

He chuckles and tucks the ring back into its holder. "As was I, but also...not. Our vows explicitly said in this life and beyond. That lust yeh feel." He comes closer and brushes his fingers down my arm. "The insatiable need to jump my bones." He links his hand with mine and brings my knuckles to his lips. "That is this world giving us her blessing again."

I shake my head, trying to push away a new fog of desire. If I didn't know any better, I'd say we were back in Neverland already because being there intensified everything I felt, both good and bad. But I can feel the literal weight of this world pulling down on me. It anchors me to the moment while pushing me toward him all the same. "Wendy is Peter's soulmate. I belong to him."

"A soul is meant to love millions. It fractures and splits to give itself away over and over again, but it only has one life mate." James's lips curl into a sad smile, and I feel the weight of his suffering. He knew how much Wendy loved Peter, how potent her feelings are for him that run through me, and still he fights for even a chance at there being an *us*. "Love is always a choice. I chose my wife knowing her heart was torn, and she chose me. Yeh are not Wendy, Sunshine. Yeh can forge yer own path in whatever way yeh see fit. I will be by yer side, wherever it may lead. That is my blessing and burden as her husband."

I open my mouth, unsure of what to say. Last night I went to bed a hollow version of myself, desperate to find my way back to Mira. Today I woke with a fighting chance of reaching her and feeling like a human again, ready to move on and stop loving a ghost. It's crazy. Impractical.

And so fucking confusing.

My stomach growls, breaking the tension of the moment. James chuckles and says, "Seems I wasn't able to satiate all yer hunger." He kisses my blushing cheek and drapes his arm over my shoulder. "Come on, Sunshine. Let's get yeh fed. We have a grand voyage ahead of us."

CHAPTER 16

Wednesday

Walking into the galley is like being the new girl at school all over again. Everyone looks at me, their eyes judging me for wearing James's clothing. Their faces tight, letting me know, without question, that I was not expected.

All of which makes me painfully self-conscious.

James slips his hand in mine and a man with a fishhook as an earring arches his bushy brown eyebrow. That man shakes his head and then goes back to eating a piece of toast with jelly.

"Crew," James says in his ish-accent. I still don't know where it stems from, but now that I've traveled and spent the last year in England, it doesn't feel English to me. "This is Wednesday. She'll be joining us on our voyage back to Neverland."

"Why?" another crewmate, with woven dreadlocks that reach his back, asks. There are eight people at the table. A total of ten crew members, if I count James and Smee. "She's alive with the world at her feet." The man cocks his head and narrows his eyes at me. "What's so shitty about your life that you'd give it all up for eternal damnation?"

"Rodgers!" Smee snaps. Her voice is commanding, and by the

reaction everyone gives to her outburst, I'd say she's earned the respect of the men in this room. "We don't question the captain. Remember?"

"Aye," Rodgers says, begrudgingly.

James leads us to the other side of the small space and motions for me to join him near the head of the table to a seat that looks like it belongs to Smee. I get the feeling that skipping line in the pecking order isn't going to do me any favors. I've already been thrown off a boat once. Re-living that experience is not high on my to-do list.

"I'm not hungry. I think I'll just go back to my—"

"Sit, new girl," Smee insists.

There's a murmured chuckle somewhere to my right, but I don't know which crew member made the sound, and James seems uninterested. So, I let it go. This is a pick-your-battle situation, and a little laughter at my expense isn't worth challenging a pirate over. If the stories are true, they should be ruthless sword fighters. Whereas I have never even been in a fistfight.

The breakfast spread is simple—scrambled eggs, toast, and sausage—but there's enough of it to feed an army. Everyone's plates are full, with some reaching for more. I watch as everyone, Smee included, eats more in this sitting than I do in a day. It's fascinating the way they almost inhale their food. A strange thought drags my mind to a pirate movie I saw in high school, and I can't help but wonder if their other needs are also insatiable. Before James, no one—man or woman—had been able to satisfy my physical needs. But what if the dead's curse runs deeper? What if they are always hungry? Always longing for the affection of another? Always wanting something they can never have?

"Eat." James sets a platter of food in front of me and it's more than I can finish.

I stare at it, wide-eyed, unsure of where to start. My stomach is rolling, possibly from the motion of the ocean. Possibly from the alcohol I drank last night. Whatever the reason, the only thing that looks the slightest bit appetizing is the bread. "This is too much."

"The crew doesn't stop for lunch," he says as he makes himself a jelly and egg sandwich. "Yehr next meal won't be until dusk. Fill yehr belly while you can, love."

Looking at all the food makes me nauseous, but I nod and eat as much as I can. Even if I were feeling fabulous, I'm not used to stuffing my face like this. I thrive on multiple small meals a day. A snack here. A coffee there. A bagel or whatever floats my fancy here. I eat and eat and barely manage to get a quarter of my plate cleaned before my stomach is bloated and hurting.

"I can't," I say, leaning back into the wooden chair. "I'm done."

All the other crew members have already left. It's just James and I alone in the galley. He chuckles and reaches for a slice of toast, the fourth out of six on my plate. "I'll have Ben put this on ice for you. Yeh'll be wanting it later."

"How does someone who looks like you eat so much?"

He clasps his hands over his stomach and grins. "I burn the calories. Want me to show yeh how?" He winks.

My cheeks flush and I don't know why. That man has already seen and had more of my body than I ever thought possible, but my mind strays. It mixes Wendy's past with the last twenty-four hours and I am ashamed to admit I want to know if he can make me feel good again. I press my lips together, a smile lifting them, then pretend to be annoyed as I say. "You're insufferable."

"Perhaps, but a small part of yeh loves it."

I do. And I hate myself for it. "What's the plan, James? Why am I here?"

"That's the million-dollar question," Smee says, emerging from the shadows. "What is the plan, Cap? We can't go back the way we came. The rules are different with a beating heart. You know this."

"Dammit. Do I have to die again? I was really hoping there was another way."

"What?" James looks at me, shocked. "No. Of course not. Wait... again?"

"I can't swim. Peter pushed me off a boat," I say with a shrug like it's no big deal when really being at the mercy of the ocean again has me more than a little freaked out.

"Fucking hell." James runs a hand through his hair and pushes back the long strands that have fallen into his eyes. "We need to work on teaching you then."

I find the tassels of my sweatpants and twist the strands between my fingers. I've tried to learn, countless times, and it always ends the same. The moment my head goes underwater, I panic. I can't help it, and believe me, I've tried everything. I even tried learning to doggy paddle with my head above the water like little kids do. My ass sinks like lead and, even though my arms move, it's like they invite the water instead of moving it. I'm hopeless.

"It's not a bad idea," Smee says. "Then she'll be one of us."

"I'm not a murderer and she's not dying," James says, his tone final.

"Pa...Peter said that the Bermuda Triangle is a gateway. Ships get lost there all the time. We might have a shot at making it through the barrier under the full moon tonight." I've also tried this already, but maybe James's ship will be different. This boat has already crossed the barrier between their world and this one once. My rental from Bob's Boat Yard had never seen a speck of Neverland magic and did nothing but run out of gas.

James gives me a look that sends my tummy butterflies a flight. I've seen it before, only I can't recall where, and I wonder if it stems from a memory Wendy had locked away. He reaches for a necklace tucked beneath his shirt and opens the small pouch. He holds a golden acorn, sparkling like a glitter-covered craft project my students used to make, only instead of being coated with specks of plastic, it's covered in gold dust.

I shiver as a chill takes hold of me. The sensation is like

walking into a standing freezer. Goosebumps pepper every inch of exposed skin. Something deep inside me recognizes the acorn. I wish I knew why.

"Tell me, Sunshine," he says with a wicked grin. "What's yehr happy thought?"

CHAPTER 17

Wednesday

What's my happy thought?

Now that's the question of the day because it can't be *just* a thought. It has to be a memory, something so pure that it resonates to my core. A singular defining moment that carries enough joy to lift this ship literally into space and cross the galaxies.

No pressure.

I pace the space of James's cabin and try to think. There are only a few hours left until sunset. I've spent all day trying to come up with some great moment in my life and I've got nothing. The few tiny moments I've thought of—graduating at the top of my class, earning teacher of the year—they're great, but I don't feel like they're enough.

There's a knock at the door. I stop mid-pace, my heart in my throat. I glance out the window and note that the sun is still up. Time hasn't run away from me yet. At least, I don't think it has. It's hard to tell when there are no clocks, no shadows, and only an endless canvas of blue to look out at.

The person outside knocks again and that second rap has my lips lifting in a smile. There's only one person on this ship I can think of who has the decency to wait for permission before entering. "Come in."

James pops his head in. His dark eyes skim over the room before they find me in the far corner, chewing on my thumbnail. He lets himself into the small space and closes the door behind him, an unassuming smile on his face. "Hello, Sunshine. Yeh've locked yehrself away all day. Are yeh all right?"

Agony has me on the brink of tears. How do I tell someone who crossed the barrier between space and time to find me that I am going to let him down? I don't want to talk about me or my happy thought. I don't particularly want to talk about him and Wendy either. I could talk about us... if we are an us. "Why do you call me that?"

"What?" James reaches for the strand of hair that's fallen over my shoulder. He twists it between his fingers, looking one hundred percent at ease with being this close to me. As if us being together doesn't make his heart race or his skin tingle. Or like it's not a constant struggle to look me in the eyes instead of at my lips.

He seems perfectly fine.

Whereas I am a complete mess. "Sunshine. Everyone else calls me *the Darling.*"

"Ah." James walks to a wall at the side of the room and presses his palm to the lateral siding. A hidden door releases and swings outward. He tugs on a sliding shelf, opens it all the way, and exposes an old polyphon. He winds the handle and adjusts the needle so a pleasant melody can play. "Dance with me."

I laugh because, of course, he wants to dance while I'm having a minor freakout. Why wouldn't he? And even though I feel overwhelmed and anxious, and I know that feeling his skin on mine again will be a mistake, I take his hand and let him guide us into an eighth-grade-style sway. We take tiny steps, from side to side, not able to spread out due to the lack of space.

"Wendy Darling was a shooting star in the sky. Beautiful but utterly unreachable to Peter. He gazed upon her with wonder, never satisfied with the pieces of her he got." James spins me once, then pulls me tight against his chest, his hard muscles pressing against my soft skin. "For me, Wendy was the center of life. My world revolved around her happiness and I basked in the smiles I earned, but yeh were an unexpected ray of light in the darkness that had consumed me. Yeh are everything Wendy was, but brighter. The shining light I gravitate toward, even though I know my chances of being burned are high."

"Sunshine," I say, unable to fight my smile. These Neverland men and their riddles. I've never met anyone else who could wrap a compliment in such pretty words while still making me wonder, "*What the hell are they saying?*"

"I never liked being called *Darling,* but I don't mind Sunshine." I press my head to James's chest and listen to the music. Like Cass and the Lost, he has no heartbeat, but that doesn't scare me like it used to. James is living and breathing. He is as real as the sun in the sky and the wood under my feet.

"Yehr struggling with a happy thought," he says without a hint of judgment in his tone.

I bite my bottom lip and look down at my feet. The shame of failing is almost as bad as the embarrassment. "Is it that obvious?"

"We would be flying right now if yeh weren't." More facts. Not judgment, but the truth hurts. I could be halfway to holding my daughter again if I weren't such a failure.

"Oh." I step out of James's arms and hug myself. I don't know what to say. I had a good upbringing with two parents who loved me. Nothing tragic happened to me—besides dying at the hands of a living legend—and I didn't live a miserable life. But I didn't have anything *great* happen to me either.

Mira's birth should have been the best day of my life, but it turned into the worst when Cass stole her.

I've loved one mortal man, but all of my memories with him are tainted because he cheated on me and married my sister.

And any happy moments I could have had with Peter or Cass are stained with lies, murder, and distrust.

I *really* need to do a better job at picking who I give my heart to. At that thought, my gaze drifts to James's face again. His lips curl into a sympathetic smile and I think back to the time we've spent together. It hasn't been much, but from what I can tell he hasn't tried to manipulate or hurt me even once. Which is more than I can say for the other Neverland men.

"Yehr overthinking this, Sunshine." He reaches up and cups my cheek. "Relax."

"Easy for you to say. No one is counting on you to power a flying ship."

"True, but everyone here expects me to guide it and keep them safe." James walks to the edge of the bed and sits. He moves his pillow aside and then taps the mattress. "How's bout I tell yeh one of mine?"

I find a space beside him and cross my legs. Peter never talked about the past, and Pan was more interested in me than all things Wendy. Since being back in this world, I've seen so much through her eyes. Her memories almost feel like mine, but they are only one side of the story. Her life is a book with the back of each page missing. I don't have the context or background for the visions my dreams give me. I'm piecing together the pages of her life, but I don't know if they're in order or what bits might be missing.

"I knew Wendy Darling loved Peter. Hell, everyone knew. Yeh could tell from the time they were kids that she was enamored by him."

"This doesn't sound very happy, James."

He chuckles and takes my hand. His fingers trail along the thin lines on my palm, both tickling and soothing the skin. "I didn't care. She was a child, six years younger than me, and I was set on making my father proud. While Peter played in the trees, I was shadowing Father to learn the business. He was in the finance industry, and as the eldest son, it was my duty to follow in his footsteps. When I was eighteen, I was drafted into the war. Wendy was twelve, not even a woman yet but, even then, she was kind. She wrote me letters while I was away, mostly because her father made her, but eventually, we forged a friendship. It was platonic in every sense. She would tell me things about her life she couldn't tell anyone else, ask me questions she was too shy to voice to her family, and I would tell her about the places I'd traveled."

Flickers of Wendy's memories flash through my mind. I see her hand excitedly penning letters and feel her heart race when a new one came. What started as a chore turned into an unexpected friendship. But James was right. That's all it was. I don't sense any romantic inclinations when she reads what he wrote her.

"I knew the moment Peter had won her heart." James's smile falls. "I was due to return home in the fall and months had passed since my last letter. I wrote her every week up until I got my notice of discharge and not once did she write me back. It hurt more than I expected. Wendy had become a constant in my world where not even the next day was guaranteed and without warning, she was gone."

I close my fingers and hold his hand in mine. I feel this memory too, only from Wendy's point of view there wasn't just sorrow but also guilt. Understanding firsthand what abandonment feels like, I sympathize with the pain James must have felt and hate knowing what she put him through. "You don't have to keep going. It's okay."

He chuffs out a breath but continues. "Wendy Darling stood beside Peter, her hands delicately folded in front of her when the driver brought me back to my familial home. She had blossomed from the little girl I left behind into a woman as beautiful as the sun is bright. I was so excited to see her, but she acted as if the last five years we'd written to each other never happened. We were strangers and, unbeknownst to us, about to be engaged." James stands and walks to the window. He stares out at the sea, watching the sun's darkening rays glitter against the rolling waves.

His words pull at memories buried deep in my soul. I find that day in Wendy's archives, too, buried beneath layers of guilt and despair. She was also excited to see James. So much so that it threw her off guard. He was the brother to the man she'd sworn her heart to, someone completely forbidden, yet he summoned an excitement that outshined anything she'd experienced. She was confused. Didn't know how to act and decided putting a wall between them would be best.

And then life threw a curveball at her she wasn't ready for.

"My homecoming dinner was a disaster," James finally says. "Peter threw his glass of wine across the table when Father made the announcement that he'd arranged for Wendy and me to wed. My brother stormed out of the room, leaving his shaking lover behind. I remember being torn because a part of me wanted to respect Peter's feelings and rebuke the engagement, but I was so jealous of the way Wendy looked at him. I wanted to know what it felt like to be someone's whole world."

"Did she ever make you feel that way?" I know the answer before I even ask the question, but I want so badly for him to have felt that kind of love, even if she didn't.

"Wendy tried. Later that week, she arranged a candlelit dinner on our rooftop under the stars. She wanted to make her parents proud and so she agreed to the marriage. That dinner was her peace offering and our chance at a blank slate. It was our beginning, but not her and Peter's end."

I've seen the night he's talking about, more than once over the years. The moon was so big in the sky, the stars so bright, Wendy thought she could count them all if she tried. There wasn't a single cloud to cast a shadow, and she felt that it was a good omen. She was so nervous, torn between running away as Peter suggested and staying to try and make things work. She knew she could be happy with James. He was a good person with a kind heart. Marrying him would secure the merger her father needed and provide stability for the whole family.

Whereas a life with Peter would tear her family apart. She'd be alone in the world, living like a pauper. She feared love wouldn't be enough to get them through the hard times, and that doubt was enough to make her want to stay.

"She kissed me that night." James touches his lips and laughs under his breath. "I was so nervous I almost botched the whole thing. At twenty-four, I'd had more than my share of lovers, but holding Wendy in my arms that night was nothing short of magic. I fell in love, right then, and knew I'd do anything to make her happy."

"She's your happy thought."

He nods. "My happy thought. My damning thought. She was my everything."

I realize all I've ever wanted was to be someone's happy thought. I didn't even know that could be a relationship goal, but now that I know what it is—when I find someone worthy of trying to fall in love again—I want it. "I don't have a love like that. I don't have anything."

"That, Sunshine, is where yehr wrong." James strides to me and threads his fingers through the hair at the base of my neck. His head dips and his lips brush against mine. "Yeh could have it all. All yeh need is to ask. Ask me to love yeh. Ask me to be yehr happy thought."

I close my eyes, waiting for a kiss that doesn't come. "That's a lot of commitment. What if I'm not ready?"

"I'll wait for yeh. I'll share yeh. I'll do whatever yeh need, but yeh have to explicitly tell me what yeh want."

What I want is an impossibility in this world, but so should be James's existence. By the laws of logic, I shouldn't want a man more than a hundred years my senior. I shouldn't feel guilt tied to another's past. I shouldn't believe in magic, but I do. And while I don't have a happy thought I believe in everything. I just hope it's enough. "I want you to take me to Neverland."

"How?" James asks, his breath warm on my cheeks.

"I want your ship to fly me there. I want to arrive in one piece, and I—"

James's lips crash against mine. We fall backward onto the bed again as the ship jolts beneath us. He ignores the deep swaying of the ocean, solely focusing on me. His hands glide up my shirt as his mouth begins to worship me.

James's hands are heaven. His lips a sinful delight from hell.

He's everything I want and shouldn't have wrapped up into one delicious package. He kisses his way down my stomach, removing my sweatpants along the way.

I try to focus on the pleasure, but my mind keeps circling back to the unfinished sentence. There's an urge I can't explain, begging me to finish. I can't relax until I whisper, "And I want my daughter back."

CHAPTER 18

Wednesday

"Cap!" Smee shouts.

I recognize her voice through the haze of lust and wish she would go away. I don't want this to stop. I think I might be addicted to how good James makes me feel.

His fingers dig into my thighs as his tongue ventures as deep inside me as it can possibly go. He gives me everything and nothing at once because all I want is more.

More pleasure.

More of him.

Just. More.

Smee pounds on the door over and over again, demanding James pry his attention from me to her. At this moment, I hate her and I can't say that about many people.

He groans, just as irritated as I am, and yells, "Not now!"

"Captain!" Smee fires back with a sense of urgency. Something is wrong. There's no arguing that whatever it is probably demands the *Captain's* attention. But I wish he didn't have to go.

James holds up one finger and wipes his mouth with the back of his hand. He stomps over to the door loud enough that if there was any question as to if he's annoyed it's been answered. I reach for the thin white blanket that lays across the mattress as he yanks the door open. "Something better be on fucking fire because I said— "

"We're airborne," Smee cuts in with as little emotion as possible. She looks past James to me as I try to cover myself with his bedsheet. There's a fire in her eyes that makes me wonder if Smee is going to be a problem for us. I hope not, but I've got this feeling I can't shake that something bad is coming and pray that it's not by her hands.

"Good," James says as if he expected as much and couldn't care less. He pushes the door closed, but Smee sticks the toe of her heeled black boot in the frame before it can latch shut.

"Don't you think you ought to get out here and guide us?" she counters as she shoves her way into his quarters. "No one has seen you in hours. The crew is spooked. She's a distraction and you are never distracted."

Hours? That's not possible. We were just talking for a few minutes before he and I...

I twist the fabric around myself and tuck an end between my chest, creating a makeshift toga-style dress. There aren't many steps to the window and I can see it's not bright outside anymore, but the thought of losing time again is chilling. It makes me question if my mind is slipping again and that doubt is unnerving.

A never-ending span of darkness sprinkled with little specks of light surrounds us. From my vantage point, there is no up or down. Just an endless night.

Or is this a void like the one I'd fallen into before? Has all of this been a dream? Am I still trapped in the in-between from when Cass spiked my drink?

I try to take a breath, but the air is sticky and hot. It fills my lungs while leaving them painfully hollow. I search for more and more oxygen, trying to find some sense of normalcy while my thoughts spin out of control, but even an easy breath is out of reach.

What if it is a dream? What if I never made it out of the ocean after I fell and this is some wicked version of hell? All I've ever wanted was to be loved and in this fucked up afterlife, love has been taken from me at every turn.

My stomach twists and a knot lodges itself in my throat as the theory sinks its claws in me. No one knows what happens after we die. We could be reborn or simply cease to exist. We could be stuck in a nightmare where nothing and everything makes sense all at once and—

Something cold touches my arms. The icy sensation travels to my fingertips and my head whirls. I hear a voice calling my name, but it's so far away and distorted. It tickles my brain, feeling familiar, but it's not strong enough to lift the feeling of dread.

More thoughts push their way into my conscious stream. Whatever this is, wherever I am, I don't know if I can keep going. I'm exhausted and if Mira wasn't real... I don't want to live.

A jolt of energy shocks my system and I'm finally able to fill my chest with a cold breath of air. I suck it in, greedily looking for more, and specks of light fill my vision. Little by little, the room comes back into view. It's the same wood-lined walls and the same oversized window, only I'm not standing anymore. Somehow, I've fallen and James is on his knees in front of me, a worry line forming a wrinkle on his near-perfect face.

"There yeh are." James touches my cheek and I instinctively lean into him. "Yeh fell out on me for a moment. What happened?"

I worry my lip between my teeth. Every thought I had while in the darkness sticks to me. I don't know up from down anymore. Real from imagined. I wonder if this is what the Lost felt like when they died and found Neverland.

I huff out a heavy breath and glance down at my tattoo. Seems like I branded myself as one of them, even before I realized it could be possible.

"Wednesday?" James queries, his voice laden with worry.

"I don't know what's real and what's not anymore," I admit, and the shame of feeling so broken nearly swallows me.

"Yeh feel this?" James takes my hand and presses it to my

chest. My heart beats steadily beneath my palm. He waits for me to respond, but my words are caught in my throat. All I can do is nod once, and he says, "Good."

James reaches for something in his back pocket, a modern-style blade with an orange hilt, and flips it open. He takes my hand and presses the tip of his knife to the pad of my finger. I wince and try to pull my hand back, but he holds it tight. "Yeh feel that, don't yeh?"

"Yes." I find my voice again. It's weak and cracks, revealing how fragile I am. I hate it. I hate not knowing where I stand. But mostly, I hate straddling that line between belief and insanity.

"Dreams don't hurt. When yeh wake, yeh feel all the emotions built up in the journey, but dreams. Don't. Hurt. Yeh can't bleed. Yeh can't love. Yeh can't live." James presses my finger to his mouth and kisses the wound. The few drops of blood I lost stain his lips like rouge, but he doesn't lick it away.

"We need to feed yeh." He takes me by the arms and helps me rise to my feet. "Yehr weak, both physically and mentally. Nothing some bread and stew can't fix."

The ship rocks in the sky more than it did at sea, and I loose my balance. James notices and holds me steady. "I'd forgotten how frail the living are. Magic takes a lot out of yeh, Sunshine. We need to be careful not to use too much until yehr ready. It likes balance and will seek payment for every ounce we use."

He shifts to my side and wraps his arm around my waist. I don't want his help. Looking weak around the pirates makes me nervous, especially where Smee is concerned, but the muscles in my legs shake with every step. My body is exhausted and as much as I don't want it, I need James's help.

"I don't have any magic."

Smee opens the double doors that lead out to the deck. She latches the one and then stands beside the other, waiting for us to come out.

"Are yeh sure about that, love?" James winks and then looks up at the sky.

I follow his gaze to an endless span of twinkling stars. The dark void that threw me into a tizzy is filled with rich hues of purple and blue. Streams of deep green and orange connect constellations. And the stars… they're so bright. So unbelievably beautiful. My thoughts may be questionable, but my mind isn't creative enough to make something as intricate as this sky up. It's real. Every tear-filled night, every desperate attempt to go home, all of it was real.

I walk out onto the deck, wanting to see more. James is at my side with every step, his big brown eyes on me while I take in the evening's beauty. I try to find the words to describe the night and the hum beneath my skin but nothing comes close.

It's beyond stunning.

"Are yeh daring enough to look over the taffrail?" James asks.

His hand slips from my waist to my hand and I let him guide us to one side of the boat. He waits for me to levy my stance before placing himself behind me and caging me in with his arms. There's no chance of me falling overboard. He's made sure I feel safe and secure, unlike the last time I found myself in this position.

I grip the wood railing and look down. The same span of darkness that stretches above us floats beneath us. We're flying, somewhere in the depths of space, leaving a trail of golden dust behind us. "It's incredible."

"Yehr incredible."

I spin in James's arms and lean against the railing. He takes a step forward and presses his body against mine. He's not making a move, but taking another wordless action to prove to me I'm safe. Warmth blooms in my chest. This man is the complete opposite of his brother. Protective. Supportive. And honest. He's offered more to me without asking than Peter Pan did combined. "Thank you."

"There's no need to thank me. I haven't done anything worth yeh debt."

"You found me."

"Sunshine, I will always find yeh." He looks into my eyes and I see the depth in his words. In this life and the next. Beyond the constraints of life that not even death can yield, this man is and forever will be mine. "Come. Yeh need to eat and then rest. We'll be in Neverland by sunrise."

I yawn, feeling the fatigue of the night again, despite my excitement.

Tomorrow, I'll be home.

Tomorrow, I will be one step closer to finding my daughter.

CHAPTER 19

Pan

"We'll be safe in here," Emmit says, one hand around Xyris's waist to help him balance.

He woke from Belle's time-stop about a half mile ago and while he is moving, he's groggy and sore. His muscles are fatigued from lack of food and hanging by their arms. Belle's dust may have stopped Xyris from dying of starvation, but it didn't prevent the wear and tear on his body from being held captive.

A strain we all feel.

After an hour of walking through the underground tunnels, Aria finally stirs in my arms. She shifts and her skin sticks to my shirt. She winces and then groans, but as the dust fades away her groans turn into cries, which echo into screams when she fully wakes. Tears fill her eyes as she tries to climb out of my arms, but her legs are weak. She falls to the ground, crying even louder.

My stomach sours. I want so badly for the Island to heal Aria's wounds, just like I wanted it to bring Heidi back from the brink of death, but its magic is still out of reach. The electric hum that should be rolling through my veins is a cold wash of nothingness. The darkness of the cavern won't listen to me. I can't even manage to create a mage light to guide our way through the tunnels. If not for Emmit and his wielding abilities, we'd be stumbling around in the dark because I am utterly useless.

I drop to my knees and gently pull the hair off Aria's cheek. The strands have stuck to her paper-thin skin and peel back a layer when I move them. She screams again, not even able to form the word *stop* because it hurts so bad.

Emmit helps Xyris balance himself with the help of a wall, then hurries over to us. His gaze drifts over the burns. There are so many. Her back, arms, and shins are the worst from how she was hiding in the bathroom, but the rest of her body is burnt, too. Her skin ranges from red to blistered to oozing.

"Shh," Emmit coos, trying to soothe Aria's cries. He takes her palm in his left hand and touches her head with his right. "I know it hurts, but you will be all right. I promise."

Aria's sobs wane to quiet cries as Emmit absorbs her pain. His own pale skin turns red with irritation while his magic burns him from the inside out. Aria's open wounds and blisters melt away before my eyes. In minutes, her burns shift from fourth-degree trauma wounds to first and second. She's still in a considerable amount of pain, but she's no longer screaming.

"Scar, can you help Aria walk?" Emmit grunts as he straightens his spine.

"Of course," she says, rushing to take his place.

"I'll get Xyris," I insist.

Emmit flashes me a look of gratitude, then washes all emotion from his face. I get it; in a world where magic reigns supreme, the slightest sign of weakness can wipe you off the board. Even though it's just the five of us, and not a soul here would defy the circle of trust, the Island is always listening. I don't know who she belongs to now. If it's Belle, and she finds out about Emmit's new weakness, I have no doubt she'll kill him.

"It's eerie down here without the glow bugs," Aria says, huddling close to Scarlett. She's trying to be light-hearted and pretend like she's okay, but her words are clipped.

"Just pretend it's a cloudy night. We're used to those," Scarlett adds, offering her own words of comfort.

Before the Darling came, Neverland was stuck in an eternal twilight, but once she and Peter reconnected, the Island shifted. We saw the sun and the stars for the first time in decades. Most nights, the sky was clear and bright. The dark clouds must have come after we left when the magic began to change.

We follow Emmit deeper into the darkness. It feels like we're in a maze of tunnels beneath the mountain with more caverns the further we go. I survey the path, trying to find landmarks in case we need to run back, but the ground is smooth and the walls are blemish-free. Too perfect to be natural. *Why didn't I know it existed? I thought I knew everything about Neverland...* "What is this place?"

"Caves," Emmit says curtly. He looks over his shoulder and flashes me a look of warning before adding, "Don't tell me you've lost your sense of adventure?"

"Peter?" Xyris says through a forced laugh. "Never."

I mimic the sound but don't comment. I never understood Peter's need to make everyone think he was carefree. The only time he left Neverland was to fetch the Darling and he rarely went beyond his side of the Island. I was the one who went everywhere and saw everything, but no one knows. How could they? The only person who ever heard my voice was Peter.

We walk for what feels like an eternity to the sound of Emmit's humming. I don't recognize the melody, and since no one else has chimed in to sing or hum, too, I'm guessing it's a ballad from his people. There's a lot of unknown about the Fae. I've only ever met the triplets. Everyone else either died or disappeared before I came to be, and it's not like I could ask any questions.

The burden of being a shadow. Always there, but no one minds your existence.

Emmit slows as we approach an opening I recognize. We've reached the Neverpool, a small clearing in the mountain surrounded by stone. It's a little piece of heaven with a peephole view of the sky and a direct connection to the Neversea. Triton created it as a safe space for his land-loving wife to sunbathe without risk of exposure. When she died, he left the magic that keeps it hidden from above in place. We can look up and out into Neverland, but nothing from above the barrier can fall within.

Before us is a glittering night sky and calm seas, but above the night is at war with bursts of red flickering through the overhang of vines. We all step onto the sandy shore of the Neverpool and look up. Scarlett covers her mouth, tears falling down her cheeks as she stares at the fire ravaging our Island. Smoke wraps around the trees as bright red flames swallow them whole. My heart sinks thinking about all the innocent lives being lost. All the creatures who had just come out of their slumber... gone.

"What are we going to do?" Aria asks.

"There's nothing we can do," Emmit says, defeated. "Belle will burn the Island to the ground before losing it."

"I'd say she's definitely losing it," Xyris mumbles. I think it's safe to say we all agree, but no one voices their opinion.

"Scar, help me get Aria into the water." Emmit peels off his shirt. It's sticky with sweat and blood and takes a layer of burned skin with it when he tosses the fabric to the shore. The new wound is bright red and angry, but you'd never know if it hurts. Emmit's face is a mask of indifference, even as he absorbs all of Aria's weight.

"Peter said never to swim in the grotto," Scarlett cautions. She looks at me for guidance, and for a moment, I almost agree.

But then I remember that I am supposed to be Peter and while I agree with the warning, I am trusting that Emmit knows what he's doing. I have no other choice.

"The waters are healing," Emmit says as he and Aria wade waist-deep and then sit. Their heads bob above the surface and he sighs, the tension he held visibly releasing. "Hold your breath," he says to Aria right before pushing her head under.

I count the seconds. *One. Two. Six...* before she finally resurfaces at ten. The red tint to her cheeks is gone. Her honey-colored skin is a crisp golden, as if she's tanned all day, and her fried black hair is wet but lush. They walk out of the grotto's waters, drenched but able to move with ease. Both of them look as good as they had on Neverland's beach the night before Peter and I left. Happy. Healthy. And alive.

"What did that cost?" I ask because nothing comes for free. Magic wants payment for what it gives. Being made from it, I gave freely without repercussion because I could. But for everyone else, it comes with a price.

"Nothing," a cheery voice says from the center of the pool. There's a splash of water and then silence. I wait, too many painful heartbeats to count for the creature to return.

I don't like mermaids. They're unpredictable. I never know if they're going to play with their kill before drowning them or make their suffering seamless with a quick death. Either way, all souls know to stay out of the water because these monsters are just as blood-hungry as Belle.

"But you should find the princess. Time is running out," the creature says.

She uses her arms to crawl onto the water's edge. She lays on her belly and flexes her seafoam green tail until her fins poke up through the murky brown, while long blonde hair falls over her shoulders, concealing her bare breasts. Her skin is the shade of sand with glittering green scales on her forearms that match her tail. I've only seen a mermaid this close once and hoped to never again, but through Peter's eyes, I can understand the desire to draw near. She's one of Neverland's rarest beauties.

And one of its most dangerous creations.

"We have a princess?" Aria asks with childlike wonder. She takes a step toward the water's edge. I grab her wrist and tug her closer to me. Their voices are magic in themselves, designed to lure prey to them. They volley between this world and the connecting realms, feasting on whoever is foolish enough to get close.

The mermaid cocks her head to the side. "Can you not feel her? She's strong but young and in need of guidance." The creature turns her black eyes to me. "He watches over her, but his power is not enough."

"Who is *he*?" Aria asks. Her lack of fear for the creature is concerning. She looks at the beastly like she is a jewel to behold. Not a monster who could rip her throat out.

The creature holds out her hand, her voice a lullaby in the air. "Come. I'll show you."

Aria takes another step toward the seabeast, but I hold her back. "Leave my Lost alone," I demand.

The mermaid frowns at me. "A wolf in sheep's clothing is still a wolf, Dark One. The queen is coming and when she finds you..." The creature's lips pull back into a razor-sharp smile. "I want to be there to see what she does."

"I'm not afraid of Belle." I might be, just a little, but only because an idiot wouldn't fear her. Without my powers, I'm as mortal as the Lost. I may have fed on the souls of the living to keep my strength in the other world, but I meant what I said to Wednesday. I reap death, not succumb to it. If I'm going to die it will be because I chose to sacrifice myself. Not to because I'm some demented fairy's dinner.

"The Fae?" the mermaid scoffs. "She wishes. That one will get what's coming to her, too."

"Who is the queen?" Scarlett asks. She inches forward, but I'm not worried. There are a dozen feet between her and the water's edge. Not to mention Emmit. With as hard as he's fought to keep everyone alive, I doubt he will allow her life to be risked.

The mermaid ignores Scarlett's question and turns her attention to Emmit. "They've tipped the scales of fate and Daddy is not happy. Both must die or everyone will."

He nods. "Understood."

"I could stay," the mermaid holds out her hand again, "If someone wants to play with me. I have so much more to tell."

"You've given us plenty, Serena," Emmit interjects, his voice firm. "Your debt is paid."

The mermaid frowns but pushes herself back into the water. In seconds, she's deep enough to swim away and disappear. The tension in the room snaps, Serena's spell lifting as soon as she's out of sight.

"You know her?" Xyris asks. He's walking better. A little stiff, like he's sat too long, but able to support himself solely and no longer limping. I don't know if the Island has chosen to heal him or if Emmit absorbed enough of his pain too, but I'm glad to see everyone starting to feel like themselves again.

"I was there the day Belle killed Athena." Emmit walks to the water's edge and dips his toes in.

Without the pull of magic, it's just a grotto. A beautiful piece of scenery meant to be enjoyed under the sun, but this land has blood on it. I could feel the heaviness when I was in shadow form and avoided this part of the Island. Like calls to like and it reminded me that I was made from the pieces Peter rejected. The hatred. The obsession. The darkness in him.

Emmit stares out at the vastness of the night. "She would have killed Serena, too, had I not interfered."

Aria gasps and touches her chest. "Why?"

Emmit chuckles darkly. "Why save her or why kill her?"

"Both."

For the first time tonight, he lets raw emotion bleed into his features. Sadness. Pain. And regret. All feelings I've felt too fully since being grounded in this body. "Belle needed the tears of a mermaid to create her time dust and I could only save one."

"Shit." Xyris puts his arm around Emmit and pulls him closer. "That's rough. Sorry you had to go through that, babe."

"That's life with Belle. She doesn't care who gets hurt so long as she wins. Hence the fires." He looks up at the dome above us. The fire rages on, so fiercely there is no darkness. Just the light of death. If not for the magical dome, we'd be dead. "She's trying to flush us out."

"What do we do?" Scarlet looks at me and then so do the others.

One by one, desperate eyes find mine. They're looking at me as their beacon of hope. Like their savior. Like I should be the King of the Island with a magical shadow that can put an end to everything.

I'm not any of those things.

I swallow hard and try to think of what Peter might say. He always had a way of cheering the others up when they were at their lowest. He understood what true darkness felt like and never wanted anyone else to be where he was.

But I lived in darkness. I relished in the cold and the anger. I fed off the fear and the worry. I used his weaknesses to make myself strong. I made the Island listen to my wishes because it knew all I wanted was to keep it safe. We were on the same page when I was a shadow.

Yet, as a man, it wants nothing to do with me. It's rejected me. After all these years of camaraderie, everything I've ever known has turned upside down. I don't have soothing words. I don't have the fighting skills, that muscle memory as well as every memory Peter formed on these lands has left me. I am like the Lost, hopeless in a new world, wanting nothing more than for my life to be what it once was.

"Peter?" Scarlett asks again. "What do we do?"

Yes, Peter, I think to myself, the Island, and whoever else might be listening. *What do we do?*

CHAPTER 20

James

I laid with Wednesday through most of the night, despite not sleeping. I should have been at the helm guiding us home, but my clock is ticking. I can feel something coming, the dread clings to me like fog on the water, and I can't shake it. All I can do is prepare everyone for what comes next and relish the moments I've been given.

Smee doesn't bother knocking. She never has because there's no point. That woman has seen every inch of my body and helped close wounds in places blood should never seep from. She's been loyal, worthy of my trust, and in turn I've kept nothing from her. But from the way she watches Wednesday, I sense there's something she is keeping from me. "We've crossed into Neverland, Cap, but you're going to want to see this."

I kiss the side of Wednesday's cheek. Her skin is so soft. I could touch her every day and not be satisfied. Returning to the land of the living broke her. Not nearly as much as it had Wendy, but enough. The few updates I could pry out of Peter about my late wife were heartbreaking. Mental institutions and medicine became a factor in Wendy Darling's everyday life after leaving Neverland until she learned to keep her stories to herself. It was only then that she was able to start a new family that she found happiness again. She let us and everything to do with her past go.

Whereas this Darling girl is a fighter. I doubt she'll ever give up on what she believes in, which is why I think the Island chose her. I don't have proof, not yet. But I suspect the changes Neverland is undergoing have everything to do with it crowning a new queen.

The tether that binds us together pulls tighter the further I drift, but something else tugs at my core, too. Grey smoke fills what's left of the night sky. I pull the neck of my shirt over my nose and try to keep from coughing. Black clouds are everywhere. They cover the moon in the sky and reach down to the water like the hand of death.

"Where's all this coming from?" I ask.

Smee points to a small flicker of light in the distance. "Neverland's on fire."

"Oh my gods," Wednesday whispers from behind me. I turn and pull her into my side. This isn't the kind of shock she should bear alone. She covers her mouth and stares at the blaring red light that swallows the horizon.

"Your gods can't save you here, Darling," Smee comments. She steps to the guardrail and rests her elbows on the wood. "Can't save them either."

"Smee," I warn. If Belle's pillow talk means anything, the gods of old could be near, and if that's true, the last thing I want is to piss them off. The stars above know we already have our work cut out for us.

"Who could have done this?"

"Who do you think?" Smee chides. Wednesday lets the venom roll off her back, but I'm not having it. I don't believe in punishment by shame. Unless it's a capital offense, all reprimands are dealt with on an individual basis. I'm going to have to have a word with her about her attitude. Like it or not, so long as I am captain, the Darling is a part of our crew.

"Cass," Wednesday says, and there's a shake to her voice that's troubling.

"The Fae prince?" Smee scoffs. "That boy is as useful as tits on a bull." She turns her ire to me. "This has Belle written all over it. We never should have left the pirates alone with that crazy bitch."

She's right on both accounts, but agreeing with her in front of others would signal that I am unfit to be captain. While my crew is loyal, Smee has made another good point. I have been distracted since Wednesday came aboard. One strike on the leaderboard is fine. Two is treading thin waters. But three—letting anyone know about the poison in my veins or how I haven't healed yet—could lead to mutiny. "It's only been a few hours."

"And look what she's done to our home?" Smee shouts, gesturing to Neverland.

I press my lips together into a fine line. I see the damage and hear the silent screams that echo in the night. I don't need to witness the carnage to know we've lost almost, if not every, soul we saved. Their deaths are infinite. They forfeited their chance at an afterlife when they climbed aboard my ship. Something else I never mentioned because so long as Pan was the Never King no one could die.

"I have to get to the Island," Wednesday says in a panic. She pushes my arm away, takes a few steps, pauses, looks at the fire again—her eyes wide with worry—then turns her attention back to my ship.

"We can't bring the Jolly Roger to port," Smee scolds as if the Darling were a child. "It's not safe."

"I'll find another way." Wednesday spots what she's looking for and runs across the deck to where the rowboat is tied. It hangs off the port side, secured tightly by a pair of pulleys. She tugs at the ropes, hastily trying to get them undone, without a clue as to how the system works.

"Everyone is probably dead by now, Darling. If you go over there you will be, too, but please." Smee folds her arms over her chest and leans against the taffrail. "Keep working those knots."

"You're wrong!" she snaps as tears fall down her cheeks. I've never heard the Darling yell. Even Wendy was cool-tempered. Her cheeks would flush red and her mouth would press together until her lips were barely a thin line, but she never raised her voice. It's startling to hear Wednesday speak with such raw emotion.

But it's not anger that fuels her fire. It's fear for a loved one. The blow of knowing I am one step closer to losing her stings, but I meant what I said. Whoever she chooses, I will support her. Even if she doesn't choose me. "He's fine."

"Who?" Wednesday snaps her gaze up to my face.

"Peter," I say, although by the way her brows push together, I'm not sure that's who she's worried about anymore.

"Peter can take care of himself. I need to get to Cass!" She hastily tugs on the ropes again. If she'd slow down, she'd see the pulleys are engraved with arrows and she is trying to move the wrong rope, but people tend to let fear wipe logic from their minds, and while I don't doubt the Darling could figure out the mechanism under normal circumstances, she is struggling.

"The prince?" Suddenly, it dawns on me that I might already be too late. The other half of her heart, the space I once filled, the only chance I had at winning a place in her life, might already be occupied. "Oh."

"You've got it wrong," Wednesday says hastily, then changes the subject with "And why do you keep calling him a prince?"

"His father was the late Never King," I say reactively. I wait for a flicker of excitement or some kind of acknowledgment that she could be the next princess to register, it would make sense that Neverland wants her as a queen if she is already destined to be royalty, but when her face remains expressionless, I rethink her words and ask," What do yeh mean I've got it wrong."

"I don't care if he lives or dies. I just need what he stole from me." She untwists the wrong rope and the lifeboat starts to slide over the side, without her in it. Panic flashes in her eyes.

I grab the end of the rope and wrap it around my hand. The

rope pulls, burning my flesh, but the vessel doesn't crash into the water. "What's worth risking your life for?"

Wednesday chews on her lip. Those tears flood her eyes again. I can see her fighting with them, not sure if she can trust me with her secrets. I understand that war. Some are worth dying for, while others are worth risking. The question is, what kind of secret is this?

A long beat of silence stretches between us. Just when I think Wednesday has given up on me and decided I'm not trustworthy, she looks at me and says, "My daughter."

Wednesday

Everything smells like death.

Ash floats in the air, mixing with smoke. It's impossible to breathe without a bandanna over my face, let alone see more than a few feet in front of us. The deep blue water fades to an ugly gray the closer we get to shore, but thankfully nothing dead floats on its surface. It might not count for much considering how many lives have been lost on the Island, but I am glad the sea seems to have been spared.

James rows us to shore. My gaze darts from the sky-high flames and his flexing muscles. I try not to look at either option, but I can't help myself. One sight has me anxious with anticipation. The other... well, James makes me anxious for many reasons. He's barely said anything to me since I mentioned Mira. Beyond offering to help me get to the sand and asking if I was ready, James has been painfully quiet.

I don't know why, but his silence hurts.

Despite the awkward tension and a weird desire to climb onto James's lap every five minutes, I'm grateful he's here. Sexy sailor needs aside, I'm not sure I would have been able to navigate from the ship to the Island on my own. The Neversea fights him with every row, using its waves to try and push us back out into the ocean, but James is strong and takes us to the only spot on the Island that hasn't caught fire—a plot of land just south of Peter's treehouses.

The sun peeks over the horizon as James climbs out of the rowboat and jumps into knee-deep water. He grips the wood siding and pulls me to shore. As soon as the bow meets the sand, I hop out so he can drag the boat up the bank and away from the ocean.

James wipes the sweat from his brow with the back of his arm. His gaze bounces from the rowboat to the water a few times before finding peace with his thoughts. "If the tide shifts, it should be safe."

He analyzes the boat and situates the oars and ropes while I face the Neverforest. From the Jolly Roger, this section of the woods looked small. I thought it might be a few dozen feet in each direction, but now that I see it up close, it doesn't look so manageable. The dense greenery is vast. I can't even see the glow of the fire. It's like there's a magical barrier protecting this section of the Island.

My toes sink into the sand as I walk toward the furthest edge. I think I know why this land hasn't been swallowed by the fire yet, but I need proof. Something solid to go on because a theory won't bring me closer to Mira.

I walk along the water's edge and recognize the picnic table we used to party at—tiny gray flakes cover it like a blanket. I try not to think about the last time I sat there or everything that came after. If I do, doubt will creep in and I refuse to believe all of this is anything but reality. My daughter is real and that wall of fire ten yards away is also very real.

I stop walking and let my brain catch up to my racing heart. Logically, there should be a line of forever frost on the ground. Or maybe a blanket of it on the other side of the trees. Perhaps an ice wall? No... I would see the ice shimmering in the sun, there's something here. Some form of Cass's magic and I'm determined to find out what it is.

The fire may not be moving, but whatever the magic is that's holding them back doesn't work on the heat. Waves of hot air stick to my skin and lungs and I'm still twenty feet from the fire line. My arms feel like I have a sunburn, only I haven't been in the sun. They hurt even though they aren't red.

"I don't think so." James grabs me by the shirt collar and pulls me back a few feet. The temperature difference in the air is staggering.

"Let me go!" I twist free of his hold and glare. "I wasn't going to walk into the fire. I just wanted to see the edge and find out why it hasn't crossed over."

"That's not happening," he scoffs. "Fire isn't the only thing that kills, Sunshine, and yeh are too important to risk. Magic holds the flames back. Don't try to understand it. Just accept it."

"I have to know why the fire isn't moving!" I shout, feeling every bit like a child having a tantrum, but he doesn't understand. There's a need too strong. I feel like I might explode if I don't discover whose magic is saving Neverland. In my mind, it can only be Cass keeping the Island safe. I *need* it to be Cass because that means Mira is safe. If someone else saved Neverland but didn't save my daughter, my heart would break.

"Yehr letting fear shift yehr focus, Sunshine. Yehr not here to save the Island. Yehr here to save yehr daughter while yeh still can." James grabs my shoulders and looks me in the eyes. His determination tickles at a memory, but I can't find which one. I try to search the archives of my mind, but everything is gone. I can't access Wendy's past now that I'm back in Neverland.

"Don't lose yehr daughter like I lost my boys, Wednesday." He swallows hard and takes a minute to say, "Yeh'll hate yehself if yeh do."

James never says my name. I've been Sunshine since the moment we met. Hearing him call me anything else is like a crack of thunder on a summer's day. Loud. Purposeful. And out of place.

"You're right," I admit. I push my hair back with one hand,

gather it in my palm, then let it go. Shit. I thought losing my cat was heartbreaking. I thought it helped me understand the suffering Peter went through when he lost his nephews, but an animal isn't the same as a child. And a secondhand loss, while horrible, doesn't come close to losing your child. James lost two. "Help me. Please."

"Close yehr eyes, love." James waits patiently for me to find my bearings again. It's hard to choke back the constant worry and need to cry, but I can't be weak forever. Mira needs me, and I am too close to fuck this up.

I close my eyes and James says, "Yehr her mother. The magic tying yeh to yehr daughter is in yehr veins. All yeh need to do is tap into it. Reach for her. Call out to her. Find the thread of life that binds yeh and pull it tight. Make the Island tell yeh where she is. It will do what yeh say. All yeh have to do is ask."

Ask.

Ask the Island to tell me where my daughter is. Yeah. Okay.

I feel silly, but I use my thoughts to call out for Mira. *Where are you, sweet girl?*

In the real world, all this talk of magic would be crazy, but this is Neverland. Anything is possible. I traveled on a flying ship. I've dined with people whose lives were lost before I was even born. I've crossed through space and time, somehow skipping three years of my life. I lived on an island that should only exist in storybooks. I've fucked and fell in love with the man, the Shadow, and have very strong feelings for his brother. None of it should be possible, but here I am. Living proof that if you believe in magic the world is at your fingertips.

I choose to believe Neverland listened to my pleas and brought me home. Just like I choose to believe it will lead me to my daughter.

The invisible string James mentioned pulls tight in my chest. It guides me, physically moving my shoulders and twisting me to my right. I imagine myself yanking on the rope and whatever is on the other side fights back. I snap my eyes open and point. "There."

"Good. She listens to yeh."

"Who?" I open my eyes. "Mira?"

James grins and I see a flicker of resemblance between him and Peter. The mischief. The madness. Perhaps even a little magic. "No, Neverland."

"That's absurd." I laugh. Neverland belongs to Peter Pan. If it listens to me, it's because I am tied to him. The other half of his soul it feels obligated to entertain.

"Prove me wrong," he says with a challenge. "Ask the Island to bring yeh something. If it does, we have our answer. It helps many but only serves one."

And what should I ask for? Breakfast? I roll my eyes. Even though I am hungry and would love a mango or some toast and cloudberry lemonade, this distraction is exactly what James said we should be avoiding. "We don't have time for this. After we find my daughter, I'll play your game, but we need to go."

I take off into the woods, following the pull of the thread that binds us. With every step, it pulls tighter. I'm a fish on a string. A yoyo to its master. I can physically feel her calling to me.

And I'll do whatever it takes to get to her.

CHAPTER 22

Wednesday

It's funny how different a memory can feel when you're staring at its origin.

I often dreamed of the Lost's treehouses. Each built from wood harvested from the Neverforest or found on the Island's shore. At least ten feet off the ground, they are connected by wooden rope bridges, with Peter's being at the center of it all like a spider with its web. Heidi's house was the closest, a mere twenty feet from the web's center, with the others spreading out to offer privacy.

Cass's treehouse is smaller than the rest. He only had the one bedroom. All the others had at least two. Emmit's even had three, although I'm not sure why. It's not like he could have kids and up until recently, the Island only seemed to welcome adults.

Cass's treehouse is also furthest from the rest. It's bridge to the group's center feels miles long. I never cared enough to count my steps or to wonder why he'd want to be so far from his friends, but now I'm curious if the distance is intentional. If he always planned to betray Peter, or if his plan came to fruition after I arrived.

The last time I was on the Island, he said he'd been trying to reclaim his home for centuries. Hundreds of human years of failed efforts, with the last hundred—give or take—having Peter thrown into the mix. I can't imagine knocking up a mortal was where he saw his life going. Then again, I can't imagine him doing all the other terrible things he's done. Had I not been the victim or seen it with my own eyes, I wouldn't have believed it.

"Yeh alright there, Sunshine?" James looks at me and I swear all I've seen in his eyes since stepping foot back on this Island is worry. I'm sure the pain he feels is because of what happened to the pirates. He lost one family to Neverland and now it's claimed another. I just happen to be his current focus so he doesn't break down.

"Yup," I lie because I most definitely am not. I'm guessing this is what those *Law and Order* victims feel like when they confront their attackers. I always felt bad for them, but excited at the same time as I watched the characters finally get their justice. But I'm not looking for justice. I'm looking for Mira and I'm a bundle of nerves out of fear that she might not be here.

"What's yehr plan?" James asks.

That is a great question. I never thought I'd get this far. My plan stopped at getting to Neverland because that felt next to impossible. "Don't have one. Figured I'd knock on the door and play the surprise card. Worked well enough for him."

"He won't hurt yeh," he says, seeing through the mask of bravery I'm trying to wear.

I raise my eyebrows and force a laugh. "You clearly don't know him well. Cass is a psychopath."

"Must be a familial trait." James rubs the scruff on his cheek. "But the prince *can't* hurt yeh. If what I think is happening is happening, then he's in for a world of shit."

"Did coming back to the Island tie your tongue or something? Because you're starting to sound like Cass."

"Gods, I hope not." James laughs and despite the severity of where we stand, it sounds genuine. "Just trust yehrself. No thought is too crazy, no wish is too far-fetched. Yeh want him dead...then strike him down. Yeh want him to suffer...imagine him in pain. Or if yeh just want to grab yehr daughter and go we can do that, too. Whatever yeh choose, I'm here if yeh need me. No questions asked. I've got yehr back."

"Thank you, James." I touch his arm and a sizzle of heat passes between us. "I'm really glad you're here."

I step in front of the rope ladder that leads to Cass's porch and stare up at the path I need to climb. The last time I was here, a small part of me locked up every time I had to work my way up or down a ladder, but this time, I'm not afraid. Falling to the ground feels trivial compared to everything I've been through.

So, what if it hurts? Who cares if I break a bone? Life hurts. Living has been the most difficult and painful experience, but it's had some great moments, too. I never thought I'd become best friends with my sister. I never imagined the warmth and joy growing a child would give me. I didn't expect the pain of losing a lover to amplify the excitement of finally finding another. I've traveled the world and done things I never thought possible.

This stupid ladder is nothing.

I grab the first peg and pull myself up. Eighteen steps are all that separate me from Mira. Eighteen notches, each about a foot apart, and then I'll finally have my baby girl in my arms again. I climb, reaching one arm up to the next peg before moving my foot. It's easy enough, but I don't rush the process. I take my time, going what probably feels snail-slow to James, but he doesn't say anything. He climbs beneath me, patiently waiting for me to make my next move.

The middle peg about halfway up is slick. My foot slips, throwing me off balance and the bravery I felt is gone. In a split second that fear of falling and the anticipation of pain floods my senses. James grabs my waist the moment my balance wavers and steadies me. "Easy, Sunshine. I don't think yehr ready to fly yet."

I force a laugh, feeling my heartbeat everywhere, and light-heartedly say, "That'll be the day."

James holds me tight while I get my bearings again. I don't take long, just a minute at most, then keep making my way up to

Cass's platform. I peek my head through the panel cut into the patio floor, searching for any sign that he saw us coming. Seconds tick by without movement. When I feel confident it's safe, I finish climbing the last steps and then hoist myself back onto solid ground.

James pops up like a daisy, effortlessly finding his feet again and taking his stance just outside of the front door's view. He draws his sword, holding it in his right hand, ready to fight. "Are yeh ready?"

"Is that necessary?" I ask, eyeing the two-and-a-half-foot piece of metal.

"Hopefully not, but yeh never can be sure which is why it's made from iron, not steel. Metal will cut a Fae, but it won't slow them down. They'll be bloody and pissed off, but still standing whereas iron will incapacitate them. It's one of the few weaknesses these creatures have."

"Good to know. What's another?" I'm stalling. I don't know why. I should be knocking and preparing to face off with Cass, ready to go full mamma bear on him. Instead, I'm wasting precious minutes, trying to muster up the courage to see him again while hoping I don't puke all over myself.

James reaches in front of me and pounds on the door. He gives me a silent nod, then steps back into the shadows and out of sight. He knew I needed a push, just like he knew I needed saving. I smile at him, yet again grateful for his presence. I almost wish it was him I had met at the bar, and not Peter, all those moons ago. But the thought feels wrong as soon as it crosses my mind. I may not understand or fully like the path I was thrown on, but it is mine. For better or for worse, this is where I'm meant to be.

"I swear to the stars, Belle," Cass's voice carries from deep inside his treehouse. "If you hurt a single hair on her head, I'll—"

The door whips open and Cass's words die. He stares at me, eyes wide, all the color draining from his face. A nervous smile tugs at my lips, but I hold it back by pressing them tight together.

My feeble heart races at his beauty, but my mind reminds me that he is deadly.

And apparently, an idiot who can't keep track of the most important thing in both of our lives.

I place my hands on my hips and level my stare with his ice-blue eyes. "Whose hair are you worried about, Cass? Because I swear to every star in the sky, if you lost our daughter, I'll kill you."

CHAPTER 23

Wednesday

"Thank the stars." Cass grabs me by the wrist and pulls me inside. He slams the door shut and then wraps me in a hug. I lock up for a moment as he buries his face in my shoulder, holding me like I'm his long-lost lover and not the girl he knocked up and tried to kill. "I never thought I'd be happy to see you again, but damn it, Darling, you're a sight for sore eyes."

Anger simmers under my skin. How dare he use me to soothe his agony when all he's done is cause mine. I press my palms to Cass's chest to shove him away, but the narcissistic prick is immovable, probably under the delusion that I'm here because I forgive him. I arch my back and push harder, barely able to make an inch between our bodies. "Get off of me, asshole."

No sooner than the words leave my lips does the front door swing open and clamor against the wall. Cass moves with a speed that can only be explained as Fae because, in less than a second, I am tucked safely behind him, his right hand is spread wide while a small flurry of snow plays in his palm.

James steps into the open space, his sword drawn and pointed at Cass's face. The sight is breathtaking. Every fantasy I had as a girl about Orlando Bloom has flooded my brain again. I swallow hard and try not to stare at the corded muscles of his arm or think about how this man is every bit of the fairytale prince I always dreamed of. Wendy's novel about Peter Pan painted James as the villain, and maybe, in some ways, he was in her story, but in mine he's the unexpected hero. The love interest that snuck up on me. The man I almost wish I had met first.

"Yeh heard the girl." James tips his wrist and motions for Cass to move.

"Interesting." Cass takes a large step to my left. His hand relaxes and the tiny storm in his palm dissipates. His gaze bounces from James to me, twice, then settles on the purple marks peeking out beyond the collar of James's shirt. "Very interesting."

I swallow the heady desire I seem to fight whenever James is near and turn my focus to the treehouse. The living room is the same, the wall shelves are still filled with too many trinkets to count, and he's still got the same tattered oversized chairs and driftwood-carved end table. At quick glance, there isn't a single hint in the main space to indicate that Mira is here, but I know she is.

I can feel it.

The anticipation of finally reuniting with my daughter twists my stomach into knots. I'm nervous. Excited. And terrified. I don't know how to be a mother. I read all of Tyle's old *What to Expect* books because she swore they prepared her for all the ups and downs of her pregnancy. I found them boring and hardly helpful, which is why I never graduated to the next stage of the series. And after Mira was taken, I didn't see the point. Not until I had her in my arms again. Now I wish I had read them because that moment is here and I am low-key freaking out.

"Mira?" I call out while walking toward Cass's bedroom.

Less than twenty paces and I'm through the hallway and into his tiny space. It was always the barest room out of all the treehouses, having only a bed and minimal necessities, but it's fuller now. There is a small cradle carved from wood with a rocking base near the far wall and some odd-looking bottles on the bedside table. Cloth squares are laid out on the dresser top that I think might be diapers and he's hung some dried branches with woven flowers from the ceiling above the cradle. Little by little, I find clues that confirm this is where Cass brought Mira.

But she's not here.

I search every inch of the room, just in case he's hidden her somewhere. Under the bed. In the bathroom. Beneath the pile of dirty clothes in the corner, not likely, but I can't leave a single inch untouched. I refuse to believe that she's gone and that Cass is stupid enough to have lost our daughter. I make my way to the kitchen and open every cabinet just in case Cass hid her somewhere in there on the off chance that he could sense my arrival. I empty everything, throwing it all behind me until each shelf is bare.

Pressure builds in my chest as I sit on the kitchen floor, surrounded by everything Cass owns, and my heart races. Something wraps itself around my lungs until I can't draw in a clean breath. The air physically hurts my chest and my skin feels like someone is poking it with a thousand needles.

I traveled the world, literally crossed the universe to find my daughter, and she's not here.

The room spins around me. Everything swirls and tilts to one side like it does when I'm on a carnival ride. My hands sweat as a cold blanket of air washes the color from my face. Saliva floods my mouth, warning me that if I don't get my shit together soon, I'm going to puke. I try and swallow it but there's too much. I spit it on the floor and then wipe away the mess with a dish towel.

Cass reaches for my arm. He looks genuinely concerned, which is surprising. I didn't think he could care for anyone but himself. "Darling?"

"Don't touch her," James snaps. He steps behind me and pulls me to my feet. My cold body presses against his warm chest. The heat is a shock to my system, but in a good way. I feel the rise and fall of his steady breaths and try to keep my own breathing in sync with his. The weight of his arms around my belly is steadying. Everything begins to find its place again and, although I could use a glass of water, I feel a little better.

Cass tries to come close again, but James effortlessly raises his sword. "I would think twice if yeh value yehr life, mate."

"You can't kill me," Cass chides incredulously. The snarl he gives is feral, like a cat caged, ready to attack. I doubt the reaction has anything to do with me, but it's obvious he feels threatened.

"Maybe not," James quips. "But she can."

"Impossible." Cass's gaze bounces to me again. He studies my face as if it's the first time we've met, almost like he believes James. There's a hatred in his eyes, but curiosity, too.

James lowers his sword and chooses to stand beside me rather than behind me. His stance is relaxed, but his grip on the handle of his weapon is tight. "Enlighten me, Prince, did stealing the child give yeh the power yeh craved?"

"Power?" I look over to James. "What are you talking about?"

"Tell her," James insists, never breaking his focus on Cass to look at me.

Cass exhales heavily and runs his hands through his hair. He steps around the mess on the floor and finds a green bottle I set beside a pile of cups. "I need a drink for this. Wine?"

He's joking. He has to be.

But as an extra second ticks by with Cass doing nothing but staring at me, I realize he's not. "As if I'd trust anything from you again."

"Fair point." Cass pops the cork and pours himself a glass. I recognize the scent, but can't pinpoint what flavor they might be. I tried so many the last time I was here. He swallows the first round like a shot, then adds, "Sorry about that."

"Him?" James asks, reading between the lines. I planned to keep the details of who tried to kill me to myself, but with Cass's admission, there is no point in lying. I nod and a deep growl vibrates in James's chest.

"What? I said I was sorry." Cass's ignorance of how much he hurt me, Peter, Pan, and apparently James is mind-blowing. But what's done is done. I am alive, no thanks to him, and even though I will never forgive Cass, I'm ready to move past it all.

"Why did you take Mira, Cass? And where is she?"

He foregoes the glass and takes his next swallow directly from the bottle. "Years ago, Neverland was a magical hotspot. It was an island built by the gods but given to the Fae. My father ruled alongside Triton and Poseidon and frequently counseled Zeus. You wouldn't believe what it was like growing up here."

"I don't care. Get to the part about Mira."

James sheaths his sword and pulls me into his arms again. They wrap around my waist and I lean against him, our bodies molding together like they were created for each other. "Patience, Sunshine."

Cass rounds the kitchen island and makes himself comfortable in one of the oversized chairs. "The Island itself embodies the magic of the gods. It lives and breathes through its king, the magic tied to his life. When an heir is born, the power shifts to the child but the parents can siphon the wee one's abilities to keep the Island from falling into chaos until their eighteenth birthday."

"So, you were hoping to what... boost your powers through Mira?" I swear, if he thought he could draw from her life to better his, I'll put one of James's iron daggers through his heart. Magic takes from the one who uses it, that's why when Peter and his shadow reunited it almost killed him.

"Neverland was always supposed to be mine!" Cass roars. He clenches his teeth and then forces a smile before taking another sip of his wine. "Emmit had no interest in ruling, and Belle is a girl. She couldn't be king. That left me to take over my father's kingdom, and I was ready!"

"But Neverland chose someone else," James interjects. "Peter."

"Belle lost her mind when the Island denied all three of us. She challenged our father and said we lost our birthright because he was unworthy. Back then, she could command the skies. She channeled the power of Zeus and struck down half our kingdom with his thunderbolts. Father ripped her wings from her back, severing her ties to the Island and all its magic as punishment."

Neither he nor Emmit can fly. Or if they can, I've never seen it. Just like I've never seen a mark on Cass's sculpted back to indicate where his wings could have been. Although, to be fair, I wasn't looking for one the last time he took his shirt off around me. "Is that what happened to your wings?"

Cass shakes his head. "Only the female Fae are born with wings. The bigger and prettier they are, the more powerful children they can bear."

So, she's a peacock. A smile turns my lips until I realize that by losing her wings, not only did Belle lose her ties to the Island, but she may have lost the ability to have children, too. For her, stealing Mira could have a deeper purpose than it does for Cass. "But she has magic still. How?"

"Blood magic," James interjects. "The kind that sends yeh into the darkest pits of Hades hell. Yeh wanted to kill her. Didn't yeh? That's why yeh took the child."

Cass nods once.

There were more years where I hated Tyle than I loved her, but I never wanted anything bad to happen to her. No matter how much hell she put me through, she was my sister. My twin. A bond that Cass should understand since he is a triplet. "But she's your sister!"

"That creature isn't my sister! Tinkerbelle was kind. She loved Neverland. I understand being scared of change, but the shit she's done is unforgivable. Her death and Mira's reign are the only way to make this island what it was. I thought killing Peter would force the Island to choose a new leader. I thought draining him of his powers would prove him unworthy. I thought I would be the next Neverking!" He throws the glass bottle across the room. It hits the wall and shatters. What was left of the wine drips down the wall like blood.

"Where is Mira?" I ask as calmly as possible.

"Belle took her. I went out to create a barrier to keep us safe from the fire. When I came back, she was gone." He pulls open a drawer and hands me a slip of paper. "This was in her crib."

"First of all, it sucks, doesn't it? Losing your child." I grab the note from his hands. "And secondly, who leaves a baby alone? Parenting rule number one is don't forget your child!"

"You left her, too! Remember?"

"Yeah, to walk down the hall. Not alone in a house while I was out in the woods." I swear, this man will be the death of me. I fold the parchment and read the blue swirly letters.

You or her. Make your choice.

"What's that supposed to mean?" I set the note on the countertop and move out of James's arms. I'm hot, and his extra body heat isn't making me feel good. Sweat drips down my back and off my brow. Cass notices and shoots a rush of cool air in my direction. I don't understand him. One minute, he wants to be the bad guy; the next, he's trying to help.

"Belle thinks that if I die, Mira's guardianship will transfer to her. Giving her all of my powers and access to Mira's, too."

"But you don't have any extra powers," I say in a panic.

"I know."

"And there's no guarantee she won't hurt her either way." I run my fingers through my hair and pace the room. This is bad. So very bad.

And it pisses me off that all Cass has to say about the situation is, "I know."

"And if you're dead, there would be no one who can keep Mira safe."

"I know!" Cass yells, slumping into the oversized chair by the window again. "This is fucked. Everything is fucked. I thought I wouldn't care about the kid since bringing Mira to Neverland was pointless, but I can't let her go either. What the hell is wrong with me?"

"It's called fatherhood," James says sympathetically. "It's a blessing and a curse. Yehr happiness is directly tied to yehr kin."

Cass's face hardens. Regret or maybe sorrow flashes in his eyes. "I forgot you had kids."

"How long has Mira been gone?" I ask. Talking about the past won't help. Not in this situation. I feel for James, I do, but we need to stay focused.

"I don't know. A few hours at most. I searched the forest for a sign of how Belle got through the fire. Not long after I got back, you showed up."

I chew on my bottom lip. Why would the Island pull me here if this isn't where Mira was? What was the point?

Clearly, Cass is useless. He would have gone after Belle already if he could have. "What are we going to do?" I mean to ask myself, but the words fall off my lips like a plea to the stars.

"There's not much we can do until the fires die down. The only way to Belle's castle is to take a boat, but without the ability to fly we'd be trapped."

"There are tunnels that run under the mountain. We could steal Mira and escape through them," James suggests.

Cass shakes his head. "It's a maze down there. I know a few of the paths, but one wrong turn and we'd be lost."

"This is bullshit!" I shout. Everything about this is wrong. Peter wouldn't sit around and let the fires take over the Island. Pan wouldn't give up without a fight. We can't either.

"Why does Belle get to burn the place down? Why aren't the fires coming after her, too?"

Cass shrugs. "It's her island.

"No, it's not!" I yell. "She doesn't have the right to kill everything that lives here because she's what… throwing a tantrum!" I open the door and storm outside.

"Where are yeh going?" James yells, chasing after me as I scurry down the ladder.

"To find my daughter."

"You're not strong enough to save her!" Cass yells. "The fires—"

"Screw the fires!"

"Wednesday!" James yells and hearing him use my name again gives me pause. I turn to face him and something falls on my cheek.

I reach up to the wet spot and wipe it away. I rub my fingers together and another drop falls, hitting my arm.

Thunder booms overhead and then the sky opens up. Water pours from the clouds in big, monsoon-like drops. I run back to the overhang and stand under the shelter of Cass's platform.

"It's raining." I watch steam rise from the yielding flames and hope blooms in my chest. If this keeps up, the fires will be out within the hour. Neverland will have a chance to breathe and we can hike towards Belle's castle in the mountain. "It never rains in Neverland."

"Do yeh believe me now?" James wraps his arm around my waist.

I lean into him, oddly relaxed despite the hot air forming around us. "About what?"

"The Island. It listens to yeh. Yeh want the fires put out, it's doing it for yeh."

"Impossible." Cass slides down the ladder. "She only listens to Peter's shadow."

"Yeh said it yehrself, a true heir was born. That child kicked Peter off his throne and made way for a new liege."

"She's human," Cass says, shocked and angry. "She can't be the new ruler."

James steps into the rain and bows, as if that is all the proof he needs. "I humbly pledge my allegiance to yeh, Sunshine. The new Queen of Neverland."

CHAPTER 24

Pan

X yris, stay here with the girls," Emmit directs. "You know where the food and water are. Watch the sky. If we aren't back in two days, take the rowboat to the Jolly Roger. James will give you sanctuary, but move in the night. Belle's guards are mindless, but if she's given the order to execute trespassers, they will without question."

Xyris nods and leans forward to kiss Emmit. The embrace is quick, but I think it's safe to say we all feel the heaviness of this goodbye. The goal is to keep the Lost safe. The endgame, eliminate Belle and take back our Island. The plan...

I'm hoping Emmit has one because I don't.

"What happens in two days?" Scarlett asks. I'm wondering the same thing. It's a very specific amount of time, which leads me to believe Emmit knows more than he's letting on.

"Just stay together and you'll be safe." He dodges the question and takes off into the tunnels again.

Scarlett looks to me for guidance since Emmit hasn't offered any. "Everything will be okay. Xyris will take care of you both until we get back."

If we come back.

I sprint into the darkness to catch up to Emmit. The black

blanket around us is smothering. I'm not usually afraid of the dark. I lived in it for so many years that it became a part of me. I could sense the movements of the land and see tiny shifts in the air.

But in Peter's body, my senses are dulled. I have fear and worry for the first time. Worry about tripping. Worry about bleeding, wondering what that pain feels like. I'm so pathetically fragile now. I don't know how much use I'll be in this war.

Perhaps all I am is a decoy. Belle doesn't know Peter is dead or that I exist. That bit of knowledge is the only leverage we have. I just hope Emmit knows how to use it.

I bump into a hard body deep within the maze of tunnels. I swing on instinct and hit the air. The person shuffles back a step and then sighs disapprovingly. "Whatever you're going through, you need to get over it. I need the Neverland Shadow, not this pathetic version of Peter."

Believe me, I'd love to be that man again, too. Given time, I could be, but time isn't a luxury I have. I've been thrown into a magicless body and my only interaction with it in this world was bound by chains. I'm learning and trying my best to adapt, knowing that if I don't Wednesday will think I abandoned her, but it hasn't been easy. "I'm fine. Let's keep going."

I step to the side to go around Emmit. He grabs me by the back of my shirt. "I can smell your fear. You reek of it. What's going on?"

It crosses my mind to lie, to preserve what little dignity I have left, but like me, Emmit is one of the Lost. We are brothers. Bound together in this life by a pact made in blood. Who else is there if I can't trust him with my truths? "I'm not connected to the Island anymore. She's stripped me of all my magic, and I don't know how to be human."

"That's...really fucking shitty." He lets me go. "But you have Peter's memories. He learned to exist without magic. Use them."

"I can't reach them. Something is blocking me from him and them."

"Great. You're basically an oversized toddler. Cute but useless." He's quiet, probably trying to decide if I should be left with the Lost. I'd be less of a hindrance there, but I want to help. "We need to convince Belle that you're Peter. You did a good job of that back at the castle."

"That was before I knew my magic was gone."

"Magic doesn't make the man, Pan. You want to be a coward? Fine. Go back to the grotto and wait for me to return. I don't need a liability. I need a soldier. Someone who will go into battle with me and take back our home."

Every one of the Lost has gone through this moment. That's why Peter named them Lost. The souls come to the Island and don't know up from down anymore. Change will throw you for a loop like that. You can either spin out and lose all control of what's left of your life, or you can take the reins and make the best of where you've landed.

As a shadow, I never understood why the souls on Neverland were tortured. I thought they were pathetic and weak, but I understand now. Without my magic, it feels like I've lost myself. I have no purpose anymore. The island has rejected me, and I'm left to simply exist. It's a hard pill to swallow.

I imagine this is how the souls feel when they arrive. The world they knew is gone. Their families gone. That force that drove them to work and forge a life doesn't exist in Neverland. They have to learn to cope with their losses and adapt to a new way of living. They have all of eternity.

I have mere hours to get myself together.

"I need to get back to Wednesday," is all I offer because it is the only option.

"The only way that will happen is if we kill Belle. Now, let's go."

We walk and walk, turning down unmarked corridors, going gods know where. I stay close, careful not to lose sight of Emmit. The last thing I want is to be lost in this body, wondering these tunnels until I starve to death.

After what feels like an eternity, light filters into the darkness ahead of us. We've found an opening to the outside world, but we could be anywhere on the island. The Never Mountain is at Neverland's heart, split between Peter's half of the Island and James's, but neither of them goes to the east corner, where the late king's castle was carved into the stone. The land over there is in ruins from a battle that happened long before our time. Walking onto it emits a wave of fear that snakes its way into your veins. The magic warding it doesn't want visitors and so we've stayed away. Until today.

"She's here. The Island wants us to find her." He looks at me with hopeful eyes. "Can you feel the pull?"

"Who?" I stand beside Emmit and look out at the rain. I don't feel anything except the heat in the air.

"The new queen."

"Your mermaid friend mentioned her, but who is it?"

"I thought you were smarter than this." Emmit shakes his head. "It feels like she's on the west end of the Island. If we hurry, we can cross paths before they make it to Belle's castle. She's going to need all the help she can get."

I grab his arm as he starts to walk away. I'm tired of the half-truths. I know it's how he was trained to talk, but I'm grasping at straws, trying to keep my head above water. I need a solid answer. "I'm going to need you to slow down a beat, Emmit. I can't feel the Island anymore. Remember? Who are we trying to find?"

He huffs out an impatient breath and says, "Your precious Darling. Wednesday."

CHAPTER 25

Wednesday

"What's the plan?" Cass shouts as we run through the woods. His ignorance to us trying to be stealthy is frustrating. We're already loud enough, unable to control the sound of half-burnt branches snapping beneath our feet and Cass was zero help in telling us what Belle's guard is like. We don't know how far from the side of the mountain they stretch or what their orders are if they discover intruders.

The likely answer? Capture or kill. Both of which we cannot let happen.

"I don't have one."

"Of course you don't," he mutters.

I stop running and brace my hands on my knees. My lungs burn. Legs hurt. I forgot that everywhere we go in Neverland is on foot. After catching my breath, I stand upright but keep my hands over my head for another minute. "Improvising worked well with you. Maybe Belle will hug me, too."

"Unlikely," Cass scoffs. His patience grows thinner the longer we're together. I can't read him. One minute, the man is hot; the next, he's cold.

"Watch yehr tone," James warns. "But Cass is right. We can't go to the castle half-cocked. If she throws her dust, we're done for.

It's been three days since she last fed. She'll be weaker but still deadly."

"How do you know?" Cass asks.

James pulls the corner of his shirt to show the stitches on his shoulder and the purple veins that stretch from the mark. "There were no new souls in the Neversea. I offered one of my memories to keep the Pirates from having to sacrifice again."

"She did this to you?" The marks look horrible. I knew they looked wrong, but I never would have imagined they were from a bite wound. I trace over one of the purple lines with my finger. The skin is raised, similar to a burn scar. Textured, yet soft.

"You should be dead," Cass says with zero emotion.

James adjusts his shirt to cover as many of the marks as possible, but they peek out over his shirt collar. There's no hiding how she's hurt him. "It's a miracle I'm not."

The sound of snapping branches and rustling of leaves has us all turning our heads. James pulls his sword from his holster and steps in front of me. Cass flicks his wrists and a glowing blue ball appears in his palms. Both men are ready for battle and I...

I don't even have a weapon to defend myself with.

"Show yourself!" Cass demands.

"Always with the orders," someone shouts, and I recognize the voice. Emmit pushes aside a half-charred palm frond and steps into view. "Hello, brother."

"Emmit!" I run forward and throw my arms around his neck. I'm so relieved he's okay and hopeful for the others. I tried not to think about what might have happened to them in the fires. The way the flames swallowed everything in their path, I hoped the Lost made it out alright. Any other outcome was unacceptable, but there haven't been any signs of life. Everything we pass is either black or ashen and the whole island smells like death.

"It's good to see you, too, Your Majesty." He steps out of our embrace and bows. "I have a gift for you."

My cheeks flush pink and I stifle a laugh. I am the furthest thing from a queen and for some reason, even Emmit thinks I'm one. Cass rolls his eyes and puts out the snow flurry in his palm. I scowl at him as someone else steps through the clearing. I recognize the silhouette, but don't let myself get excited until I see his face.

"Peter!" I leap forward into his arms. "I was so scared something had happened to you."

Peter barely touches me. His body is like a wall, hard and cold, and his voice... It's broken. "Something did."

I look into dark eyes and gasp. "Pan?" I whisper. "But how?"

He sets me on my feet and tucks his hands in his pockets. "I don't know, but Peter's gone. So are my ties to Neverland."

I cup his cheeks and look into his eyes. This isn't the broody spirit I love. This man is broken, and it breaks my heart to see him this way. I want to pull him into my arms and reassure him that everything will be all right, but he steps back, putting inches that feel like miles between us. "Are you okay?"

He shrugs sadly. "I'll survive. That's what you mortals do. Right?"

James places his hand on my belly and pulls me back a step while he comes forward and draws his sword at Pan. "Stay away from our queen."

Pan holds his hands up. "It's bad form to challenge an unarmed opponent."

"Stop this!" I push James's sword down and the Island rumbles. "No fighting. Pan is my friend, not my enemy. I know you've had your differences in the past, but if you can't put them aside and work together, then I don't want you here. Understand?"

"Yes, my lady," James agrees begrudgingly. He sheaths his sword but doesn't move from my side.

I turn to Pan. "And you? Can I trust you to have my back with both Cass and James there, too?"

"Doesn't seem like I have a choice. I'm not leaving you." There's the fire in his eyes I was looking for. A small glimpse that the man I know is buried somewhere deep inside.

"Good." I reach for his hand and squeeze it. "Because I think I might have a plan, but it's going to take all of us to make it work."

"And what is it? Because five minutes ago, you were drawing a blank," Cass sneers.

I look at him and wonder which man is the real one. This arrogant jerk or the one who took me into the Never Caves to see their version of stars. I will never forgive Cass for all the pain he's put me through, but that doesn't mean I don't miss who he used to be when we were together. "Do you remember what you told me never to say?"

"No," he says flatly.

"Go on," Emmit encourages. I see the gears turning in his head, and I think he might be on the same page as me.

"Well, what if we get me in the room with Belle and I say it?"

Emmit paces back and forth. He knows the Fae laws better than I do. I hope he's deciding if my plan is doable because it's the only one I've got. Finally, he stops walking to meet my gaze. "It's risky, but it could work."

"I'm lost," Cass whines.

James scowls. "Of course yeh are."

"What if saying the forbidden words don't work?" Pan asks, and it's a legitimate question. My theory is based on one sentence Cass offered and the lore in Wendy Darling's story.

I squeeze Pan's hand. "That's where you come in. You can use your magic to get us out of there if anything goes wrong. I believe in you."

He swallows hard and glances at Emmit. I see the worry in his eyes, but I have faith. Body or no body, he is still the Neverland Shadow. That power is still connected to him. It has to be. He just needs to trust himself.

"It's a start," Emmit says. "We'll improvise if we have to, but I think it's a good plan."

CHAPTER 26

Cass

I always thought I'd have a big family. One where my mother helped care for my children and my brother was close, causing chaos but happy. I imagined my father standing beside me as we went over the realm maps, discussing which worlds within our multi-verse were in need of help and which we'd choose to rule beside. I pictured meetings with the gods, where we'd forge new alliances and discuss the ways of old.

I thought I'd have a wife at my side whose opinions were firm, but her heart was true. She'd listen to my concerns about Neverland and the neighboring kingdoms with open ears and a guarded heart because she would love our world just as much as me.

That dream was severed the night Belle decided to challenge the gods. She damned herself and all of Neverland to live in a near barren existence. Our people, the friends and family we'd known since birth, were slaughtered. The few Fae our father helped escape have forgotten us. If they haven't, they've turned their backs. Our home has been cast out of the light to fall within the shadows of the underworld.

Neverland rejected all three of us—Belle, Emmit, and myself —as its heirs to the throne. I was denied my birthright as the Island gave it away to an outsider.

Hundreds of years of my life have been nothing but a living hell. All because of Belle's need for power. Her fear of Wendy and the prophecy she held. And now, Wednesday, who, too many mortal years later, brought the seer's words to life.

"Stop crying, you wretched thing!" Belle yells at my daughter.

A thread inside me pulls tight. I didn't expect to fall in love with the little beast. My kind is supposed to be above those mortal emotions. We have the ability to care and nurture, but an unwavering dedication to something besides myself, the willingness to die for her, and to feel Mira's agony when she cried took me by surprise.

I wait for Mira's wail to change. Each pitch and the way she drags out the sound means something different. She's a complex little creature with so much to say without the vocabulary to do so. This cry means she's hungry. The timing is about right. Mira is due for a bottle and a nap, then will likely need to be changed once she wakes.

"Can't handle a baby?" I taunt as I stride into our father's throne room.

It looks the same as it did all those years ago. Father's chair sits at the center of a dais, Mother's beside it, their gilded grace lacking the shine they once held, but still beautiful. My seat was beside Father's, as was Emmit's. Belle was seated beside Mother. Someone has cared for them as there's not a speck of dust, only tarnish from lack of polish.

The grand room still holds the same portraits on the walls. Our family history, captured in paint, spans over a dozen generations. I'm sure the paintings have seen more horrors under Belle's reign than in all the years Neverland has been in existence. I'm grateful the murals can't talk. Father would be so ashamed if he knew the stories they could tell.

Belle's drawn the satin curtains, cutting out what little outside light Neverland has to offer. It makes the room feel colder. Or maybe that's the lingering spirits of everyone who died here.

"Tell me, sister, how do you expect to be queen if you can't control a child?" I taunt her to lure her away from Mira. Belle, while dangerous, is semi-predictable. She's a cat, and I am her prey. I'm counting on her wanting to play with me before delivering the fatal blow.

"With your powers, of course. Ready to die, brother?" As I had hoped, she steps down from the dais and ambles near the center of the room.

"Actually, we had a better idea." Emmit emerges from the shadows of the hallway. He strides into the throne room with his head held high, exuding practiced confidence.

"What a pleasant surprise," Belle says, her smile wide but her words clipped. "I wasn't expecting so much company, but having us all under one roof again is nice. Tell me, brother, what is your plan?"

Emmit tugs on a twine rope attached to Wednesday's wrists. She comes into the light, semi-voluntarily walking to his side, and lets him push her down onto her knees. My cock twitches at the submission. That woman is something extraordinary. If only she hadn't fallen for fucking Peter Pan. I could have made her my wife, the future Queen of Neverland, once I had my island back.

James and Emmit think the Island chose her anyway. I think they're full of shit.

Belle's spine straightens. She licks her lips and glides to the center of the room, leaving a trail of golden dust in her wake. "The precious Darling girl. You, dear, have caused quite the stir on my island."

"A gift," I add. The words feel like fire in my mouth. I'd never give her Wednesday. I did what I had to do to get my kingdom back. Was it ruthless? Yes, but I still care for the girl. At the very least, she's the mother of my child, but in truth, she's more. So much more. "To show our loyalty."

"You were always smarter than you let on, brother." Belle turns her attention back to Wednesday. Her long nails caress the side of Wednesday's face. "I wonder what pretty little things are inside your mind?"

"Belle!" James's voice booms from the hallway. Right on time. We want Belle to have the illusion of power. Too long with the Darling and we risk her life. Not long enough and she'll see this ruse for what it is. A trap.

"Not now!" Belle hisses.

James ignores her and carries in a hog-tied Peter, or if Wednesday's assumptions are correct, Pan. I must say, I enjoy the sight of him bound, too, but for different reasons. "This one was creeping around the castle."

Belle beams with excitement. "My, my. Two presents in one day. The stars must be favoring me. I'm going to enjoy torturing your precious Darling, Peter. You will watch her bleed and listen to her screams while I—"

"I'm right here, you know," Darling says, right on schedule. "And I gotta say, that doesn't sound appealing."

Belle whirls around, her snarl vicious. "How dare you talk back to me! I am Neverland's Queen. You will quiver in my presence."

Wednesday chuckles. She motions to stand, but Emmit pushes on her shoulder to keep her on her knees. "You think you're scary? That's cute. You're a five-foot-nothing woman who weighs what...a hundred pounds soaking wet? I have seen cats scarier than you."

"Why, you little twit, I will cut your tongue out!" Belle stomps over to Wednesday, her claws out, ready to make good on her threat.

Wednesday doesn't cower in the slightest. She glares at Belle and says, "I'd love to see you try. Especially when I don't believe in fairies."

My sister gasps and takes a step back. Her golden skin pales to the color of snow. She looks from Emmit to me, terror in her eyes. I feel her fear. Those words are the only thing that can give true death to a Fae. It's a power only a few can wield, and Wednesday is one of them. I step forward, prepared to catch Belle as she falls. She might not be the sweet girl I grew up with anymore, but she's still my sister. Despite it all, I will always care for her.

I take another step forward and a fire blooms in my chest. It spreads rapidly until it's all I can feel and consumes my thoughts. I find my sister's face as realization dawns on it. She runs to me as the ice in my veins melts. It hurts more than anything I've ever felt. I scream, unable to keep it inside any longer, until it finally stops.

Everything stops.

Wednesday

It all happens so quickly and there's is nothing I can do. As soon as the words leave my lips, I feel them reach out, cold and greedy, like the hand of death. Only, they don't grab the Fae I intended. They latch onto the Fae furthest from me, the one I hate but care for at the same time. I feel that coldness turn to fire and before I can fully comprehend what's happening, it's too late.

Belle runs toward Cass and screams, "No!" But there is nothing she can do either.

I feel her magic, too, as a heaviness reaches out to blanket her brother. It touches him, giving them an extra second to lock eyes, and then poof. Cass bursts into flames and a heartbeat later is nothing but a pile of ash.

Belle turns to me, her eyes flaring with anger. "You!"

"Think this through, sister," Emmit cautions. He steps between us, his hands out to try and slow her.

Something in my brain whispers for me to run, but I can't move. I'm stuck, frozen with shock. Knowing Cass was alive, I was content with being angry with him. He deserved that anger after everything he's put me through, but I never wanted him to die thinking I hadn't forgiven him. What if I'm the reason his soul is stuck in another form of Neverland? An eternal hell he can't escape because we never turned that page in our story.

"Get out of my way, Emmit!" Belle shoves her brother, but he's as still as a statue.

"Cass is dead," he says calmly. Too calmly. Did he know this would happen? Did he know there was a chance the words would kill either him or Cass? If so, why take the risk? We could have found another way to try and take her down.

"Exactly!" Belle wails. Her cheeks are red with fury, her eyes shiny with unshed tears.

"And where did his magic go? To you?" Emmit's words give Belle pause. She stops her tirade as he looks at Pan. "To him?"

Belle presses her lips into a tight line, letting his words process. Based on how angry Belle is and how pale Pan is, I'm guessing neither of them absorbed Cass's powers, which is what he expected. He may have been Mira's father, but she didn't bless him with any gifts.

"Get to the point," Belle growls.

"My point is that we don't know where the baby's magic will go once both parents are dead." Emmit pauses to let Belle mull over his words. "Do you truly want to risk everything you've worked for because you're angry?"

"He's right," James chimes in. "The Island is already in a state of change because of the girl."

"Exactly," Emmit pushes. "Don't tempt the gods when they've already given you such a precious gift." He gestures to me and Pan.

"There is only one god I fear, brother, and he couldn't care less about Neverland and its magic." She pauses to think. "But it wouldn't hurt to consult the fates. Lock the Darling in the study, as it seems our dungeon needs work."

"Of course, sister." Emmit bows and tugs on the rope that binds my wrists. The knot is a dummy slip. I could escape and run if need be, but I'm trusting Emmit knows what he's doing.

"What about this one?" James asks.

Belle chuffs. "If he had any power left, he would have used it. He's useless now that the child is here. End his life however you see fit, but make it painful."

"Yes, my lady." James grabs Pan by the back of the neck and leads him out of the room.

"Let's go." Emmit shortens the leash between us and pretends that I am the scum of the Earth. He's convincing enough. Belle leaves us, and Mira, without asking any questions, to go...somewhere within the castle.

I can't help but look at the pile of ash as we walk past what's left of Cass. Tears fill my eyes, but I hold them back. I will not give Belle the satisfaction of seeing me cry. I'm sure she thinks I'm a monster for uttering those horrible words, and maybe I am, but I never wanted this to happen. I knew that coming to Neverland would eventually mean forgiving Cass. Mira would need her father to guide her through the Fae aspects of her life. I figured we'd find a way to co-parent and live peacefully. None of that is possible now.

And it's all my fault.

I follow Emmit, unsure of what to do next. I won't risk saying those words again. Not now that I know their target isn't guaranteed. He leads me to what I'm assuming is the study and opens the door. I step inside. "What now?"

He closes it behind us and turns the lock. "Find something in here that could be useful."

"Like what?"

"I don't know. Anything. Our family history is in there. There's bound to be a clue or something as to what's happened to Belle." He walks to one of the walls filled from floor to ceiling with books and stars skimming over the titles.

I stand beside him, overwhelmed by the hundreds of cloth-bound books. Some have print on the spines, others are bare. From what I can tell, there's no order, and most are written in a language I don't understand. "Haven't you read all of this already?"

"No. Cass was supposed to be king. He spent years studying this shit." Emmit pulls out a red book and flips through the pages. He doesn't find what he's looking for because it's back on the shelf a moment later. "My interest lied elsewhere growing up."

Great. So not only did I prevent Mira from ever knowing her father, but I also killed the only person who might know how Belle came to be so dark and twisted. I slide down the wall and hide my face in my arms. I don't want to cry, but I can't help it. I'm no closer to getting my daughter back, and I recklessly took a key player off the board. I came to Neverland feeling hopeful, but now all I feel is doubt and worry.

"Hey." Emmit touches my arm. "We both knew the risk of you saying those words. It's okay."

"It's not." I look up but can't meet his gaze. I feel so bad. I don't know how Belle can effortlessly take a life. "I killed him."

Emmit pulls me into a hug and tries to soothe me, but it only makes me feel worse. He lost his brother. I should be comforting him, yet here he is placating the stupid mortal girl. "We have bigger things to worry about. Grieve his loss, but don't let it eat at you."

I nod but make no promises. I have a feeling Cass's death is going to be with me for a long time. "How long will I be in here?"

"For appearance purposes, a few hours. I can't spring you, but if I know a certain captain like I think I do, you'll be out sooner rather than later." Emmit's lips lift into a warm smile. I think the comment about James is supposed to make me feel better, but it just adds a new layer of worry to my back.

"You don't think he'll kill Pan, do you?"

His brows push together and he regards me for the first time as something more than a weak mortal the Island chose. "You know he's not Peter?"

I nod and can't help but wonder what else Emmit knows and has purposely kept secret. "Do you?"

Emmit runs his hand through his hair and sighs. "Did I know? Yes. Do I think he's in danger with James? No, but Pan is struggling to adjust to having a body, especially one without magic."

"Wait, he's not the Neverland shadow anymore?"

"Nope. The Island is changing. With Peter dead—"

"Oh my god! Peter's dead?" No. He can't be. He has to be somewhere on this Island. Peter can't die. He's a legend. The boy who lives forever. The man who stole my life and my heart. He can't be dead. He just can't!

"Fuck, I thought you knew." Emmit lets out a heavy breath and sits back on his heels. "Maybe. Probably. I don't know. All I know is that Pan is Peter, but with no magic. Belle is on a war path with stolen magic. Cass is dead, and now I have to go kiss the bitch's ass." He squeezes my shoulder. "I need you to find something that can help us take down Belle and fast. Can you do that?"

I wipe my nose with the back of my hand. "I can try."

"Good." He stands and looks around the room. "I should go. Belle will be consulting with the fates soon and I want to hear what they have to say. You've got this, Wednesday. I believe in you."

"Thanks," I mutter, trying to be strong, but as soon as the door closes and I'm alone, I crumble.

CHAPTER 28

Peter

Neverland once had a shadow. A darkness comprised of the worst parts of myself with infinite powers. It learned to hone all of my anger and resentment, all of the sorrow and regret, and turn it into a strength I never had. It protected our island and, from time to time, was its voice.

A voice I often wished would shut up and leave me alone.

I never understood Pan's constant need to prattle. He could talk for hours and it took me years to figure out how to block the bond to stay sane. Living with another voice in your head is maddening. Eventually, we found a balance, but I understand it now. The desperate need to be heard. For someone to acknowledge your existence. This world is cold and lonely. It's too easy to fall into the darkness and lose yourself when you feel there's no one by your side. But all it takes is for one person to listen to keep your head above water.

Pan had me.

And I have no one.

I don't know how I lost control of my body. One minute, he and I were arguing about how to care for Wednesday and the next, there was darkness. It felt like I fell asleep because when my eyes opened again, I was rejuvenated, but also empty. Literally. I floated like a spirit in the sky at the barrier of Neverland, just outside of its grasp in the land of the living. I could feel Pan drifting away. The bond between us stretched thin, but something pulled me back to the ground. A tinging. A need to find and protect. I thought the sensation had pulled me to my Darling, but I was wrong.

I was called to look after her child. The anomaly of life growing.

Watching Wednesday cry herself to sleep those first few days after Pan left was excruciating. I wanted to hold her and tell her I was still here. My hands went through her body, peppering her skin with goosebumps. I couldn't comfort her, couldn't tell her how much I cared, couldn't let her know I hadn't left her alone, and it was torture.

But all of that changed when the first full moon rose in the sky and the barrier between my world and hers grew thinner. Somehow, she could hear me just as I had heard Pan. It was exhilarating. Not the life I would have chosen for us by any means, but to truly love someone means that you adapt. Life prides itself in throwing curveballs at your face, and the choices it gives are to roll with the punches or die.

I'll be damned if I let our bond die.

Everything changed again when Mira was born. A pulse was sent out into the universe that Wednesday couldn't see, but I was sure could be felt all the way to Neverland. I hoped I was wrong. I hoped the innocent baby girl my Darling had brought into the world would be safe, but even Wednesday knew better. I think she felt the danger even though she didn't know what it was. Her stupid sister didn't understand. She didn't believe Wednesday when anything Neverland-related was spoken.

I often wonder if Darling had been in the room, if she and I could have protected Mira from Cass. The energy is wasted because as I stand unnoticed in the throne room rocking the forgotten child because I know that this is the path Neverland intended me to be on.

Footsteps echo from within the palace corridors. I ready myself to defend the girl despite my limited powers. I don't have nearly the abilities Pan did. I can't summon a storm or corral the animals. I can't wield objects with my mind or bleed into the shadows. But I can guide others, like how I warned Cass about the encroaching fires or how I drew the Darling to his tree house. I can soothe the child, my hands allowed to touch all things related to her, even though they passed through everything else.

Too many days after she first arrived, I fed and changed the girl as if she were my own, without Cass realizing what was happening because he is utterly clueless when it comes to taking care of a child.

Or should I say...was.

I recognize the voices and rub the little one's belly. She's hungry and has cried herself to sleep, something I haven't let happen since the first day Cass brought her into this world.

"Over there!" Xyris's not-so-quiet whisper draws the attention of the others. Scarlett and Aria hug the walls near the entrance. Their swords are drawn, ready to fight if they're caught, while Xyris runs across the room.

If they were smart, one would be guarding the far entrance, too, but I don't sense any danger. No need to alert them of anything just yet.

Xyris sheaths his weapon and reaches into the cradle. He scoops the sleeping Mira into his arms and rests her against his chest. I touch her back, willing her to stay asleep until they breach the walls again. Belle only has a handful of soldiers, all mindless drones she's sucked the life out of. They have no thoughts of their own anymore and exist only to serve her needs. I've never seen them do anything more than stand guard, but I wouldn't put it past her to have whispered contingency orders in their ear if there ever was a breach to occur.

"You'll be safe," I say to the child, and Xyris's gaze lifts. He looks at me, and something stirs inside. "Xyris?"

He blinks and then shakes his head. The small ounce of hope

I had that there was someone on this island besides the baby who knew I was here dies. Pan was Neverland's shadow. Seen but not heard. Acknowledged but not feared.

Whereas I am its ghost.

I let them leave, keeping my senses open for any danger they might encounter, and follow the trail to the Darling. She's easy to find, which makes me wonder if it was this simple for Pan. If he was as drawn to Wednesday as I am, he could have known about her rebirth the moment she took her first breath. Something I would love to ask him about, but we aren't connected. Like the Lost and everyone else I've tried to speak with, he can't hear me.

I walk through the closed door and almost through the Darling. She's huddled on the floor, knees pulled to her chest, her head down as tears soak her cheeks. It's a sight I saw too many times back in the land of the living. My heart breaks for her. I don't know if she's mourning the loss of Cass or if there are new traumas burned into her soul since I left. Even though Cass was a motherfucker, I'm sure her sorrow is a mixture of it all. He doesn't deserve her tears, but they will still fall for him because Wednesday is a good person with a big heart. She'll let go of all the pain he caused and focus on the good times when she thinks of him beyond this day.

I crouch down in front of her and, even though I know she can't hear me, I still try to comfort her. That is my curse. Wanting nothing but happiness for this woman and being unable to give it to her. "You know what they say, Darling. What goes around comes around."

Wednesday lifts her head. Those big eyes meet mine, tear-stained red and glossy. "Peter?"

CHAPTER 29

Peter

I stumble back and fall, half expecting to go through the floor. It takes effort to walk and act like I am still myself. Pan never cared. He floated and flew around like a feather in the night, whereas all of this is new to me and I still want to feel like... me.

"Peter?" Wednesday sniffles and her gaze darts around the room. "Is that you?"

"You can hear me?" I ask for the second time today. I don't expect a response. No one can ever hear what I have to say, but that doesn't stop me from being hopeful.

Wednesday's lips lift into the most beautiful smile I've ever seen. It's warm and bright and so full of life. "Yes! Oh gods, Peter, I missed you so much. Emmit said you were dead. Are you dead?" She waits less than a second for me to respond before dropping her face to her hands again. "I'm losing it again. Aren't I?"

I reach Wednesday's arm, expecting it to pass through her like it does every other person I touch in Neverland. To my surprise, my hand holds steady on her skin, goosebumps raising her little blonde hairs.

Wednesday looks up again, her lips parted lightly. "I feel you."

She reaches her hand out and I lean into her touch. I feel her, too. She's warm and soft and damn it, if I had tears, I could cry. I'm not alone in this world anymore, and it makes me so happy that it's my Darling who knows I'm here.

"I want to see you."

"Me too," I tell her.

"Oh, my stars! Peter!" Wednesday lunges forward and wraps her arms around my neck. I fall backward onto the floor, not through it, and hug her back. I don't even get the chance to process that we're hugging before her lips find mine. I thread my fingers through her hair and pull her close. I don't know how this is possible. I don't care either. I'm just glad.

Wednesday laughs as she crawls off me. "How?"

I wipe the tears from her cheeks, hoping happy ones are mixed in with the sad, and say, "I don't know. Neverland magic, I guess."

She sits cross-legged on the floor across from me. Her eyes trail over my body, taking in every inch. I hope it's the same as before and that she still likes what she sees. It's not like I have a reflection anymore to know what I look like. "But you're not a shadow."

"No, I'm not." And never was. "I called myself the ghost of Neverland for a minute. It was funny until it wasn't." Being a ghost is more depressing than it is funny. Maybe if I could have scared Cass or tormented Belle it would have been more fun, but all I could do was look after the little one. A task I am grateful to have been given, but sometimes I wish I could do more.

"But you're here."

"I know."

"No, Peter." Wednesday scampers to one side of the room and empties a silver serving tray resting on an end table. She wipes the dust away with her shirt and holds the metal up so I can see my reflection. "You're actually here."

"That's not how it works." I am grateful she can see me too, but I have no body for the image to reflect. I try to tell her as much, but then I see myself. The warm glow of my cheeks. The dark hue of my hair. I reach up to touch my face and even the tattoos on my arms are there. The clothes I wore in the world of the living, simple jeans and a short-sleeved shirt are as clear as the day is bright. I touch the fabric of my shirt, and it lifts. It's not a part of my body anymore, but on it.

I lunge at the Darling and lift her off her feet. She laughs as I lean down and claim her lips again. I kiss her until she's breathless, then move to her neck, and she lets out a sigh. That sound will be my undoing. If we weren't under the roof of a psychopath, I'd take Wednesday now and make up for all the time I've lost, but there are other more important matters to attend to.

Despite wanting to stay in her arms forever, I take a step backward to create distance between our bodies and try to fit the pieces together. "This shouldn't be possible."

"Neverland shouldn't be possible," she says with a laugh, "but here we are."

I can't argue with her logic, but something still seems amiss. If I have my body again, where is Pan? What happened to him?

The door handle jiggles, ending any further conversation. Wednesday looks at me with wide eyes. I'm not supposed to be here, but maybe I am to keep the Darling safe now that the little one is in good hands.

I back myself against the wall, hiding myself from the intruder's sight once the door opens. I ball my fists, ready to fight. There is no hum of magic in my veins anymore. I don't feel the Island's warning, just like I can't feel Pan's presence. I'm not worried. I lived most of my life here without magic. I don't need the Island's help to kick someone's ass.

Wednesday takes a step back and grabs a pillow. It was the closest thing to her, so I understand reaching for it, but the down-stuffed fabric isn't going to save her. Then again, she's got me now. So, I guess her choice of weaponry doesn't matter.

"Really, Sunshine?" my brother asks, humor in his tone when he enters the room. "What are yeh going to do? Smother me to death?"

"Asshole," Wednesday teases as she throws the pillow at his face.

James effortlessly swats it away. He peeks into the hallway again, then extends his hand. "Everything is in order, but we need to leave."

"What about Mira?"

"Xyris and the girls grabbed her a few minutes ago." I step out of my hiding place and tuck my hands into my pockets. It's a strange sensation having them again, both pockets and hands.

"I left yeh at the boat. How did you...?" James's brows knit together as he takes in the subtle differences between me and my shadow.

"Not Pan," I say because there's no other explanation.

James processes what I said and then grins. "Fuckin' brilliant, but there's no time to explain. We need to leave."

He steps forward and takes Wednesday's hand in his. Something twists inside me as I watch their fingers intertwine. I see it, just like I did all those years ago, the bond between my brother and the woman who holds my heart. I don't hold it against her if she's fallen for him or anyone else. I've been a ghost in this world for weeks. The stars only know how many years it's been for her in the land of the living, but seeing that she's moved on stings.

Wednesday turns to look at me as she and James pass. She takes my hand and smiles, pulling me along with them. A strange glimmer of hope that the Darling could love us both warms my veins. Wendy would never allow herself the satisfaction. It was always one or the other, even though we both knew her heart was torn. James got the bulk of Wendy's love while I got the stolen moments and scraps, but for me, it was enough.

I follow her down the dark tunnels beneath the castle, holding her hand while she holds James's. Only it doesn't feel like I'm a tag-along. Wednesday holds me tight and something tells me that this time around, things with the Darling will be different.

CHAPTER 30

James

"I'm putting my foot down, James," Smee shouts from the deck of the ship, hands on her hips.

We should be the last to arrive if everything went according to plan. Xyris and the girls should already be on board with the baby. I hand-delivered Pan to his quarters—that situation is a mindboggling miracle that needs to be addressed, but not now—and Emmit stayed behind, working as a spy behind enemy lines.

"And when the hell did that one leave the ship?" she screeches, pointing to Peter. "I told Rodgers to keep an eye on him at all times."

I fight a frown and work to keep my face as expressionless as possible. I understand Smee is concerned. Bringing everyone here is a risk, but it's one I'm willing to take. Outside of the small plot of land Cass saved, and Belle's castle in the mountain, Neverland is in pieces. Our ship is the only safe space for survivors. Not just Peter's friends, but ours too. We found thirteen survivors throughout the cove, all with various stages of burns to their bodies and so many more that were unsaveable. I can't begin to understand the pain my crew is feeling. They carried on the search while I went back for Wednesday, but I'm sure the weight of our loss hangs heavy.

"I have!" Rodgers protests. "He's right here."

Smee turns to look over her shoulder. I know she'll find Pan obediently beside Rodger because that's what I ordered him to do. Be a wallflower. Cause no waves while I'm gone, or he wouldn't be welcome to stay once I brought Wednesday back. My brother's shadow was more amicable than I expected. The beast is relatively tame for a creature that held all of Peter's darkest desires.

I cross the plank, guiding us from what's left of our dock onto the deck. Wednesday is behind me, with Peter following her. I hold her hand while he steadies her waist. There's no chance she will fall into the water. I've worked too hard to let Triton claim her. Stars above only know what he'd do with a soul as pure as hers.

"There are two of them!" Smee shrieks. Her blatant observation draws the attention of everyone on the deck, which is more people than I'm used to seeing aboard the old girl. Majority of the pirates are below, resting in their quarters, but there are four faces I recognize up here waiting. Them, plus six of the crew, and Peter's Lost make for a crowd to witness our arrival.

"Have I not mentioned that Peter is a twin?" I offer light-heartedly. I need to speak to Wednesday, Peter, and Pan alone to see if they agree with my theory before I offer it to listening ears. God knows I don't need to instill false hope into anyone at this point.

I help Wednesday navigate the steps onto the deck. She offers me a brief smile before her gaze searches the crowd. She finds her treasure, happily tucked into her friend's arms, and runs to the Lost. I watch, feeling my own form of joy as she reunites with her child. The moment is bittersweet because I remember the days when my boys were young. Wendy loved them with every inch of her being. She glowed with pride every time they were around and wilted when we washed ashore without them.

I don't think Wendy realized that losing John and Michael broke me, too. She was too deep in her own grief to realize that I shut off my pain to protect her. We had a handful of survivors with no food, no shelter, and a pissed-off Peter who offered no help. I had to shoulder all the burden, and when I finally reached a point where I could open up and be the emotional support Wendy needed, she was gone.

I'd lost my wife.

I'd lost my kids.

My brother hated me and pulled away.

I couldn't even be mad at him because it was all my fault. If I hadn't taken us on the stupid voyage to try and find an uncharted island to bring Wendy's stories to life we would never have fallen into the whirlpool. My boys would have lived full lives and my wife would have grown to old age by my side.

But giving Wednesday the gift of finding what was lost and reuniting her with her child eases the guilt I feel for what I did to Wendy.

"This is going too far, Cap," Smee insists. "I won't allow it."

I drag my gaze from Wednesday's reunion to my first mate. Anger rolls off of her in waves, and she is trying my patience. I never corrected her for disrespecting me before the Darling and I left for Neverland, and that error is coming back to bite me in the ass. "Mind yourself, Smee."

"No!" she shouts and takes a challenging step toward me. "We trust you to do what's best for the crew. That's why you're our captain, but you've gone too far. The Lost have a target on their backs."

"Be careful with yehr words," I warn.

"There's not one Neverking, but two, and you've captured them both. I understand they are your brothers, but the girl and the child..." Smee pauses to glance at Wednesday.

I shake my head, wishing she'd shut her trap and listen to reason. By the laws of our code, mutiny is punishable by death. Despite being a fool, Smee thinks she's looking out for the crew. I won't hurt her for doing what she thinks is best, but I'll have to punish her. If not, my hold as captain will slip. "Think hard, old friend. You're about to do something that can't be undone."

"They are who Belle wants most," she continues, not having heard my warning. "Having them here is a death sentence for us all. They can't stay."

"Every person on this ship is now a member of our crew. As the captain, it's my right to allow them into our home, and as my first mate, it's your job to see they feel welcomed."

"She doesn't belong here!" Smee insists. Her shouting startles the baby, and she cries.

I can take the verbal lashing, and I can handle the beratement of Wednesday, but hearing the child cry does something to me. My anger seized control and I finally snap. "That's where yehr wrong! Wednesday has always belonged here! Her home is by my side, and I will always offer it to her. She is my wife in this life and the next. Beyond life and death. Those were my vows and I will stick by them until the day my soul rots and there is nothing left. Her child. Her friends. They all fall under that umbrella because they are an extension of her. Yeh don't have to like my decisions, Smee, but as yehr captain yeh have to accept them."

"I can't." Smee looks at me with tears in her eyes. It hurts because she is my friend, the closest person to me in this world as much as I want to, I can't comfort her.

"Then this can't be yehr home anymore."

"I've been by your side for years, James." Her voice cracks with emotion. Her heart breaks before my eyes, and still, I hold my ground. "You were supposed to choose me."

"It was never a choice. It is and will always be Wednesday. I'm sorry, I thought yeh knew."

"I'm going to grab my things."

"Smee..." I reach for her arms, regret sinking in. Maybe I was too harsh. Maybe if given time, she'd understand.

Smee twists out of my reach and shakes her head. "Don't. You've done enough."

She walks with her head held high to the stairs that lead below deck. I feel terrible, but there are more pressing matters at hand. We still have to deal with Belle. Once she's out of the picture and Neverland is safe, I'll find Smee again. Once a pirate, always a pirate. We'll get through this as we have done everything else.

Wednesday puts her hand on my arm. "I'm sorry, James."

"I'm not." I stroke the soft blonde hairs of her daughter's head. The little thing seems at peace in her mother's arms. It radiates warmth into the air. The girl is pure magic. Even an idiot can sense that she's special. Which means it won't take long for Belle to realize she's gone. "But now isn't the time to dwell on my loss. We need to talk." I look at my brother and his shadow come to life. "All of us."

"Agreed." Peter steps forward. "Lead the way, Captain."

CHAPTER 31

Wednesday

Mira is the most beautiful baby I've ever seen.

She's grown since I last saw her. Her legs are a little chunkier and her belly is a touch rounder but, essentially, she looks almost the same as the day I had her. Perfect.

I haven't put her down since boarding the Jolly Roger. I know people say that holding a baby too much makes them clingier and more dependent on their parents, but those people, whoever they are, never lost their child. They don't know the fear that comes with wondering if your baby is all right. They don't understand the constant worrying, and they can't imagine the relief when that nightmare comes to an end.

I will hold my daughter and I will love her every second of every day that she lets me because each minute we have together is a gift.

I rock her back in forth. James was ready for her before I even came back to the ship. I don't know how he did it, but he had a rocking chair, cradle, and a changing table crafted and moved into his room. In a span of hours, he rescued the injured, saved Peter and me, and still found time to prepare for a infant. This man blows my mind in the best of ways.

"Can I hold her?" Pan asks.

Fear wraps itself around my bones. The last time I let my baby girl go she was stolen from me. I want to tell him no and kick everyone out of the room, but this is Pan. My Shadow. My friend. I know with full confidence that he and everyone else in here would die before hurting me or Mira. I'm not alone anymore. I'm with my family again and the only way we're going to keep Mira safe is by trusting each other.

I stand and lay her in his arms. It's nerve-wracking to let her go, but watching the emotions play out on Pan's face is fascinating. Fear. Excitement. Then pure adoration.

"You're good at that," I say, and Pan beams up at me. I don't know if he existed in the years John and Michael were alive. By Neverland logic—which is that anything is possible—there is a chance that the memories of Peter holding and loving his nephews have been imprinted on Pan's soul because he is a natural. Mira hasn't woken since the handoff and she looks more than content in his arms.

"Can I address the elephant in the room?" Scarlett says. "How the hell are there two of you? And don't even try that twins-bullshit. I know Peter only has one brother. Your crew might be fine accepting that you've kept secrets from them, but Peter told us everything."

"I have a theory." James walks to the liquor cabinet and pours himself a glass of scotch. He takes his time, letting the flavors roll on his tongue before swallowing. "But I want to hear how it happened."

"There have always been two of us." Pan hands Mira back to me. She's warm and smells like morning dew and sea spray. I set her in the cradle, torn between looking at her forever and joining the conversation. The choice is made for me when Pan says, "But you all have only ever acknowledged him."

"So, you're Peter's Shadow?" Aria pokes his arm.

I glare at her and come to his side. I understand that he is a lot to take in, and I have had time to see Pan in person before today, but there is a way to handle the distrust and curiosity while remaining tactful.

"Yes."

"Then how are you here?" Xyris asks, and that is one question I am curious about, too.

I understand that Peter and Pan are two separate people. I know they share one space when they are on Earth. Pan was a voice in Peter's mind, but Peter was the one in control of his body... Until Pan became the dominant personality and Peter went to the back burner, but I thought things would go back to normal when they returned to Neverland.

"The better question," Pan turns to Peter, "is how are you here? This is your body. How did you get one of your own?"

"I don't know. When I came back to Neverland, I wasn't a shadow like you. I couldn't talk to anyone or control the Island. I had lesser magic, but it was only helpful in protecting Mira." He glances at the crib and it dawns on me that I couldn't hear him anymore because he left me to take care of her. "Wherever she went, I went. I was there when Cass died. I saw you," He looks to Xyris. "And the girls take the baby. I knew she would be safe with you, so I went looking for Wednesday, and the next thing I knew, I was me again. Flesh and bone."

"That's how it went on my end, too," I add. "Emmit knew Pan was in Peter's body. He said Peter died, and I... well, I lost my shit. I was crying when I thought I heard his voice. I wanted so badly for him to be real and to be with me, and then *poof* he was."

"If there were any doubts that you are Neverland's new queen, they should be gone," James says proudly. All eyes turn to him as he sips his crystal glass filled with brown liquor.

"Come again?" Aria asks.

"Cass was an ice wielder, Emmit is a healer, Belle, before she became corrupt by blood magic, was sky bound and could control the sky. All of the royal Fae had powers that tied them to the Island. Peter, being human-born, couldn't wield the Neverland magic, so his soul was split and Pan became a shadow self. Each legacy of the Neverking is given a gift, and you, Sunshine, by being Mira's mother, were given one, too. The gift of life."

Pan crosses his arms and shares a glance with Peter. "Go on."

"Only one person has ever existed in Neverland with a beating heart." James holds his glass and points to me. "The same person who insisted the Island wasn't Belle's and made it rain so as not to let it die. A beautiful, powerful woman who willed Peter back to life."

"I wasn't dead," he chides.

"But you weren't alive either. You were caught in between, like all of us. Only your prison lacked shape and forced you into isolation. Do you disagree?" James prods.

"No," Peter mumbles.

"Point proven. Wednesday wanted you to be with her and so you were." James saunters over to Mira's cradle. "But most importantly, let's not forget about the child. The true heir to Neverland, a soul born of both worlds that should never have existed because the Fae can't breed with humans and yet, here she is." James tosses back the last of his drink and sets the tumbler down. "Neverland chose you, Wednesday. Not Wendy. Not any other soul. You."

James's statement is a lot to process, and I've heard half the speech before. He comes before me, drops down to one knee, and takes my hand. "The Island knew it needed a savior. It couldn't have picked a better one."

"I cannot be the savior." I cross my arms and hug myself. "I can't fight or fly or do anything useful. I am just a mother who wanted her child back. Saviors are special, and I'm just...me."

Peter steps in front of me as James rises to his feet. "You don't honestly think that? Do you, Darling?"

I shrug.

He pulls me into a hug, one I needed but damn sure wasn't about to ask for. Today has been too much. Cass died. I was a prisoner. Peter went from not quite dead to very alive, and now this. A declaration that I'm destined to save us all.

I can't.

I don't know how.

"Even on your darkest days, when you feel worthless, never forget that you are everything." Peter cups my cheeks and wipes away my tears with his thumb. "I crossed through time and space for you. As did Pan and James. Do you think we'd do that for just anyone?"

"And we felt it the moment Peter brought you to Neverland," Scarlett adds.

"There was a ripple in the air, a legit wave across the water the other night. We just didn't know what it was," Xyris says. "But it was you. You changed everything, and I think that's why Belle has gone a little crazy."

"She's always been crazy." Aria snickers. "But she's definitely amped it up a few levels since we last saw you."

Someone twists the handle of James's double doors. When they don't open, he pounds against the stained glass over and over until James nods to Xyris to open them. The two seconds of tension that fills the room is thick. The boys' stances change, readying themselves to fight, while the girls step closer to the wall, out of the way.

Pan puts himself between Mira and whoever is outside while Peter protectively stands in front of me.

Emmit rushes in, panting, covered in sweat. There's a general breath of air released as the tension falls away, until he says, "We don't have a lot of time. She's coming."

Peter

"Stay with the baby," I tell Pan. This may be James's ship, and he may be used to giving the orders, but this is my fight and my family on the line.

"Why?"

"Because Belle doesn't know there are two of us and your hand-to-hand combat skills are probably shit considering you haven't had hands long."

If something were to happen to me, Mira would need a guardian, Wednesday will need a partner to help her, and I need to guarantee that at least one of us survives.

"I'm not leaving her," Darling insists. She grips the edge of Mira's cradle so tightly that her knuckles turn white. I nod, understanding her choice, and don't hold it against her. She was robbed of her child once and fought tooth and nail to have her again. She shouldn't be on the battle front, anyway. Wars aren't fought by kings and queens. Wednesday is our queen. She shouldn't have to risk her life for a world that's only just become hers. That's our job.

"All the more reason one of you should stay." James hands me a sword. A thin piece of metal with a black handle. The smallest in the bunch he carries, but just as deadly as the rest because it's made from iron, not steel. As are the daggers he's strapped to his chest. "I don't care who stays, but I can't protect the girls and the ship. I need help on all fronts."

"I won't let anything hurt them." Pan takes a sword, but it's clear he's never held one.

I adjust his grip and then look around, making sure everyone is armed. We are an army of six going to war with a woman who singularly has the power of ten, if not more. The odds are against us in every way. If I were a believer in the gods, I'd pray, but they abandoned Neverland long ago. I can't see them helping us now.

"It's been three days since Belle last fed." James tucks two more daggers into the holster on his chest and slips another into his boot. "Her dust will be weak, lasting minutes if not seconds, and every burst she throws will weaken her."

"How do you know?" Scarlett asks. She looks uncomfortable holding her weapon. I scan the room and find two other swords in a barrel behind James's chart table. These are smaller, almost half the size, but they'll be lighter. I offer a trade, her heavy sword for these. Scar hesitates but then wordlessly switches.

"Because I was the last soul she fed on," James admits. His brows furrow as he tries to hide his shame. His gaze finds mine for the first time since entering this room. To everyone else, he looks angry, but I know my brother. He's hurting both inside and out, and I wonder why I never saw it before. He didn't have to sacrifice himself. He could have sent one of his pirates to bleed for his former queen. It crosses my mind that I may have misunderstood his place among the pirates.

"The marks," Wednesday gasps. "Are those from her?"

"Poison." He nods.

Emmit touches James's markings and wrinkles his nose. "This isn't poison. I could take some of it if it were. This is magic. I think she bonded with you."

"What does that mean?" I ask.

There are only two types of bonds the Fae can create. An imprint, where they siphon energy and life from their bonded, and the mating bond. Both options require the bonded to sacrifice, but only one might work in our favor.

"I'm not sure." Emmit casts a glance at me, and I read the silent message. *We need to talk.*

"Everybody ready?" I ask. There's a murmur of yeses and nods, but in truth, none of us are prepared. For the first time since coming to Neverland, the Lost face death. Be it now by a sword or later by the hands of a tyrannical queen, if we don't fight it's imminent.

Wednesday hugs each one of us as we leave the room, offering "Be safe" and "I'd better see you after this" to us all. Her words are kind, but don't pierce the emotional armor our family has put up.

James is next. He takes Wednesday's chin between his fingers and pulls her in to kiss her goodbye. Pan looks away, but I can't. It's obvious that she cares for him, maybe even loves him. I can't help but wonder if the feelings are solely hers or if they are mixed with Wendy's emotions. I guess it doesn't matter. The original Darling loved us both. This one can too.

"The light in my darkness," James says against her lips. "Thank you."

Wednesday nods and wipes a tear from her cheek. James doesn't linger. He turns and heads out onto the deck to give a pep talk to his crew. He leaves the door open, wordlessly reminding me to join him. As if I could forget.

"This isn't fair," Wednesday says. She sniffles and tries to fight a new wave of tears. "I just got you. Both of you."

"And you will always have us," I insist. I can only imagine how difficult this must be for her. Walking away, even knowing that she and Mira will be safe and that Pan is the final leg of defense should anything happen to us out there, is still one of the hardest things I will ever do. But I am doing it for her.

"All of us. One of us. Whatever you choose, we're here for you," my other half adds.

Even without the bond connecting us, Pan knows where I stand. It's clear Wednesday's heart is full and only a bastard would force her to choose. It's not ideal. I want her to myself, but with Pan living and breathing, that's not possible. My brother is just another layer to bring into the mix I'll have to adjust to as well. "Agreed."

"I should have told you about me and James," Wednesday says, ashamed. "There just hasn't been time and I honestly wasn't sure how."

I pull her close and try not to dwell on the fact that this could be the last time I hold my Darling. I wish we could have had the reunion we deserve, but the stars didn't favor us in that respect. Still, if this is all I get, I am grateful. "Hey. It's okay. We aren't making you choose. I just figured that whatever happens out there, you should know I love you. I can't remember if I've said that yet."

"I love you, too, Peter." She holds me tight, then reaches a hand out for my shadow. "And I love you, Pan."

"I know, Darling," he says resoundingly, then looks at me. "I'll guard them with my life."

Ah, my cue to go. Seems my shadow can still read me despite us losing our bond to communicate. "I know you will."

I shut the door and listen for the clink of the lock behind me. *She will be safe*, I remind myself. *They all will be.*

James's ship is sprinkled with soldiers. He's arranged the crew and the Lost in a fanned-out triangle, as if he were at war again, with him at the point near the bridge. Emmit stands on the port side, waiting for Belle to arrive.

He doesn't wave or motion for me to join him, but I know that's where I need to go next. "Tell me about the bond," I whisper.

"I have a theory," he says, "but you're not going to like it."

I force a laugh because that is the undertone of my life. Nothing has worked out the way I hoped, and I've had to adapt. My father never regarded me as someone worth his time. The love of my life married and fell for my brother. My nephews—one of whom I would have bet my life on as being mine—were ripped from this world while I was forced to live forever in a realm constantly being invaded by a crazy, magic-hungry fairy. Me not liking something isn't new. "I don't like anything when it comes to your sister."

"If Belle dies, James might, too."

My smile falls and my heart sinks to the bottom of the ocean. James may be a lot of things, half of which I don't like, but he is the only true family I have left. It's taken years for us to find our way back together. I'm not ready to say goodbye. "Could you bring him back?"

"From death?" Emmit rubs his chin and mulls over his words. "No, but depending on how *she* dies...maybe. The swords are iron cast. If we stab her in the right place, it could kill her without taking James's life too. It'll hurt like a bitch, but I can delay his death and take the pain away, and after a few days heal him to where it never happened."

"Got it. Avoid the heart," I say as Belle emerges through the smoke with ten mindless soldiers, all dressed for battle and one painfully familiar pirate. "James isn't going to take Smee's betrayal well."

"I figured. Thought it best he sees her true nature for himself. No one wants to hear that someone they love stabbed them in the back."

I know the feeling. I loved Cass like a brother and he betrayed me. He tried to take the only thing I've ever wanted and end her life. That kind of backstabbing never heals, but the ache eventually shifts to a dull throb. Especially now that he's dead. "I'm sorry about Cass."

"Don't be." Emmit stares at the treeline and watches his sister approach. She follows behind her line of soldiers, walking in a gilded dress, shining like the sun herself and just as deadly. "The scales will always be balanced, one way or another. I warned him his plan was shit. He didn't listen when I tried to talk him out of it."

"You knew he wanted to kill Wednesday?" Anger burns my throat. I swallow the heat, but only because today isn't a day to make new enemies. I need him by my side. Even if he, too, can't be fully trusted anymore. "Why didn't you say something?"

"Because I would not pick one brother over another." He looks at me and claps his hand on my shoulder. "You, Pan, and I are born from the same magic. Wednesday is, too, and her child is the purest of us all. My weight in the battle for Neverland was even; I couldn't pick sides, but now it's swayed. Belle threatens to destroy my home and what's left of my family. I can't sit by and let it happen."

I grunt, wanting to hold onto that anger, but let it go. I understand. He and I may be brothers, but Cass was blood. He couldn't betray him, and I guess I should be grateful that he didn't help. Although, now that I think about it, Emmit never offered to help heal Wednesday when she was sick either. This explains why. "I appreciate you siding with us, but you're still a mother fucker for letting things get this far."

Emmit chuckles and shoots me a knowing look. "Wednesday's destiny was written before you even existed. I did nothing but let fate guide her path."

"So, you're saying this fight is all a part of Neverland's plan?"

"I feel like it is, which is why I'm not worried. Today will go how it's meant to." He winks and draws his sword. It's nearly time.

I ready my stance and do the same. I wish I had Emmit's confidence. Fear, something I rarely felt before bringing the Darling into my life, tethers itself to me. I glance back at James's quarters and Wednesday peeks through the curtains. I wish she would stay out of sight, but I don't fault her. I'm sure she's just as nervous as we are.

Belle's soldiers run up the plank and spill onto the ship. They fan out, protecting their queen as she boards the Jolly Roger.

Our numbers are close, but most of James's crew is readied to fight below deck, tasked with protecting the injured.

I take a deep breath and walk to stand beside my brother. This is it. The moment we live and claim Neverland for ourselves, or we die.

CHAPTER 33

Wednesday

I run to the window as soon as Peter shuts the door. Pan locks it behind him, as if the tiny metal latch is enough to stop the crazy Fae princess. It's not. If she wants in this room, she'll get in. That I have no doubt.

I pull the curtain aside and peek out. My friends and James's family stand on the deck. Ready. Waiting.

My heart races with anticipation, but I can only imagine how nervous they are. We have an idea of what Belle brings to the table, though I'm sure she has at least one surprise up her sleeve... unless she feels this battle is a waste of time and that it will end quickly.

I hope not. I know I said I would protect my daughter, but I don't know if I can stand here and watch everyone I care about die. If they fall, I'm going out there. James thinks I'm the savior, so that's what I'll do. Save them if they need me.

I hope they don't need me.

"You should get back." Pan reaches for my arm. His touch is gentle yet commanding. "We don't want Belle to see you."

"If Mira is as magical as everyone thinks she is, Belle won't need to see my face to know where we are." She'll be drawn to her. All the more reason to stay put. Just in case, but I'm torn. Half of my heart is in here, safe. While the other half is out there ready to die for me.

Peter walks to the center of the deck and stands beside James, who is dressed to kill. Literally. He has a sword in each hand and a dozen daggers strapped to his body. Peter twists his wrist, showcasing that his singular weapon is just as deadly.

"Well, well, well." Belle's gaze skirts across the deck. I watch her attention bounce from each one of our men to the next, probably counting us and weighing her odds, before focusing on James. Fire flares in her eyes, but her words are as sweet as honey, thick with condescending undertones and meant to cut. "How predictably disappointing. I worried your ties to Peter would come between us one day."

"There was never an us!" James growls.

I wish I could see his face, to read if he truly means the words. I've put the pieces together. I know he and Belle have been intimate, and while I shouldn't be jealous, I am. I don't like knowing her hands have touched his body, and I hate that her teeth have ravaged his skin. She's a parasite. One I pray he never had feelings for.

"Awe." She covers her heart with her hands. "You wound me. Here I thought we had something special."

James chuffs and challenges her. He raises his arm and points a sword at her face. One of her soldiers hunches down low, preparing to launch himself at James if given the word. My captain pays him no mind as he addresses the Fae. "You used me, just like you used all the souls in Neverland, but not anymore."

"Leave, Belle. You aren't welcome here," Emmit adds. Belle's gaze slices to her brother. She scowls, realizing his deceit, but holds her tongue.

"On this boat or our Island," Peter adds, driving their statement home.

That seems to tip her over the edge, the three of them united. She stomps her foot and yells, "I am Neverland's Queen! How dare you disrespect me!"

"Not anymore, you aren't." James's words are cold and cruel. He leaves no room for argument in the statement. I half expect him to fling a dagger at her heart and end the battle before it begins, but beneath his rough exterior, James is kind. If he can avoid bloodshed, he will. "Go, Belle, while you still can."

"You won't kill me, James. You can't," she says with a snicker.

In one swift movement, he hands a sword to Peter and grabs a dagger from the holster on his chest. It flies through the air and sinks itself into Belle's shoulder. She pulls it out, and blood drips off the golden petals that make up her dress. "You're a fool, James Panning!

I can't see James's face, but I'm sure he's got a wicked grin as he says. "That was a warning. My next dagger will be at your heart."

"Guards!" Belle screeches. "Kill them all, but leave the captain and the baby for me." A murderous look glints across her face as she searches the ship. She finds me a second later and smirks. I step back from the window and grab my sword.

"What happened?" Pan asks. He pushes the curtain aside with one finger and peeks out. I don't need to look to know what he sees. Our friends, the Lost and the Pirates, engaged in a battle.

"She's coming," I warn him.

"No." He shakes his head. "She's not. She's just standing there. Watching."

I make my way back to the window, this time with my sword in hand. Not that I know how to use it, but I can swing a baseball bat. If need be, I can severely hurt someone. Once. Because I doubt I'll get my sword back once it's in someone.

Not like the Panning brothers. Stars above, they are merciless. They swing and strike and stab every soldier that comes at them, but Belle's souls are monsters. Peter's sword cuts the head off of a red-haired woman, but she doesn't fall. She swings blindly, attacking without yielding. Aria tries to push away a set of legs bent on kicking and stomping her to death. Scarlett runs from an arm that is creepily *Thing* like. Everyone either fights a body or part of one, if not more. The scene is maddening, but not messy. The souls don't bleed like the Lost and Pirates do.

One of the souls lunges for James. He jumps back, avoiding being stabbed by a one-armed zombie, and finds the edge of another monster's sword. The metal slashes his arm, and Belle screams. Bright red blood drips from his shoulder down to his wrist. The gash is two inches long and I don't know how deep, and Belle has one in the exact same place.

"I said leave that one alone!" she shouts.

There's a change in the air and a cold chill that slithers to all corners of the ship. Time slows to almost half speed. I see it, the moment Peter puts the dots together. It's seconds after me.

"What are you doing?" Pan asks as I reach for the locks on the door.

"Let me out," I say, unable to twist and pull and make my fingers work. I need to get out there. I need to save him and stop Peter before it's too late. "Let me out!"

Pan flips the lock and I yank the door open, then step out into the madness. There may not be blood, but the smell coming off of Belle's soldiers is nauseating. I hold my breath and look for Peter. He's here, somewhere. I can feel him. I just... Can't... there!

I run into the center of the madness. I don't have a sword or any way to protect myself if one of the monsters were to notice me but adrenaline has me dogging blades and weaving between fights as I span the length of the deck.

I'm almost to him.

James shoves one of Belle's soldiers, a creature with no head and one arm away. He sees me running to him and stops fighting. "Sunshine?"

"James!" I shout, but I'm too late.

CHAPTER 34

Wednesday

Peter comes out of nowhere, his body as stealthy as the Shadow, Pan, used to be and as swift as Cass. He takes his sword and shoves it through James's stomach, then rips it out. "I'm sorry."

"No!" I scream as my captain, my unexpected savior, a man I never expected to love, falls to his knees and blood pours out of his mouth. I catch him and ease him to the ground.

One by one, Belle's army falls around us. There isn't a single soul of hers intact. Carved and cut torsos cease fighting while limbs go limp. Metal clanks against the teak as her soldiers finally die.

I don't feel relief that the battle is over because all I can think about is James. I stroke his face and hold him to my chest. He coughs, spitting blood as he gasps for air and the sound of his struggling breaths rip me to pieces.

"It's okay," I tell him. "Everything will be okay."

"You stole everyone I've ever loved. I hate you," Peter says from across the ship. He stares at Belle, who's in just as bad of shape as James. She holds her stomach, trying to close the wound, but crimson leaks out of her. She's bleeding too much to survive, which means...

"Emmit!" I cry as Peter's blade rises into the air. I look away, searching for our friend. He steps forward after a *thump* rolls behind me. "Can you help him?" I ask, refusing to look at Belle.

Emmit takes in James's condition. He has a long gash on one shoulder, deep enough to see bone. The stab wound on his stomach is open and leaking, and a new line of red gathers around James's neck.

Emmit shakes his head, worry wrinkling his face. "I can't take all this on. Not without risking my life."

"You have to try," I beg, my voice cracking. That line, the little one that matches Belle's injury darkens. Whatever happens to one, happens to the other. Peter knew and still he killed her. He knew she was hurt and that we could have found another way, and still, he took her life. If James dies because of his selfish impulsiveness, I'll never forgive him.

"My magic will only drag out the inevitable." Emmit shoots Peter a wicked glare but places his hand on James. "But I can ease his pain so you can say goodbye."

Smee runs across the dock bridge and drops to her knees beside us. She didn't fight her old crew. She led Belle and her soldiers to us but didn't raise a sword against her family. Her morals are fucked, following a twisted line, but she never broke the code James laid out for her. "I'm sorry," she cries, falling apart beside him. "You weren't supposed to get hurt."

"It's okay, Smee. I forgive you." James coughs and more blood pools out of the corner of his mouth. It's a deep, dark purple, pulled from the furthest points of his body. His skin loses its sun-kissed hue as a cold sweat blankets him.

I wipe the blood from his cheek with my shirt sleeve, refusing to accept what is coming. "No! This isn't okay. You're not allowed to die!"

James doesn't have much time left. I can feel it, just as purely as I can feel my bond with Mira. He looks at Peter and croaks, "Take care of her."

"We will," Pan says in unison with Peter. He looks down at us, a frown pulling at his lips, showing so much more than Peter, who seems to have shut us all off.

James's breaths slow. I cradle him to my chest, not caring about the blood ruining my clothes as my tears that flow freely. He's worthy of each one shed. This man was nothing but kind to me. He offered me friendship when I ventured into his cove, unaware of who he was and what our meeting meant. He journeyed across the universe to find me and bring me back to Neverland. He stuck by my side, his belief in me never faltering, even when I didn't believe in myself.

He's a good man that I will mourn and love and, dammit, he doesn't deserve to die!

"You can't die. I won't let you. Please," I beg as another second passes between each inhale. One turns into two and then three until there are too many seconds to count.

I wipe my eyes with the back of my arm, the only part of me not covered in James's blood, and look up at Emmit. "Tell me how this works."

"How what works?"

"My gift. James thinks I can bring things to life. How do I do it? How does this magic work?"

Emmit stops touching James and rubs the back of his neck. He's quiet for a beat and then sighs. "It's different for everyone. I have to touch people to heal them. Belle's moods affected the weather. And Cass...his magic came on demand."

"Well, I'm an emotional mess, touching James, and I demand he comes back to me." I fall over him again. This pain hurts so much more than losing Cass. Perhaps it's because we shared a bond, or maybe it's related to our vows. In this life and the next. Next not being an option if you die in Neverland, but the dam he built inside me that filled the holes Peter and Pan left has been ripped open.

"Darling," Peter coos. He reaches for my shoulder to try and comfort me, but I shift out of his touch. I don't want to hate him, but this is his fault. He took someone I care about away.

"No!" I can't listen to him say James is gone. I won't. I'm the savior. My gift is life. There has to be a way to bring him back. "He can't die," I insist. "Not yet. Not until I'm old and ugly, and even then, he has to outlive me! Come back. Please."

"Yeh'll never be old or ugly," James rasps. "But you are a little heavy."

I sit upright and lift my arms off his body. I watch, awestruck, as James shifts from lying in my lap to sitting on his knees. The dark mark around his neck has fades into a light purple and the hole in his shoulder is closed. James coughs and something makes a squeaking sound. He lifts his shirt to look at where Peter stabbed him. The wound is an ugly, bloody mess, but it's not leaking. It's just red, and raw, and angry. "A little help with that would be great, mate."

Emmit steps between Peter and Smee. He places his hands over the hole in James's stomach. Blood stains Emmit's shirt red as James's skin heals. He doesn't fully close the wound because it would transfer to him. Instead, Emmit takes enough so that James's insides aren't at risk of falling out. They both need stitches and possibly a shot of scotch to take the edge off, but they're alive.

"How is this possible?" Aria asks.

Pan extends a hand to help James to his feet. He wobbles but finds his footing a moment later. "Wednesday has the gift of life. She can create it." James glances at the cabin where Mira sleeps. "And return it." He looks at Peter briefly, not an ounce of resentment in his eyes, before finding me again.

"I told yeh, Neverland will give yeh anything yeh want. All you had to do was ask, Sunshine." He touches my cheek and I lean into his hand.

I enjoy the warmth of his touch, but only let myself linger in it for a heartbeat. I look at our crew and the lifeless souls on the deck. Our people have survived with some cuts and bruises, but overall, they seem okay. The same can't be said for Belle's soldiers. "Can I save them?"

Emmit presses his lips into a tight line and shakes his head. "You could try, but their souls left their bodies a long time ago. Might be best to let them rest."

"What now?" Smee asks. She hugs herself, out of place as she's the only one of us besides Pan not covered in blood.

"Yeh betrayed me," James says, his voice cold and emotionless.

"I know, and I'm sorry." Smee hangs her head low. I can feel the shame rolling off of her as well as the resentment being shot at her from the crew. It seems as if Neverland hasn't just given me the gift of life, but also made me an empath. The Lost's emotions are waves of color. Blue for sorrow. Purple for resentment. Whereas Smee's are black with fear, orange with desperation, and a smidge of white. Hope.

"Sorry is not enough, Smee. Yeh need to earn my trust back."

"How? I'll do anything," she begs and that orange aura around her burns brighter.

James grunts, but I can see this is all an act. He does not hate Smee or even resent her for her actions. He feels sorrow but he's also hopeful. "For starters, you can help clean the mess you made. Each body deserves a burial."

"I'll help," Xyris says, stepping forward. "I dug graves before I died. Been a long time since I've worked a shovel, but I'm happy to lend a hand."

"I will, too, but I'd like to handle the burning of Belle. Her soul will be tortured if it's not burned to ashes... and I'd like to reclaim my father's old castle." Emmit looks at me. "If that's okay with you."

Belle could use a heavy dose of torment considering all the suffering she's caused, but I agree. Who am I to dictate what Emmit does with the remains of his last family member? So long as she can't come back to life or haunt me, I don't care what he does with her. Or the castle.

"That home belongs to your family. I don't want it.

Although, I'd love to peruse the library if you're willing to teach me your language. I'm a sucker for a good book."

"My home is yours, your majesty. You are welcome any time." He bows.

"Don't say that. It's creepy." I'm about to add that he should not bow either when Mira cries from within James's quarters. Like a true princess, she's avoided all the drama and decided it was time for everyone to focus on her. Warmth blooms in my chest at the thought of finally settling down and enjoying these moments with her.

"I'll fetch her," Peter says, a step ahead of Pan as they both race back to the captain's quarters. "She's probably hungry."

James chuckles and watches his brothers leave with a far-off look. "He was always good with the kids."

I nod because Peter is good with Mira. He and Pan both are.

I walk to the side of the ship and lean against the taffrail facing the ocean. I can't look at Neverland, not when she's given me an impossible decision to make. Do I go home to the family I left behind, or do I stay here with the family I chose?

"We can set sail at sunrise...if that's what yeh want," James says, coming up beside me. "I'll need help with steering the ship through the mouth of hell again, but I promise I'll get yeh back to yehr sister."

"No," I say resoundingly. "This is my home now. I worked so hard to be here again, I'm not ready to leave yet."

"Then what seems to be the problem?"

I stare at my hands because looking at him is too difficult. I don't know how I'm going to give any of them up. I don't know if what I'm feeling is love, but the thought of having to let go of him, or Peter, or Pan kills me. "I don't want to say goodbye."

"Why would you say goodbye?" Peter asks, holding Mira in his arms. He's fashioned a makeshift bottle out of a teapot and while it looks absurd, Mira is drinking from it. He whistles once, catching Pan's attention, who comes over to join the conversation.

I turn and lean against the railing to face my boys. The asshole who took my heart without asking. The dark knight who's had my back from day one. And the savior who brought me to life again. How can I let one go and not the others? How can I choose which of them deserves my heart the most? I can't. But I can't string them along either. "It's not right for me to be with all of you."

"Why not?" Pan asks. "I'd rather have some of your time than none of it."

"Same," Peter adds. "I told you before, I won't make you choose and I stand by my word."

"Wendy married me and, eventually, loved me, but she was never truly satisfied. Her heart beat for me but bled for Peter," James says. "I won't be the cause of yehr pain. Love one of us or all of us. The choice is yehrs."

"You don't mean those things," I say, because they can't. They don't know what they're signing up for. Hell, I don't know what they're signing up for. I've never had someone love me enough to put their needs aside and think of me first. I've always been the second choice or an afterthought. And now I have three men willing to do whatever it takes to be with me. "This is crazy."

"No." Pan takes my face in his hand. "This is love. We love you enough to share you with not just each other but with Neverland." He kisses my forehead and then looks down at me. "Besides, who better to teach you how to rule Neverland than me? I am her shadow."

"Was her shadow," Peter interjects. "And what about me? I built every tree house. Are you going to show her how our plumbing system works?"

"Hey now! Who rescued souls and created the cove?" James says.

"Rescued?" Peter guffaws. He glances at Pan, having a conversation only they hear, before turning his back to James.

The boys walk toward the dock together, bickering the way

siblings do—about nothing and everything all at once—and my heart is full.

The End.

THE NEVERLAND NOVELS

BONUS CHAPTER

It's been weeks since Bell's tirade against Neverland and I don't think I'll ever get used to seeing the damage she inflicted on our island. Nearly every inch of our land was burnt to the ground, hundreds if not thousands of animals—some I recognized, some whose carcasses were so twisted and mangled I couldn't even tell what they were, and others who had just come out of their magic-induced slumber—dead. It was a horrifying sight, and that doesn't take into account all of James's friends, his makeshift family, whose lives were lost.

So much death.

For nothing.

But even in the darkest of days, there's always a ray of sunshine. That moment when you can finally breathe,when it feels like everything you've been through might be passed, and life is ready to go back to normal. We aren't there yet. So much of our land needs to be rebuilt, but that's what Neverland made me for.

It's a rejuvenating bit of sunshine.

I press my palm to the charred bark of another maple tree. Mira's magic hums in my veins. It's a tingle, a prickly sensation that skirts down my spine, but it's not uncomfortable. It's warm and exciting and made from love, fueled by the Island's love for itself and our love for each other.

But Neverland's magic is just as punishing as it is giving. Every time I use it, it drains a little more of me. Some days, I can bring twenty trees to life before feeling the effects. Other days, I can't even manage to revive ten. I don't know why or what makes each day different. I just know that there are times when I feel like I am a breath away from death, and then there are times when I simply feel tired and need a nap.

Today is an in-between kind of day. The number I'm settling on is seven. If I had set out sooner and rested midday, I probably could have revived double. But just as the land needs healing, the cove needs rebuilding and that doesn't require any magic.

James's people lost everything. Their houses are ash in the sand. Their affects nothing but whispers in the dark. Friends have perished and loved ones were buried. Emmit healed as many as he could, more than I thought possible, but we had no place for them to go. James' ship was overcrowded and emotions were high.

We started with one building, something big enough that people could spread out but also be under one roof. When that was done, we began working on the treehouses. With the exception of my family, no one is allowed to move out of the common house until we have a home for every soul. Mira made some of the pirates anxious and everyone agreed it would be best to keep her out of the cove until things went back to normal. As for everyone else, how do you choose this person over that one? There was no fair option to offer private housing until they are all complete.

And so my mornings are spent with Pan rebuilding our city and my afternoons are with Peter, healing the land.

I look to the few new bursts of green within a never-ending sea of grey. Guilt gnaws at my insides for how little I've accomplished. I could push myself to heal more of Neverland, we've only just begun to touch the trees outside of the cove, not even an eighth of this island, but today is Friday, the one day a week I cross through the realms to see my sister.

James worries that if I overextend myself before a voyage, the magic needed to cross between worlds will be too taxing. He fears the whirlpool we portal through will claim my soul and send me to the afterlife. He could be right. We don't know how far my magic reaches or what lengths it will go to keep me alive. I'd like to think Neverland won't let me die until I've healed her, but over-exerting myself to test the theory isn't a risk I'm willing to take. So, on Fridays, I don't push myself as hard as I do the rest of the week.

"Is this the last one for today?" Peter asks, taking in the little details I'm not sure the others would notice. The extra fraction of a second I take to keep my eyes closed when I blink, the way my pace has slowed, the sweat pooling at my brows. I'm fine, but I know he sees the toll that today has taken.

I ignore the question and try to bring my focus back to the maple tree I'm working on, but my thoughts stray to Peter and his worrying stare. He comes into the forest with me every day, no matter how much I insist I don't need his help or guidance. I haven't started healing parts of the Island I haven't already seen. I haven't stumbled across anything so horrifying that it's given me nightmares. And even if I had, there's not much he could do. Neverland stripped both him and Pan of their magic when Mira was born. I hold it all, despite wishing I could share my gift with them. I see the longing in their eyes and the guilt they both bear for wishing they had magic again.

I let out a heavy breath, feeling a bit of my life transfer into the tree and watching as the bark builds new layers upon itself. It shifts from a bare stick, charred and black with scars from Bell's assault, to a lively shade of brown with blooms of bright green. The exchange of energy takes less than a minute, but when it's done my head is woozy. I brace myself against the newly brought-to-life tree until the world steadies itself again.

This happens with every revival; we know to expect this response, and Peter still worries. He sets a hand on my lower back, just in case my legs give out and I need him to catch me. That only happened once. The first day, I tried healing a palm tree, but he's always ready should I need him.

"You're pushing yourself too hard," he warns. The pressure of his palm shifts from a steady presence to a soothing rub as I find my legs again. "Slow down, Darling, there's no rush. We have all of eternity to bring Neverland back to life."

"I'm fine," I insist because I am. From the start of his warning to now I feel better. The magic may take from me, but Neverland knows I'm trying to help, and so it, in turn, heals me as well. Something it didn't willfully do for Peter when he needed help. More guilt.

Peter looks up at the sky, noting how the orange hues bleed into the bright blue canvas. It won't be long before twilight and we still have to reach the mirror pool before the final ray of light dips behind the horizon. "We should head back."

I nod, agreeing reluctantly. I want to stay and keep working. No one else can do this, not even Emmit. His gift only works for beings with beating hearts. All of these plants are still alive. Their roots run deep beneath the Island's surface, grasping at any shred of life they can, but because they don't have blood flowing within them Emmit's powers are useless. The Island is solely dependent on me, but I need to eat. Take a shower. And hopefully, have a little fun before our voyage.

After all, it is Friday.

I haven't seen James since he sailed into the sunrise on Monday. He's been forging new deals with the God of the Underworld and working with Emmit to bridge the broken bond between those of us left in Neverland and the Gods of Old. Emmit has cautioned that someday soon, I'll be expected to meet with them too, and when the time comes, I will. But until then, I will happily stay rooted between this world and mine.

Peter and I are out of the woods within minutes of deciding to leave and walking up the ramp to our new treehouse. Ours. Not just mine.

The first treehouse we built is the largest on the Island, having five rooms, a kitchen, a living room, and two bathrooms. The plan is to build two smaller ones on either side of me once the cove is redone. One for Peter. The other for Pan. Just in case things get weird or one of us needs some distance, I want them to have somewhere that's their own.

Although if someone had told me a few weeks ago that I would want this big house all to myself, I would have called them crazy. I fought with Peter and James for days about who would be sleeping where. They both insisted that I needed my own space and were willing to stay on the Jolly Roger or in the common house until all the treehouses were finished, but I wanted them close.

It didn't take much convincing. Pan hated the idea of not sleeping by my side and truthfully, I think the other two only pushed because they worried something might happen if I were alone at night. After three days of a pathetic attempt at arguing, they conceded. We designed my tree house so that each of my boys could have their own room while making mine big enough to hold us all should we choose. We also decided to skip the rope ladder entry. The concept was great for keeping critters from making their way into the living quarters, but most of the Island's creatures are dead or in hiding these days.

And it's damn near impossible to maneuver up one of those things while carrying an infant.

Plus, the way the ladders were orchestrated left a hole in the floor. We probably could have put a hatch of some sort and kept the original treehouse design, but I didn't want to risk someone accidentally locking me out or, worse, forgetting to close the door. It would be my luck once Mira starts walking that she would fall through a hole and break something. The last thing we need is a hospital trip in the human world and to have CPS called. So, we decided that a ramp with chest-high and knee-high railings on both sides was a better option. Are the double railings overkill? Probably, but better safe than sorry.

Peter opens the front door for me and the smell of freshly

baked bread wafts through the air. My stomach rumbles as Pan greets me with a slice of avocado toast and cloudberry lemonade. I smile brightly, both excited to be home and greeted with food. I eagerly take the offering and moan when I take my first bite. It's heaven in my mouth, and I am starving.

"You're back early," Pan grins, watching me sink my teeth into the afternoon snack. "And famished."

"I'm going to take a shower," Peter strolls past us and smirks, those blue eyes lingering on my mouth a little too long before he shifts his attention away.

I can tell he doesn't want to leave, but he's respecting that we've spent the last three hours together, offering Pan a few uninterrupted moments before James arrives. My boys are good like that. They respect my desire to be together while granting each other the chance to have their own needs met.

At first glance, all three of them seem to have the same love language—protection—but in reality, they're vastly different.

James is my golden retriever. Loyal. Protective. And craves affection. When he's home, he likes to sit on the floor between my legs or lie on the couch with his head in my lap so that my fingers can run through his hair. His love language is touch, and I give it to him every chance I can.

Peter doesn't require as much. We spend our afternoons together, reviving the Neverland forest and our nights talking about books. He likes the classics, although I guess that makes sense since that's what he was raised with. He tries to convince me that they're better than my romance novels, but he's wrong, and one day, when he finds a book that makes him want to set the world on fire, he'll realize it. There's nothing wrong with the classics. Many of today's stories are based on them, but due to the era in which they were written, they lack that spark that modern books bring. AKA the spice.

Pan's love language is life. He wants to explore all of it and has no hesitations. His current fascination is food. He cooks everything and insists on feeding me. It's weird but also kind of cute, so

I let him. Besides, I like watching his reactions. The curiosity. The joy. Occasionally, a hint of fear when he thinks I don't like what he's made. Pan has the eyes of a child and the body of a man. Sometimes, I wish I could see the world the way he does.

"What do you think?" There it is—that flick of nervousness. I wonder how many variations of guacamole he made this afternoon before choosing this recipe as today's favorite. But as fast as I see the emotion, it shifts to excitement, and I can't help but smile. "I tried a different seasoning in the avocado when I smashed it."

"It's divine," I tell him. As far as guac goes, it's good. Not as good as yesterday's pumpkin bread, but I enjoy it. "Thank you."

"Avocado is the worst," Peter says dismissively as he walks into the room. Droplets of water trail down his chest as he rubs a towel through his freshly showered hair. My gaze follows those beads down the divots of his sculpted stomach, all the way to his bare cock, hard and ready to be ridden.

"Says you. I rather like it." Pan snatches the last bite from my fingers and shoves it in his mouth just to prove a point. He glares, always eager to remind his brother that they are no longer one. They have different needs. Different likes. Different desires.

"Whatever." Peter snakes toward us with a hungry look in his eye. My nipples pucker and my body prepares for what's about to happen. "I'd rather eat something else."

Peter wraps his arm around my waist and effortlessly lowers me to the floor. He wastes no time as my back settles against the cold wooden planks and shimmies my pants to my knees. He spreads my legs and kisses up my thigh, running his tongue against my sensitive skin as I push myself onto my elbows and try to remember to breathe. It feels good. So deliciously good. It hasn't been that long since we've fucked, less than twenty-four hours, but the way my body is reacting to his touch, you'd think it's been years.

Peter pulls my lace panties aside, and it's not until he presses his lips and tongue against my center and the air is forced into my lungs that I'm able to take a breath. My heart races as I struggle to bite back a groan of longing while he teases me, licking around but never finding that one perfect spot. Caressing but never entering me with either his fingers or tongue. I claw at his head and try to force some part of his face inside me but Peter is calculated. His moves purposefully slow and drawn out. It's torture.

"You'll never make her come like that." Pan stands over us, his cock hard in his shorts, watching. "I'm happy to show you what she likes."

Peter shifts, placing all of his weight on one arm and gives Pan a vulgar gesture. One that ends with the raised finger buried inside of me. I bite back a smile and try to contain the bliss that comes from him playing between my folds. The first orgasm of the day is unlike any other. It's stronger and deserves to be relished, not lost in the heat of the moment, but this one builds so quickly. As much as I want to hold onto the feeling, I can't. Satisfaction releases in a burst of hot pleasure and I melt into a puddle on the floor.

Peter smirks and brings his fingers to his mouth, tasting my sticky sweetness. "So much better than avocado."

My gaze drifts up to Pan. At some point, his shorts ended up on the floor, boxers too, so his fist could wrap around his length. He strokes himself. Slow. Steady pumps. Never taking his eyes off me. "Maybe I should taste her for myself."

"I think you should," I taunt.

Peter chuckles and lifts my foot. He unlaces my boots, then tosses them and my pants aside. He steps back and then gestures for his brother to take his place, adding a mocking look that says *as if you could do better.*

Pan doesn't give Peter the satisfaction of a rebuttal. His sole focus is on me and my wet pussy. I tremble with anticipation, wanting so much more than the tease Peter gave me. Pan kisses me, his tongue moving with tailored precision, having learned exactly what I like. If he were any other man, I'd worry about having been the only woman he's experienced, but Pan never makes me feel like he needs more. Or different. He grabs my hips and flips me onto my stomach. I wiggle my ass, lifting it higher into the air and bending low. From afar, it looks like I'm bowing to my men when really it's them who worship me.

I wasn't sure how this was going to work out, loving multiple men at one time. If I'm honest, it was intimidating. I never wanted one to feel left out or less than the other. But these two... Peter and Pan are an extension of each other. They hit differently, neither better than the other, satisfying parts of me the other didn't reach.

Pan grips my ass and spreads my cheeks open. He sucks on my clit while his tongue licks, and laps, and pokes my center. The pressure building inside me is greedy. It wants more. I need more. I moan Pan's name, my eyes fluttering as the word leaves my lips. His fingers press tighter into my hips and he pushes his tongue deeper.

Peter, never wanting to be left out of the fun, knees in front of me. He reaches for the back of my shirt and rips the collar until the hole is wide enough that the fabric almost falls off of me. He unclasps my bra. I shift my weight from one side to the other so my breasts can fall free and Peter reaches for them. He grabs one, carefully massaging while holding my nipple between his fingers. My back arches as I'm getting close again, so beautifully close. Pan senses my release and chuckles. The sound vibrates against my lips and then there's nothing.

I've been cut off.

I bite my lip to keep from whimpering. I'm not above begging if that's what Pan wants, but I don't think it is. He doesn't have an ego that needs to be fed. So why?

I get my answer as the head of his dick presses against my center. I wiggle and inch backward, wanting to feel him, but Pan only teases. I hear him pop a finger into his mouth and wait. Seconds feel like hours and he gives me nothing. I back my ass up more, hoping to spear some part of him, but all I find is his leg. I shamelessly rub myself against it. If either of these boys knew what they were doing to me, truly knew, they'd understand.

Peter smirks. He wraps my hair around his hand and pulls me to look up at him. "Such a filthy, darling girl." His thumb brushes the pillow of my lip. "Are you ready for us?"

"Please," I say, looking up into Peter's ice-blue eyes.

"Open wide, darling," He instructs, and I listen, like the good little girl he wants me to be, but instead of waiting for Peter to decide when I get rewarded, I take my prize. I wrap my fingers around the base of his cock and lean into his length. Peter grabs my hair again, moaning my name. It must finally break Pan's reserve because he pushes into me. My pussy is slick, wet from waiting. His fingers curl around my hips until they dig into my skin just hard enough to hurt. There's such a beautiful line between pleasure and pain, one I find myself dancing often, and I love it.

I suck Peter hard, pulling him as deep into my throat as I can, struggling to breathe while Pan takes me from behind. One of my boys moans, a throaty, low, rough sound, that tells me the waiting was just as tortuous for him as it was for me. Pan's strokes quicken. He hits me harder, deeper, touching the sweet spot that only he seems to find. I suck Peter harder, matching the intensity for as long as I can. He groans my name again right as Pan's thumb presses into my ass. That does it for me. I come all over him, and shortly after, I feel a warmth inside me. We don't try to prevent the unlikely. All of them have come inside me multiple times since we took Neverland back. We aren't hoping for another baby, but we wouldn't be unhappy if we had one, either.

I grab Peter's balls, wanting him to find the same sweet release. They're tight, so he's probably close, too. I suck and suck while Pan continues to stroke me with what's left of his hard-on. My gaze drifts upward to Peter as he looks down at me. He oozes confidence, reminding me that he was once a king, and in a roundabout way, he still is.

"You could join," Peter says gruffly.

I lift my head and replace my mouth with my hand on Peter's cock as I look up. James leans against the doorframe, his dark-lined eyes glistening with delight as I lick the taste of pre-come from my lips. I leave both my boys, run over to him, and jump into his arms. I bury my face in his chest, ignoring the warmth dripping down my legs and the two naked men patiently waiting for my return, and enjoy having him here again.

"No need to stop on my account." He leans down and presses a chaste kiss on my forehead. "I want her all to myself when yehr finished."

I look up, wanting him just as badly as I want the others. Each of my boys has a piece of my heart, and while I love them all wholly, I'm never complete unless we're all together. I touch James' cheek. "We don't have enough time tonight, though, do we?"

James grabs my wrist and turns it to kiss the inside of my palm. "'Fraid not, Sunshine, but there's always tomorrow."

"I'm not waiting until tomorrow." I grab James by the shirt and tug him over to the couch.

He follows without asking what I want, letting me be the one in control. I don't often tell my boys what I want. I like being dominated and relishing in the way they worship my body, but I've waited five days for this man. I'm not wasting a precious night because we have to leave in forty-five minutes. A quick fuck done right can be better than a long, drawn-out one and, if all goes the way I hope, I can satisfy each of my boys in half of that.

"Lie down," I instruct. Again, James does what I say. I glance over at Peter and Pan, fearful they'll think I've abandoned them. I haven't. I have a plan, one I'm hoping James doesn't freak out about. I just need a few minutes to get everything in place.

I unzip James' pants and grab his dick. It's hard, the way I like it. I lean down and wrap my lips around him. James' eyes flutter closed and he exhales a breath of pleasure. I don't know what he's been through out on the open water, but I do know that he hasn't been with anyone since he left.

I climb onto James' lap and slide onto his cock. James pushes upright, shifting the angle, and kisses me. He kisses me without worry of what his brothers will think or giving any acknowledgment that I was between two naked men a moment ago. That is the beauty of what we have. There's no jealousy. No judgment. Just love.

I give him my undivided attention, letting him savor my heat. I think this feeling, sinking inside me after being gone for so long, is similar to what my first orgasm feels like. I can come over and over again in one session, each release different than the last, but a man only gets that one release. It's a cruel trick of fate from the Gods, which is why I think this moment, the first few seconds after entry, is the closest they get to an orgasm without achieving one and ruining the experience.

James buries his face into the side of my neck, his lips feverishly tasting my skin. He grips my hips and guides me up and down his length. My lashes flutter as my fingers dig into his back, making new marks on his already-marred skin. I love Peter and Pan, but something about James makes me feel safe, like I could curl into his arms and never have a care in the world again.

"I missed yeh," he says, moving me at a pace that is more tortuous than anything else. He worships my body with his hands, sliding a palm up my back, holding my ass with the other until his control finally breaks.

"I missed you, too." I press my palm to his chest and push James to lie back. "But I'm in control tonight. Will you let me do what I want?"

"We can do anything yeh'd like, Sunshine."

I smile, relieved and excited. James has no idea what he's agreed to, but his word is his bond. He won't take it back no matter how uncomfortable he feels. "Good. I was hoping you'd say that."

I ride him, trying to find the perfect angle that still feels good while I lean over James. Sweet James, who has no idea what I'm about to do.

"Peter?" I call out seductively.

There's a flash of heat in his eyes. He strides over without me needing to finish my thought and climbs onto the couch behind me. James stills, realizing he's about to take place in his first three-some, and drops his hands from my hips.

I grab his wrist and move his fingers to my chest. "Do you trust me?"

"With my life," James replies, but I hear the hesitation. I lean down and kiss him, hoping to ease his nerves.

Peter grips my ass and lifts me to a better angle. We've done this a few times already and have figured out what works, what hurts, and what sends us both over the edge. But we haven't tried it with anyone else yet. This will be a first, something the four of us can share together. Something I'm hoping that goes well and we can do again.

Peter enters me slowly, careful not to push too hard or too fast. This first feeling, the stretching is the most uncomfortable. It borders that line between pleasure and pain, but also has a hint of awkwardness. My brain doesn't know how to process what's going on until Peter is fully inside.

"James." My voice cracks. I can't help it. I have so much built-up anticipation and he hasn't moved since Peter entered me. I can feel them both, one pressing against each other through my walls, and even that has me on the edge of coming. "I'm gonna need you to fuck me now."

He rocks his hips slowly at first, gauging how each movement affects us. Spots fill my vision within seconds as a whole-body orgasm claims me. Peter feels everything tighten, my ass included, and begins to take his pleasure. They find a rhythm, working together, that would bring me to my knees if I weren't already on them. Everything is perfect. This is what I wanted: feeling full and satisfied in a way we haven't had yet. All I'm missing is Pan.

I reach my hand out and invite him to join us. He stands at the edge of the couch and lets me decide how I want him. I barely need a second to choose before pulling him closer and into my mouth. I was wrong. *This* is perfection.

Peter finishes first, pulling out and coming on my ass rather than inside it. He leans over and kisses the small of my back before stepping off the couch. I glance at him and Pan pulls his cock from my mouth.

"What?" I whimper, wanting to satisfy him, too.

Pan drops to his knees and kisses me, our tongues finding a practiced rhythm that sends a wave of warm shivers down my spine. "I'm not to come again, beautiful, but thank you." I nod as he steps away, too, heading down the hallway and to the bathroom to start a shower.

James pulls out, too, and my heart stops. He hasn't come, and for a moment, I wonder if I've fucked things up. I bite my lip as he lifts me off of his lap, tears on the brink of falling. It felt so good. We were so perfect.

"On yehr knees, Sunshine," James says, and the relief I feel in that moment has never been so great. I lean onto the armrest of the couch and pop my ass up again. I don't know which hole he wants. He could take either. I just want him to come. I don't feel right leaving him unsatisfied.

"That was cruel, my love." James smacks my ass. He barely gives the sting time to settle before pushing inside me again. His strokes are punishing, and maybe I deserve them, but they're amazing, too. "I know that to love yeh I have to share yeh, but yehr mine when yehr with me. Understand?"

He drives into me, catching a desperate moan as I say, "Yes."

He fucks me hard, claiming what's his. Releasing the tension he carries that I've yet to ask about. I let him use my body as his release because I've already used his for what I needed. His hips drive me into the the side of the couch and I claw at the fabric to keep myself grounded. He waits until I've come one more time, always careful to meet my needs before satisfying his own.

I collapse on the couch, satisfied and exhausted.

"You look like you need this." Peter extends a glass of water to me. I thank him and swallow half of it in one breath before offering the rest to James. Peter's lips lift into a lazy smile and he tilts his head toward the hallway. "The shower is hot. You two should get cleaned up. We've got to leave soon if we're going to cross over tonight."

"No time. I need to get Mira ready." Changed. Fed. A bag packed. There are a million and one steps that have to be taken when traveling with a child. Car rides. Magical boat trips. It's all the same. Kids make going places so much more complicated than simply walking out the door.

"Pan's taking care of her. I'll pack the travel bag." Peter steps forward and kisses my forehead. "Stop worrying for five minutes and go take a shower. We've got this."

He's right. We do. Me, Peter, Pan, and James.

I used to think Wendy was a fool for leaving Neverland when I believed the lies woven into the fairytale and thought she only had one man loving her. I didn't know how wrong the story was or how the choice to leave was never hers. And I never could have imagined that when I got my tattoo all those moons ago that I would become one of Neverland's Lost, let alone its Queen. Yet here I am, living an impossible life, loved by three amazing men in a world that shouldn't exist. Is this life perfect? No, but I wouldn't choose any other.

"Go," Peter says, stepping back. "Or we'll be late for our next adventure."

He winks and I can't help but laugh. My Peter. Always ready to go on a new adventure.

Mini blurb:
Find the Looking Glass.
Don't get caught.
Don't die.

It should have been a simple plan until she crosses into the Wildlands and came face to face with the one monster she was never meant to survive.

Readers who love:
- A Girl Hunted and not just by the Crown
- A deal she can't take back
- He Falls First
- Forced proximity
- Who did this to you
- Slow burn
- Reluctant allies

Might enjoy this twisted Beauty and the Beast retelling. Coming Soon.

All I Want For Christmas

Tinsel Evergreen didn't get a say in her future. As the Grand Elf's daughter, she was signed, sealed, and delivered to the next Santa before she hit kindergarten...destined for sugar cookies, sleigh rides, and a picture-perfect happily-ever-after she never asked for.

But two weeks before the holiday that defines her family, Tinsel steals a little magic and runs. She lands in Winter Key,

Florida—a fishing village trying to reinvent itself with twinkle lights and tacky holiday contests—and discovers freedom for the first time. No expectations. No fiancé. Just sunshine, salt air, and the terrifying possibility of figuring out what she actually wants.

Mason Kraus isn't looking for complications. His family's bait shop is shuttered, his father's legacy weighs heavy on his shoulders, and he's barely holding his sister's bar afloat. Letting a runaway stranger crash in his spare room is the last thing he needs, but when a booking mishap leaves Tinsel with nowhere to stay, she ends up in his spare bedroom.

Living under the same roof is supposed to be temporary. Instead, it feels inevitable. One look across the kitchen counter, one brush of his hand, one late-night conversation on the dock— and suddenly, the line between roommates and something more is impossible to hold.

But Tinsel can't hide forever. Her future is waiting at the North Pole. And Mason knows better than to believe in miracles.

Still... when the one person you weren't supposed to fall for becomes the only one you can't walk away from, rules and even Christmas start to feel negotiable.

Resting Grinch Face

Welcome back to Winter Key. Santa Claus has to find a bride before his thirtieth birthday or risk losing Christmas for the whole world.

Readers who love:
• Grumpy Sunshine
• Smal Town Chaos
• Forced proximity
• Magical Mischief
• Fast fun and slow feelings
Might enjoy Resting Grinch Face

Coming November 2026

Falling for You

Josh Andrews hadn't expected to meet the girl of his dreams in a church parking lot—especially not while his best friend was hooking up in his truck. But there she was, parked two spaces away, pretending not to notice his predicament. Layla was gorgeous, sharp-witted, and completely immune to his charm.

He should have walked away. Instead, he couldn't stop thinking about her. Layla wasn't like the girls who usually fell for his easy smile and smooth lines. She challenged him, saw right through him—and he liked it. For the first time, he wanted more than just a fleeting connection. He wanted her.

Winning her over won't be easy, but Josh has never backed

down from a challenge. And Layla? She might just be the one risk worth taking.

In Too Deep

A wedding. A lie. And regret.

I'm in over my head with not one but two ex-boyfriends at the same wedding. Both of which I haven't seen in over a year. When the one who ripped my heart into pieces backs me into a corner, I grab the other and kiss him.

Yup. This is how I ended up fake dating Noah Ruckers, and let me tell you, it's an emotional roller coaster. I thought I'd put my feelings for him behind me. We spent years as friends after our break up, nothing more. But no matter how hard I try I can't forget what his lips feel like. Or the way his arms wrap around me.

In two days, I'm walking away. There is no future for us. But that doesn't mean I can't pretend.

Lucky In Love

Holly Flynn is a leprechaun who grants wishes but with a dangerous twist. Each wish comes at a price: once it's fulfilled, the "victim" forgets everything before their wish and her.

When a gorgeous stranger asks for one unforgettable night, things take an unexpected twist. The chemistry between them is electric, and soon, Holly's struck by a terrifying thought: She doesn't want him to forget her.

Then, a week later, he knocks on her door. And he remembers everything. Why does he remember, when no one else does? Is it fate—or is her magic betraying her?

Breakups and Bouquets

Emma Evans had the perfect wedding planned until her fiancé dumped her a week before the big day. Now she's heartbroken, homeless, and stuck with a non-refundable, high-end wedding package she can't return... or use.

So she does the unthinkable: gives the whole thing away in a viral giveaway.

What she doesn't expect...The winning groom is best friends with her frustratingly attractive landlord, Matthew Anderson. The same man who catches her illegally crashing in her office with a bottle of wine and a Taylor Swift playlist.

Matt has every reason to evict her. Instead, he makes her a

deal: fake date him to help sell the love story, and he'll look the other way. It's outrageous. It's risky. But if pretending to be in love for one week keeps her business afloat, Emma's in.

Only, somewhere between staged kisses, scorching chemistry, and one very real wedding, the line between make-believe and something more starts to blur.

And Emma's about to find out that the best love stories never go according to plan.

Say You'll Be Mine

Ariana Hart is officially done with Valentine's Day.

Another breakup. Another year of watching couples cuddle in the courtyard of her apartment complex. Another reminder that every guy she dates disappears before the six-month mark.

At least she has one thing to look forward to: the *mysterious Valentine's card* she's received every February for the past five years from a Valentine who refuses to reveal themself. Sweet notes. Soft promises. Just enough hope to keep Ariana believing love might not hate her as much as she thinks.

This year, though, the card comes with something new—
an invitation to finally meet her secret admirer.

Suddenly, Ariana finds herself spiraling between nerves,

excitement, and the uneasy suspicion that stepping into the unknown might be a mistake. And Miles, her best friend and frustratingly attractive roommate, is no help—teasing her one minute, protective the next, and acting like he has a personal stake in whoever she's meeting at eight o'clock.

Between mystery notes, unexpected gifts, and Miles's suddenly unpredictable behavior, Ariana starts to wonder if she's been missing something that's been right in front of her all along.

A sweet & flirty Valentine's Day short story full of mutual pining, anonymous notes, and the surprise confession she never saw coming.

Beautifully Broken

Most people don't think about the day they'll die. They coast through life, blissfully unaware of how their time is ticking away. I wasn't like most people. I welcomed death, wanted her to take me away from the prison I called life, but she refused. I tried twice only to survive. And then, when I thought I had nothing left it came.A reason to live.Rex was a small, unexpected ray of light my world of darkness that blossomed into a beam of sunshine. I thought, maybe this was why Death didn't take me. Maybe she knew that if I held on a little longer things would turn around. But the third time Death came to my door wasn't by choice. Someone else brought her, and I fear this time she might take me.

2 BOOKS

The Love Hate Duet

She's beautiful. Fierce. Nothing at all like the girl I used to know, which is absolutely terrifying because Danika Winters is the only person outside of that room who knows the truth. She could ruin me, and I'm not talking about my reputation. I couldn't give two shits about what the kids at St. A's think. I'm talking major, life-altering, jail time ruined. I'll do whatever it takes to keep her quiet. Even if it means destroying the only person I've ever cared about.

Unexpected

Asher Anderson is a dick.

We aren't friends, so when he seeks me out in the cafeteria on the worst day of my life, I'm suspicious. When he tells Liam Heiter that we're dating, which couldn't be farther from the truth, I want to kill him...Until I see Liam's reaction.

Liam—my best friend, the guy who crushed every hope of us *officially* being together—is jealous. He has never looked at me this way and I love it.

So, I play along. Maybe watching me with someone else will make Liam suffer like I have the past four years. And maybe, just maybe, he'll come to his senses and realize we belong together. It's not like I actually *like* Asher. At best, I tolerate him. What's the worst that can happen?

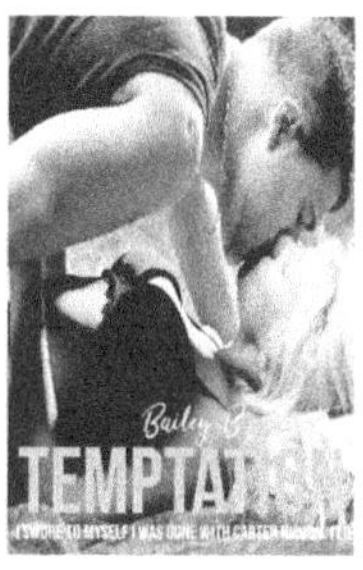

Temptation

I've sworn off men forever! Okay, not forever, but for a few months. After my last hook-up, my vag needs a reset because the last man to touch me broke it in the worst of ways. Not a problem until my new dance partner comes into the picture. He's turning into my forbidden fruit, tempting me in ways I didn't know possible.

I have three months of celibacy ahead of me and eight weeks to whip my new dance partner into shape.

Someone save me.

Love Me Like You Mean It- A collection of big love in a small town.

Welcome to Brooksville, where summer nights are warm, old feelings resurface, and love never stays simple.

The *Summers in Brooksville* anthology brings together four short, sweet, and spicy romances set in a small town that knows all your secrets... and isn't afraid to stir them up.

Inside, you'll find:

Kiss Me Like You Mean It: a fake date that turns into very real feelings, fast

Hold Me Like You Mean It : a forbidden slow burn that crackles under summer fireworks

Miss Me Like You Mean It : a second chance that still hurts... and still wants

Want Me Like You Mean It (bonus story) : when almost finally becomes forever

From friends-to-lovers and second chances to small-town tension and heart-tugging chemistry, these bite-sized romances are perfect for readers who want big feelings, swoony moments, and a little heat—without the long commitment.

Short. Sweet. Spicy.

Come spend the summer in Brooksville... you might not want to leave.

The Cerise

I had a plan. Find the soldier who killed my family and make him pay. It should have been an easy feat. I'd done it over a dozen times, taking out each member of that regiment one by one, but the mission went sideways. It all started with the man in the woods. The one my webs of magic couldn't sense even when he stood before me. Then my partner made a mistake, and now he's lying in one of the Crown's dungeons, fighting for his life. I couldn't leave him to die, but I couldn't just walk into the castle either.

Or maybe I could.

With the help of some unexpected allies, I entered the Culling —a one-in-a-lifetime chance to become queen. I have no interest in winning the prince's heart, or the crown. My only goal is to get into the castle, find my friend, and get out before someone realizes I'm a Cerise.

But when the welcome ball turns from a grand event into a nightmarish dance of death, all eyes are on me. As if that's not bad enough, the soldier, the one who took my family, he's here.

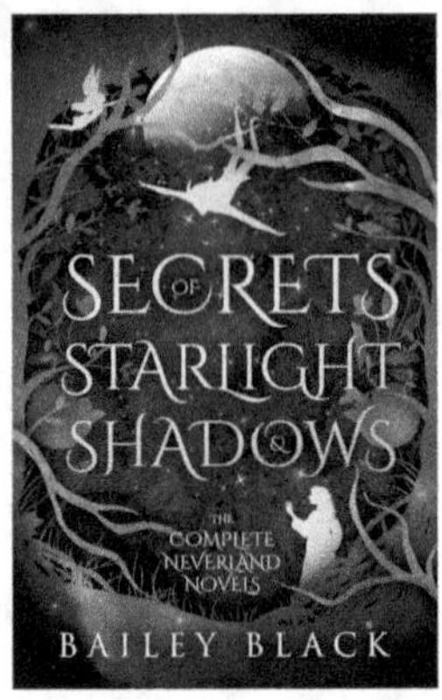

Secrets of Starlight and Shadows

"There are a million women in existence throughout the universe, but there is no other soul in all the galaxies like yours. I would choose you over her every day, with every breath."

I wasn't looking for anything serious the day I met Peter. I needed someone to make my sister jealous and help me forget the shit-storm that my life had become. Peter was just the man.

Handsome. Immune to my sister's Bullshit. And solely focused on me.

I didn't know he was Peter Pan.

I didn't realize the cost of going to Neverland.

I couldn't have imagined how my life would change once I got there.

But I wouldn't take any of it back.

This is the complete Neverland Novels Collection with the bonus MMMF chapter you didn't know you needed.

Thank You

Sometimes I think the Thank You section is the saddest part of the whole story because it means it's over.

A special thank you to Heather Douglas for being my star beta reader. All of the beautiful quotes on IOTL's graphics are all because of her.

Thank you to Ashleigh Blakely for being my final set of eyes before publication. Her attention to detail is immaculate.

To my editor Beth at Magnolia Author Services, I don't even know how many books we've worked together on at this point but as long as you want me I will forever be a repeat customer. (Indie authors...if you're looking she's the shit!)

To my husband who says he wants nothing to do with my books but hounds me when I haven't written anything in a week... I love you.

To the bloggers and bookstagrammers who bring my stories to the world. You are amazing! I cannot begin to express how grateful to you I am.

Finally, I'd like to thank my readers. Every time you open one of my books, you make my dream come true.

Thank you.

Xoxo

Bailey

Bailey Black is a romance author with a love for all things romantasy and contemporary. She began her writing journey as Bailey B before embracing her full name with the start of her Neverland Novels. When she's not lost in a world of words, she's busy playing chauffeur to her teenage daughters—though she wouldn't trade the chaos for anything. A firm believer that coffee needs cream, cheesecake deserves strawberries, and bread is a love language, Bailey finds joy in the little indulgences of life.

Find her everywhere @baileyblackbooks or join her facebook-group Bailey Black's Book Nook